To my darling girls,
Samantha and Tabitha

Sherlock Holmes
&
The Ciphered List

Simon Trelawney

Breese Books

THE Publisher for Quality Murder Mystery Books &
Home to the Breese Books Sherlock Holmes Collection

First published in 2022 by
Baker Street Studios Ltd for
Breese Books
Endeavour House
170 Woodland Road, Sawston
Cambridge, CB22 3DX, UK

ISBN: 978 1 901091 83 0

Cover Concept: Antony J. Richards

Cover Illustration: Whitehall – Looking North: The Treasury Buildings on the left
(*Round London,* 1896). The spy ring uncovered by Holmes included several persons
working in Government departments in Whitehall.

Typeset in 8/11/20pt Palatino

Contents

Editor's Note

I found the foregoing account amongst the voluminous memoirs, notes, files, cuttings, and photographs of the estate of the late Dr. Watson, and have kept it for posterity. Abiding by his wishes I too had not allowed it to be published, but with the death of the great detective some years ago, outliving his chronicler by a decade, and the recent passing of Diana Conquest-Romanoff (at the age of a hundred) all parties are now deceased, and I feel justified in letting this exceptional story see the light of day.

Simon R. Trelawney

England, July 1966.

Chapter I

The Client

"Confound it Watson! I can forgive the London criminal almost anything except lack of imagination. In heaven's name, the cases that people present me with these days are so utterly footling and so totally lacking any spark of ingenuity that even those dunderheads at Scotland Yard could solve them in an instant. Where are the mysteries of days gone by that stimulated the intellect and challenged one's powers?"

With this ejaculation my friend Sherlock Holmes sprang from his chair, flung his newspaper to the floor, and started pacing about the room in agitated fashion.

It was a chilly, gloomy Monday morning in November, and this sudden outpouring of discontent did not come as a surprize to me. I had been forced to endure Holmes roaming restlessly about our chambers over the last few weeks and months in a state of frustration, and saw his eye stray more than once to the morocco case on the mantelpiece. I had scoured the newspapers and periodicals to see if I could find something that would divert him but, alas, as Holmes had declared with all too much veracity there was very little that would have seized his attention. It was the usual round of politics, finance and social gossip, none of which was of interest to Holmes unless it had some direct bearing upon the criminal or notorious.

"But you are still working on the Confratini affair, are you not, and then there is that business of the Chinese laundryman, the parrot and the fire engine that so intrigued you. These must surely be matters of some substance?"

"Pah, mere bagatelles. I have wound up the Confratini imbroglio to my satisfaction and given all the evidence to the police, who are, I am advized, shortly to make a whole series of arrests on the basis of it. I may have to make a statement but that will effectively be the end of it. No, I don't think that that will sustain me through the long, lean winter months. And as for the other matter if only our friends in the constabulary had thought to look in the cistern of the outside lavatory then all would have been explained. No, Watson, this is thin gruel indeed. I need something with some meat on its bones."

I sighed and wandered to the window overlooking the street when my eye was caught by a rather grand coach drawing up outside.

"I say, Holmes, this may bring us something."

"Is it a pale blue carriage with a crest surmounted with a tiger rampant emblazoned on the door, driven by a liveryman dressed in a scarlet coat and pulled by a pair of young stallions?"

"Holmes, even by your standards that is astonishing. Have you developed the ability to see through walls?"

"No, my dear fellow, but we have an appointment with a certain personage from a House of which that is the coat of arms, and whose carriage I have seen about town on several occasions. I heard the trot of horses and from their loudness and frequency calculated that it was a young and vigorous pair. I also have the benefit of a mirror from which I saw the carriage round the corner of the Marylebone Road a few seconds ago."

"Very droll Holmes, but perhaps you could have informed me of an impending visitation."

"I only received the telegram requesting an interview this morning and you had already left the breakfast table. Anyway, I could not presume upon your presence."

"But as always I should be only too happy to sit in, assuming, that is, you wish me to be involved."

"Why naturally. How can I survive a day without my Boswell? And you must be running short of material for your chronicles given the doldrums of late."

8

"Then why all the vexation on your part when you have the prospect of a new case? Surely a richness of horizons opens up before you."

"Oh, but it is probably some silly tribulation of high society. A skivvy has gone missing for a day or two, or is behaving oddly, or can't manage to dust the furniture properly or some such tripe, and all because of some romantic disappointment. Must I be forced to waste my energies on things like this?"

"But you never know, Holmes."

He dismissed my protests with a wave of the hand and slumped back in his chair to await the arrival of our visitor, snatching up his newspaper from the floor to resume his perusal.

The carriage was as Holmes described; a very elegant five-glass landau, drawn by two fine white stallions and driven by a red-uniformed coachman and bore the aforementioned crest. Its gold-plated lamps shone like beacons in the murk of the street. My gaze was transfixed. A very large, powerfully built young man in the same livery as the coachman alighted from inside and opening the door wide he drew down a small flight of iron steps from which there descended a young woman attired in, even to my inexpert eye, the height of fashion. Even at a distance I could see from her dress and deportment that she was no ordinary lady. My heart jumped to see them approach our front door, and shortly after there was the rap of Mrs. Hudson's page boy, Billy, delivering a calling card.

"Please show them in." I said, taking control of the situation, since Holmes appeared singularly unenthused.

There entered at first a petite and rather plain young woman modestly dressed in a beige shawl, who bobbed at us, and who I took to be a maid, and then following shortly behind, much as an ocean liner is preceded by a tug boat, the lady I had espied. She was statuesque and graceful in movement, and dressed in a sumptuous yet rather sombre gown of bombazine black and an exotic, vaguely oriental design. Her bearing was regal. Lifting her veil as she entered she revealed herself to be a lady of quite breathtaking beauty; her eyes of a Mediterranean azure, a flawless complexion and a face framed by the proudest of cheekbones. She glanced from side to side at the two of us.

"Do I have the privilege of addressing Mr. Sherlock Holmes?" she enquired. Her address had fallen upon my friend, who had risen, and, from his former indifference was now somewhat more engaged.

"You do indeed, madam. Pray take a seat". He gestured towards the armchair by the fireside. She glided over, followed closely by the maid, and sat with an expectant air, her maid standing dutifully by her side.

"And how may I assist you, Lady Diana?" I gasped slightly, for I had not read her card, but now recognized our visitor as none other than Lady Diana Conquest, only daughter of the fifteenth Earl of Tewkesbury, celebrated society hostess, philanthropist and, one might add, campaigner for a host of causes including the highly questionable one of female suffrage. And it was evident that the photographs of her that sometimes appeared in the public prints did not do justice to her stunning looks.

"May I offer you some refreshment? Tea or coffee? Perhaps I can even prevail upon our landlady to produce some cake?" I effused. I could sense Holmes's irritation at these fripperies.

"Thank you, no, Dr. Watson. You are most kind but I have very little appetite in my present straits and I should prefer to outline matters without delay." Her voice was soft but commanding.

Holmes had seated himself opposite her in a familiar pose of intense scrutiny, his hands steepled together in front of his face.

"I see, my lady, that you are a member of the Olympia Society."

"Yes, indeed, Mr. Holmes," she answered with some disquiet. "May I ask how you know?"

"You are a wearing a bracelet bearing the insignia of that organization upon your left wrist."

"Oh, yes so I am. I had forgotten I was still wearing it. I see that your reputation for perspicacity is not unjustified, sir." she replied.

"And were you, by any chance, in attendance at their recent meeting at the Albert Hall?"

Our guest seemed taken aback by this further observation.

"Yes, but I was not aware that my presence there had been reported in the newspapers, for I did not speak at it."

"It had not, to my knowledge, but I notice that the link of your bracelet looks to have been repaired recently since it is made of a different metal and I speculated that it was due to it having suffered damage in the course of the scuffles that occurred there."

She evinced further surprize and looked distinctly flustered.

"Well, there was a bit of a melee at one point in the proceedings from which I was unable to extricate myself in time." she said with a hint of embarrassment. "I am wondering what else you may divine about me, Mr. Holmes, for I did not realize how transparent a creature I was?"

"Transparent only to those who look hard enough; but I must offer my apologies if I have caused you any unease. It was not my intention but it is sheer force of habit for me sometimes to give voice to my findings."

"Yes, I realize that, sir. It is not unease but wonderment." she said admiringly.

I was astounded not only at my friend's acuity of perception but also at the extent of his erudition, extending apparently into such unlikely spheres as the politics of female advancement.

"So, in what way can I be of service, dear lady?"

The niceties of introduction over the lady seemed to lapse into despondency. For all her self-possession and composure there was an air of deep perturbation about the woman. Holmes settled further back in his chair, his concentration upon the interviewee even more intensely focussed than usual.

"As to the reason for my presence here, it is because a strange set of circumstances has overtaken me and it may be that you are the one man in the land who can extricate me from my current predicament". Holmes was never averse to flattery, much as he might seek to disavow it, and I could see he was warming to his new client; though, knowing the man as thoroughly as I did, I supposed it actuated by the prospect of intellectual challenge rather than the undeniable physical attractions of the lady.

"Pray proceed." He closed his eyes and leant back.

"Let me begin, Mr. Holmes, by saying that these are matters of the utmost sensitivity, and anything I say here must not extend beyond these four walls. Do I make myself clear?" She glanced at me as she said this.

"Abundantly. The fact that you have engaged my services, or I presume wish to do so, surely implies that you trust in my discretion as well as my expertize, and anything that may be said in front of me may be said in front of my learned colleague." Saying this, he glanced briefly at the lady's maidservant.

"In terms of trustworthiness Elsie is to me, what Dr. Watson is to you, Mr. Holmes." Holmes nodded his assent.

She cleared her throat and paused for a moment. Holmes remained impassive.

"Mr. Holmes; a few years ago whilst travelling around Europe, we; that is to say my aunt, Lady Marjorie Anstruther and I; made a lengthy sojourn in Germany and there I made the acquaintance of a young gentleman of noble birth. He was then a professor at one of that country's leading universities and quite a brilliant scholar. Our paths crossed socially on several occasions."

She hesitated before proceeding with her narrative, seeking as if to overcome some slight embarrassment.

"It may be fair to say that we became intimate with each other, though our opportunities for liaison were of necessity somewhat limited, mine by the careful chaperoning to which I was subject at all times, he by the necessity of attending to his academic duties. In due course I had to depart from that city to continue my tour of the Continent and though we corresponded subsequently there was no further meeting though, I cannot deny, my heart yearned for it.

"Much more recently, I discovered to my great and overpowering joy that he had taken up residence in this country and I hoped ardently that I would be able to renew my acquaintance with him."

"May I know the name of this individual?"

"I should prefer not to divulge his identity at this stage, Mr. Holmes."

"My dear lady, I must know all pertinent facts or I fear that I can be of little service to you and that our interview must be at end."

She havered slightly.

"Very well, Mr. Holmes", she sighed; "it is ... the Count von Runstedt."

Holmes jerked forward in his chair as if galvanized, any vestige of his former jaded demeanour shed.

"Continue." Holmes, I could see, was now enraptured.

"I, at first, renewed my correspondence with Wolfi ... that is to say ... the Count. You must pardon me if I lapse occasionally into the familiar. I alluded to our former friendship, and expressed the sincerest wish that we might renew our acquaintance. He was more than enthusiastic in reply and we arranged to meet at a social engagement upon the following Saturday. I had very largely dismissed him from my thoughts in the intervening years and I suppose assumed him to be a now a married man, but I discovered that he was still a bachelor."

She paused before continuing her narrative.

"We, at length, reignited our passion for each other." There was the merest suggestion of a blush about her lovely cheeks.

"We continued our liaison over the next few weeks and months, our relationship becoming deeper and deeper."

The lady seemed to find the story harder to narrate the further it progressed.

"I had said to you that the Count was a bachelor but I gradually became aware from certain sources that he was in fact engaged to a lady in his native country, of a similar station in life to his and of similar background and stock. One day I confronted him with this knowledge. He admitted as much, telling me that family connections and social expectations made it very difficult for him to break off the engagement, but that his passion for me was such that he was prepared to do so. However, the ground would have to be prepared for such a momentous decision on his part. Our romance continued and yet could never blossom in the sunshine of public acclaim as I so devoutly wished. It was a secretive affair, conducted hugger-mugger, an affair of shadows and mirages. We met very largely at his own residences in London and Berkshire and nowhere else. On occasion I had had to be smuggled in through a back door. Even when he held a party to celebrate his forty-fifth birthday the Saturday before last I was not invited." She smiled wanly.

"Only a few trusted confidantes of his and mine knew of our affair. I pressed him time and again to break off his engagement and commit himself to me but he said that it was at present impossible but he assured me nonetheless of his total devotion."

She started to breathe heavily for it appeared that the narrative was progressing towards a climax the nature of which the lady found difficult to confront. Her maid clutched her mistress's hand consolingly.

"But, Mr. Holmes, my hopes and plans were thrown into disarray for, one day when I was at his townhouse, but whilst he was out attending to business matters of some description, I was approached and taken aside by his secretary and right hand man, a vile and repulsive creature with whom I had crossed swords in the past and who seemed to resent our alliance."

We sat captivated by her narrative.

"Who was this man?"

There was a pause for she seemed almost reluctant to pronounce his name.

"Kellmann. Dieter Kellmann." she spat the words out as if he were an extinct species of reptile. I could see from the flickers of reaction that Holmes's interest had been piqued for the second time by the mention of a name.

"He had been with Wolfi for many years and was often at his house on official matters, though he had his own lodgings, somewhere in North London I believe. I was glad that I did not have to endure his presence too often.

"Though, from snatches of abrasive conversation between them that I had overheard and the little that Wolfi was willing to divulge of official matters I gathered that there was a growing rift between them. I am not sure of the cause. At any rate, whatever the reason, he seemed to despize me. Perhaps it was jealousy of his master; I cannot really say and do not wish to speculate.

"However, on this occasion his approach was at first friendly and courteous in its own way though I suspected he had his own designs. He had a superficial charm which he could turn on when it suited his purposes. He tried to put me at my ease inviting me to have a drink with him, but I was wary, and was right to be so. After a few offhand comments he came to the point. He said that he knew all the details of our affair and that if it became public knowledge it would not only ruin my reputation but have disastrous consequences for the Count. At the very least the Count would be discredited and might have to leave the country and I would never see him again. I could not bear the thought of that. He said that he could easily prove everything by means of letters and notes that had passed between us, of which he had had copies made, and by the observations of some of the servants who were in his confidence.

"I was deeply shocked. I reacted furiously and told him that his master would hear of our conversation and that he would be lucky to escape a horse-whipping. But he just laughed and said that I might say whatever I liked. It would not prevent the truth getting out and the consequences would be far worse for me and the Count than for him.

"I had to recognize the element of truth in what he said. He then told me he was prepared to overlook everything if I was prepared to meet his terms. These were, as you might suppose, of a monetary nature for he knew that my family has accumulated considerable wealth. He said he was sure we could easily arrive at an agreeable settlement. But that I must not say anything to the Count. He would know immediately if I had and our understanding would be at an end. He tried to put me at my ease again, perhaps fearing that any mental agitation on my part might betray itself to the Count. He said that his demands were really very modest, that he would never press me again, and that he would allow matters to continue undisturbed thereafter. I was not sure that I could believe him but I felt I had little choice in the matter.

"I played for time and said that I would have to arrange for the withdrawal of funds from my bank and that there might be a slight delay in arranging the transaction given the largeness of the sum. He accepted this and suggested that matters be brought to conclusion in a week, but no longer. I demurred very sharply at this but he persisted, and finally I relented and agreed to his timetable. He said that he would contact me again to finalize our arrangements. He once more tried to solicit my sympathy and even started to force his attentions upon me, but I resisted fiercely, throwing off his advances and storming from the room. As you may imagine, Mr. Holmes, I was in a state of utter turmoil and confusion. I felt I could not stay any longer under the same roof as this barbarian. After the briefest of preparations I left for my own home, hastily scribbling a note to Wolfi that I was unwell and needed rest."

Holmes interjected. "Did anybody overhear you whilst you and the man Kellmann were together?"

"No. Most of the servants were out I think, except possibly for the elderly butler who is rather deaf and whose room is on the other side of the house. But anyway almost the whole conversation was in German, a tongue with which I know none of the servants is familiar, all of them being drawn from the local pool of domestics."

"Pray proceed".

"You may imagine my emotions over the next few days, Mr. Holmes. I was not sure where to turn. I confided only in Elsie." she turned her head upwards to smile at the faithful servant standing beside her, their hands clenched ever tighter together in mutual support.

"I decided not to say anything to Wolfi as agreed and to have little or no contact with him for the next few days upon the pretext of indisposition. I sorely needed the respite to consider my position. Though my whole soul rebelled against it, I came to see that the wisest policy was to accede and to pray that this would put an end to my torment. Who knows what this man

Kellmann might say or do? Actually, his demand was relatively modest and fairly easily met from my own funds."

"Precisely how much did he demand?"

She hesitated.

"It was a thousand pounds. It is a sum well within my means. I realized that he might have tried to coerce me again but if so I would have faced him down! I went to my bank and arranged for the withdrawal of the sum agreed which was to be paid over to me in three days time. I awaited further communication from him. Surely enough, upon the next day, he called at my house to further our discussions. I received him very coldly and treated him with the utter disdain he merited. I ensured that my manservant, Meadows, you may have seen him downstairs as my coach arrived, was present throughout. This, perforce, required our conversation to be somewhat cryptic, though at all events I was not keen to prolong our dialogue beyond the necessary.

"I proposed that we conclude our dealings at my house, but for some reason he insisted upon an address elsewhere, where he said we would not be observed and at a time and a date four days hence upon the following Saturday; that is to say the day before yesterday. He demanded also that I come alone. I very reluctantly agreed, for I felt I had no choice, and matters were left there.

"May I trouble you for a glass of water, Mr. Holmes?"

The lady's throat was understandably somewhat parched after this lengthy and trying account and I sprang forward to bring over the carafe and a glass for her, Holmes remaining motionless in his chair in a penumbra of concentration. After a brief draught she resumed.

"We are coming to the terrible ending of all of this, Mr. Holmes, and I am sure you will understand if the details are a trifle hazy and confused." Her voice was starting to falter. The grip on her maid's hand tightened yet more and the latter was now crouching before her, staring up into her mistress's eyes as if willing her on to complete the ordeal of narration.

"I drove to the venue agreed upon and at the time and date."

"Which was?"

"An address in Shepherd's Bush, of all places, the day before yesterday, at eight o'clock in the evening. It was already dark when we arrived. I say we because I had brought both Elsie and Meadows, but to comply with the understanding I ordered them to stay in the coach unobserved, which was left around the corner and out of sight from our point of rendezvous. I should say that I travelled not in my official coach which you may have observed outside today, but a plain one that would not attract any attention or identify the owner.

"'Please be careful, ma'am' came the cry from my little Elsie. If only I had taken her advice!" The two women exchanged the most heart-rending of looks.

"Well, Mr. Holmes, I ventured alone into the building. I need not pretend other than that I was in a high state of trepidation. It was not the most salubrious of establishments, and I was beginning to wonder if I had gone to the wrong address, but the street sign clearly indicated that I was correct. It appeared to be a scrapyard of some description, the wooden gates of which were swinging open in the breeze of the evening, giving on to a ramshackle and dilapidated three storied abode, the like of which I had never seen before. It had several broken windows and there was no sign of habitation. The whole area was very isolated with not another house for fifty yards or more on either side and the street lighting was very poor or non-existent.

"I made my way across this wretched courtyard which was scattered with a variety of discarded metallic contraptions and various decaying objects and everywhere a pungent smell. I began to wish I had worn something rather more practical than my evening gown, for I had to tread through puddles of oil and water to get to the house within. It took all my nerve to proceed.

"I rapped sharply on the front door, which gave way before my touch. I stepped inside. It was in complete darkness and there was no sign of any means of lighting. There was a foul stench. Cobwebs abounded and I found myself kicking up against cans lying about the floor. I heard the meow of a cat from somewhere. I called out but met with no response. I delved further inside still calling out. I felt the strong urge to turn on my heel and run away."

She took another long draught of the water, her hands trembling slightly as she raised the glass to her lips. The maid was staring up beseechingly into her mistress's eyes.

"Screwing my courage to the sticking place I crept further inside. 'Good evening'. I was so startled I almost fainted. From somewhere inside the room a man emerged with a lighted candle. 'I wasn't sure you were coming.' I recognized all too well the harsh metallic tones I had come to dread. 'I almost didn't come. What is this hideous place and why have you brought me here?' 'Don't be so unkind, *liebchen*. Why, it is a lovely meeting spot.' He sneered. 'Have you brought the money as agreed?' 'Yes.' Did you come alone?' 'Yes.' 'Excellent, come with me.' He gestured towards the staircase which I could now see dimly from the candlelight. 'No, here is the money'. I produced a pouch with the money from my reticule and prepared to hand it to him. I warned him that any attempt to fleece me further or to threaten to expose me would result in my telling all to his master, whatever the consequences for myself."

She gulped hard at this point and was obviously struggling to control her emotions. Holmes maintained his silence to allow her to recover. I felt as if I should intervene in some way to console the lady but knew that such a move on my part would only vex Holmes.

"He did not take the pouch but signalled for me to mount the staircase ahead of him. 'We must go upstairs' he repeated, and I foolishly, *foolishly* complied thinking perhaps some document was to be handed me in return for the money. Oh, how utterly ridiculous! How stupid of me!

"I nervously climbed the stairs with him directly behind carrying the candle. The upstairs quarters we entered were scarcely more congenial than the downstairs and were generally in a filthy condition, old furniture consisting of a few tables and chairs and a dreadful musty odour, but were at least better lit with several candelabra which I assume he had set up in advance of my arrival. How I longed to be clear of the wretched place. I placed the pouch down upon the nearest table. 'Here are your pieces of silver. Take it and let it be an end of the matter.' I said putting on as bold a front as I could muster. I cast a look of utter contempt at him and turned to leave.

"But he urged me to stay, suggesting we could have a drink to celebrate the successful conclusion of our business. The foul creature seemed to be deluded into thinking that there could be some amity or even intimacy between us, despite everything that had gone before. It was obvious he had imbibed plentifully for I could smell the drink on his breath and he was slightly unsteady on his feet. He proffered a glass of wine from a sideboard. I demurred and took to leave again but the beast then blocked me, pushing me back, forcing himself upon me, grabbing roughly at my arms and ripping my dress as he did so."

The lady's breasts were heaving at these dread recollections.

"I resisted with a strength born of alarm and terror and a fierce struggle ensued. I cried out but there was no-one in the vicinity as the fiend well knew. How I wished I had taken Elsie's advice or at least had she and Meadows accompany me, but it was too late."

Our client's account seemed to be moving to a terrible climax. She was breathing harder and harder as she relived the horrors in her mind's eye. By now Elsie was cuddling her mistress and sobbing.

"I fought back hard, kicking at his shins and clawing manically at his face. After what seemed an eternity but was probably only a few seconds of this awful tussle he suddenly stumbled backwards in his intoxication and under the impact of my blows, feeble though they may have been. He tripped and fell, cracking his head upon the edge of the wooden table. He groaned and lay motionless upon the floor."

Her voice was quavering, the words coming in an uncontrolled flood.

"At first I was relieved beyond description to see him prostrate, but then the blood started oozing from him, crawling across the floorboards and forming a sort of ghastly crimson lake. I rushed over to him, but realized there was nothing I could do. I couldn't bear the sight. In my frenzy I knew I had to run and had just enough of my wits left about me to grab the money pouch from the table. I flung myself down the staircase, spraining my ankle as I went, half hobbled and half raced out the door, across the courtyard and around the corner to my carriage. I have never been happier to see it in all my life. I was retching uncontrollably. I grabbed onto Elsie and shrieked at the coachman to speed us away."

"It was just like what she says, sir, she was in a God awful state, pardon my language, sir, but she was crying and howling and wailing something terrible, and I never seen her act nothing like it before, sir." burst out the maidservant, acting as a chorus for her mistress.

"Yes, alright Elsie, that's enough." she said patting the girl on the shoulders with a benevolent tolerance at this unprompted outburst.

Holmes and I had heard many a grim and harrowing tale in these chambers but we were both gripped as never before by this extraordinary narrative.

"What could I do, Mr. Holmes? I could scarcely go to the police with such a matter. How could I explain it all away? I meant no serious harm to him and my actions were in self defence and no more. But I have been in a woeful state all day yesterday, not knowing which way to turn. I felt unable to attend morning service as is my custom, nor to do anything at all, until finally I resolved upon throwing myself upon your services, knowing your eminent reputation, Mr. Holmes."

Her composure was now crumbling. She started to cry into a lace handkerchief pulled from her bag. She and the maid were cuddling each other even more tightly, the maid almost throwing herself upon her mistress. I moved over to comfort her, and I could see that even Holmes was shaken from his customary inscrutability.

"Dear lady, if matters are as you describe then you are entirely innocent of any wrong-doing and I would urge you most strongly to go to the police and make a clean breast of it." Holmes said softly.

The lady pushed the maid gently aside for a moment, her eyes now red-rimmed.

"But, Mr. Holmes, my position is such that it would be acutely embarrassing for me were anything to come out to my discredit. And how can I be sure the authorities will believe me? It might all look so terribly suspicious, and where would I be then. I am so terribly afraid, Mr. Holmes. And another thing, I … I cannot really even be certain he is dead. Supposing he was not killed at all, but survived his injuries! Then I would be confessing to something that never happened. And I really cannot bear to go back to that ghastly place to find out."

Holmes seemed momentarily torn.

"I understand your quandary entirely, but you cannot really suppose that the laws of England are so unfair as to make it a criminal matter for a lady to defend her honour under such circumstances as you described; however unwise your conduct may have been in entering into dealings with such a man. Much as I may sympathize with your predicament, I really cannot see that there is anything I can do for you, other than to offer the advice I have already given."

The lady appeared profoundly downcast at this rejection of her plea, her head slumping against the cushions. But Holmes after a pause, designed I fancy more for show than as the product of mature reflection, added, "But, given the enormity of the matter, if you insist on engaging me I will not refuse."

The lady's demeanour was transformed.

"Oh, thank you, thank you, Mr. Holmes. I am so inestimably grateful to you!"

Her exhalations of relief seemed to fill the room. The atmosphere perceptibly lightened, but Holmes, typically, wrenched affairs back onto a business-like footing.

"It is essential that I am in possession of the full facts. Are you prepared to answer my questions?"

Lady Diana had re-composed herself and drying her tears she sat upright once more to address herself to Holmes's scrutiny, the maid now slipping aside.

"Now, firstly what is the precise address where these events took place?"

"Anticipating your query I have written it down for you. It is Oil Drum Lane, Shepherd's Bush, an address I shall try to avoid for the rest of my life!" She handed Holmes a note plucked from her bag.

"And have you told your friend the Count any of what transpired?"

"No, Mr. Holmes, I feel I cannot possibly do so. I said nothing to him beforehand as this man insisted, and I feared what my dear Wolfi's reactions might be, for though he is the most charming and thoughtful of men he has a fearful temper when crossed. Having said nothing to him of my first encounter with Kellmann then I could hardly tell him of what occurred later. He may in some way have blamed me for allowing this to happen. I cannot say what he might do. I have had no communication with him for over a week now and he must imagine me still to be convalescing from my feigned indisposition. But in any case I know that he intends to go overseas in a few days time to attend to matters in his native country. He may be away for as much as a month, but I am not sure I can ever face him again." She was once again struggling to master her emotions as she said this.

"And may I ask for the Count's addresses?"

She seemed slightly disconcerted to be asked this, but hastily wrote down two addresses in her little notebook and passed this note also to Holmes.

"And you say he is soon to go abroad?"

"That is so."

"And when he is in this country, what is his normal routine?"

"I am not sure why you would ask me. As you might suppose, he leads a very active social life, frequently attending dinners and balls, and academic conferences and the like, though alas I have not been able to accompany him. He often works in his office during the day; I believe he is currently engaged upon researches for a work on Frederick the Great, upon which he is acknowledged as one of the foremost experts. As I mentioned to you, he was a professor of history at the University of Wurttemberg before inheriting his title and retiring from public life to devote himself to his estates."

"Please go on."

"Well, I really don't know why you seek to elicit these details, but of late he almost invariably dines at his club, and then attends the theatre or otherwise occupies himself, returning quite late to his house at ten to ten thirty."

"And who, besides yourself and your doughty servants, are aware of these occurrences?

"Why no-one at all."

"Not even your close family?"

"My dear family do not reside in London and I have had relatively little contact with them in recent months, profoundly to my regret and my discredit, but it would surely be impossible for me to say anything of these terrible events to them without invoking their horror at my conduct."

"I see. And are there any other pertinent facts?"

"None, that spring to my mind."

Lady Diana had recovered much of her composure, the crisis point of her story now over, but still she and her maid clung to each other.

"May I presume upon your privacy a little more and enquire as to whether you have yourself entered into any engagement?" The lady blushed slightly again and replied haughtily that she was a free woman, and that she would scarcely have been intimate with the Count had that not been the case.

"Very well. Please be assured of my most urgent attention to this matter. I will inform you of any significant developments and in the meantime may I respectfully suggest that you do not allow distress to overwhelm you. Distract yourself with whatever amusements are to hand. I cannot promise a successful outcome but I pledge my most earnest endeavours on your behalf."

With that they both rose.

"Oh, I am so very, so very grateful to you, Mr. Holmes. You have taken at least some of the great weight from my shoulders. I shall await your summons as soon as you have any news." She paused. "We have not discussed the matter of remuneration."

"Since I am unsure as to whether I can render any useful service, I cannot in all faith charge any fee, at least unless matters take a turn that may require further action on my part."

"Oh, but sir, I really cannot allow you to enter into such a grave undertaking on my behalf without some recompense. I am not without means, as you know well. You must permit me to make some sort of gesture." she implored.

"I have stated my position and I will not go back on it."

"Then I can only redouble my thanks and await your first report with the utmost keenness."

She said no more but proffered a velvet-gloved hand for him to kiss. He took her hand and bowed slightly but no more. She behaved similarly with me and I obliged her. Her fingers were long and slender.

With that and a fleeting nod of acknowledgment she and her maid departed our rooms, the latter bobbing and curtseying frenetically and mumbling her thanks as she went.

I gazed wistfully from the window as they re-boarded the coach which rumbled away up Baker Street towards Regent's Park.

"What a very remarkable woman." I said.

"Remarkable indeed. Well, I think it may be a most absorbing case at all events."

"I must say Holmes; I was surprized that you agreed to accept the commission, for you were surely right in saying that she should have put her faith in British justice."

"Well, that may be so Watson, but I must admit to an ulterior motive."

"Aha! I thought that you were somewhat taken with the lady."

"Not quite what I meant, my dear fellow." he replied with mock asperity. "No, I was rendered agog by the fact that her paramour is none other than Wolfgang Siegfried von Mecklenburg, the Count von Runstedt, a man whose extra-curricular activities I have been following with the greatest possible interest for quite some time now."

"Really Holmes? I cannot imagine why. I have only read of him but I can scarcely believe he would be a magnet for your attentions."

"Ah, but for all his imposture as a retired academic, and an aristocratic man of leisure, he is, I am convinced of it, at the centre of a web of intrigue spreading right across the Continent from Bantry Bay to the Bosphorus. He is the puppet-master pulling the strings of a hundred agents, all of whom dance to his merry tune at the slightest flick of the rods."

I was taken aback by the vehemence of this diatribe against a man whom I had only ever heard referred to in the most approbatory of terms.

"But Holmes, I am not personally acquainted but this fellow is, I am given to believe, a figure of great probity and rectitude, and no little academic distinction. Surely you cannot suppose him to be some sort of international criminal mastermind. Are you sure you are not craving for another opponent to replace the late and unlamented professor of mathematics?"

Holmes reacted acerbically.

"You do me a disservice, Watson! No, not a bit of it. I am convinced this man von Runstedt is behind many a dastardly deed in recent years, both in these islands and on the Continent. So often my investigations into a great variety of different crimes and mysteries have led me from one clue to another to the same point of nexus. A murder here, a theft there; and an act of sabotage in a third place. And it all leads back to the Count! He is a threat to every realm in which his minions operate. And this fellow Kellmann I have heard much of too. He is, as our lady says, the Count's right hand man and I strongly suspect his chief means of liaison with his country's embassy; which I believe he frequents often. And yet I cannot prove a thing." He cast a glance in my direction and saw my look of incredulity.

"You don't believe me?"

At this Holmes sprang to the bookshelves near his desk and seized one of the alphabetized box files wherein he kept his coveted archives. I could see from the spine it was the one covering the letters P-Q-R. He plonked the file down upon his desktop and blew the dust from it. He flicked fervently through the contents, until his eyes came to rest, and I could see even from a distance of several yards that he was gazing at a cluster of photographs as well as documents. I was avid to know more.

"You have prolific documentation on this fellow then, Holmes?"

"I should say. Have a look for yourself at all of this. Documentation galore, collected over a course of many years and from information gleaned from diverse and reliable sources of mine, but the one thing I lack is hard evidence; evidence that could give this man his just deserts, or at the very least force his exile from these shores and an end to his malign influence."

I strode over to peer at this wealth of paperwork. It was seldom that Holmes permitted sight of these records of his to anyone, even to me, and I felt almost privileged to be given sight of his treasure trove. Much of it appeared to be Holmes's casebooks detailing in his spidery hand observations and deductions and so forth. And interspersed amongst the sheaves were photographs of varying quality and definition depicting several figures and one in particular; a tall, distinguished, stern-faced character. I picked up one such specimen.

"Our friend the Count." Holmes declared. "Taken two years ago at a meeting of the Anglo-German Historical Association of which he is an honorary member. And this one here." he said, picking up another; "Taken more recently of him in Hyde Park."

I peered at the likeness. It showed in addition to the Count a second, rather unprepossessing figure; shorter, squatter and uglier, gazing up at the Count and apparently deep in conversation with him whilst keeping stride.

"Herr Kellmann with his master." Holmes explained.

"And what, pray, is this sinister organization of which he is the chief?"

"It is known, colloquially, by many names since it has no official status, but if it has to be given a designation then it is the Federation of the Black Eagles; or *Die Bund der Schwarzen Adler.*"

Holmes flicked through more sheets before alighting on a sheet of cartridge paper with the symbol of two black eagles upon a red background foregrounding crossed swords and pistols. "Their activities are highly clandestine and it is rare for a document emanating from them to surface but here I have managed to obtain a small sample." He handed me the sheet and I cast my eye over it. It was filled with impenetrable German script and a few sketchy diagrams of some bizarre contraption.

"I cannot be sure but I think it is the design of a new flying machine being developed at some establishment under the auspices of the War Office of which the Bund may have gained some knowledge." Holmes explained. I stared hard at the document trying to make sense of it. "It just emphasizes the extent of their penetration into affairs in this country." he declared solemnly.

"The Bund's tentacles extend far and wide and deep, even I fear into crevices of government ministries. Below him in the hierarchy of this body are several of his countryman resident here, including Herr Kellmann, but it has recruited to its ranks through bribery, blackmail or other such nefarious means gangs of home-grown members of the underworld to do much of the dirty work." I handed things back to him and he replaced the various papers and photographs more neatly than before into the box file.

"I fear that von Runstedt may, even as we speak, be extending the scope of his machinations beyond the Continent. I see already a dark Teutonic hand casting itself over the affairs of southern Africa."

"Well, Holmes, I am completely taken aback. I know this fellow only very slightly and solely by reputation and yet could never imagine him to be the orchestrator of some sinister conspiracy such as you describe. And you have never mentioned any of this before, though you are often prolix on such matters."

"No, that is true Watson, but I have never been sufficiently sure of my ground to express my beliefs openly."

"Have you unburdened yourself to the police or the authorities?"

"No. There would be little point. Nobody in a position of power or influence could nor would take action unless I had incontrovertible proof, which I conspicuously lack. Some of my sources in the underworld could not possibly give evidence for they would surely forfeit their lives in the process. No, this is a dark business indeed, Watson and I have a way to go yet before I can settle accounts."

"Well, I am flabbergasted by all this. And what an extraordinary coincidence that your new client should be involved with this man."

"What a coincidence indeed."

But how does any of this affect the predicament of your client?"

"Perhaps not at all but it may at least grant me a new means of penetration into the heart of this devilry."

He replaced the box file upon his shelf and then, as if mindful of some unspoken threat to its security, placed it instead in the bottom drawer of his desk which he locked, placing the key in his waistcoat pocket.

"Well this is all very extraordinary. So what do you propose to do, Holmes?"

Chapter II

The Scene of Death

"Holmes?"

I repeated myself for I had received no answer to my last question which I had addressed to him whilst momentarily facing away and when I turned around I found he had vanished noiselessly from the room. I shrugged my shoulders and busied myself with personal affairs for the next few minutes. I knew anyway that it was a fruitless exercize to try to draw the man out as to his intentions until he had settled upon a firm course of action, and often not even then. But my query was at least partially answered when within a quarter of an hour he re-emerged having effected a complete change of apparel and now clothed in a long, dark overcoat, a muffler wrapped so tightly as completely to obscure the lower half of his face and a cloth cap pulled down over his brow.

"I think it advisable to remain as unidentifiable as possible for our forthcoming expedition, Watson. Oh, I do apologize for assuming your readiness and willingness?"

I indicated that I had no pressing engagements, my medical practice all but dried up if I were to be honest about the matter, and my days now spent chiefly in idleness and triviality. In truth, I thirsted for action and excitement almost as much as did my friend.

"Excellent, Watson, I knew my man. And by the way perhaps you would be good enough to bring your box of tricks with you?" he said alluding to my medical bag, "for if so it may be greatly to our advantage." I grabbed the black leather case and hurried after him as he bounded down the staircase with me in his wake. He had hailed a hansom and barked instructions to the driver before I had scarce gained the pavement. In an instant we were rattling off.

"May I enquire as to our destination?"

"Shepherd's Bush must be our first port of call. We must inspect this corpse of ours to ensure it has not somehow regained the power of motion and wandered off."

"You are not suggesting, surely, that this whole thing is a figment of our client's imagination?"

I supposed a jest on his part but my friend's face betrayed nothing.

Shortly, Holmes rapped with his cane upon the roof of the cab, bellowed to the driver to step it up a notch or two, and that there would be a shilling in it for him if he got to our destination within the half hour. The man complied so eagerly that we found ourselves rocked from side to side with the motion, the vehicle weaving its way through the chaotic midday traffic of Paddington, Bayswater and Ladbroke Grove and thence to Shepherd's Bush and down the Goldhawk Road. Our journey was punctuated by the cabbie's bellowed oaths at other road users so impudent as to cross his path, and the periodic crack of his whip upon the poor mare's back. A hard, cold rain was now lashing down. Gradually the broad thoroughfares of the West End gave way to the meaner streets of the western suburbs.

Holmes said little during the journey but the deeply furrowed brow spoke of a fast-gestating plan of campaign. I attempted to draw him out but to no avail, for when in these deeply contemplative moods on the precipice of action it was impossible to penetrate the carapace of his mind. At length his face lightened and he suddenly broke into a disquisition upon the music of Mendelssohn, a subject to which he had devoted much attention, but which bore no relation whatever to the business at hand, and yet it was so typical of the man's protean nature to segue off as he did.

By late morning we had arrived at the charmingly appellated Oil Drum Lane. Holmes paid off the cabbie at the end of the street and we wandered down the road to find the object of our quest, Holmes desiring to scout the whole neighbourhood before focussing upon the house in question. I was glad at least that the rain had eased off. He scrutinized intently the unprepossessing and poorly maintained buildings that lined our route as we passed them, but what clues he gained thereby I cannot begin to imagine. I was more concerned with my own well-being and constantly tried to hug myself warm, rubbing my shoulders briskly and wishing I had donned an extra layer. The bitter cold was gnawing at my innards and causing a recrudescence of the old shoulder wound that was now increasingly finding a sympathetic response in my leg. A change of weather could be guaranteed to have this effect, especially one towards the inclement. My humour was not improved by the dreary, forbidding appearance of the street.

It was indeed an ill-appointed neighbourhood, with row upon row of terraces of dour and crumbling tenements which met our sight, until at length we passed some open waste ground and came to a sprawling, dilapidated house set well back from the street and fronted by a small yard with its large wooden double doors flapping open on creaking hinges.

There was a coal vendor's dray parked opposite, covered with heavy, brown canvas sheets.

"This must be our mark. I can understand our lady's reluctance to embark on a rendezvous here!" for indeed it was a dismal dwelling. Ensuring we were unobserved we negotiated the outer doors and picked our way through the clutter and rubbish littering the yard to the door. The smell described by our client was unmistakeable. To one side were the stables, though no horses were in evidence, and to the other the fearful abode. Its front door gave way after we had made a few forceful shoves and we crept in warily scouring the interior with our eyes. There was no sign of any habitation.

"No sign of life here, Holmes."

Holmes signalled to me to keep my voice to a whisper for who knew who or what might be lurking within the intestines of the house. The downstairs rooms were shabbily and basically furnished, and shed no light on matters. At the front of the house was a dingy and dirt encrusted kitchen, its sink containing a number of pots and pans indicating that there had at least been some human presence here within recent times. It gave off to a scullery and a lavatory. At the back was a drawing room that was equally unappealing to the eye, with some rickety furniture, cobweb strewn, and displaying no signs of recent occupation, nor any attempt at cleaning.

Having satisfied ourselves that there was nothing of relevance to be discovered downstairs we ventured up the rickety old staircase, Holmes leading, and treading carefully upon the creaking boards which we feared might give way, or betray our presence to any lurking malefactor. My heart was pounding so hard I felt it must be audible. We moved very slowly along the landing and stopped at the first door we came to, which was slightly ajar. I could see that even Holmes's normal bravado had deserted him, for there was a quiver about his lips such as I had rarely witnessed. He flung the door open and the sight that met our eyes was as hideous as any that could have been imagined from the lady's account.

"Oh my God, Holmes!"

The body of a man lay in a twisted posture in the centre of the floor, a ghastly contorted smile upon his face, his tongue lolling out of its mouth, mad staring eyes seeming to search for an escape and a hand outstretched as if in supplication. A pool of congealed blood encircled his head.

We exchanged distraught glances. It took a few moments for us to recover our nerve, Holmes more rapidly than I. For all my military background and long experience of medical practice it had been quite a while since my professional duties had led me to an encounter such as this, and I was still not totally inured to such a grisly spectacle. We squatted awkwardly on either side to inspect the corpse. I had to gird myself even to look at him and I could see from the almost imperceptible twitch of his facial muscles that Holmes was similarly affected, though as ever he would not own to it. There was a gash to the back of the corpse's skull clearly visible, which was no doubt the proximate cause of death. I took his pulse and applied my stethoscope, but these were absurdly redundant exercizes.

"I should say this man has been dead for at least a day or two but it is hard to be certain in these matters." I ventured. "*Rigor mortis* has long since passed."

The man was conventionally if rather untidily clothed in heavy overcoat over a tweed suit and had brogues on his feet. He was, or rather had been, of about medium height, a fairly portly build, fair haired with pale blue piggy eyes, rather a pudgy face and a clipped moustache. He now wore a deathly pallor. His body was already cold.

The room showed little sign of recent human habitation, the furniture being rather quaint and dated and with few amenities. Lighting had been by means of candelabra, for there was no sign of any gas supply. There were a few plates, one containing a half-eaten meal of cold meat and vegetables upon a large dining table in the centre of room adjacent to our cadaver, plus a few bottles of wine, a couple of bottles of whisky, one open and half-empty and a decanter. There were two glasses laid out, one full, one empty. The heavy, moth-eaten brocade curtains were drawn, casting a pall of gloom over the whole chamber.

Once he had taken a moment or two to regain his composure Holmes threw himself into the business of forensic investigation with all his old customary vigour and exactitude. He set about inspecting the scene in the minutest detail, flinging himself to the ground, lens in hand, supplemented by a measuring tape; flying hither and yonder; first the body, then the table, the glasses, bottles and decanter, the plates, then the furniture, the walls, the floors and the windows, the staircase, the landing, the hallway, the outer door and the yard. He left nothing uninspected.

Whilst he was thus absorbed, I made a further, more extensive, examination of the deceased, loosening his clothing sufficiently to inspect the body which was quite heavily bruised in places, though there were no signs of serious injury other than the terrible head wound. Whilst Holmes continued his activities, I occupied myself by investigating the rest of the house. There were three more rooms on the first floor, two bedrooms and a bathroom-cum-lavatory. None showed any sign of recent occupation. Furniture was minimal and basic in the form of beds, wardrobes, cabinets, side tables and chairs, and all were in a filthy and neglected state, evidently not having been cleaned for years if not decades. What had led Kellmann to select this ghastly hovel as a point of rendezvous heaven only knew.

There was a wooden ladder leaning against a far wall ascending, I supposed, to an attic. It was distinctly unsteady and in a similar state of disrepair as the rest of the abode's fixtures and fittings, but curiosity beckoned. I ascended the rungs very gingerly, some of which were missing or gave way, until reaching a trap door which I levered open bringing a shower of assorted light debris down on my uncovered head. Ducking and shaking my head vigorously to sweep it away, fearful of letting go of the ladder, I pushed hard upwards and flipped the door wide open, causing it to slam down on the floor above. I peered into the tenebrous cavern thus revealed and immediately heard rapid scuttling noises, which so unnerved me that I nearly clattered back down the ladder. The attic was evidently host to a colony of rats, of which variety I did not stay long enough to ascertain, but not, so far as I could glean, a great deal else. I hurried down the ladder, mission accomplished, considerably faster than I had climbed.

All the commotion elicited a voice echoing from somewhere. "Are you alright, Watson?"

"Yes, fine." I said, with less than total accuracy. I had grazed my hand and bruised my leg slightly in the descent, neither of which improved my temper.

I rejoined Holmes in the main bedroom, trying to avoid gazing at the corpse and yet finding it an eerily compelling sight.

"Discovered anything of note in your travels?"

I was brushing bits off my hair and dusting down my coat.

"Only some rats and a lot of dirt."

"Rats, eh?" Holmes seemed momentarily intrigued, working some idea over in his mind.

He renewed his inspection of the dining table, perched alongside it with his magnifying glass scanning every square inch. I wandered into another bedroom and peered out of its windows, its timber frame rotting away with age and crumbling at the touch of my fingertips and the curtains thick with soot. Through the grubby and bedraggled net curtains I viewed the neighbouring dwellings, though the nearest was perhaps some thirty or forty yards away on the far side of the waste ground. They were almost equally depressing in aspect, and showed few signs of habitation either, though one presumed there must be occupants. I strained intently in the hope of seeing some form of humanity, but could see nothing save a couple of street urchins playing on the wasteland, and the road with its intermittent stream of vehicles. Screwing my eyes I thought I spied the glint of something in a window opposite, but it may just have been my imagination playing games with me. After what I had just witnessed phantoms rose and fell before me. It was in any case difficult to see with the light already fading and the gas lamps in the street not yet lit.

I returned to the fateful bedchamber where Holmes was concluding his investigations by producing some pouches and phials from the commodious holdall he had brought with him. Using tweezers, he placed samples of the man's hair and fibres from his clothing into the pouches, and very small samples of coagulated blood from the floor and the festering blood from the skull into the bottles. I knew his methods all too well and I confess I could not help deriving a grim amusement, though I could not imagine what he hoped to learn from any of it. He went through the man's pockets and quickly scanned some papers retrieved from the inside pocket of his jacket. He also tore a cufflink from the man's shirtsleeve, which action quite stunned me.

"Holmes, what are you up to!?"

"I have my reasons. Well, I think we have discovered all we can for the moment, Watson. What do you make of the corpse?"

"As I say, deceased for at least a day I would hazard. Cause of death undoubtedly the blow to the skull. There is considerable bruising about his body, but no other ostentatious injury or wound. As I said, *rigor mortis* has long since passed and, moreover, *livor mortis* has set in with some purplish discolouration of portions of his lower torso."

"My conclusions precisely."

"So, our client was not fantasizing!"

"There is a corpse to be sure."

"We must alert the police at once."

"Watson, no!"

"But Holmes, we must inform the authorities at the earliest possible moment. You know the law as well as I do."

"And I know the law to be an ass as well as you do! I don't want all of Scotland Yard blundering in here and trampling the evidence to oblivion. Besides, I may have other plans for our corpse."

"Whatever can you be thinking of, Holmes. This is outrageous. It is a serious offence to conceal a death like this."

"We are not concealing it, Watson, merely omitting to reveal it."

"Oh, Holmes this is preposterous!"

"Just abide with me a little longer, my dear doctor. After all, a slight delay will scarcely cause any further deterioration in his health."

"This is surely not a matter for levity, Holmes." I chided. "You have bent the law on occasion but this is going too far!" What game are you playing?"

"A long one, I fancy. Bear with me, Watson. If the law is pliable enough to be bent then we may see if we can try it a little more without it snapping."

He gathered up all of his accoutrements into his bag and ushered me out.

"Come, Watson, if you please; there is another venue on our itinerary before the day is out."

With that we hastened from the premises, not a moment too soon for my liking, and emerged back through the yard and onto the street. I breathed a long hard sigh of relief to be free of that accursed place and drew as much clear air into my lungs as I could. Traffic in the road was sparse, the odd lumbering cart and trotting carriage, and the coal merchants dray still stationary and unattended on the other side of the road. No-one, I earnestly hoped, had observed our entry or exit, which was well if we were to feign ignorance of the horrible corpse closeted therein. My watch showed it to be two thirty, which meant we had been there for between two and two and a half hours though in my state of shock and disorientation I had completely lost all track of time.

"What now?"

"Let's find ourselves some transport."

"Do you not want to question neighbours?"

"Probably a futile exercize. All the houses seem nearly as ill-favoured as this, and given that it all happened late at night I doubt there were any witnesses."

I could not pretend I was displeased at this reluctance on Holmes's part to spend any more time than strictly necessary in these morbid environs.

"No, we have another port of call." he declared.

We walked briskly back along the road to the end and down another before we caught sight of a hansom, they being somewhat thinner on the ground in these outlying districts than in the heart of the metropolis. We hailed the first that hoved into view.

"Kilburn, please cabbie." Holmes shouted, and we were once more cantering along.

I tried to engage Holmes in conversation but to no avail. I was desperate to know his conclusions upon all that we had discovered but he was sunk in thought and doubtless working on some scheme upon the likes of which I forbore to speculate.

We were swishing through the late afternoon traffic, along the route we had come but then veering off to the north for some considerable way until we came at length to Acol Road, a drear thoroughfare of respectable if architecturally unimaginative houses stretching along either side for as far as the eye could see.

"Pull up here, cabbie."

We had stopped outside a sizeable three storied double fronted townhouse of brown brick with a generous drive-way and bay windows.

"So where are we?"

"The abode of our dear departed friend, Herr Kellmann. Some correspondence I found on his person confirmed for me that these were his lodgings."

Holmes knocked at the front door and after a wait it was answered by a forbidding lady in her sixties of a grumpy disposition and sour countenance.

"Good day to you, madam. May we call upon Mr. Kellmann, we are friends of his." Holmes announced cheerily, doffing his cap.

"He ain't at home."

"Any idea of when he might return?"

"No, he doesn't tell me nothing about his comings and goings and I doesn't ask him."

"I see. Well, madam, would it be permissible for you to admit us to his rooms, for as I say we are very good friends of his, and would like to catch him unawares."

The woman cast a deeply disapproving eye over the pair of us, and perhaps being in a good mood, she opened the door just wide enough for us to get through.

"I suppose you'd better come in then, but make sure you wipes your feet properly; I had these carpets cleaned only yesterday."

We wiped thoroughly.

Still eyeing us suspiciously she escorted us up to the first floor landing and along the corridor.

"I'm getting sick of all these visitations. Damned foreigners up and down the stairs at all times of the day and night. How am I supposed to get any work done. Women as well. If my Albert was still alive, God rest his soul, things would be a bit different I can tell you."

She delved into her apron pocket and retrieved a jangling bunch of keys from which she selected a long thin specimen and opened the door, favouring us once again with a look of displeasure.

"Make sure you don't make no noise, and let me know when you're gone." She tramped back downstairs, casting a final backward stare before disappearing into the bowels of the house.

"What a charming lady. And so hospitable."

"Dammit Holmes, what is this wild goose chase?"

"This, as I said my dear doctor, is where Herr Kellmann resides, or rather resided. I fancied that we might pick up some more useful information here."

"Do we need any more information, Holmes?"

"I find one can never get enough of the stuff."

He cast his eyes eagerly around the sitting room in which we found ourselves.

"We don't want to outstay our welcome here so let us be quick about our business."

The room was rather plain in its furnishing and adornments and utilitarian in its amenities, though clean and well-ordered and a decided improvement over our previous place of visitation. The carpet was thinning, with small segments missing in places and the curtains drab. There were a few undistinguished prints upon the walls. The establishment had evidently seen more prosperous days.

"One might have thought someone of Kellmann's stature would be able to afford better accommodation." I mused.

"Perhaps the Count pays him a less than generous salary."

Holmes had commenced his familiar routine of examining the furniture, the carpets, the walls and the windows with the same assiduity as he had only an hour or two before in a very different setting. A door gave off to the bedroom and another to a bathroom. Holmes roamed swiftly through these before returning to the sitting room.

Of greatest interest to him, however, were the occupant's desk and cabinets. Swiftly but methodically opening and closing drawers and cupboard doors Holmes rifled through their contents, glancing briefly at each and issuing forth with little cries and mutterings at each new offering.

I availed myself of the only easy chair in the room and sat smoking and reading a local newspaper that was to hand; almost the only reading material I could find apart from a small shelf of German language volumes. After a quarter of an hour or so of his ransacking Holmes had satisfied himself with a small sample of documents, and he motioned for us to leave. Ensuring that all had been left exactly as we found it he shut the door loudly behind us and we made our way downstairs to be greeted by the landlady emerging from the back.

"It seems that Dieter left a note to say he will not be returning home until much later, so we must take our leave. Perhaps we will come back another time." Holmes ventured.

"Please yourselves, but don't expect me to be constantly letting you in and out." she grumped as she led us to the door. "You wasn't smoking was you?" She cast an accusatory glance at us, keening in on me as the probable culprit. "I can smell tobacco. I don't abide that, especially not from visitors."

"Must be wafting in from outside, madam." I improvized, though her look of sheer malice signalled disbelief.

"We are most grateful to you, madam, for your forbearance." Holmes gave as his parting shot, cutting off any further invective, before doffing his hat and striding out with me in his wake.

The front door slammed with a thud behind us.

We exchanged looks of wry amusement and hastened to the roadside. Hailing a hansom a few minutes later we made our way back home. I was grateful that there was nothing more on the agenda that day for I was profoundly shaken by everything. Holmes's demeanour was now a little more light-hearted and conversational, though still unforthcoming upon the central issues of the matter in hand. It was evening by the time we reached Baker Street and I cannot deny I was very happy to be back in our own comfortable nest after all the travails of the day. I poured myself a large brandy and slumped into my fireside armchair.

"What a God-awful experience! After my retirement from the colours, I had hoped I would never see another corpse."

"Does not your practice bring you into occasional contact?"

"Scarcely, I freely admit. I haven't lost a patient yet."

Holmes was pre-occupied with decanting the items from his holdall procured at Shepherd's Bush and Kilburn.

"So, what do you make of it all so far, Holmes?"

"I make quite a lot of it. I think our little expedition has been quite fruitful."

"Fruitful! That's one word for it I suppose. Well, we have certainly ascertained the truth of the lady's account, though I cannot for the life of me see why you found it necessary to go to his lodgings?"

"I find it yields dividends to examine every possible aspect of matters for you never know what you may discover." With that he slipped away to his bedroom, leaving me brooding heavily and as perplexed as ever.

Chapter III

Mycroft

I slept fitfully that night, exhaustion battling for my soul with recollected horrors. I awoke and arose early, contrary to my usual custom and natural inclinations, meditating grimly upon the events of the previous day. Had it all been a terrible dream or all too real a nightmare? And what was to happen now? I was deeply troubled by Holmes's decision not to inform the police and my thoughts rambled over all the possible permutations that fate might deliver.

To my surprize Holmes had beaten me to the breakfast table and was already perusing his correspondence over toast and marmalade, a characteristic insouciance contrasting sharply with my own bleak mood. It was almost as if we had exchanged dispositions with each other overnight. To Holmes a corpse was a mere object for forensic examination, just another case study, to be dissected upon the post-mortem table in search of clues; whereas for me it was a stark and brutal reminder of my days in Afghanistan and the hellishness of war. I knew all too well the lead up to death and the agony of it.

"Good morning, Watson." he said breezily, upon my appearance. "Why the haggard visage?"

"Oh, for God's sake, Holmes, you know perfectly well why!"

"Be of good cheer, my dear chap, for all will be well. I have a great sense of events unfolding to our advantage."

"I can scarcely see how. We have found a cadaver and now face the choice of continuing to conceal it, unlawfully I may

45

stress and for purposes best known to yourself, or going to the police and effectively handing our client over to their tender mercies. I presume you are going to apprize Lady Diana of developments? I certainly hope so."

"It would be derelict of me not to do so. I mean to go over to her townhouse this morning and give a report. I also have a number of other minor errands to run. Alas, it is so long since I last had a case in hand that demanded any sort of scientific analysis that I much fear I no longer have the necessary tools. I propose a visit to Bart's this morning to see if I can procure the necessary chemical re-agents and, if I am very lucky, a newer more powerful microscope. The innovative Köhler model is a vast improvement on existing instruments I am given to understand, and I believe they just may have at least one in stock. My old collaborator, Quennell, is still in charge of the laboratories there and I feel I may be able to call in an old debt or two to secure his co-operation."

"I was going to ask what you are going to do with all these blood and other samples. I suppose then I must brace myself to you turning our living quarters into some sort of hellish bio-chemical factory once again."

"Just like old times."

"We'll see what Mrs. Hudson has to say about that. I remember the last occasion. She was beside herself what with the smells and the fumes percolating through the whole house. It's a wonder she didn't kick us out there and then without a minute's notice."

"I have squared it with our good landlady. A small increase in our rent will satisfy her."

"Our rent? You mean I have to pay for you making my home unliveable! And in case you hadn't noticed, Holmes, my practice is not exactly lucrative at the moment, my army pension does not grow any larger and you seem to make a fetish out of not charging your clients!"

"It will only be temporary and quite painless I assure you. Smells and fumes will be notable by their absence. Oh, by the way, we are going to see Mycroft for lunch at his club today. I say we because I very much hope you will see fit to accompany me, and I requested the invitation for us both."

This sudden announcement took me aback since it had been several years since he had made any reference to his brother, still less evinced any desire to draw upon his expertize, vast and all-encompassing though it was reputed to be.

"You believe it will advance our cause?"

"It can scarcely retard it and, as you know from his role in a few of my little cases in the past, his erudition may be of no little benefit. If there is a man alive who can penetrate to the inner core of any subject it is he."

"What precisely is his job? Is he something in government?"

"Something indeed. He is employed on a consultancy basis these days; his role to think the unthinkable, imagine the unimaginable, conceive the inconceivable!"

"You make him sound like some sort of magician."

"And perhaps he is. I propose we shall walk over there at twelve when I have returned from my little jaunts. The exercize will do us a power of good. Now, you must excuse me."

And without further ado Holmes departed the breakfast table to discard his dressing gown and re-emerged minutes later fully dressed and was off out of the house, cane and hat in hand, leaving me to ponder the inexplicability of it all.

I tried to settle down to read the morning papers, but I found it impossible to concentrate, as my mind raced over the events of the previous day and flashed forwards to the manifold and not altogether appealing prospects now opening up before us. At length I gave up the unequal struggle and set off for the Criterion to fortify myself and in the hope of bumping into an old acquaintance or two who might cheer my sinking spirits. And I was fortunate, for I met up with young Chapman whom I had known from Afghanistan where he was a dresser under me. It transpired that he was no longer in receipt of the Queen's shilling and was studying for a new career in book-keeping, upon which I congratulated him, opining that business was potentially a more lucrative sphere than either medicine or soldiering – and a safer one!

I returned at about a quarter to midday, and in better humour, and found Holmes was already *in situ* and swiftly establishing his forensic work station in a corner of the drawing room, arranging phalanxes of complex instruments including an impressive looking microscope, and row upon row of test tubes, gas jars and other such chemical esoterica.

Seeing my entry, he saluted and bid me be patient whilst he completed the construction of his laboratory.

"You will forgive me while I set out my stall. You have been to the Criterion I see." He had not looked up from his desk.

I was so used to this party trick of his that I barely registered surprize, but knew he expected me to react and so I played along.

"Alright, Holmes" I said wearily, "how do you know? The soil on my shoes perhaps or the soot on my hat."

"No, by virtue of the fact that I saw you there as I was passing *en route* to the post office."

I smiled. "I see. The mirror business again."

"You were deep in conversation with the left-handed book-keeper and former army lieutenant."

I couldn't prevent a slight gasp escaping.

"Go on, amaze me."

"Simple enough. He was holding both his drink and his cigarette in his left hand throughout, had an accountancy textbook protruding from his pocket, and the bar there is a well-known watering hole of ex-army types such as yourself. As a professional man I supposed him to be of the officer class but since he was younger than yourself and a tad deferential towards you, Captain Watson, I made a stab at his rank."

"Very impressive." I sniffed. "What else have you done this morning?"

"I went to the Gloucester Walk residence of our good lady client to apprize her of developments and reassure her of our continued devotion to her cause. It is a very smart and fashionable townhouse. I believe she lives there alone but for her staff which is quite small."

"And how did she take the news?"

"Alas, she and her devoted maid were absent for the day upon some mission of mercy to a sick relative in Hertfordshire according to her valet, and so I left a message summarizing our findings and promising to contact her further in due course. I also made a detour to St. James's where I had a brief interview with Langdale Pike." He was still peering with screwed-up eyes at one of his test tubes as he gently shook it.

"Langdale Pike! That mountebank. Why the man is an absolute bounder, with his scurrilous scribblings in the gutter press about those of good repute. Why ever would you associate with such a creature?"

"For enlightenment, what else? He is a veritable mine of information about the doings of the upper echelons of society and his sources are, I believe, impeccable. Did you know for example, that Lady Diana had a very brief career on the stage? Apparently, she wowed them with her Desdemona at the Haymarket a few years ago."

"No, I did not. She is evidently a lady of many talents, but is that relevant?"

"Perhaps not."

He had now completed his scrutiny of the test tube, and placing it back in its rack, at last turned to me.

"Are you ready for our luncheon engagement?"

I had almost forgotten. Within minutes we were off on foot in the direction of Pall Mall, the brisk pace of my friend's step heating our bodies against the chill of the morning. We reached our destination by twelve forty-five and entered through the august portals of the Diogenes Club, an oasis of tranquillity amidst the hurly burly of the capital. Holmes presented his card. We were ushered into the Strangers' Room where we were met by the jowly and rubicund figure of Mycroft. Recalling him somewhat hazily from the problem of *The Greek Interpreter* some years ago, and his cameo role in the problem of *The Empty House* a few years later, I observed that he had, if anything, gained even more in weight, and that his general demeanour was even more ponderous and saturnine than hitherto, almost as if lethargy had taken possession of his soul.

He bid Holmes and me a mildly querying welcome in hushed tones and led us to a set of armchairs by the fireplace and some distance from anyone else in the sparsely populated sanctuary. He plonked himself down, his body seemingly folding in upon itself. The sepulchral tone of the room was broken only by stertorous noises emanating from a slumbering member at the other end, his spread newspaper covering his front and floating up and down with the gentle rhythm of his breathing. Mycroft ordered brandies from the steward.

"Well, what an unexpected pleasure, Sherlock. I see that you have been dabbling with your foul chemicals yet again."

"Doubtless, you spotted the potassium nitrate stains upon my sleeve. Damnably hard to remove. Yes indeed I have, in pursuit of enquiries dwelling upon a matter of some moment I might stress. I see that you have deviated from your normal routine, dear brother, in that you have evidently widened your habitual radius of activity to take in the law courts, for I perceive mud stains on your coat of a variety which is often to be found in the Strand, which is currently undergoing extensive building works, and nowhere else within your purview."

"Quite so. I regret I was summonsed to attend there a day or two ago in connection with a lawsuit which an acquaintance of mine is contesting."

I sat bemused by this fantastical exchange of minute observations and obscure deductions, as so often in the past when these two got together. I tried to imagine what it must have been like in the Holmes's household when they were growing up. Were their parents like this?

"And you, Doctor. I trust you are well, though you have evidently been through travails lately, with flecks of plaster in your hair and a graze on the back of your hand."

I had supposed I had brushed my hair thoroughly that morning and gave no thought to the graze but these were evidently as plain as a pikestaff to Mycroft's penetrative scrutiny. I felt a tad abashed.

"Oh, yes, had a bit of a scrape yesterday." I bumbled, casting a quick look at Holmes and reluctant to divulge anything of our escapades without his say-so.

Holmes's face betrayed only the merest hint of mirth as he listened to our exchange.

Mycroft turned his attention back to his brother.

"But I suspect, Sherlock, that your visit is not purely social?"

"Alas, you are correct for much as I enjoy the pleasure of your company, Mycroft, I have been presented very recently with a little nugget of a case. Whilst straightforward in essence, albeit unsavoury in character, it presents certain features which require a rather broader canvas of knowledge than I possess."

He paused and then exploded his little bombshell.

"What do you know of the Count von Runstedt?"

Mycroft's face lit up at the mention of this name, much as Holmes's had when the name was first scouted the previous day, his sunken features re-awakened. The world-weary cynicism fell away in an instant to be replaced by a vibrant, expectant air. His grey eyes almost twinkled.

"That is indeed a name to conjure with. I know of his activities, or suspected activities, and that he is believed to be at the centre of a large but covert organization, and the recipient of a multitude of governmental secrets."

"Anything more specific?"

"He appears to be a connoisseur of naval intelligence in particular. The Admiralty's been a bit leaky of late, only trifling stuff though, no real evidence of any theft but certain Continental powers seem to know rather more than they ought about our affairs. Senior chap, Tremayne, had to resign over it though I don't think he was the source of the leak, just a scapegoat. He was on the verge of retirement anyway. May have been a case of *cherchez la femme*."

"Anything else of note in government circles?"

"Papers going missing here and there, I seem to recall. But nothing has been proven against von Runstedt, and I believe the consensus is that it may be better to leave him undisturbed the better to keep a very close eye upon him; see who his associates are the better to understand the full scope of his operations. Give him enough rope and, though he may not actually hang himself, he may succeed in getting some of his confederates hanged. Beyond that I cannot really say. Why your sudden interest?"

"He is, as I said, a key figure in my present case. What else can you tell me about doings in high government circles?"

Mycroft's tones became even more *sotto voce* than before, and he glanced around to ensure there was no-one within earshot.

"I can tell you that there is a tremendous flap in the Colonial Office. Missing documents etc, and all and sundry running around like headless chickens. Not sure if it might have any connection to our Teutonic friend, however, and contrary to what you might suppose, Sherlock, I do not know the details of every government scandal or blunder. I just pick up a lot of stuff on the grapevine. You think there may be a connection with your case?

"There might be. What more can you tell me about these goings on at the Colonial Office?"

The snoring of the slumberer on the far side had reached a crescendo, his newspaper suddenly slipping from his lap as his body jerked. We all three turned toward him, but he was still asleep. Mycroft lowered his voice almost to the point of inaudibility as he strained forward in his chair.

"Disappearing tricks and all that, the usual hurrah. Whisper is it's a collection of papers bearing upon the South African question, known collectively I believe as the Transvaal Dossier. More than that I am unable to say."

"Unable or unwilling?"

"Unable. As I said, even I don't know everything. Word is it's a lot of contingency stuff, position papers and so on, plus some other bits, even the text of telegrams. If you really press me the whisper is that it emanated from the very top. Could be a major embarrassment if it got out or, heaven forfend, got published in the foreign press."

"Has the source of the leak been traced?"

"Theft, not leak, because for it to be effective it has to be the original document. But, no. Everyone's in the dark. The police haven't been notified, since H.M.G. are anxious to deny even the existence of the document which, if it became public would be awkward in the extreme, or so I hear. It might be supposed the object of the theft is precisely that, to make it public knowledge and leave H.M.G. red-faced."

"Exactly when did this occur?"

"Less than a week ago, so I understand."

"Do we know who might have an interest in getting hold of it?"

"Well, all the usual suspects. There are several powers eager to see London squirm, but I am sure you know the favourite. There have been desperate and unavailing attempts to retrieve it. The usual niceties have been waived aside by having diplomatic baggages intercepted and searched before leaving the country, but with no success. Everyone's flummoxed and getting more and more desperate."

"Fascinating. Anything else you can tell me?"

"Not really. But tell me about your case. These confidences can't be all one-sided you know. What has put you on the track of this von Runstedt fellow?"

"All I can say at the moment is that there is a corpse, and a fairly prominent one at that, but it is too early to theorize."

"And von Runstedt has a hand in all this?"

"Perhaps."

"Look, Sherlock, I give you gold nuggets and you fob me off with matchsticks in exchange. This isn't fair, you know." he huffed. "It's always been like that between us. I initiate you into the darkest arts and get nothing in return. If you do know something then you must be candid. I need scarcely stress the vital importance to H.M.G. of recovering these wretched documents, so if you do know something let's hear it."

"I know nothing that bears on this Transvaal business, I promise you."

"Very well, but if you do glean something …"

"You have my assurance, dear brother."

"Well, well. What a turn-up." he wheezed.

He settled back in his chair, the excitement over, and gulped down the last of his balloon of brandy.

"Care for another? Rather a good Armagnac, wouldn't you say."

"Kind of you, but if you have nothing else to tell us we must be off." Holmes announced to my dismay.

"You won't stay for luncheon? The beef Wellington here is quite excellent."

"No, but you have given me plenty of food for thought."

"But you can't say anything more about this case of yours. If I knew the details, I might be able to help." he wheedled, but to no avail.

"Sorry, dear brother, but work to do, unlike some. I will keep you apprized of the situation."

"Oh well. Have it your way." Mycroft harrumphed, now returning to his usual disposition. "Some of us work but more discreetly. We don't go rushing around showing off."

Holmes did not riposte and we rose to leave.

"Oh, before you go, Doctor, you don't know of anything good for gout do you?"

"Well, not really my field, but have you tried less Armagnac?" I meant the suggestion helpfully but the man fixed me with such a baleful expression that I wished I had remained silent upon the question.

After this badinage we departed, Mycroft seeing us out of the Strangers' Room into the main lobby and then galumphing back to his armchair. We were escorted out by a steward and back into the relentless noise and bustle of the street. I was disappointed at being cheated of a good lunch.

"Did we have to depart so peremptorily? And have you learnt anything relevant?" I chided.

"Sorry to rob you of a free luncheon old chap, but ideas are bubbling forth too fast for me to contain my patience any longer. This sudden agitation at the Colonial Office may have some bearing. I cannot be sure at this stage."

We had returned to Baker Street by the early afternoon and Holmes was back to his former hyper-active self, despatching further telegrams for Billy, the page boy, to trundle off to the post office with, and labouring intensively over the blood samples at his newly constructed work-station. A telegram arrived for Holmes in the late afternoon, brought up by the breathless Billy, and it produced a cry of exultation.

"Watson, I have managed to obtain a meeting with our illustrious friend, the Count. It is tomorrow at ten o'clock sharp. Do you wish to attend?"

I was astounded.

"Well, yes, if you think I can be of some use. But how on earth did you manage to achieve that? It can't be easy to get to see this exalted fellow. His time must be very precious."

"Quite simple. I dropped a note to him at his Mayfair residence this morning claiming to be an academic who has by pure chance come into possession of the Sansoucci flute that belonged to Frederick the Great, and offering to sell it to him or indeed, in my unworldly way, to give it to him *gratis* in exchange for information upon my own field. But I stressed the urgency since tomorrow is my last day in London before I return home to Scotland and to my post at the University of Aberdeen where I hold tenure. I fancied he could not resist the bait. How is your knowledge of eighteenth century Prussian history, Watson? You are a most erudite chap. I am sure you must know something."

"I know very little. History is scarcely my field, as you well know."

"Try to bone up the subject; I know you to be a quick study on all matters, and we can present ourselves tomorrow for our appointment. You can pose as a friend and fellow academic but you can leave the talking to me, though it might help if you possessed a little knowledge. I have taken the trouble to dig out a book or two that you may find of use in your scholarly enquiry. Perhaps you might care to peruse them for the rest of the day."

"And, pray, what is the object of this convoluted exercize?"

"We will beard him in his lair. 'Case the joint' as the underworld argot has it. See where he might keep valuable or confidential material. In the meantime, I have further errands to run."

With that he disappeared for the rest of the day, and I was left to plough my way through the tomes presented to me.

Holmes returned in the evening and enquired as to my progress. I was able to inform him that I could at least pass for someone with a superficial grasp if no more, but that a deeper probe would inevitably reveal to me be a complete ignoramus.

"That will do fine. Oh and, by the way, I have arranged a little diversion that may allow me to have a bit of a rummage around, if matters go to plan."

Holmes then retreated to the other end of our not very commodious living room and started beavering away again in his self-constructed laboratory with its plethora of microscopes, test tubes, vials and scientific instruments. He was thus occupied with characteristic intensity of purpose for the next few hours, as the harvest of his earlier investigations was evidently being subjected to chemical analysis of the most extensive kind. The various specimens of blood were poured into tubes, mixed with other liquids, had drops of potions applied to them, tubes shaken and detailed notes made in his indecipherable hand. These and his other samples, the hair and the fibres, were subjected to microscopic scrutiny and a panoply of procedures which, even I, with my medical training was unable to follow. These procedures were punctuated by the occasional muttered exclamation at each new discovery.

Finally, I could contain my curiosity no longer and, putting down my books, sought to draw him out upon the nature and purposes of these experiments, being not wholly unacquainted with diagnostic medical techniques myself. Holmes alluded loftily to the work of a Professor Landsteiner of the University of Vienna with whom, apparently, he had been in private communication. This fellow was, he gave me to understand, working on blood analysis and his researches were so far advanced that he felt able to distinguish between human and non-human blood, though his work was, as yet, unpublished. Holmes boldly asserted that this presented a potentially huge advance for forensic science, though, he admitted, these researches were still at an embryonic stage and could not yet be wholly relied upon. He was also fascinated by the work of a Dr. Piotrowski of Krakow who, he averred, had published a treatise upon the dispersal of blood in instances of trauma, again causing him to expound upon the deductions this made feasible.

I was profoundly impressed though sceptical as to the practical application of any of this in the field of detective work. But, being unable to compete with Holmes in the field of forensic knowledge, I retreated to the opposite corner of the drawing room to re-acquaint myself with the tomes presented to me in the hope of acquitting myself satisfactorily upon the morrow, though I could not begin to divine my friend's true purpose in all of this.

Chapter IV

The Count

Holmes and I were up early in eager expectation of our forthcoming encounter, Holmes affecting a most complete and compelling makeover of his appearance to include pince-nez spectacles, a wig of wispy greying hair, combined with a rather shambolic wardrobe of scruffily maintained jacket and trousers of clashing hues, a nod perhaps to his notions of the attire to be expected of your typical professor. I as usual went as myself, my celebrity being somewhat less than that of my friend.

We arrived by hansom, slightly early for our appointment at ten o'clock at the Count's rather grand establishment in the heart of Mayfair; a large, square, whitewashed mansion, bounded by well cultivated gardens of laurel and eucalyptus at the front and courtyards and stables at the back. We knocked at the ornate, colonnaded front doorway and were ushered inside by a rather pompous and elderly butler who treated us with a sniffy condescension, taking Holmes's calling card and holding it between his fingertips as if it were a dead fish. He evidently regarded us as a pair of ne'er-do-wells scarcely respectable enough to be allowed through the tradesman's entrance let alone the main portal.

Once safely ensconced inside I was able to admire the decor of the house which, even to judge solely by the entrance area, was exquisitely furnished in a rococo style with paintings, sculptures and *objets d'art*. The butler escorted us solemnly and a trifle reluctantly into what we presumed to be the inner sanctum of his master's study-cum-library, and bid us to be seated pending the Count's arrival. This office was magnificent in its fixtures and fittings with several cherry-wood bookcases holding impressively entitled academic tomes, chiefly of German and Prussian history, their gilt-edged spines telling of their Teutonic origins, and a number of paintings, chiefly portraits, including several of Frederick the Great, by Graff, Ziesenis and Therbusch. But pride of place was held by the portrait above the fireplace directly behind the Count's chair on the far side of his oak desk. It was a stunning and romanticized depiction of Frederick on horseback, by Richard Knotel, showing the great man in the refulgence of martial splendour, tricorn hatted, be-ribboned and be-medalled. There were portraits of other historical figures and battle scenes, but this room was clearly a shrine to the man's hero.

We had to wait a while before the Count's appearance, but I could see Holmes occupying the time purposefully, avidly scanning the room, probably taking in every detail for storage in his mind's eye, though to what end I could not imagine. I tried to make conversation but Holmes would brook no interference with his survey. At length the Count made his presence felt in the corridor outside, as we heard his guttural tones berating the butler for allowing visitors into his office without his permission, and a faltering apologia from the elderly retainer.

Then the man appeared, and strode purposefully into the room; a tall, broad-shouldered figure in his mid-forties, handsome in an austere way with cold blue eyes, closely cropped blond hair and sporting a resplendent upturned moustache with waxed tips. He had what I took to be a faded duelling scar on his right cheek. He was formally dressed in an impeccably tailored dark grey frock coat with the most exquisitely designed waistcoat and a multi-hued cravat, elaborately knotted in the Parisian fashion and held in place by a gold tie-pin. He bowed to us briefly and seated himself in the chair behind his desk, flouncing the tails of his coat in an exaggeratedly precise way. His manner displayed an icy charm but one got a distinct sense of a darker subterranean side if he were crossed.

"I am very sorry to have kept you waiting gentlemen, but I had urgent matters to attend to." He glanced from side to side at the two of us in an expectant manner.

"May I offer you a cigarette?" He proffered a silver box from his desk, but Holmes declined and I took my cue from him.

"Thank you, no, I suffer from asthma you realize and I find they are awfully bad for my health." Holmes piped in the quavering Scots accent he had perfected for the role.

"Ah yes, it is this accursed British climate and the poor heating and ventilation in your houses. You will not object if I indulge." He lighted a cigarette, striking the match against the box in a precise manner, and leant back surveying us keenly.

"So, how may I help you, or perhaps I should say how can you help me?" His English was very good, if strongly accented and syntactically suspect. There was a heady whiff of scent emanating from the man. He glanced down at the calling cards we had presented. "Professor McTavish and Dr. Wilson, I see, from the University of Aberdeen. And you are conducting research into mid-eighteenth century Prussia and your letter said you have something of great interest to me, I am believing?" His eyes gleamed and he leaned forward again in eager anticipation.

Holmes held forth in a slow and pernickety manner, pince-nez perched on the end of his nose, adopting a curiously hesitant tone of voice with a distinct highland brogue.

"Ah, yes, My Lord. Let me explain the background to my story. Whilst on my current vacation to London I was touring some of the many art and antiquities shops that abound in this fair city, as is my wont ... some of them are really such enchanting places you know, and you never know when you may be able to pick up some unconsidered trifle that turns out to be of exceptional historical interest ... when I came across a particular article, in point of fact a musical instrument, even more particularly a flute, that I did not at first deem of great antiquity or value, but which on closer inspection I began to suspect may be a hidden gem. Now I used to be proficient on the flute as a wee lad but have not alas kept up practice on the instrument …"

The Count's eyes were starting to roll in exasperation at these circumlocutions.

"Yes, yes, will you please come to the point. I have not got all day. You are in possession of the Sansoucci flute, *nein*?"

"If you will forgive me you are running ahead of me a wee bit. I was explaining that upon closer examination of the flute I concluded that there was a distinct possibility that it was the long-lost flute depicted in the portrait by Menzel …"

"Yes, you said all of that in your letter. Now may I see it please." his voice betrayed increasing impatience with his interviewee's prolixity.

Holmes started to rummage in the cavernous bag he had brought, ostensibly searching for this invaluable item of musical arcania.

He suddenly broke off the search with an appearance of distraction.

"That is a most intriguing trinket you have there on your sideboard." He pointed with wobbling fingers at a small ornament consisting of a bronze horse. "May I enquire as to its provenance?"

"Oh, just some little bauble I picked up in a sale at auction recently. Now, you said you were in possession of the Sansoucci flute depicted by Menzel. May I see it please?" His eyes were alight with expectation, his fingers drumming impatiently upon the desk top.

Holmes/McTavish continued to rummage. The Count's frustration with this pantomime was getting overpowering. Holmes now bore a look of embarrassed puzzlement.

"Well, I rather fear that it seems as if I may have omitted to pack the item." Holmes was delving ever more feverishly into the depths of the holdall which was sitting on his lap, his glasses almost falling off his nose in the endeavour. "Now I am sure I put it into this bag just before I left the hotel this morning, or did I perhaps put it into my other bag. It is so easy to get confused you know; they look so similar. I remember when I left my house in Aberdeen last week …"

"It is no use to me if you do not have it." the Count boomed.

Holmes pretended to be taken aback by the vehemence of the man.

"Er, well, I rather fear that I must confess that the item does not appear to be currently in my possession, but I am absolutely certain that it must be somewhere back at my hotel and I do most earnestly assure you …"

"This is ridiculous. You are trying my patience to the limits."

I was finding it hard to maintain a straight face during this performance and had to bury my face in my hands on the pretence of removing something from my eye.

"But, perhaps I may be of assistance to you in some other respect." Holmes delved even more ponderously into the large grey holdall. "I recently obtained this item at a shop in the Portobello Road which may be of considerable interest to your lordship." He was starting to remove some object in brown paper, and very carefully unwrapping it. "I came across this picture of the Teutonic knights of the Saxony region in the thirteenth century which might be of great interest to Your Lordship …"

"I am a scholar of eighteenth century Prussia, and not medieval Saxony as you would surely know if you had taken the trouble to read any of my books or monographs."

"Well, I do most humbly apologize to you, My Lord, if I have been unable to be satisfy your scholarly requirements but …"

"Gentlemen, I believe you have wasted my time and your own. Tell me, Professor McTavish, that is a Scottish name I am thinking. Where did you say are you from?"

"The University of Aberdeen. A most splendid establishment of learning consecrated in …"

"I have never heard of the place. Is this some elaborate charade on your part? I feel that you have trespassed upon my generosity for too long already, and my time is precious since I leave for the Continent in a day or two. So, unless there is anything else I must bid you *guten morgen.*" he said dismissively.

He rose abruptly but at that point there was a sudden commotion coming from the street, and all three of us were diverted. I had noted Holmes's anxious glances in the direction of the window at several points in our discourse and supposed him to be awaiting such an event. The Count muttered an oath and strode to the window overlooking the street to see the cause of the disturbance. From our seats away from the window we could observe something of a fracas breaking out, with an assemblage of ruffians disputing possession of some item, an outbreak of fisticuffs and the throwing of objects picked up from the road. The Count left the room briefly to locate a servant to investigate the matter. We could hear him barking orders at an underling. He could not have been absent for more than a minute or so but the instant he left Holmes sprang from his seat, lens in hand, and feverishly examined the office, focussing his attention particularly upon the far wall behind the Count's chair, and the area around the Knotel. The Count re-entered moments later by which time Holmes had resumed his seat and was sitting casually as if he had not moved. So swift were his movements that even I who was seated there would barely have noticed it.

"Some problem?" warbled Holmes innocently.

"Oh, just some hooligan element. Nothing of any great concern. It seems to have died away. Now, gentlemen, I believe you were about to depart." He motioned us to the door, cupping Holmes's elbow in his hand to speed the process.

"Yes, well thank you so much for your indulgence. I must repeat that I am most contrite that ..." Holmes mumbled.

"Yes, yes. Good day to you."

The butler was summoned and instructed to escort us out, with which instruction he obliged with some relish and we found ourselves back on the street, the door slammed firmly behind us. I felt as if we were naughty schoolboys having been given a stern reprimand from the headmaster, and lucky to have escaped a thrashing.

There was no sign in the roadway of the brawl of moments before, the miscreants having melted away into the general populace. We walked some distance and turned a corner into the next street to assure ourselves that we were no longer visible from the Count's residence before Holmes straightened up and settled into his normal stride. After a while we could contain ourselves no longer and broke into fits of laughter. But I decided to chaff Holmes over the futility of the whole exercize.

"All very amusing and I suppose that that little interruption was orchestrated by you, Holmes?

"Assuredly so. A detachment of the Baker Street Irregulars hired for the occasion. Rather well staged, though they left it so late that I had to engage in thespian mode for rather longer than I had prepared for, but I improvized rather well don't you think?"

"Yes, but all rather a waste of effort and resources."

"Quite the contrary. It has been most productive. We have discovered the location of his office. And did you notice the positioning of his Knotel above the fireplace?"

"No, should I have done?"

"If you had been more observant you might have noticed faint finger marks upon the wall by its side, which is highly suggestive is it not?"

"Suggestive of lack of a good cleaning by the staff perhaps."

"Or of the location of a safe."

I scoffed. "All very interesting I am sure, but what of it? Are you proposing to burgle the place?" I joked.

"Yes, I am." he said in a matter-of-fact tone of voice.

Chapter V

The Bull's Head

"Holmes, have you taken leave of your senses!"

I glanced around anxiously to ensure that no-one on the pavement had overheard our last exchange. We had been striding along briskly and I was relieved to see that there was no-one within earshot.

"I am in firm possession of them. We now know the location of the office, and possibly of the safe. We know roughly the plan of the house. What more could a successful burglar require, except perhaps a knowledge of the routine of the household?"

"And how can you be so sure that he has a safe or that if he does it might not be located elsewhere in the establishment?"

"No, I think his evident displeasure at the servant's allowing us in unaccompanied is sufficient proof that any private and confidential material is indeed held there. And I cannot imagine him dividing his spoils between two different safes and two different rooms."

And when do you plan to commit this outrage?"

"This evening, around midnight. Are you free?

We had slackened our pace and slipped into a side alley which, thankfully, was bare of pedestrians. I stopped in my tracks at this last sentence, and stared at my friend in utter disbelief.

"I am free. But I suspect I won't be for very long thereafter if I go along with this crazed notion of yours. Are you really serious?"

"I have never been more serious in my life. And I cannot really make headway with this case without some further and more detailed examination of the Count and his domestic empire. But I do not wish to expose you to any danger, my dear fellow, and I will understand perfectly if you choose to withdraw from the whole enterprize."

"Withdraw" I spluttered. "I didn't know I was party to it in the first place."

Holmes was poker-faced and had lighted a cigarette from his case, as he looked casually around. I pondered for a few seconds.

"But dash it, what have I got to lose, except perhaps my liberty and my reputation. Alright, Holmes. I am with you all the way!"

"Excellent. Oh, but there is just one more thing. I need more knowledge of the staff and their retirement times. And if I may trespass upon your services once more that is where you come in. I would like you, Watson, to do a little research on my behalf, engaging in a spot of intimacy with the servants in the household."

"Holmes, really. What are you asking of me?"

"What better source of information about the innards of a household can there be but those who work in it. Now, I rather fancy that a handsome fellow such as yourself would have no difficulty in making the acquaintance of a young chambermaid or scullery wench who, under your charms might let slip a few details of the house routine. How many servants are there; do they live in; what times are they up and about; that sort of thing?"

"Good God, Holmes, do you imagine to me to be some sort of Lothario. When am I supposed to be doing all of this?"

"Early this afternoon, at about one o'clock. I have it on good authority that many of the servants from the area around Wessex Gardens refresh themselves at the Bull's Head in Nightingale Square around the corner. If you were able to insert yourself there you might enhance your prospects."

"Really, Holmes! But might some of them recognize me from our visit this morning?"

"Possibly but I don't think it will matter and may even ease your passage. Just say you are an old friend of the Count who was paying him a social visit and it may gain you enhanced respect in their eyes."

I acquiesced with a shrug of my shoulders. "In for a penny."

"Splendid fellow."

We lunched frugally at a local café, and then Holmes announced he had to return to Baker Street, if for no other reason than to shed the bizarre accoutrements in which he was still garbed. And he urged me, in the meantime, to seek to engage with the staff in line with his request. I agreed resignedly, bade him farewell and made my way to Nightingale Square wending my way through the bustling, prosperous streets of the neighbourhood. I soon located the Bull's Head, a pleasant enough public house, attractively bedecked with hanging plants and tubs of foliage on the outside and bursting at the seams on the inside with local domestics and tradesmen. Upon enquiry of the barman, he pointed out me to a large, raucous knot of humanity in the central tables of the room several of whom were apparently from Wessex Gardens and the Count's residence.

Thanking him I sidled over to the group, tankard in hand, in the hope of striking up a conversation. It consisted of a dozen or more; a mixed bunch from appearances and probably from several different establishments in the locality; a few fairly senior but mostly junior to judge by their dress; footmen and maids, cooks and ostlers. Sizing them up as best I could I diffidently approached a pert and rather attractive young woman on the fringes of the group in animated chatter with a friend. I made my apologies for butting in and asked for directions to number 4 Wessex Gardens and upon her telling me that that was a coincidence because she worked there as a chambermaid, I offered her and her friend a drink. She seemed a trifle flattered at the attentions of a man of an evidently higher station, and waved her friend away with some disdain, saying she would resume their conversation later, before slotting her arm through mine and steering me towards a table. I was pleased with my efforts so far but chagrined to find that her tastes ran to slightly more expensive intoxicants than I had anticipated. I was soon plying her with large gins modestly laced with water.

"And might I know why a gentleman such as yerself is interested in going to number 4?" she asked as she downed the first of my offerings with surprizing ease.

"I should like to renew my acquaintance with your employer, the Count." I said.

"Why, yes, sir, but I thought I seen you there earlier with another, older geezer; that is gentleman, I mean."

"Oh, er, yes, but we did not manage to get to see him on that occasion."

"But then you already know where he lives?"

"Oh, er, yes but, er … er … would you like another drink?"

Distraction seemed to be the only means of preventing her from picking away further at my flimsy deception.

"Oh, that's really nice of yer. I'll 'ave another gin and water please." she said handing me her glass with some alacrity. "But easy on the water." she chuckled. I swiftly sank the rest of my own pint of beer and taking the glasses I struggled my way back to the crowded bar, and wedging myself between two rather surly workmen who resented my intrusion, I ordered again. Returning to the table she smiled sweetly at me as I proffered her the glass.

"So why *was* yer asking me his address?" she was looking at me very quizzically. Flustered, I changed my story to adapt to reality. Perhaps it was just the drink but she really was very pretty in a gamin sort of way, notwithstanding the hint of a blackened tooth or two and a rather sallow complexion, but there was something fetching about the whole package with her bright green eyes and the unruly tumble of reddish hair protruding beneath her mob cap.

"Look, I am most dreadfully sorry, but I saw you standing there, and er, well, you reminded me of someone I used to know and, well, er … I couldn't help but want to talk to you just in case you were her, if you see what I mean." I babbled.

"That's alright luvvie, yer don't 'ave to say sorry." Her eyes twinkled in a knowing way. She seemed already to be slightly tipsy. "My name's Molly. Molly Carter. What's yours?"

"Wats ..., er ... Wilson, I mean. Dr. Wilson." I said.

"Yer don't seem to know your own name." she giggled.

"Just had a frog in my throat. Pleased to make your acquaintance, Miss Carter."

"Call me Molly. What's your first name?"

"Oh, er, John."

"Can I call you that?"

"Why, yes, if you wish."

"Don't get many like you in 'ere, John."

"Like me?"

"You know; a gent."

"Oh, well, just wandered in. Rather glad I did." I smiled at her again. She looked amused.

"Bit of a charmer, you." I became aware of her scent, cheap but beguiling.

"So, what is it like working for the Count?" I said remembering my mission.

"E's very strict, 'e is. Don't let yer get away with nuffing. Like yesterday he gave Tom ... that's him over there." she pointed out a tall, thin young man in noisy disputation in the centre of the group at an adjoining table. "He docked his wages, he did, just for not having his jacket buttoned up proper in the dining room. He's a right so and so, so 'e is, but that's like what it is with these foreigners, ain't it? They got strange ideas about fings."

"Yes, indeed, I suppose that is true."

"Then there's that other foreign bloke what's always round there; His Lordship's scattery or whatever they call him.

"Scattery? Oh, you mean secretary?" I ventured.

"Yeah, that's it; secretary. Really don't like 'im. Fancies himself, you know, always feeling you up, but he's a slimy little git ... er ... I mean bloke, begging your pardon John, but I told him to push off I did. Pinched his elbow good and hard. He didn't like that." she giggled again.

"Really. What more can you tell me about this secretary of his." I felt I was making decided progress.

"Well yeah, like I said, he's always round there and you could hear him rowing a lot with His Lordship about stuff, though I don't understand none of it cos it's all in that funny foreign language of his."

"What about the other servants?"

"Well, there's Mr. Fairbrother, him's the butler, like, a bit old-fashioned, he is, and he's really old, and he gets a hard time from His Lordship but just seems to put up with it; and then there's Jack; he's another footman like Tom; well he's the under-footman actually; and Edna, she's the downstairs maid, and there's Mrs. Cracknell, the cook and Sophie the kitchen maid, and then there's ..."

"Yes." I said interrupting her flow, "and do all of these live in? I mean, do they sleep there overnight?"

"Well, yeah, course they do, except I don't cos I lives round the corner with me mum and dad, except my dad's not there at the moment cos he's in the clink. But they wanted me to sleep there, but I says no cos it's only so they got me at their beck and call at all hours of the day and night, and I says well I've got me own life to lead, ain't I, and, and Edna says she don't want me to stay there anyways cos then she'd have to share her room with me and she says I snore like the one time we did share, and I says no I don't, and she says yes I do and then she says I nick stuff from the house and she'll tell on me and I said no I don't you rotten little fibber, and she says ..."

"Erm, yes, yes, all very interesting but, er, I mean to say, do they all sleep upstairs?"

"Well, yeah, of course; I mean where else would they sleep; in the kitchen or the coal cellar; no I don't reckon so. I mean it'd be a bit uncomfortable wouldn't it. You don't 'arf ask some funny questions. Oh, sorry, John luvvie, I didn't mean to be rude or anyfing and I'm going on a bit aren't I, but you's did ask."

"No, no, that's quite alright Miss Carter ... er ... Molly. No, I was just a bit curious, that's all. I mean it's always interesting to hear about what goes in these grand establishments. I must say it seems extremely well-staffed."

"Oh, yeah, well His Lordship is very demanding. Has to have everything just so all the time. And he's really rich they say. Well, I suppose he must be to live in a palace like that and all of us servants running round. Alright for some ain't it."

"Indeed."

"And plenty goes on, I can tell yer. There's that posh lady what comes round nows and again. Mr. F says she's an *acquaintance* of his lordship and one should *ignore her presence*." She mimicked the butler's pompous tones. "But she's a bit of a close acquaintance I reckons. I saw her coming out of His Lordship's bedroom one time and when I told Tom about it Mr. F over'eard me and told me I was to keep me trap shut or it'd be out the door without a reference; well 'e didn't use quite those words but that was what he meant; so I tells him I don't care; I'll say what I bleeding well like; I don't need your rotten job anyway and if yer try to get rid of me I'll tell about you and that delivery boy in the pantry. That put a spoke in his wheel, I can tell yer!" she giggled hard, causing an outbreak of burping.

"Oh, sorry I'm talking out of turn a bit ain't I; it's just the drink talking; don't take no mind."

"No, that's quite alright. There's really no need to reproach yourself for any indiscretion. It's all quite fascinating." I was feeling rather pleased with my progress.

I was supping slowly on my pint but my companion had already downed another glass and was peering at the empty tumbler in a meaningful way, wiggling it to and fro in her hand.

"Perhaps you would care for another?"

"Oh, yer very kind." She flashed her sweet smile at me again. I was feeling increasingly that it would turn into a costly afternoon.

After returning from the counter once more I found her snuggling up to the young chap to whom she had earlier alluded. For some reason I felt slightly disappointed but, then again, I felt having two servants to question might aid my enquiries.

"This is Tom, what I told yer about."

"Good afternoon Tom." I shook his hand. His grip was very firm.

"Dr. Wilson here knows His Lordship." Molly said, "And he's being asking all sorts of questions about the house."

"Well, just a few. I understand you are a footman at number 4."

"Yeah, that's right."

"So, you both work for the Count. A strict disciplinarian I hear."

"A strick what?"

"Dis ... I mean he doesn't let you get away with breaking the rules."

"Too flipping right there, mate. Had a cushier time of it in the army. Wish I was back there."

"Oh, really. I was in the colours myself. Afghanistan, don't you know. What about you?"

"Never got further than Aldershot. You see any action in Africastan then mate?"

"Er, Afghanistan. Yes. Battle of Maiwand in fact." I said proudly, and a tad disingenuously for my actions were solely in a medical capacity.

So you on leave then?"

"Alas, no. I was wounded and got shipped back home, but that was a long time ago now."

"Wounded, eh? Where?"

"In the shoulder." I rubbed it to enhance the veracity of my story, not that I didn't feel the need for massage on many occasions.

"What d'yer do in the army then?" queried Molly.

I pondered and so no reason to falsify the record.

"I was a doctor."

"So how do you know the Count then? Was 'e a patient of yours." she chirped.

"Scarcely. Er, no I know him from quite some time after that."

"How?"

"Oh, um, met him at Ascot I think a year or two back. Chap really knows his horseflesh."

The conversation was not running down the tramlines I had set for it so I attempted to wrench it back onto its desired course.

"So, er, the household. Molly was saying there is a dozen of you, and all but she live in."

"No, actually I live round the corner from her."

"Oh, really. So how do you get on with the other staff, Tom?" I uttered as a spur to further conversation.

"I get on okay." He turned sideways to the girl. "I get on fine with some." He winked at her and they both giggled.

"You're a right nosy one you are, ain't you?" Molly teased me again. "Like I said I lives round the corner and Tom lives round the corner from me. So why do yer wanna know all this? You planning a burglary?" The two of them dissolved in another fit of giggles, rocking back and forth in their chairs.

I joined in the laughter as convincingly as I could manage.

"Ha, ha, yes, very funny."

After what seemed an interminable bout of this merriment, rather forced on my part, any hopes of advancing my knowledge further were dashed.

"Look, we gotta be off." Molly said firmly.

"But won't you stay for another drink?"

"Nah, we got the afternoon off, ain't we Tom." She winked at him and they got up together, she discarding her cap and straightening her tousled hair.

"Ta for the drinks, Mr. Wilson; oh sorry, I mean Dr. Wilson. We'll buy you one next time your 'ere."

I rose to say goodbye. As I did so, Tom was momentarily waylaid in chatter by one of the other group members at the next table. Molly, seeing him thus engaged, leant over to me and whispered in my ear that she lived at Wessex Lane, number 69, if I really wanted to know, and I was welcome to come round any time. I barely caught it such was the commotion in the bar and had to ask her to repeat. Close up her perfume was overpowering and blended weirdly with her breath, hot and gin soaked. Moments later they had left, Tom draping a proprietary arm around the girl's shoulders as they stumbled out the door, still bantering with other customers. I sat down and, after pondering for a few seconds, I found myself writing the address on a beer mat which I slipped into my coat pocket. I am not sure why I did so.

The rest of the group was by then dispersing to return to their labours. It was obvious that I was unlikely to learn anything further and so, feeling my presence redundant, I decided to make my way back to Baker Street for my rendezvous with Holmes. I wandered out into the fresh cold air, a pleasantly bracing contrast to the fug of the bar. I was disappointed not to have learned as much as I had hoped about the household and its regimen, but even so thought I had garnered enough to impress Holmes.

Walking off at a brisk pace to shake my head clear I took a slightly circuitous route and, passing through a side street, I was accosted by a heavily painted and garishly dressed woman of the sort known to ply their trade in that neighbourhood. Her thick make-up looked as if it was designed more to conceal her ugliness than to enhance any possibly favourable aspects of her visage.

"Allo, darling, you look like a nice gentleman, I'm sure; you in the mood for some fun?" she croaked at me in a weird high-pitched voice.

I politely declined and walked briskly onwards, cursing myself for choosing that homeward trajectory, but the wretched crone followed me and would not leave me alone. Eventually I dived down a side alley to escape her attentions, but still she followed.

"Come on dearie, don't be shy, I'm much cheaper than them over in Shepherd Market, and I'll give you a better time."

"Madam, please, will you leave me alone, or I will be forced to call a constable."

"Not a very chivalrous way to address a lady, Watson."

"Holmes, how the devil!"

"The devil had very little to do with it. Sorry to startle you, my dear chap, but I thought I would try my own approach. Once I have cast off these effects, we can make our way homewards and compare notes."

It took me a while to recover from my astonishment at the turn of events.

"Do you never go anywhere other than in disguise?" I spluttered.

"I do on occasion go as myself as you well know, but it is less amusing and I find generally less productive of confidences. But I trust you have made some headway?"

"I have learned a little. What about you?"

Holmes was swiftly divesting himself of his feminine garb and adornments which he deposited in a nearby dustbin and wiping away the war-paint in the semi concealment of the alleyway. In seconds the familiar gaunt, masculine figure had re-emerged. I looked around furtively and was relieved that there was no-one to witness any of this outrageous performance.

"I find this disguise enables me to inveigle myself into places where a gentleman may fear to tread. I have overheard a lot of interesting conversation, not all of it totally relevant, but intriguing all the same. I have also learned rather a lot from a dim-witted and very short-sighted footman at Wessex Gardens, when in his cups; though I fear I arranged an assignation which it would be unwise to keep."

"I don't know how you do it, Holmes; the stage really lost a star when you turned to detection." We made our way back on foot and at Baker Street I unburdened myself of my gleanings at the Bull's Head. Holmes was scornful.

"Really, Watson, I do think you might have done better. I peered in through the windows of the hostelry at one point. Perhaps if you had spent less time carousing with that maid and more time on some of the other servants you might have emerged with more information. I rather think I have learned much more than you and in less time."

"I fancy I rather impressed Molly with my debonair charm. I found her most forthcoming." I stroked my moustache in satisfaction.

"Molly, is it? Impressed more likely with your pocket book than your debonair charm." he snorted. "Sounds to me that she learned more about you than you about the household." he added derisively.

"Must you pour cold water on all my efforts!"

"Cold water is what results when hot air gets onto thin ice." he said tartly.

"Well, I do most humbly apologize for being so incompetent in my allotted task. I shall try to do better next time I am asked to prepare for a burglary."

Holmes's demeanour changed as he saw my irritation, and his abrasive tone softened.

"I am most sorry, dear chap. You must know me by know. I am most grateful for your endeavours, as always. They may not be productive of quite the desired effects but their entertainment value is guaranteed."

I was not entirely assuaged by this less than fulsome apology but before I had had a chance to riposte, he had switched into professional mode.

"I shall tell you of my intelligence. I have enough anyway to enable me to navigate around the mansion with minimal chance of detection. The servants, I understand, all retire before eleven-thirty and their sleeping quarters are upstairs in the attic above the second floor and on the far side of the house from the office. The Count himself generally retires before midnight and often takes a sleeping draught which makes him a very sound sleeper. All well and good. It seems, incidentally, that our noble friend has been much vexed of late by his secretary being incommunicado for some inexplicable reason, particularly annoying given that he is due to depart these shores in a couple of days and needs to make arrangements. I feel it makes it all the more essential for us to do the deed without further delay for if he is in possession of this so-called Transvaal Dossier he will surely take it with him or arrange for its disappearance out of the country by other means. I cannot imagine him allowing it to fester in his safe during a prolonged absence. Perhaps also it would be good to do so before he makes enquiries into the existence or non-existence of Professor McTavish of the University of Aberdeen." he chuckled.

"Indeed. But will this document be in his safe at all?"

"Well, we cannot know but, at all events, I fancy I may pick up some trifles that will tell against his activities. So let us fortify ourselves for our night's labour with whatever Mrs. Hudson has to offer for dinner."

I did not share Holmes's enthusiasm for the task ahead and had altogether lost any appetite. I admitted as much to him. But he was re-assurance itself and expressed the utmost confidence in the success of our venture, whilst tucking into roast chicken. I could only pick at my food and for the rest of the evening I tried to contain my nervous excitement, attempting to read but without success, and could do little except pace about our rooms. Holmes had once again disappeared into his room and only emerged when we were close to the appointed hour.

"Are you ready for our little jaunt? I fancy we might set off at midnight so that we may be *in situ* by half past or one o'clock at the latest. I suggest you bring your revolver and a lantern for we don't know what we might encounter. I shall supply the other tools of the trade."

I gawped at the man in dismay and breathed a sigh of resignation.

"Very well, Holmes, if you are really set upon this perilous and unlawful course then I am sure there is nothing I can do to dissuade you, in which case it is best that I accompany you to at least try to keep you out of any further trouble."

"Excellent, I felt sure I could rely on you. You have never let me down and I felt certain you would not do so now, and, Watson, I can assure you there has never been a nobler cause in which we may indulge our taste for the outlandish adventure."

I nodded my assent, and I could not deny that for all my foreboding there was a tantalizing aroma of derring-do about the venture in prospect. Holmes disappeared again into his room.

Chapter VI

Wessex Gardens

Upon the chimes of midnight Holmes had re-emerged from his room, once again heavily in mufti. He carried a voluminous black bag containing, I presumed, all the necessary paraphernalia for the well-equipped modern burglar and housebreaker. I shook my head in incredulity. Thus armed we set off.

We crept downstairs on tiptoe, so as not to wake Mrs. Hudson, into the biting chill of the November night. All was silent in the road for London had gone to sleep. Holmes had resolved that we should walk all the way there so as not to leave any evidence of our movements. And we took a decidedly circuitous route to Mayfair, taking several side-streets rather than the main thoroughfares giving Holmes the maximum opportunity to throw anyone who might conceivably have been trailing us; a possibility which he evidently considered not to be lightly dismissed.

We said little to each other during the walk, Holmes as so often secluded in a self-contained prism of contemplation, doubtless planning every step, and as usual I did not dare to interrupt the flow of his thoughts, though I was sorely vexed by so many features of the whole deeply questionable enterprize. What if we could not gain entry? What if a constable was on his beat in the vicinity? Did we have a cover story to justify our presence there at that time of night? What if we were to be sprung upon by a servant in the house? Were there any savage dogs likely to be set upon us? These and countless other questions tumbled over and over inside my head as we strode briskly along.

We arrived on the outskirts of Mayfair at about twelve-thirty by my watch. We walked as noiselessly as humanly feasible through the deserted streets, speaking if at all in the most hushed tones, I at least making frequent anxious glances for any signs of another person, but none was evident and we were the beneficiaries of a black moonless night, and a cloying, cloaking London fog that shrouded our activities. I sensed Holmes's irritation at the furtiveness of my manner which might betray a guilty purpose to anyone who did by chance materialize out of the darkness.

After a further walk of ten minutes, we had reached the object of our quest. The grand house looked slightly less imposing than it had some twelve or more hours before, and yet even more impenetrable. Certain that the neighbourhood was totally deserted, and that not a single wakeful soul but ourselves possessed the night, Holmes motioned me to follow him to the back of the house, which was enclosed only by a low and easily surmountable brick wall. Within a few seconds, and without too much effort on either of our parts, we had dropped down into the rear courtyard. Stables abutted. There was total silence, not so much as the rattle of a carriage nor the whinny of a horse. I was trembling both from the cold and in anticipation of the dangers that lay ahead, but Holmes was a model of calmness and authority, though I could not imagine how he intended to gain entry. Handing me his leather bag he clambered nimbly over the iron railings enclosing the downstairs quarters, and gripped a drainpipe, shaking it slightly to assure himself of its fixity.

"Do you feel like joining me or shall I let you in via the back door?" he queried in a hoarse whisper.

"I should very much prefer the latter, for my joints are not as supple as yours."

"As I thought. See you in a few minutes."

With that he began to shimmy his way up displaying a feline agility and sinewy strength with which I should scarcely have credited him. In no more than thirty seconds he had clambered inside via a first floor window that had been conveniently left wedged slightly ajar. I was grateful for somebody's desire for fresh air in the middle of the night even at this late autumnal date. I clapped my gloves hands together to generate some warmth and to bide the time before Holmes's hoped for reappearance and kept a constant nervous vigil, expecting at any moment to see the dreaded sight of a constable on his beat rounding the corner of the building, but there was no-one. I waited and waited, watching my breath as it exhaled and feared the worst, but after five minutes (that had seemed like thirty) I heard the slight click of a latch and the man had re-appeared by a downstairs door, just below ground level, close by the rubbish bins. I clambered awkwardly over the railings, my coat catching on a spike, to Holmes's evident annoyance, before dropping to his level as silently as I could contrive.

He beckoned me inside and I snuck in through the door as he held it open. There was a deathly silence pervading the house, with everyone resident apparently deep in the arms of Morpheus. The relative warmth of the house was a welcome contrast to the chill of the open air, but a stark reminder of the perils that might be encountered within. We wound our way up the service staircase with only the most minimal of creaking of floorboards and gained the main hallway. I recollected immediately the interior of the dwelling, though it was eerily strange in the darkness. I lit our lantern and we crept along, Holmes with his bag and me with the light. I was, again, awestruck by the magnificence and ostentation of the premises, lavishly furnished and thickly carpeted throughout which at least muffled our footsteps, despite a maddeningly squeaking sole of mine. There was a hushed grandeur about the place.

The long, broad entrance hall gave off to a number of rooms on either side. Though there was little sign of our being disturbed we had our escape route firmly fixed in our minds if we encountered opposition. Holmes, I scarcely need say, knew the room he was looking for from our earlier visitation, the last door on the right hand side. Reaching it he tried the handle gently, but unsurprisingly it was locked; but here my friend displayed yet another hitherto undisclosed skill; that of his proficiency in breaking and entering, as he levered open the lock using a jemmy or some such metal device plucked from his capacious holdall. The door gave way with little resistance. We slunk in. There was still no sound of anyone or anything save for the steady ticking of the clock in the hallway.

We were inside the office again. It was in total darkness, and we dared not turn on the gas for fear of its hiss giving away our presence, and chose to rely on our lantern. I vividly recalled the furnishings and adornments from our interview, and by the fireplace was the Knotel which had been such a cynosure of Holmes's attentions on our earlier visit. Holmes swiftly removed the painting and located a sliding panel behind it which he deftly drew back to reveal the presence of a safe, the face of which had a long iron handle on one side and large knob with numbers around its grooved edge on the other.

"A Sargent and Greenleaf!" he croaked in consternation.

Answering my look of bafflement, he elucidated.

"These are locks which can be opened only by entering the correct combination of numbers and in the correct sequence."

"And do you know them?"

"No, my dear fellow, or I would not be standing here scratching my head!" He produced a stethoscope, of all items, from his bag, one which he had asked me to provide for him to my great perplexity. He took the instrument and started to twiddle the knob to and fro whilst listening intently to the sounds emanating from the mechanism, his head pressed tight against the safe door. This made for a fascinating and slightly comical study. After a while Holmes paused in exasperation, the exertion and concentration had yielded a river of sweat on his brow.

"Watson, rather than study the side of my head make yourself useful and position yourself by the office door to listen for the approach of intruders."

I did as bidden, pushing the door slightly ajar to peer outwards for signs of anything bestirring. To my immense relief there was not a sound other than that of the clock. I stood sentry by the crack in that door glancing back from time to time to watch the glimmers of frenetic knob twiddling from Holmes. I maintained that pose for what seemed an eternity, my ears pricked to detect even the slightest sound and my heart thumping every time I heard so much as the meow of a cat or the occasional rattle of a carriage in the street. At one point a hefty thump emanated from somewhere and my heart leapt almost out of my chest, but after a few seconds during which we both held our breath in fearful anticipation no sequel was heard and I realized it must have come from the street, a box falling out of a passing vehicle in all probability. After about fifteen minutes of this torment, which seemed to me like the longest quarter hour of my life, Holmes summoned me back. I clicked the office door shut and discovered to my delight the safe door wide open and Holmes rifling through the contents.

"Holmes, you've cracked it?" I gasped wondrously, my voice rising above the necessary whisper, and eliciting a fearsome shush.

"I am a simpleton of the first magnitude, Watson. People, even the cleverest, are not really very imaginative when it comes to selecting numbers for secret combinations. After trying every possible permutation under the sun, I recalled our client say that the Count had celebrated his forty-fifth birthday on the Saturday before last, which was the 26th of October, suggesting the numbers 2-6-1-0-5-0. And hey presto!

"So, our man is a Scorpio. Very apt."

"Thank you for your astrological observations, Watson. Most illuminating. Now, what do we have here?"

He was evacuating the safe of its contents, its interior being considerably larger than one might have supposed from the small door, and which was divided into compartments of different sizes, each containing sets of documents and paraphernalia. He strew the contents upon the desk, sorting through them in his gloved hands. There were several sizeable bundles of documents tied with black ribbon, plus several smaller bundles and many single sheets, some envelopes and bits of stationery such as stamps, embossers and elastic bands.

"Let us take no chances and take the whole lot. Perhaps we can leave him the rubber bands. There must be plenty here for our delectation."

Grabbing the documents, he thrust everything into his holdall, and then, in a mysterious addendum, paused briefly to scratch the inside edge of the safe door with a small object which I couldn't quite see, which he then placed inside the safe before closing and locking it. He slid the panel back into position and replaced the painting upon the wall. I marvelled at the speed and proficiency of this performance.

"I think we will not presume upon our luck any longer and hasten away as fast as humanly possible. There cannot, I wager, be a great deal more to offer itself up."

I was relieved that our little venture was coming to a close; not a moment too soon for my taste.

The pair of us retraced our steps, Holmes making sure to leave everything as he had found it and to close the office door which did not seem noticeably damaged by his forcing of it. We strained to hear the slightest sound as we crept back along the hallway, down the stairs and out through the scullery door, and clambered back over the railings, the effort of scaling it being almost too much for me with Holmes having to half drag me over. I did at least manage to avoid a collision with the dustbins. We took a moment or two to dust ourselves down and once again cast around nervously praying no-one was in the vicinity.

There were no lights to be seen anywhere in the house or in adjacent buildings, and the only sound the somnolent whinny of a horse in the stables. We surmounted the enclosing wall and scuttled back to the road and hastened along. We both breathed the more easily, the deed accomplished, the sweat cascading from our brows notwithstanding the cold of the night. We walked as briskly as our tiredness permitted all the way back to Baker Street, a journey of only a mile or so as the crow flies but considerably lengthier via the circuitous route we adopted to evade any possible sighting. Very sensibly under the circumstances we did not seek to hail a hansom, not that there would have been any about at two or three in the morning, and at the merest hint of an approach from anything whether on foot, wheels or horseback we scurried into the nearest passageway or behind a tree to avoid being seen.

At Baker Street we crept up the staircase so as not to awaken Mrs. Hudson, for we knew our estimable landlady was a light sleeper. I felt the most overwhelming sense of relief upon our regaining our chambers and, flinging myself down upon the couch, I permitted myself a cathartic outburst of laughs and tears, part jubilation, part joy at deliverance. And I could see that I was not alone for Holmes, too, looked overweeningly pleased with himself, a beam quietly playing about his normally inscrutable features. Even he could not suppress a squeal of delight at the successful outcome of our enterprize.

"Watson, I do believe we've pulled it off! Our little booty here may be as good as gold-dust to us and to those in authority. We will have to see precisely what gems our swag may contain."

"The Transvaal files?"

"If we are lucky, but who knows? But, if you will forgive me, I fear it may have to wait until morning for some rest is definitely called for. I store up my energy, but I have drawn very heavily upon it in the last twenty four hours as I am sure you will agree."

I heartily concurred. He prepared to make for his bed, but paused.

"Watson, I fear that sometimes I presume too much upon your loyalty, and that in my zeal I have lured you into actions that must be abhorrent to your law abiding and peaceable nature, but you have never flinched nor failed for a second. You are the truest friend a man could have."

I found myself moved by these seldom expressed yet obviously heartfelt expressions of his gratitude and in my heightened state replied in kind.

"Holmes, we have been through a lot of high water together, but I know that you have never done anything, no matter how outré or irregular, without good reason and a noble heart. And I too must make a confession, for I have never thrilled to anything so much as tonight. To be truthful, I fear I may be developing a taste for this sort of thing. If our alliance continues for much longer, I may find myself on the Scotland Yard 'Wanted List'."

He said nothing, but clapped me on the shoulders, and retired to his room. And I am not sure that I didn't see a slight tear in his eye.

Chapter VII

Murphy

I slept very soundly that night, in sharp contrast with the disturbed attempts at slumber of the two previous nights, sheer physical exhaustion adding to a general sense of relief at escaping discovery and a deep sense of satisfaction at the successful outcome. I did not awake until mid-morning. Stumbling ataxically down to the breakfast table I found Holmes had already been long astir and was drawing heavily on his briar pipe, the one he favoured for the brownest of brown studies, his ham and eggs only partly consumed. I had expected him to be in buoyant mood after the success of our venture, but to my surprize he looked morose.

"Do you never sleep, Holmes?"

"You know me well enough by now, Watson. I go into hibernation for prolonged periods and store up reserves which I then draw upon in the throes of a case."

"True enough. You seem fresh as a daisy. Have you had a chance to go through all the documents you purloined?" I queried.

"I am working my way through them. Much of it, as one might expect, is in the Count's native language, and my German is a little rusty so I may require the services of a translator for some of the more obscure passages. Nonetheless, I have been able to interpret quite a bit. There is a lot of intriguing stuff to be sure, much of it seeming to bear upon matters of State, though nothing that could be described as stolen material, but much that speaks volumes of our noble friend's keen interest in the minutiae of military and naval affairs. But no sign of this bothersome Transvaal Dossier, or anything approximating, which is most vexing. And there is a particularly intriguing specimen consisting of scores of pages of typewritten script held together by a paper clip, which seems to be a list written in code. I have wrestled with it for hours without even getting on speaking terms."

"May I take a peek?"

"By all means bring your analytical faculties to bear." He tossed a sheet of paper across the table at me. I ignored the barely concealed note of irony in his tone and scrutinized it with what I hoped was an expression of emerging insight. Out of the corner of my eye I caught Holmes's amused look as I sat and pondered. It was, as he averred, a typewritten page on the Count's headed notepaper with its elaborate crest of twin eagles surmounting crossed swords and pistols, of high quality paper, and, on the face of it, consisted of nothing other than a very lengthy, undifferentiated sequence of numbers, line after line after line of them. On the first line of the page, for example, there were the digits:

```
2 3 0 4 4 1 0 2 1 1 3 9 1 8 0 7 5 0 1 6
```

Twenty digits. And on the next line another twenty digits, and the next and the next, for the entire page. Numbers, numbers and nothing besides.

I could not conceal my bafflement.

"What about the next page?"

Holmes slid another sheet across the table to me. It was scarcely more enlightening than the first in being composed of nothing but numbers on every line. I looked up and Holmes slid across a third sheet. The same.

"Are they all like this?"

"Yes, every single one of them. Dozens of pages of about thirty lines each of twenty figures each. A grand total of tens of thousands of digits. Quite a monstrosity. So, good doctor. What is your diagnosis?"

I cleared my throat and attempted a look of erudition. "Well, they are typewritten notes. It is on the Count's headed stationery. And they are apparently lists of numbers."

"Brilliant! Yes, I had got that far myself. To be precise it is typewritten using an 1890 Remington 146X model, precisely the model I observed in the corner of his office. And the paper is an expensive weave of a type produced I believe only in Frankfurt. But what of the numbers, eh?"

"Alright, Holmes, I give up. What do they portend? It is seemingly nothing but an interminable list of random numbers."

"But probably not random. That is the point. I do not imagine that our friend entertains himself by drawing up random lists. There must be more absorbing pastimes. No, the figures must symbolize something?"

"Perhaps they are references to the page or column numbers of a book?"

"Must be a very lengthy book! Or a lot of different ones. No, we are on the wrong track. But there are slight clues. You may have noticed, Watson, that the list was not all typed at the same time since some of the figures are rather faint and getting fainter where the ribbon has evidently worn down, and then others are much clearer where a new ribbon has been inserted at some point. And the gap between the lines is variable, as if the sheet has been removed and then re-inserted at various times into the typewriter. This strengthens the hypothesis that it is an inventory of some sort; perhaps of agents or accomplices, added to from time to time to take account of new entrants to the club."

"Well, anyway, what are you going to do with all this documentation? You cannot exactly hand it all over to the authorities without some enquiry into how you obtained it."

"A point that had not escaped me, my dear fellow. But as I said there is nothing here that appears actually to have been stolen, so far as I can ascertain, and so nothing that would inform decisively against him in a court of law, though much of it would undoubtedly be of interest to the government."

"But even if your intention is merely to acquaint the authorities with the Count's complicity in espionage you still require the documents as evidence."

"Exactly. A more oblique stratagem may be necessary. And anyway there is no point in handing over this list. I hope you will not accuse me of vanity if I say that if I cannot crack it then nobody at Scotland Yard, or any other centre of officialdom, can do so either."

"I think I may accuse you of a little vanity. Is it not possible that someone somewhere may know something you don't?"

"*Touché*, Watson. But it is not knowledge *per se* that counts but the ability to make appropriate use of it. Whitehall may be choking with weighty tomes but that will not avail unless one can crack the code."

Holmes plucked the notes back from out of my fingers and lapsed back into contemplative mood, refilling his briar with a pungent mixture that he favoured for especially intractable problems.

"By the way, Holmes, there are a couple of points about our little escapade last night."

"Fire at will."

"How did you know there was going to be an open window on the first floor?"

"Part of the intelligence I gleaned from the footman whose acquaintance I cultivated. He must, I fear be rather disappointed at the non-appearance of his little lovebird yesterday evening." he chuckled.

"You cad, Holmes!" I joshed. "And what was it you deposited in the Count's safe?"

"Merely Kellmann's cufflink. It may be well to let suspicion fall upon him for the burglary. Even if von Runstedt does not believe him responsible it will at least sow confusion in his mind and divert any suspicion from our good selves. And I think he is scarcely likely to report the matter to the police if he has even the merest inkling that it was an inside job."

"In other words you had the burglary in prospect even as we were inspecting the corpse at Shepherd's Bush?"

"It was not totally absent from my calculations."

"Well, I must say, you play a very deep game."

"And it may get deeper yet."

"How do you mean? Are we to plumb even greater depths of iniquity and lawlessness?"

"Let us hope not, but we may find ourselves treading even murkier waters before we are finished."

"By the way, what about the Count's other residence? Didn't the lady mention he had a house in Berkshire? Perhaps he keeps his higher grade stuff there? May be worth a visit, though not I sincerely hope with a view to burgling the place!"

"Well remembered, Watson, and a good point but somehow I don't think so. It would be risky for him to be conveying top secret documents from one house to the other and it is so far away. What would be the purpose? But if all else fails we may have to consider that option."

"Well, I think I have had enough adventure in the last few days to last me a lifetime. I sincerely hope you will not need to call upon my services for the rest of today, for I am tired indeed and propose to spend the rest of the day in glorious and unashamed idleness once I have finished breakfast. My batteries are in dire need of re-charging, even if yours are not."

"A wise decision, Watson. I intend to spend the day continuing my researches into this list and other matters. Plus I have a few more errands to run. I promise I shall not disturb your well-earned relaxation."

"Excellent. I shall leave you to it, Holmes." I said as I retreated to my bedroom, fell onto my bed and dozed for a few hours. I rose again and returned to the drawing room just after midday to discover that Holmes had ventured out I knew not where.

Upon his return at about one o'clock I quizzed him.

"Anything significant to report?"

"A few things. I thought it might be to my advantage to renew acquaintance with our charming Kilburn housekeeper once again."

"You didn't go back there! To confront that old harridan!"

"Oh, quite the contrary, Watson. I found the estimable Mrs. Agnes Grimthorpe to be most amenable. I presented myself as a sterling fellow who had been friends with Herr Kellmann many years ago and was looking him up after a long absence to repay an old debt. Luckily, she did not recognize me from our previous visit, when you recall I had affected disguise of sorts. Offering to give the money to her for safe-keeping since I had to depart immediately for foreign shores, she was suddenly most accommodating and inveigling myself into her kitchen to arrange the transaction she became extremely loquacious on the topic of Herr Kellmann. Her tongue was lubricated, I may say, as she partook increasingly liberally of her cooking sherry. I contented myself with cups of her Earl Grey. As a consequence, I learnt a great deal about the activities at Acol Road, and particularly those of last Saturday."

"Really? What exactly?" I asked eagerly.

"I will explain all in the fullness of time."

As so often I was exasperated by my friend's unwillingness to share with me the full extent of his knowledge; preferring instead to store it up for revelation at the climax of affairs, like a conjuror producing a rabbit from a hat. For a man who disowned any aspiration to celebrity (and who repeatedly disparaged my accounts of his cases for their tendency to allow narrative effects to obscure the cold, hard forensic skills deployed) it must be said that he was unduly fond of a certain staginess of presentation himself.

My curiosity was piqued and I ploughed on in the hope of enlightenment on other aspects of the case.

"And you still haven't said what you are going to do about the body in Oil Drum Lane? Surely we must do something or the corpse will be discovered by other hands or be starting to decompose." After the high drama of Wessex Gardens, I had allowed the Shepherd's Bush and Kilburn angles to recede to the back of my mind but now they came surging to the forefront like a tidal wave.

"I need a day or two's further reflection." he said cryptically.

I tried a different tack.

"Have you had any further communication with Lady Diana? I seem to recall that she is your client and must be thirsting for news of your progress."

"Alas, I have not had a window of opportunity. But again another day or two may place me in a better position to advize her. Oh, and by the way, I am expecting a visitor later this afternoon."

"Anyone interesting?"

"Interesting to me, certainly. A man called Murphy. Declan Murphy. He may be a bit rough around the edges for your tastes, Watson, and you may prefer to absent yourself, but I hope to find his visit rewarding."

"So, who is this paragon?"

"A small-time crook; thief, pickpocket and receiver of stolen goods. I had the handcuffs on him a few years ago for some petty crime but rather than hand him over to the tender mercies of Scotland Yard, I offered him alternative employment as an informant, and I must say he has been very useful to me over the years."

"I see. A nark of yours, and a common thief. Coming here."

"Yes, a common thief; not an uncommon one such as you or myself. Oh, but don't worry. I shall try to ensure he does not pocket any of your valuables, but as I say he is a walking almanac of the doings of the underworld, and moreover, as fortune would have it, he is a somewhat peripheral member of a gang of thugs who I know to be in the service of the Count. I think I had mentioned to you that von Runstedt employed these for some of his rougher doings. I sent Murphy a telegram using our customary code and arranged for him to meet me here. He is due any moment."

There was a loud knock on the front door.

"And unless I am very much mistaken that is my good friend now. He has many failings but unpunctuality is not one of them."

In a few seconds Billy had ushered the man into our rooms. He was a small, wiry unkempt personage of vaguely Romany appearance, scruffily dressed and with the face of a half-starved hamster, furtive and untrustworthy. A dishonest fellow if ever I saw one.

"Murphy, how goes it?" Holmes had stepped forward to greet our visitor with outstretched hand and ushered him into a hard-backed chair by the window.

I was reluctant to soil my hands on the man, since he did not look as if he had bathed for some months. I resolved also to keep a close eye on him, unostentatiously busying myself about the room whilst listening closely to the conversation.

"Keeping out of trouble I hope, Murphy."

"Oh, well you know how it is, Mr. 'Olmes. Just a bit of minor stuff. Can't dodge all the heavy lifting." he muttered in his unprepossessing blend of Cockney and Irish.

"You are no good to me in prison. I need you as my eyes and ears on the outside. Why else do I pay you?"

"Understood, but you know me; I am very quick on me toes. So, what can I do for you, Mr. 'Olmes?"

"The Bund."

"At this the man blanched.

"I see from your reaction that you are familiar with the organization."

"I pick things up on the grapevine."

"It is more than a grapevine though, isn't it? Your mob and theirs are intertwined as I hear it."

"I don't know what gives you that idea, Mr. H."

"I, too, pick things up on the grapevine."

"Well, maybe I know a little about them."

"I think you know a lot, and even if you don't you must have cronies in your outfit who do, or who can find out."

"I'm not saying yes, and I'm not saying no, Mr. 'Olmes."

"It would be greatly to your advantage to say yes."

"So, what do yer wanna know?"

"I am particularly interested in documents that may have disappeared from certain government ministries in recent days and which I suspect are being spirited away out of the country. Would you know anything about that?"

"Don't know nothing about any of that, Mr. 'Olmes. I just stick to honest thieving; none of this government malarkey."

"Well, malarkey or no, you must know something about it, or know someone who does and I should appreciate fuller and better particulars."

"Well, I'll do what I can Mr. H, but I can't promise nothing. I mean I'm taking a risk coming here today. I sometimes think they are on to me." At this he craned his neck to peer out the window, and his pallor grew even more deathly. I wandered to the window myself but could see no-one sinister and nothing untoward.

"You are probably getting paranoid, Murphy. You weren't followed were you?" A note of concern had crept into Holmes's tone.

"Well, I sometimes think there is someone shadowing me."

"Well, just be careful."

"Care costs money Mr. 'Olmes. Just as information does," the man added pointedly.

Holmes smiled indulgently at the man as he casually produced an envelope from the drawer next to him.

"Let me oil the wheels of your machine. Here is five pounds on account and there may be more if you come through with something worthwhile, but it had better be worthwhile!"

The man's eyes lit up like a torch as he sprang forwards to grab the envelope being waved enticingly in my friend's hands, but Holmes withdrew it from his grasp.

"But, I want value for money, Murphy, or you may find your source of funding being cut off or worse. I believe that Scotland Yard is still very keen to track down the culprits responsible for the Hatton Garden job last year."

The man's demeanour tensed and his tone became profusely co-operative.

"Oh, don't you worry Mr. H. I will get you something. Only I never had nothing to do with that Hatton Garden job." he added plaintively, but unconvincingly.

"Hmm. Well, take your money and I want to hear from you within the week. Do you understand?"

Holmes's manner was stern as he handed over the money and I could see the blood drain from Murphy's face.

"Oh don't you worry Mr. 'Olmes," he said pocketing the envelope.

"You may count it if you wish."

"No, I trust you, Mr. 'Olmes."

"Then, I think there is nothing more for us to discuss." Murphy rose to leave.

"Oh, but there is one thing. I should appreciate it if you returned that little ornament you picked up from the side-table on the landing on your way up the staircase."

Holmes held out his hand with the palm upwards.

The man looked shamefaced and slowly retrieved something from his hip pocket and handed over the bauble.

Holmes tutted in mock disapproval.

"Old habits die hard, Mr. 'Olmes." pleaded the man.

"They don't have to die, but do need to take a holiday whilst you are dealing with me here."

I viewed this last display with misgiving. With that the man slunk out, and I watched him from the window as he scuttled away down the street, eagerly counting the notes, licking his fingers as he went.

"Really Holmes, do we have to entertain such creatures?" I said brushing down the seat of his chair, now rather soiled, with the back of my hand.

"Such specimens are my stock in trade. Do I reproach you for liaising with sick people all the time?"

"Scarcely comparable!"

"Quite so. You or I may catch something from a patient, but I don't think you will catch a criminal disease from associating with the likes of Murphy."

"I think I already have caught the criminal disease, as you deem it, and direct from you, Holmes! So, will this fellow be able to supply you with anything useful?"

"I can only hope so, since I am not making headway with this wretched list, and I am fast exhausting other avenues. I fear I may, perhaps, have been a little too hard on him, though, and I was troubled when said he might have been followed here because he is my only person on the inside of this damnable organization. He is too great an asset to lose. One has to squeeze to yield juice, but I may have squeezed too tight. I pray I have not placed him in danger."

Holmes's confidence in his man seemed to wither and he appeared increasingly worried, pacing about our living room, and then disappearing into his own room. He re-emerged some minutes later and declared he was going out for a walk without being more specific as to his destination. I watched him go and returned to my newspaper.

Half an hour later he had returned, dashing up the staircase and bursting in through the living room to make a dramatic announcement.

"Watson, I am convinced I am being followed!"

Chapter VIII

Surveillance

This sudden outburst from Holmes took me aback, though after all the alarums and excursions of the previous few days I should by now have been inured to any such emotion. But nonetheless it was rare for Holmes to exhibit such a confession of vulnerability.

"And what convinces you?"

Over the past few days, I have felt a presence on my shoulder, unseen yet dogging my every step. I felt it particularly today during my sojourn to Kilburn, perhaps because I had more leisure to scout the terrain, though I have had a sense of it for several days since we began this investigation. And you know that I am not easily deceived nor prey to irrational fears or impulses. And now, with Murphy's suggestion adding to my own suspicions, I decided to test matters by taking a turn around the park."

"And?"

"And now I am absolutely certain of it. I took a circuitous route and darted hither and thither to evade surveillance, and yet always there was this shadow, now one person, then another, but on my tail I am convinced.

"Dare I suggest an element of the irrational creeping in all the same? Perhaps after the, shall we say, rather dubious activities in which you have engaged, a sense of misgiving is clouding your judgment and making you see things that are not there?"

"Balderdash, Watson. No such misgivings have clouded my judgment, as you put it, nor ever shall. No there is nothing irrational or fantasized about it. And it is not only surveillance, for I fear even greater invasions of our privacy have been contemplated."

"Whatever do you mean?"

"Mrs. Hudson reported to me earlier today that she had caught a man loitering within the precincts of our rear courtyard and trying the handle of the kitchen door. Her formidable presence was sufficient to frighten the fellow off, but there may be another attempt."

"A burglar?"

"It looks that way. All of this strengthens my belief that we are under surveillance."

"Do you mean to say there might have been someone on our tail even during our activities last night?" I said with alarm growing in my breast.

"I don't think you need have apprehensions on that score for we were very careful to ensure we were unobserved. But on other occasions I am convinced of it. And now we have Murphy evincing the same intuition. If they can follow me, they can follow him, and the one may lead to the other. But I need a witness to prove matters beyond peradventure. Will you venture out with me today and we can put matters to the test?"

"I thought I had been given the rest of the day off." I groaned. "Very well, then. But whose agents are they, supposing them to be not merely phantoms of your imagination? The Count's men? Does he already suspect you of being on his trail?"

"Very possibly, perhaps even probably. So many times our paths have nearly crossed in the course of my investigations that it would be surprizing if he were not conscious of the hunter tracking his footprints. And now that he has been burgled his antennae must be even more acutely tuned."

"Will he have discovered the burglary already?"

"Probably. I think surely, for it must be evident to him from the broken or forced lock that there have been intruders in his office and that will lead him immediately to the safe."

"Will he suspect you of the burglary?"

"Difficult to say at a distance. I have as you know tried to deflect him to his own man, but he may not be fooled by that."

"But are you the hunter or the hunted?"

"Often it is both at the same time."

"So then, what do you propose?"

"A walk. A brisk, health–giving spree across Regent's Park."

"When?"

"Now."

With that I found myself tagging along beside the man, walking at far too rapid a pace for my liking up Baker Street and to the southern fringes of the park. The afternoon was chilly and breezy, but the exercize soon warmed us. I was breathing hard which made conversation a chore.

"What is going to happen? Are we about to be attacked?"

"Not attacked. Not a bit of it. No, just shadowed. Shadowed, shadowed, all the way."

"Well, where is our proof? There are lots of people thronging about but none look like they are following us."

I had cast around at several points during our ramble but could espy no-one who looked remotely sinister; merely assorted groups of everyday folk; family groups, courting couples, individuals going about their business.

"They would not. I am sure they know their craft well enough to remain inconspicuous. There may well be more than one, probably working in relays and relieving each other at strategic points along the route so as to avoid recognition."

I sighed and ploughed on, my breath coming harder, and my leg starting to ache.

"And please, Watson, do not keep peering about. We do not want to frighten our bird away with the fear that we are on to him."

"I shall endeavour to look straight ahead and not allow my head to turn so much as one degree to the east or west."

"You may be satirical, but I fancy we shall soon have all the proof we need."

We had travelled a considerable distance, up past the bandstand, deserted at this time of year, and along past the boating lake, similarly bereft of people on such a cold and blustery day. We had outpaced the knots of humanity that we encountered and passers-by were now few and far between. We had reached a more remote and boskier part of the park.

You see that clump of trees over there." He pointed to a coppice of beeches a hundred yards ahead.

"Yes."

"Good. When we get there, I want you to carry on walking just as you are at present and to take no notice of my actions or inactions. Do you understand? You must follow my instructions to the letter or the whole exercize will be futile."

"Very well, but what are you going to do?"

"We are going to close in on our suspect with a pincer movement. You may see me walking some way behind you but take no notice and proceed towards that further coppice over yonder." He pointed out another cluster of beeches some two or three hundred or more yards further on from the immediate coppice. "And when you get there conceal yourself as best you can and wait."

"Very well; but where is our assailant? I have seen no-one suspicious."

"You will not have. I imagine not looking suspicious is part of their tradecraft."

We gained the first clump mentioned and as I proceeded onwards at my customary gait and pace Holmes suddenly darted out of sight behind some trees. I was momentarily fazed but Holmes bid me sharply from his place of concealment to carry on as if nothing had happened towards the aforementioned second coppice. I did as instructed, maintaining what I hoped was an air of normality as best I could under the rather bizarre circumstances. I emerged from the clump and marched ahead resisting with all my might the temptation to look behind.

I had proceeded for a further hundred yards or so and, Holmes's sternest injunction notwithstanding, I could not resist the urge to survey the scene behind me, and thus disposed I bent down ostensibly to tie my shoelaces, contriving to turn slightly sideways as I squatted. I caught sight of a thin, pale looking man dressed in a slightly shabby grey suit with a bowler and umbrella some fifty yards back, sauntering with apparent nonchalance. I recalled him vaguely as someone I had perceived earlier on our little trek, though I had given him little consideration at the time since he was but one of many, but now he was the only person in view. He was, himself, peering about a little uncertainly and though it may have been my fancy he seemed to turn his head slightly to avoid my glance and to slow his pace as I crouched. But the more surprising sight that met me was that of Holmes some fifty yards behind him. I rose and carried on, a sense of thrill now coursing through my veins. Was this the man Holmes suspected?

Nearing the second spinney my sense of expectation led me to quicken my pace and it took all my willpower to avoid a further glance backwards and to desist from some similar stratagem as previously. As I ventured into the spinney, I was aware of the bowler-hatted man still fifty yards behind. As bidden by Holmes I dived behind a clump of trees to await events. The man hoved into view, slightly breathless and evidently bemused by my disappearance. He stopped and, mopping his brow with a handkerchief, looked left and right, fore and aft in growing despair. I felt almost sorry for him. At this point Holmes had raced into the area and running up behind him accosted the man by tapping him sharply on the shoulder with his cane.

"Now, sir, who are you and why have you been following us?" he demanded in tones that brooked no contradiction. The man was understandably startled and took a step or two backwards trying vainly to regain his composure.

"Watson, break from your cover, if you please." Holmes barked, as I revealed myself. The man was hemmed in on either side in a very confined area by the two of us. It was fortunate, or perhaps it was carefully arranged by Holmes, but there was no-one else in the vicinity.

The man's discomfiture at being so besieged was all too evident. He stuttered, stammered and faltered, looking around for an avenue of escape.

"I don't know what you are talking about." he spluttered in weak, unconvincing tones. "I am merely taking a walk through the park as is my custom at this time of day, and do not expect to be waylaid. What is your purpose? Are you trying to rob me? There are constables and park keepers who patrol here you must realize and I will not hesitate to call them if needs be." His voice strove to achieve mastery of the situation, but his nervousness and air of defeat were all too apparent.

"It is I who shall call for the forces of law if you do not explain your reasons for following us all the way from Baker Street."

The man attempted to move away but Holmes and I barred his passage with our sticks and shuffled him against a tree in as menacing a manner as we could contrive. I was unused to disporting myself in so aggressive a mode, but felt obliged to act the part as best I could. I must say I was astounded at the vehemence of Holmes's demeanour, something I had not witnessed previously though I had been through briar and thicket with him over the past few days.

Having cornered the man Holmes again demanded an explanation in even more uncompromising terms than before. The man was clearly torn between further protestations of innocence and an admission of his culpability as a means of extricating himself.

"I ... I ... really don't know what you are talking about. Now get out of my way immediately or I shall call for assistance." He pushed hard against the two of us but we had him tightly cornered and he was no match for the pair of us in terms of physical strength. He was sweating profusely, lank strands of his wispy, sandy hair falling across his face. Alarm and distress were writ large across his features, though whether due to a genuine apprehension of personal harm or merely humiliation at having been exposed was unclear.

"You must think me a booby of the first water if you believe it possible to tail me for miles without my noticing. I say again, who are you and why have you been following us?" Holmes was almost bellowing at the man.

"I have told you, I was doing nothing of the sort. Now let me go."

"Very well then. If you will not admit to it." So saying Holmes grabbed the man's lapels very roughly, yanking his jacket backwards over his shoulders and delved into his pockets. The man protested loudly, jabbering oaths and made a token resistance before Holmes had retrieved a small bundle of papers from his inside breast pocket.

"How dare you. This is theft and I shall assuredly report you." he stammered.

"Report me and be damned." cried Holmes. "If you will not tell me anything then be off with you. And do not dog my steps again or I shall not deal with you so gently the second time around. Go, go!" Holmes barked as the man gathered as much of his shredded dignity as he could muster, crudely adjusting his attire and departed, part shambling, part running, casting a furious glance back at us from a distance.

"I say Holmes, that was all a bit rough, wasn't it?" I exclaimed. "How do we even know this fellow was actually spying on us? And did you have to treat him with quite such violence?"

"Tush, tush, my dear doctor." He chuckled, seeing now to find the whole affair one of sport and entertainment. I have no doubt he was following us. I had seen him from afar not long after we set out on our little journey, and I am sure I had spotted him on my previous little jaunt around the park. So I have no doubts on that score. And I know I laid it on a bit thick with him, but I desired to impress upon him my displeasure. No harm was done and we have here some documents of his which might enable identification."

Holmes had crouched down to examine the purloined papers more closely.

"Are you sure this chap will not summon the police. Shouldn't we make ourselves scarce?"

"He will no more summon the police than I shall, but you are right. We can best inspect our booty at our rooms, and at our own leisure. The wind is getting up." And indeed a sudden gust threatened to scatter the papers to all points of the compass. There was now no sign at all of the man we had accosted. We had started a brisk canter back towards Baker Street. The light was already fading fast and the cold closing in.

"It was fortunate no-one else passed by or else they might have come to his aid or fetched help."

"I chose my spot carefully. There is rarely anyone about in these far reaches of the park at this time of year."

I was sceptical, once again marvelling at my friend's insouciance in the face of danger and his confidence that matters would turn to his advantage. We maintained silence for the rest of the walk home.

Once back to Baker Street I voiced my apprehensions.

"If your fears are correct then there may be others watching us."

"Very possibly. But then again he may have been the only one on the case today, for certainly I was unable to spot any other likely candidate."

"Is he one of the Count's men, do you think?"

"Most likely."

"Then you mean to say that this diabolical organization knows of your investigation. And has done all along? Are we not placing ourselves in grave danger? All the more so, now that you've effectively put them on alert." I couldn't wholly disguise my deep misgivings.

"We are in no personal danger, I feel sure. I don't believe the Count would make any move against me. If you will forgive my presumption, I think I am too prominent a figure to be touched, but I am very vexed about my Irish friend."

We settled in by the fireside, Holmes riffling eagerly through the papers, as he settled into his armchair with his calabash refilled with acrid tobacco. Mrs. Hudson looked in briefly to ask if we required supper, but was shooed away to her annoyance (and mine). I could not still my apprehensions.

"But I say, Holmes, was it wise to confront our man like that? Wouldn't it have more prudent to pretend ignorance, for now the Count will know of your suspicions of him and perhaps redouble his efforts at surveillance."

"That is likely. But if he suspects me already of being wise to his villainy then it will make little difference, and it might have seemed out of character for me not to have been aware of his attentions. And moreover, it may be best to try to ward off any such surveillance at this critical juncture for who knows what further adventures lay ahead for us."

"But Holmes, if you have been followed then how often has this occurred? Have we been trailed on every little expedition over the last few days. If so it may look black for us."

"I cannot be certain but I think we may have been a mite too quick on our feet regarding some of our little jaunts, and I can vouch I was not tailed everywhere, and definitely not to number 4 Wessex Gardens, let me put your mind at rest on that. And if our enemies know of our movements, well I am not sure it is necessarily to our disadvantage. I do not intend it to let it cramp my style, but in future I may have to tread a little more carefully."

Holmes scanned the documents, which consisted chiefly of correspondence.

"It seems this man is Frederick Beecham, and he resides in Camden Town."

"What do you intend now?"

"I may make some enquiries of our stalker and perhaps even reverse our roles and spy upon him. How does that sit with you?"

I heaved a sigh.

"I don't know what to make of anything at the moment. It has been such a whirligig of events."

Holmes chuckled again.

"The world seems to rotate faster and faster does it not with every passing year?"

Shortly after that Holmes bounded out of the house without a word and did not return until late in the evening.

I stared at him from over my book with a questioning glance.

"And?"

"And what?" he grumped.

"Have you been to Camden Town?"

"Yes, and a fruitless exercize it was too. A man of that name is not known at that address and though I circulated a description of him to neighbours and tradesmen in the area no-one seemed to know him." He slumped grumpily into his chair and reached again for the calabash.

I could not wholly suppress a smirk at the barrenness of my friend's labours, deriving some small measure of satisfaction that not everything worked out as he predicted.

"I shall quiz Mycroft on this cove when I next get the chance, but for now the trail has gone cold. And anyway, this fellow is probably but one of many in the pay of the opposition. They must rotate them like bus conductors."

That, at any rate was the end of our adventure for that day, but little did I suspect what was yet in store for us before this whole affair had concluded.

Chapter IX

The *Rendezvous*

The lightning pace of events over the previous few days, not to say their macabre unfolding, had started to tell on my nerves and I yearned for some respite from all of this. I had nearly made it to the end of the week, and as chance would have it I had a couple of appointments at my practice booked for the Friday, which being rare enough events these days were eagerly anticipated, not to say potentially lucrative. I was relieved that no further major incidents occurred to distract me from my professional duties that Friday and I spent a relatively conventional day in Harley Street with my patients. Returning to Baker Street that evening, I found Holmes busying himself once again at his newly constructed laboratory.

"Anything dramatic during my absence today, Holmes? Have you stumbled over another corpse, or perhaps you have committed a train robbery?"

"Sarcasm is the lowest form of wit, Watson, but no, you will be gratified to learn that I have spent an easeful, but not altogether fruitless, one without leaving this room."

I was relieved to be answered in the negative.

"Were you able to treat your cases of gallstones and, what was it, osteo-arthritis successfully?"

"Oh, for God's sake, Holmes, don't you let up for a moment? Is it the stains of some medication upon my coat?"

"No; merely that I inadvertently caught sight of your diary with its list of patients and their ailments the other day, which you had left open upon the table."

"I see. Not so clever after all."

"I don't know. I thought it moderately clever, but have it how you will."

"Do I get the weekend off or do you have some further mischief planned requiring me as an accomplice?"

"I have nothing planned, neither of a mischievous kind nor even a straightforward."

"I am pleased to hear it for I had thought to visit my cousins in Eastbourne from whom I have had an invitation."

"Then go."

"Thank you. I shall."

And I duly departed for the south coast on the Saturday morning from Victoria returning late on Sunday evening. I attempted relaxation over those two days but the events of the week just ended were swirling around in my head with such demonic insistence that it was impossible to blot them out. Upon my return I found Holmes still ensconced in the far corner of the drawing room as if he had not moved an inch for the whole two days. And perhaps he hadn't.

"I trust you have had a restful weekend and found the sea air healthful, Watson?"

"Scarcely, for I cannot stop dwelling upon recent events as I am sure you realize all too well."

"Perhaps the coming week will be more advantageous to your wellbeing."

"I somehow doubt it."

And come Monday and the headlong passage of events resumed with even greater intensity.

"Telegram for yer, Mr. 'Olmes. Just arrived." Billy, the house-boy announced.

It was about ten the following morning and I had been coming and going, engaged on a series of minor personal matters. I had returned to the drawing room. Holmes was still deep in cogitation, poring over the list of his at his desk.

Holmes clicked his fingers at the boy for him to bring the telegram over to him and snatched it from him with such peremptoriness that I realized it must be something he was expecting. I could see from his avid scanning that its contents were setting him athrall. He rushed to his bedroom without a further word, carelessly letting the telegram flutter to the floor. I scooped it up in his wake and took the liberty of glancing at the missive before his return and saw that it was a plea from someone signing himself simply 'CELTIC CITIZEN' to meet him without delay at 'THE USUAL PLACE', with no further elaboration.

Holmes was evidently so impressed by the urgency of the situation that he threw on his coat, snatched his cane from the hall rack and, with barely a word of farewell or explanation, swept from the house. I was disappointed at not being let into his confidence, especially after all we had been through together in the last few days, and intrigued to know what was afoot. From the window I saw him in the street directly below brandishing his cane left and right in the hope of attracting a hansom.

Still being very much at a loose end and, as I say, miffed at being excluded from this latest of his outings I decided to follow him as best I could, if only to sate my curiosity. I bounded to my room and hastily pocketed my revolver and some ammunition from the drawer, deeming it expedient to go armed for who knew what this encounter might involve. I congratulate myself on my prescience.

I set off in pursuit, hoping I could at least catch sight of Holmes's hansom before securing one for myself but I was resolved to do so as covertly as possible and not to bring myself to Holmes's attention for fear he might withdraw from the whole enterprize out of concern for my safety, but in truth I feared more for his safety than my own. Was he, or indeed we, still under surveillance from this shadowy organization, as Holmes seemed convinced? Had the spy or spies been frightened off by Holmes's drastic actions of the previous week, or would it merely cause them to redouble their efforts? Or was it all a figment of Holmes's overheated imagination under the impact of so many dramatic events?

By the time I had reached the pavement, Holmes had found himself transport and was already being whisked away in an easterly direction down the Marylebone Road. Luckily, another hansom was along in a trice; they thronged these areas with its multiplicity of offices and businesses. I bid the cabbie to keep a good distance between myself and Holmes's cab which was readily identifiable by the slightly unusual blue cloak of the driver and a vulgar advertizement for soap pasted onto the rear. Both cabs maintained a good lick of pace which would at least shake off any tail, assuming it existed in the first place. We cantered, unobserved I hoped, all the way along the Euston Road, down Gray's Inn Road, into Holborn, through the City of London, and past the Bank of England. I reflected upon the contrast between the solidity and respectability of that institution and the madcap and probably dubious escapade upon which I, or rather we, were now engaged.

The streets were teeming with traffic as always at these times of day and as we swung this way and that I marvelled at the ability of my driver to maintain contact with the object of our pursuit, though these involved frequent and hair-raising near collisions, once with a barrow-load of vegetables, on another occasion with a sedately trotting carriage which had to pull up sharply and another time locking and scraping with the wheels of the hansom of a rival company invoking a sharp exchange of pleasantries. A yelp of alarm escaped me more than once, only to be greeted with a cheery "Alright, guvnor?" from behind and above. "What yer wanted, weren't it?" "Yes, fine, keep going."

The great and recognizable edifices of the main thoroughfares of the City gradually gave way to the *terra incognita* of the East End and its more unpretentious facades. As we passed through Aldgate High Street and hit the grime of the Whitechapel Road we were still bustling along at a mighty old clip. I pondered our likely end point and began to worry if I had enough money on my person to pay what was likely to be a rather steep fare. I mused upon Holmes in the cab ahead and wondered what he was thinking and planning. What new escapade had he embarked upon, and what was I now choosing to involve myself in?

At length we turned off the Whitechapel Road, and after a few hundred yards more slowed as the hansom ahead did likewise. "What do yer want me to do now, squire?" Holmes's cab had come to a halt outside a row of drab, nondescript offices.

"Stop here please, driver." I instructed.

The parked vehicles in between our two hansoms made it difficult for me to see clearly, but I saw Holmes jump out, pay off his man and then stride off towards a side alley. I was thankful that we had succeeded in tailing the right hansom all that distance, and that Holmes had not somehow given me the slip by disembarking at some point in our journey. Leaping from my hansom, I enquired the fare, to be relieved that it was within the bounds of my pocket. Handing over the coins whilst endeavouring to keep an eye on Holmes I spilt hard-earned shillings into the roadside, apologetically bidding the man to retrieve them as best he could. As I darted off in pursuit of Holmes, my legs almost buckling under me after prolonged idleness in the back of the cab, I could hear the expletives of the poor cabbie now grubbing in the gutter for the remainder of his fare.

I turned down the alley that Holmes had taken and saw him fifty yards or more ahead, striding in very determined fashion, his cane tapping the pavement hard in time with his walking. I followed trying to maintain the same distance between us, near enough to maintain vision, but far enough to remain inconspicuous, and found I needed to gird my energies merely to keep within striking range. After a while Holmes came out into another street, crossed it and strode down another alleyway, and another, crossing several lanes such that it was increasingly hard for me to keep contact, almost as if he were trying to shake me off.

Finally, he came to a temporary halt as he reached a squalid tavern, its windows filthy and one of the panes broken. It was frequented, to judge by those lounging outside, predominantly by idlers, scroungers and petty crooks rather than honest workmen. Having evidently arrived at his destination Holmes cast his gaze around such that I had to slip behind a bollard to avoid him spying me. He then nipped smartly around the back of the building, down another siding. I baulked slightly at following him around for fear he would see me, and all my concealment be undone. What fateful assignation was he resolved upon and with whom? I fumbled inside my coat pocket for the re-assuring metallic feel of the Webley which I had gripped to my side the whole trip. I summoned the courage to move stealthily around the side of the public house, raucous guffaws and oath-laden banter issuing forth from inside.

Reaching the back corner of the building I stopped abruptly and peered round. Partially obscured in a dingy little alcove no more than twenty yards from me Holmes was in deep and earnest colloquy with none other than Murphy, who I recalled all too well from his visit to our chambers. Clearly the telegram had emanated from him, and 'Celtic citizen' his codename, and under pressure from Holmes he had evidently gathered some information to pass on, but probably feared to travel again to Baker Street because of the risk of being trailed. This obscure and inauspicious location was presumably regarded as a safe, and perhaps regular, point of *rendezvous* for the two of them, a long way from anywhere.

But Murphy seemed profoundly unsettled and was casting fitful glances this way and that, as if fearful of some hidden menace known only to himself. Holmes appeared to be trying to soothe his nerves and proffered a cigarette from his silver pocket case which the other seized upon with a shaky hand as Holmes lighted a match for him and tossed it to the ground. We were separated only by a disorderly collection of beer barrels and some rotting sacks of rubbish, but I could not get close enough to hear the conversation which was intense and low-voiced. I forbore from approaching any nearer knowing that this would surely reveal my presence, which I feared might even frighten the man away in his anxiety-ridden state.

After a good deal of earnest dialogue between the two men in which Holmes seemed to be imploring his interviewee for something, information presumably, the man produced a sheet of paper from his pocket and was in the process of passing it to Holmes when there suddenly erupted a terrifying sequence of events, which even to this day, at a distance of decades, is etched so deep in my memory as to be capable of bringing me out in a profuse sweat, as if I were in the grip of a fever.

As if from nowhere, two men leapt onto the scene. Such was the whirlwind pace of the ensuing actions that it is difficult to say precisely what transpired. The men, neither of whom I could describe with any great accuracy save that one had a livid scar running diagonally down his face from his left ear to below his nostrils, were bulky of build and unsavoury in every regard, and were armed with primitive weaponry of sorts; cudgels and hammers. One, the scar-faced man, sprang upon Murphy striking him brutally about the head with the hammer, causing him to slump to the ground, and seized the piece of paper from his hands.

Holmes reacted with the reflexes of an aroused tiger and struck out at the assailant with his cane, catching him in the centre of his chest with the point and sending him reeling backwards onto the pavement under the force of the blow. The man let out a squeal of anguish, and half-sat, clutching at his ribs. The other ruffian, following up behind, struck out wildly at Holmes in turn with his cudgel, which intended blow Holmes blocked with his cane horizontal before aiming a retaliatory swipe which caught the man amidships and sent him, too, staggering sideways against the wall.

I was so stunned by the drama unfolding before me that for a second or two I froze, both physically and mentally, and stood as if rooted to the spot and did not even think to draw my revolver. But, getting a grip upon myself I raced over to them for the drama was by no means concluded. The first blackguard had by now recovered sufficiently to take the opportunity afforded him by Holmes's momentary distraction at my appearance to strike him a hefty blow with his club to the side of the neck, felling him in an instant. I had now gathered my wits and steeled my nerve to intercede on my friend's behalf seeing him outnumbered and in grave danger, but before I had the chance to do anything a gunshot rang out. The shot came from a revolver in the hands of the first man, produced I think, from a holster concealed inside his jacket. It seemed to be aimed at Holmes, already prone on the ground. A terrible cry rang out and I feared the very worst.

The pair, now satisfied with their handiwork, dashed away as suddenly as they had arrived in the direction of buildings opposite. I feared desperately for my friend's life but to my indescribable relief Holmes staggered to his feet, rubbing his neck, and moved over to Murphy, now nothing but a crumpled heap. "Holmes, are you alright?" I cried as I made to steady him on his feet.

"I will live." he said gruesomely but apparently unsurprized at my own arrival at the scene.

Holmes knelt down cradling the fallen Murphy, obviously very seriously wounded though whether fatally I could not immediately determine. I squatted down beside Holmes to tend to the man who was gasping agonizingly for breath and bleeding profusely from the stomach. He tried to croak a few words and Holmes put his ear to the man's mouth but it was too late. Holmes and I exchanged a look of the blackest despair. The man held a scrap of paper in his clenched hand, evidently the remnants of the sheet he had been in the process of passing, which Holmes eased from his lifeless fingers. I could see he was still grimacing from the pain of the blow to his neck, but manfully trying to conceal it.

Holmes now berated me for not coming to his aid sooner. "Since you took the trouble to follow me all the way from Baker Street you might have intervened a little more quickly."

I protested there was little I could have done, and I knew that he realized the truth of it and was merely lashing out in the throes of grief. He acknowledged as much.

"But what of these blackguards, Holmes? Are they to get away?"

"I fear they may have too great a start on us, but if you are able we will try to catch them. I sincerely hope you brought your revolver?"

"Yes."

"Good, and it will be best if we are fast on our feet for I don't wish to be accused of complicity in the crime."

I glanced around very hastily to see if there were any witnesses to this dreadful drama, but I hoped and reckoned that there were none. We set off in pursuit of the villains. Holmes, despite the debilitating assault upon him, was still speed incarnate and I struggled to keep pace.

The report of the gunshot had pierced through the hubbub of the public house, and several of its denizens had spilled out into the street to see the cause of all the commotion. We could see as we fled from the scene that people were circling around the dead man in horror, seeking an explanation for his death and the identity of his murderer, but I was confident we were now too far off and well out of sight.

We ran to the building into which the men had vanished, which seemed to be a warehouse of some description; a huge edifice of rotting timber, and ventured, breathlessly, into the building. There was no source of light and it was apparently deserted, though noises could be heard from somewhere deep inside. We tiptoed along in crouched posture fearing the malefactors would take a shot at us.

"Now may be the moment to take out your revolver, Watson."

I had almost forgotten I had it and reproached myself for not using it when it might have been of some use. There was a sound of scuffling and wooden chests being overturned as our quarry bumped into them in their flight, and we saw a chink of light through a small doorway at the rear of the building.

"There!" cried Holmes and we set off again. A shot boomed out, echoing in the confined space, and it cracked into the walls only a few feet above me, showering me with timber flakes. We dived for cover. I returned fire in the general direction from whence the bullet had come, but could not see if it hit home. I was glad that my weapon was still functioning for I had not fired it for some time, though I had kept it oiled. It had a kick to it that sent a pang searing up my arm and into my shoulder. I winced. There were further shouts and we sighted the men flitting out through the rear.

"Come on!" Holmes was off again and in the thrill of the chase I disregarded my safety. We emerged out into sunlight through the same door the gunmen had fled and found ourselves in a small lane. Our quarry were some fifty yards off and leapt into a waiting carriage, standing off in the middle of the road, and with roars of "Go, go, go", yelled at the driver, the horse was lashed so mercilessly that the cracks of the whip might have been heard on the other side of the borough. The vehicle rumbled off at frenzied speed down the narrow road, wobbling crazily.

We had no means of pursuit. Casting about my eye fell on an unattended cart and a weary looking old horse tied to a lamp-post.

"What about that?"

"It will do!"

I untethered it and we clambered aboard the riding platform, gathering the reins as best we could in our haste. We tried to move off, Holmes exhorting the poor old beast with cries of giddy-up and furious shaking of the reins, but to little effect, the nag whinnying its reluctance to comply and no doubt wary of these strangers who were seeking to kidnap her. Eventually, after much more of this, with Holmes standing on the boards and wrenching the reins this way and that, to the evident amusement of a gaggle of onlookers, we managed a trot and something that was almost a canter. Holmes was getting ever more exasperated as our foes disappeared into the distance. He was not the most adept of drivers being unfamiliar with the skills required, and though we were just able to maintain sight of the coach ahead, it was only by urging the horse to ever greater feats of endeavour.

We wound our way up the road towards Hackney, the cart rattling precariously and in danger of spilling its load which seemed to consist of metallic junk, and only narrowly averting a series of collisions with other road users. To our horror, in the far distance we saw one of the men poke his head out from the window of his carriage and point a gun in our direction, though he was too far off for there to be reason to discharge it; probably more of a warning for us to back off and abandon the chase, which seemed hopeless in any case. Holmes turned to me, whilst still trying to control the reins and vainly willing the horse to speed up.

"Our friends up ahead seem to dislike our presence."

"I got the same impression." I cried." Do you think it wise to continue the chase?" I yelled.

"It takes more than a few whiffs of grapeshot to put me off the chase." He again lashed the horse but it was apparently incapable of achieving any significant velocity. The killers's carriage was getting further and further ahead of us and we now reached a major thoroughfare, which would at least mean it unlikely they would be threatening us with gunfire in the full view of numerous witnesses.

We cast our gaze left and right to see which way they had gone but it was futile.

Holmes steered the cart towards the roadside and threw down the reins in frustration.

"They have given us the slip, but I can identify one if not both."

The two of us were recovering our breath, and regaining our wits. Another cart passed us and the driver yelled something at us, probably cursing our horsemanship when we had overtaken him earlier.

"What now?"

"There, is alas, nothing for us but to return home."

"Should we not return to the scene of the crime?"

"Definitely not. Even if we are not fingered for the man's murder, we would be required to make statements, which would be, to say the least, somewhat embarrassing for both of us given all the circumstances. No, best hope we were not identified, and leave matters in the hands of the police. Not that they will get anywhere with their enquiries. These fellows are altogether too fleet of foot."

"And what of this wretched horse and cart?"

"I don't favour the trek back for the forces of law and order will doubtless be scouring the area for murder suspects. Let us just leave it here and it will soon be re-united with its rightful owner. I cannot imagine anyone else making off with it."

With that we alighted, finding a lamp-post to tether our equine companion who seemed glad of the rest, and we plodded off via side-roads in a westward direction.

A couple of hours later, and now mid-afternoon, we were back in Baker Street to rest our weary bones and soothe our frayed nerves; myself more than Holmes, though he was the one who had sustained injury. To speak plainly I was shattered to my core of my being. Albeit I had been witness to some of the bloodiest scenes of battle in the Afghan campaign and consider myself immunized against distress at the experience of violence, yet when it comes upon one unexpectedly and in a civil context it still has the power to shock and unsettle.

I was fearful that the injury Holmes had sustained in the fracas was graver than he would admit to. He, true to his nature, disdained any suggestion of it but looked pale and drawn all the same. I decided to call upon an old colleague of mine, Dr. Angus McKenzie, the occupant of a nearby practice in Harley Street and a specialist in trauma injury, to examine him at the first opportunity. Holmes demurred, waving aside my remonstrances and breezily declaring that he was totally unharmed, but I was not prepared to take any chances with my friend's health and insisted that he permit an examination. McKenzie was round within the hour and Holmes reluctantly submitted to a very thorough probing, his neck being twisted this way and that to his evident discomfort. To my relief no injury was diagnosed, though McKenzie prescribed a sedative and recommended a long rest, of which I felt there was little prospect. As he left, he enquired by way of conversation, the cause of the injuries but I was, of necessity, unforthcoming on the matter.

I imposed upon our dear landlady for hot baths for both of us, and we effected a change of clothes, desirable particularly in Holmes's case given that his coat and trousers were markedly blood-stained. He wisely decided upon throwing them out altogether rather than putting them in the laundry.

It has to be said that we were both too stunned to engage much in the way of conversation, perhaps fearful of unleashing our pent-up emotions upon each other. But by the early evening we had wound down just enough to seat ourselves by the fireside over a whisky or three, and to reflect grimly upon the shocking and dreadful events of the day that had just passed.

"What happened today?" I cried, interrogating myself as much as my friend.

"It is best I apprize you of all the facts." Holmes's tone was mellower than of usual. "I had arranged a meeting with my informant Murphy, whose acquaintance you had already made, and as you no doubt surmized from the telegram of which I so carelessly gave you sight. It is all too evident that the organization suspected him of divided loyalties, and followed him to our *rendezvous*, perhaps all the way from here, which if true is alarming. Murphy was a petty crook and no more. He did not deserve this fate but you see the villainous forces we are up against."

"So, this dastardly crew is in the service of the Count?"

"I have no doubt of it." Holmes bid me take down from his shelves another of his box files, marked in bold pen on the spine with the letters 'M-N-O', being perhaps too weary to do it himself. I obliged and he riffled through its contents before his forefinger came to rest at a batch of documentation. He plucked a photograph from the box and tossed it in my direction. I gazed at the likeness and could not avoid a gasp escaping my lips, for there, staring out at me as if he were in the room, was none other than one of the men with whom we had tangled only a few hours previously. For though the photograph was faded and slightly indistinct there was no mistaking that ghastly scar across his face and the leer upon his surly features which seemed to be a product of the disfigurement.

"Handsome chap, eh." he said. "Frank Nayland, the leader of an outfit of desperadoes who operate out of north London. They are behind several major robberies and run a series of so-called extortion rackets. They are what might be termed von Runstedt's enforcers."

"Enforcers?" I queried.

"Yes. Whilst the Count and his network engage in espionage, the grittier doings, the thefts and acts of sabotage, and even assassinations and beatings are delegated to Nayland and his gang."

He rummaged through the file to retrieve a few more photographs of other members of the Nayland crew for my edification. He lobbed another one at me; a poorly focussed photograph of another miscreant. "Danny Barton, Nayland's right hand man." There was little question that this was the other assailant, a slightly more nondescript but equally unsavoury looking character.

"Murphy was a minor figure within this outfit who partook in some relatively trivial villainy. He had been with Nayland and his associates for several years. But the really serious acts of terror would often be carried out by the leader himself as you are now all too aware."

"And the other chap is Barton?"

"Almost certainly." He rummaged around in the box and produced another photograph, this one rather more indistinct than the first, showing a group of men lounging malevolently against the side of a wall of a public house.

"This was taken by an agent of mine who specializes in fast action photography." He pointed out two figures in the centre of the group who bore an unmistakeable resemblance to the pair with whom we had clashed so fatally.

I took a while to absorb all of this.

"So, was this Murphy fellow able to tell you anything before his demise?"

"We held a brief dialogue, as you saw, and after much prompting on my part, for he was already deeply fearful of exposure, he was starting to tell me a few things before matters were brought to a terrible conclusion. He had written some information down for me before he set out, lest he forgot the details, and was about to hand it to me when nemesis struck. His assailants may not have realized the identity of the man he was meeting but when they saw a note being passed they decided they had to act. And act they did, with deadly effect."

"And how did you know I was there?" I added, having almost forgotten that Holmes seemed to be aware of my presence.

"My dear fellow, you can't really imagine that it is possible to follow me all the way from Baker Street to Whitechapel and me to be unaware of it. I realized that I had let you see the telegram and was not altogether surprized that you chose to follow. To be completely honest I might have been disappointed had you not. Once I knew, it was too late to turn back or warn you off, and then at the last there was your amusing little performance with the cabbie's fare which assured me of your continued presence.

"But Holmes" I added, voicing a dread thought. "If you fear surveillance, might it not be that Nayland and Barton had followed you all the way from here to Whitechapel?"

"Have no fears on that score. I am certain I, or rather we, were not followed. I think I have scared off any watch upon my person at least for the time being. No. They had lain in wait, or more likely had followed Murphy, already suspecting him of being a nark."

"If you say so."

"My apologies, by the way, for the harshness of my reaction to your slightly belated arrival, but I was reeling from the attack upon my own person."

"No apologies necessary. But why did you not ask me to accompany you in the first place after all we have been through in the last few days?"

"Again, I must offer apologies. I did not want to expose you to any further jeopardy, and was perhaps concerned that Murphy might be frightened away by the appearance of two men, when only expecting one."

"As I supposed. I am just sorry I could not have been of greater assistance."

"There was nothing you could have done. It was all too swift and deadly. No, Watson, but I reproach myself bitterly for having delivered up Murphy to his fate. It is almost as if I had personally pulled the trigger. He was very small fry and did not deserve this terrible end." Holmes sank back into a despondent reverie. "Once, I was renowned for my prowess in single stick combat, but alas my skill and speed seem to have atrophied with lack of practice."

"You were giving a fine account of yourself, but it was two against one."

"I have faced greater odds, but the passage of years, Watson." He sighed wistfully.

"What of the note he passed to you?"

"Well, you saw that I retrieved the vestige from his dead hand."

"And what do you make of it?"

"Nothing as yet."

He passed me the scrap which had a ragged top and left-hand edge, and which simply bore the following words:

> *ich*
> *bin*
> *ein*
> *Hamburg*er

"What on earth do you make of it, Holmes? My German isn't very good, but surely it says 'I am a hamburger'. What can that mean? Had your friend gone doolally in his fright?"

"Doolally. I think not. But I concede it is at present incomprehensible." Holmes was now pacing up and down in a torment of mental agitation. "I may need to sleep on it, Watson."

"If you will forgive my pointing it out but you are now burdened with two pieces of documentary evidence, neither of which presently make any sense, the list and now this scrap. You seem addicted to them." I said, hoping to lighten the mood.

"Good to see that your mordant wit has not deserted you in these extremities." I think he saw the amusing side of affairs even as he admonished me.

"What now?"

"We must await developments. But if I could only crack this conundrum!"

He sank back into his chair curling himself up into a ball in catlike manner, and sucked hard on his briar. He rubbed his neck surreptitiously, perhaps hoping I wouldn't notice.

Chapter X

Lestrade

The day had been long and exhausting enough, and yet it was not completely done with us, for the evening brought a surprizing visitation, and not altogether a welcome one. At about eight-thirty there came a loud rap on the front door, which brought me up sharp as I dozed fitfully in my armchair over a roaring fire, images of the death of Murphy garishly permeating their way into my dreams. Gathering my senses, I could see Holmes in the same posture as when I must have dropped off, still hunched pensively over his precious scrap of paper. After thirty seconds or so I heard the click of the latch and the muffled sounds of conversation downstairs, low murmurs punctuated by the expostulatory tones of Mrs. Hudson, doubtless berating our caller for the lateness of the hour. I did not savour the prospect of a guest at this time and after all our tribulations, and prepared to rouse myself to repel boarders. Holmes did not react in the slightest to this disturbance and continued to pore over his puzzle in the armchair opposite.

"Who on earth can this be, at such an hour?"

"It is our old brother in arms Inspector Lestrade with his new sergeant in tow."

I came up sharp.

"How can you tell? Have you received a communication from him?"

"No such communication is necessary for me to foretell of the presence of Lestrade. I can identify him from past such impromptu visits by the number of knocks, their volume and frequency. Three medium loud knocks at two second intervals, followed by two louder knocks at three second intervals if the first set are not answered."

"Astounding Holmes! You mean you can identify a man from the pattern of his knocking?"

"Lestrade definitely; Gregson sometimes; Athelney Jones occasionally."

"And how do you know he has a new sergeant with him?"

"Lestrade always has someone with him to take notes. It is standard police procedure, but I know that his regular sergeant has been transferred and he must surely have been allocated a replacement by now."

"You certainly keep your ear to the ground."

"I find it the optimal position."

"But what can he want with us? Can it be about today's events? What can we say?" Anxiety was beginning take a hold.

"We are about to discover, but pray do not allude to the murder, for it would be awkward to explain my presence; our presence; and we would be asked questions I would be loth to answer. Remain calm and silent."

"Do you think our appearance might tell against us, for you have a bruise visible on your neck and I have sustained a graze or two."

"Well spotted, Watson. We will make a detective of you yet." Holmes drew his cravat tighter round his neck, concealing the abrasion.

We heard the tramp of feet on the stairs, and the door opened to reveal an irate-looking Mrs. Hudson, announcing the aforementioned Lestrade and partner and favouring them with a look of distinct irritation as she ushered them in. Holmes had thrust the piece of paper that had been the focus of his study into the pocket of his dressing gown just before their arrival.

"My dear Lestrade; a truly unexpected pleasure. What can we do for you?"

"Good evening, Mr. Holmes. Dr. Watson."

He nodded briefly in my direction before turning his attention to Holmes. He was wearing a slightly shabby brown, tweed suit and his habitual frown. The fresh-faced, younger man at his side was gazing eagerly around the room, his eye falling particularly upon the workbench in the far corner.

"I must apologize for disturbing you without forewarning, but I felt I really had to come to see you at the first opportunity." he gruffed. Seeing my friend looking at the other man, he said "Oh, yes. This is my new assistant, Sergeant Parker."

"Very honoured to meet you at last, sir." gushed the junior. "I have heard so much about you and your methods from Mr. Lestrade. He says how invaluable you are to him in his enquiries."

"Yes, thank you, Parker. I'll do the talking if you don't mind."

The man was visibly abashed and shrank back.

"Yes, now, Mr. Holmes. May I take a seat?"

"Please, do forgive me."

Lestrade inserted himself into a hard backed chair near the fire and squirming to get himself comfortable, gave forth.

"We have had reports coming in from Hackney of a fatal shooting following a general fracas near the Whitechapel Road earlier today at about three-thirty. We have been able to identify the victim as ..." he glanced down at his notebook. "one Declan Murphy, a man with a very lengthy record of larceny and such-like felonies."

"Oh, really. How very interesting." Holmes replied with a yawn and the air of one who does not find it at all interesting.

"Yes, well, you see the thing is, Mr. Holmes ..." Lestrade pulled awkwardly at his collar. "The thing is, that we have had a description of two of the men who were seen in the vicinity."

"That must be satisfying for you."

"Yes, and ... er ... well, the description seems to fit you and Dr. Watson, here. In fact, someone actually said it was you." He broke into a rather nervous laugh.

Holmes joined in the laughter. I took my cue from him and managed a rather unconvincing pretence at mirth.

"In fact, somebody actually said they saw you driving a horse and cart in the vicinity!"

All three of us broke into even heartier laughter at this preposterous suggestion.

"And do you propose to put the handcuffs on me?"

"Well, no of course not. I mean it must be a mistake. You are now so well-known to the general public that people must be always thinking they have seen you, when in reality it was somebody completely different. That must be the explanation."

"Yes, I am sure it is. You have put your finger on it straight away. And if you really are in any doubt; well I am sure I can find several witnesses who can attest to my presence elsewhere at the relevant times. And as for Dr. Watson, he has such a nondescript appearance that there might be hundreds of men who could be mistaken for him."

I was not sure I liked being exculpated in quite such cavalier fashion but held my tongue.

"Yes. Well that settles that." Lestrade looked relieved.

"Have you made any arrests?"

"None as yet, though as I say we do have the descriptions of several men who were seen in the locality, including two other characters."

"Other than Watson and myself."

"Yes, yes." The policeman again made a little forced laugh.

"So, is there anything else I can help you with, Inspector?"

"Well, actually yes, Mr. Holmes. That brings me to my next point. Would you be in a position to bring your skills to bear in the case?"

"My, my! From suspect to investigator in a single bound. You do credit me with startling powers of versatility."

Lestrade looked slightly embarrassed.

"It is just that you have been of great help in similar cases in the past and you may be able to uncover one or two clues that we might have missed."

"Oh, but surely you underestimate yourself and the resources at Scotland Yard. And anyway, much as I should have been delighted to render assistance, I am at present occupied with another case that is devouring all my attention, so I regret I must decline."

"Yes, I quite understand, but I did feel moved to ask."

"Nonetheless, any murder case is noteworthy and I am always keen to learn of the goings-on amongst the criminal fraternity. Do you have any idea of the motive for this killing?"

"Not as yet. May have been some sort of gangland revenge killing. You know the sort of thing. Happens all too often these days. Or maybe just some argument that got out of hand."

"Yes, you are probably right. And you have no idea who these other two desperadoes are?"

"Again, we have not yet been able to identify them. But I feel confident it will only be a matter of time before we make arrests. Yes, you can depend upon it."

"Hmm. And have there been reports of any other murders or suspicious deaths recently anywhere in London?"

"Not within the last month as far as I am aware. The murder rate is always on the rise, but no. Why do you ask?"

"Oh, just curiosity, you know. There might be a connection if it had been, as you suggest, a revenge killing, if there had been another murder recently."

"Yes, I see your reasoning, but no."

"And, again just as matter of idle curiosity, you know, have there been any reports of major burglaries anywhere in central London very recently?"

"That is not something I would necessarily be cognizant of. There are all too many burglaries. Does any of this have to do with your current case, then, Mr. Holmes?"

"Possibly. But it is, as I say, just idle curiosity."

"There never seems to be anything very idle about you, Mr. Holmes, and if you don't mind me saying, I can't help thinking you know a bit more about this case than you're letting on? You realize you must inform us of anything significant."

"You have a very suspicious mind, Inspector."

"I'm paid to have a very suspicious mind."

There was general laughter of a more natural kind flowing from this, and the meeting ended on a more convivial note than it had commenced.

But before we parted the young Sergeant Parker, who had been earnestly taking notes during the foregoing conflab, rallied in confidence sufficiently to comment on Holmes's scientific instruments, arrayed very conspicuously if untidily along the table on the other side of the room.

"Ah yes, my little laboratory."

"Would it be relevant to your current enquiries then, Mr. Holmes, if you don't mind me asking?" Lestrade looked a trifle piqued at having his subordinate make the running.

"It is always useful to have the right tools for the job and in good working order."

"Yes, well, we won't take up any more of your time, gentlemen." Lestrade added pointedly, and I showed them out.

Upon my return Holmes was striding around and tapping his pipe against the palm of his hand.

"Well, that was intriguing." he commented.

"Indeed. I'm not sure we are totally in the clear. Lestrade is no fool and must still harbour suspicions."

"Lestrade has his suspicions, yes, but no more. But it is interesting that there is, as yet, no report of the Shepherd's Bush killing, so we can presume that no-one has discovered Kellmann's body, or at any rate, if so has not elected to go to the police with the knowledge."

"Not really surprizing, I wouldn't have thought, Holmes."

"No, I suppose not." he mused. "And it may be useful if his corpse remains there for a while yet."

"You seem determined not to let him go to rest in his grave."

"Perhaps I will try to keep him from it for a few more days, but things depend on progress elsewhere."

"How?"

"Things are taking shape in my head but if only I could parse this wretched note." He had retrieved the scrap from his pocket and was studying it afresh.

"This is the key to everything I feel certain."

He slumped back into his armchair.

I was slightly tickled by one thought. "I say, Holmes, it is funny that the one time you do not affect a disguise you are spotted."

"Merely reinforcing the wisdom of adopting one as often as possible."

After that exchange I finally retired for the evening, in a state in which exhaustion battled with morbid recollection for supremacy. Holmes remained, drawing upon his briar as he turned the scrap over and over in his hand.

Chapter XI

Molly

The following morning I found Holmes utterly immersed in the list of his once more, sucking hard on his briar stoked with one of the foulest of his mixtures and curled up shrouded in a miasma of smoke in his fireside armchair. He had evidently reverted to giving the list priority over the Murphy fragment, or perhaps he was merely alternating between the two, casting about for inspiration. He was turning the pages over and over in his hands, and running his fingers distractedly through his hair.

I decided to go to my club to escape the stench and aware that Holmes probably regarded my mere presence as a hindrance to these lucubrations. Whilst sitting at the bar pending the arrival of anyone I knew I fished around in my coat pockets and felt something small, soggy and round, and pulled out the cardboard beer mat from the Bull's Head, which I had forgotten all about until that moment. The pungent smell of the object brought the occasion back to me. I thought of Molly with her cheap perfume and her teasing ways and wondered what her life was like. Curiously it brought back also memories of my dear departed Mary. What a contrast of personalities!

I was soon roused from my reverie as an old chum bobbed up and we spent the morning in earnest chatter. So glad was I of relief from the darkness of Holmes's case that I quite lost myself in conversation. I returned to Baker Street in a lighter mood, but scarcely knowing what to expect from Holmes.

To my relief he was in a more buoyant frame of mind than earlier and, unless I was mistaken, almost sublimely pleased with himself.

"Back from your club?

"I won't even bother asking how you know. You look happy."

"Good news from the intellectual battlefront, Watson!"

"Do tell?"

"The list! That wretched, accursed list!"

"What of it?"

"It is so obvious. Our man is a historian. What else would a list of numbers be but dates! I must have been blind not to see it straight away. One merely has to segment the numbers into groups of six and it yields up a date; the first two figures being the day, the second two the month and the last two the year. I was misled by the fact that he had understandably not included the century, and the fact that there was no gap in the stream of numbers. There is no significance whatever in the fact of there being twenty to a page. He may even have typed it that way to further obfuscate matters. What a dastardly, fiendish mind our fellow possesses. Look here, my dear chap."

Holmes had avidly snatched up one of the sheets, the first, which was now covered with scrawlings and thrust it under my nose.

"You see?"

There were oblique slashes separating each pair of numbers, pencilled in by Holmes, and it was plain as a pikestaff now, even to me. Thus on that first page we had:

$$23/04/41/02/11/39/18/07/50/16$$

"Aha!"

"Aha, indeed. We have the 23rd of April '41; then the 2nd of November '39; then 18th July '50; etc. etc."

"Yes, it is so obvious."

"And the '16' is merely the precursor to the next set of dates on the following line."

"I see."

"I should have realized because there are, barely visible at a few points, slight gaps within the lines where our man had discontinued and resumed at a later date."

"All very clever, Holmes, but what is the significance of the dates?"

"An excellent question. I feared that we were not much nearer to solving the puzzle. But then something emerged from the mists. If you scan all the way down the page, you will see that these years, if years they be, are grouped between '32' and '82'."

"And?"

"And a perusal of any encyclopaedia tells us that Frederick the Great was born in 1712, and would thus have turned eighteen in 1732, and died in 1786."

I looked blank.

"Don't you see? It is highly probable that these are years and dates upon which significant things happened to Frederick, commencing at the time he gained his majority and then tailing off in old age a few years before his death."

"But what things?"

Holmes's shoulders slumped imperceptibly.

"That was even more vexing, for plough through encyclopaedia after encyclopaedia as I did, courtesy of the reading rooms of the British Museum, which is where I have spent the bulk of my day so far, many of these dates appear to have no significance at all, either to Frederick or anyone else of note."

"Then might not your whole idea be mistaken?" I was struggling to conceal my amusement at the thought that Holmes had erected a theory of dazzling ingenuity only for it to be brought crashing down upon the rocks of reality.

"I was loth indeed to let go of the notion. But then I was struck by something else."

"Go on."

"They might not have been significant things. They might just have been *insignificant* things!"

I was marvelling at my friend's persistence in clinging to a brilliant but discredited idea. How typical of the man to refuse to admit defeat even in the face of near fatal adversity.

"And where would a man's *insignificant* things be recorded?" he continued.

I thought for a moment or two.

"In a diary or journal?" I ventured.

"Exactly!" he cried triumphantly.

I was intrigued by this desperate chain of reasoning.

"So then what or where is this diary or journal?" I did not feel that we were any further forward.

"That too, was highly vexing, but then I cast my mind back to our interview. Did you not see, lying flat upon the top of the man's main bookcase, an imposing volume of foolscap dimensions bound in black leather, much larger than most of the others, and yet which gave the appearance not of a published work but rather a private volume? If I recollect it had a bronze carved elephant sitting upon it."

"I vaguely recall the elephant but not the book."

And, indeed, I would have been hard pressed to have named any of the volumes on show in the several bookcases.

"I have a very strong recollection that upon the spine of that volume was the word *tagebuch*."

"*Tagebuch*? The German for journal!" I cried out in unison with Holmes.

"Bravo, Watson. I noticed it at the time but thought no more about it."

"So these dates are diary entries, you imagine?"

"I feel increasingly sure of it, and the *tagebuch* is the key. The Count has the volume readily to hand to effect a translation whenever the need arizes. Did you notice he had a typewriter in the corner of the room?"

"Vaguely."

"This all starts to fit."

"But if this diary is the key to the code, would he have it on display for all and sundry to see?"

"But no-one would realize its significance, unless they had the list, and probably not even then."

"But even if all of this is true you cannot decode anything without the *tagebuch*."

"Precisely."

A horrible thought overtook me. "And Holmes, please do not tell me you want to burgle the place again!"

"Calm yourself. Even I would not be so bold. Von Runstedt must have discovered the burglary by now and probably has mastiffs posted at every corner."

"Then what?"

"Perhaps we can obtain this vital volume by other means?"

He looked at me puckishly.

"Whatever are you driving at?"

"You have a friend on the inside, do you not, good doctor? One most taken with your manly allure and *savoir faire*."

I was momentarily perplexed.

"You surely don't mean that chambermaid?"

"None other. Your delightful Molly."

"Oh, but this is too much."

"Not a bit of it. You made such a hit the first time around. An invitation to a dance, and a bit of dinner, and who knows what might ensue."

"Holmes, this is squalid. You do not really expect me to dally with a servant girl so as to obtain information."

"Why not? You did it before."

"But that was just a casual conversation I struck up by pure chance."

"Then resume it, but make it less casual. A few words of flattery from you upon her hair or dress and you might have her falling at your feet."

"Holmes, I flatly refuse."

"Gallant to the last, eh, Watson? Trespass, burglary, assault; all in a day's work; but take advantage of a lady? No, no, no!"

"What you are proposing is utterly despicable. I could not for one second countenance placing a servant in a position of jeopardy. What might happen to her if von Runstedt notices the diary is missing, as he surely would if it is so vital a tool?"

"But he might not. He might be absent. And he will not necessarily be able to lay the blame on any particular individual if the removal is done subtly enough, particularly as there are so many people on the staff there, and you suggested your young lady might be a bit light-fingered did you not?"

"Well yes but … but, anyway, whatever makes you think she would agree?"

"Don't underestimate yourself, my dear chap. I have seen you in action. Don't you see? We have come through bramble and thicket together and are on the brink of a successful conclusion and yet now you baulk at the merest suggestion of impropriety."

"It seems more than a mere suggestion."

"Well, I suppose, I must respect your sense of rectitude. Very admirable, I am sure. Just unfortunate that the consequences might be so disastrous for the safety of the realm."

With that Holmes snatched up the sheets of his blasted list and strode from the room. I went to my own bedchamber and spent the next hour in debate with myself. Mary's photographs were on the side-table. It had been several long years now, and I knew she loved me too much for her ever to reproach me for anything. I reached an agonized decision. I stormed into Holmes's room without knocking. He was lying back in his easy chair, cradling his violin upon his lap with a sulky, distracted air. He was startled by my intrusion and leapt up in eager anticipation of my response.

"I will get the wretched *tagebuch* for you, Holmes." I snapped. I did not await his rejoinder, but turned on my heel and marched out of the house in the general direction of Wessex Lane.

*****

The reader will perhaps forgive me if, in recounting these extraordinary occurrences in my modest journal of Holmes's cases, that I have been, thus far, rather more explicit in my descriptions of events than has been my custom. But, since the reader has borne with me with such fortitude up to this point of the narrative I hope that he (or indeed even she) will bear with me yet as I continue to record events in that same candid and forthright vein.

*****

Was it pure chance that I had happened to be glancing through my London gazetteer only recently and that it now fell open, so fortuitously, at the page where Wessex Lane was located? I was thus able to make my way to Miss Molly Carter's address without undue difficulty, deciding to go by foot so as to clear my head and plan my strategy as I walked. I often find that motion aids cogitation.

I ran through a variety of approaches sketching out each in turn in my mind's eye. Would I be bold and incisive, impressing her with my mastery? Or diffident and bashful, seeking to solicit empathy and understanding? Or affable and polite, complimenting her on her appearance and dazzling her with my charm? Or some subtle mixture? Or was all of this mere delusional nonsense on my part? She might not be at home and anyway would she even remember me, let alone wish to be wined and dined? But then again, I remembered *her*, though it was in the line of duty so to speak; and yet, if I am honest with myself, I would have remembered her in any case. There was something about her that got under your skin; there was no denying it.

To be frank I was becoming increasingly apprehensive about my prospects of success in this unsought venture of dubious propriety, and as I neared her neighbourhood my nerve was evaporating with each footstep. It took all my resolve to maintain my course. Wessex Lane was a street of relatively unpretentious dwellings, of a 'fifties' or 'sixties' vintage I would hazard, designed, I had heard tell, for the servants of the grander establishments nearby, much humbler by comparison but of sound construction typical of those decades and not altogether unprepossessing.

Locating number 69 about half way along the street I paused to clear my throat in readiness for introductions and knocked

141

twice upon the front door of the two storied, single fronted house with a firmness of hand which did not reflect my inner uncertainty. I was greeted by a slovenly looking, middle-aged woman of plain aspect and straggly, greyish hair, conventionally and drably attired. Doffing my bowler, I enquired if the young lady of the house was in and might I call on her.

The slattern seemed a bit taken aback to see me, perhaps expecting a different personage altogether, and seemed to be sizing me up with what I would like to think was pleasant surprize. Adopting a slightly more elevated tone of voice than she had initially deployed she said that Molly was still at her place of employment and might I care to call back later that afternoon, after five o'clock, when she was usually home, though, she added scornfully, such was her waywardness that she could never be quite certain. I nodded my compliance with this and paying my compliments I wandered off with no clear idea of my intentions. Candour requires me to admit that I was awash with a sense of relief that Molly was absent and even at this late stage I seriously considered cancelling the whole undertaking.

Rounding the next corner, I came upon a public house of reasonably decent appointments and my watch showing the hour to be well short of four I allowed myself to stray in. At any rate I welcomed the opportunity to shore up my crumbling resolve with liquid assistance. Over the next hour I downed several of the landlord's strongest cask ales to fortify myself for the trial ahead. Trial? What piffle was I talking? The truth was I wanted to see her again and hoped desperately that my desire was reciprocated.

I returned to Wessex Lane just as I spied Molly approaching her house from the opposite end, scurrying along from the rough direction of Wessex Gardens, and still in her service garb. I felt a slight thump of my heart when I saw her again; she was just as vivacious and pretty as I remembered from a few days before. I rushed up and clumsily re-introduced myself. She was startled to see me.

"Oh, hello! Didn't expect to see you again." Her tone evinced surprize and yet, I fondly imagined, was not wholly unappreciative.

"Pardon me for my intrusion upon your daily routine, Miss Carter, but ... well ... you did say I might come round to see you." I ventured nervously.

"Yeah, right, but I didn't really fink ... Well ... you'd better come inside then. And like I told you before, it's Molly." She smiled sweetly and ushered me in after her, into the cramped hallway of the little house that smelled of lavender and roses and cooking, and bawled up the staircase to announce her homecoming.

"There's a bloke wanting to see yer, Moll, bit of a toff I reckon; what you been up to now?" a voice shouted down.

"Yeah, thanks, ma, he's already 'ere." She turned toward me and made a mock grimace of embarrassment at her mother's indiscretion.

"I do hope I haven't called at an inopportune moment and really I should apologize for not writing to you in advance but ..." I stammered.

"Don't worry about it, Mr. Wilson. Oh, no, it's Dr. Wilson, ain't it. Anyways, you're good to come any time." She smiled at me again, more warmly than the first time. I laughed awkwardly, at a slight loss for words.

The older woman had made her way down the staircase.

"Oh, hello again", she said with a tinge of embarrassment upon seeing me.

"Ma, this is Dr. Wilson, what I told you about. He's a friend of the Count."

"Oh, right." she sounded impressed, and looked me up and down with renewed approbation.

"Do you want a cup of tea?" she asked.

"That would be most kind." The two women shuttled off into the kitchen at the back and started whispering intensively to each other which I did my best to avoid overhearing, scrutinizing the wallpaper as I swayed from foot to foot awaiting their return.

They re-emerged, side by side. "Do come through." the older woman said affecting a more refined tone than hitherto, and smoothing down her skirt as she ushered me into the drawing room; a very small, disordered chamber full of junky ornamentation and with some rather unappealing armchairs, their stuffing protruding, and a very worn two-seater couch.

"Please take a seat", said the older woman, gesturing at the couch. I levered myself down onto the ancient settee as best I could, finding it giving way more than I had expected and I sank deeply into it. Molly plonked herself down next to me with a grin, so that there was a discomforting intimacy between us. The mother scurried off back to the kitchen and I could hear a rattling of crockery and the whistling of a kettle.

"So, what brings you 'ere, then?"

"If you will forgive my boldness, I came to see you." I was scrunched very awkwardly on the settee, cheek by jowl with Molly and scarcely able to turn my head without nudging her.

"Didn't fink you'd even remember me."

"Oh, but not at all; you are hard to forget." I wondered if my words might be misconstrued and added hastily, "That is, I mean, for reasons of your charming disposition." I hoped I wasn't overdoing the blandishments.

"That's really nice of yer to say."

She was snuggling up to me, inching her way across the little sofa. I pretended not to notice and stared straight ahead surveying the cluttered room and its plethora of bric-a-brac. Some of the more expensive ornaments seemed slightly familiar. I thought I recognized one of the dainty silver bowls as one of a pair, its partner residing in the entrance hallway of Wessex Gardens. To my relief the mother soon returned carrying a tray of cups, saucers, jugs and plates of little cakes.

"How do you take it, sir?"

"Oh, erm, white with one sugar, if you please."

The woman did service and handed me a cup. She turned to her daughter.

"How's it been, Moll, them still all crazy up there at the house?"

"Yeah, ain't bleeding stopped all day."

"Oh, I'm sorry, Dr. Wilson." Molly realized the need for explanation, "Maybe you ain't 'eard but there's been a burglary at the house; well that's what I 'ear from Tom and the others, and everyone running around in circles, the Count going really off his rocker, yelling and shouting at every one in that funny voice of his, lots of words I don't even know; never seen him so furious; saying he might have to put back his going abroad and wrecking his plans and so on; poor Mr. F really getting a right rollicking, but it weren't his fault; well it weren't nobody's fault I don't reckon, just one of them things what happens; I mean if you got so much so valuable stuff all over the place you're bound to get robbed every so often ain't you; I mean you're asking for it more or less. Well, that's what I fink anyway. And I don't even really know what got nicked. I mean all the stuff is still there so far as I can see. Funny burglars they were, break in and not steal nuffing."

"Yes, I take your point." I squirmed in my seat.

"Ere; that's a coincidence ain't it, I mean getting burgled just right after I said were you planning to do a burglary. It wasn't you was it?" she collapsed into a fit of the giggles.

"Ha, ha, yes it was me. I plead guilty." I put my hands in the air in mock surrender, causing her to giggle even more hysterically than before.

"Oh, you are a caution, Dr. Wilson."

The mother had joined in the laughter, and I did my best to share in the merriment. This seemed to go on for an age before finally subsiding. Molly was spilling her tea onto my trousers in her hysterics.

"Oh, I am really sorry, Dr. Wilson, let me clean it up for you." She started dabbing my trousers with a napkin.

"Oh, Moll you are a butterfingers, let me have a go."

I flinched as they both set about me. "That's quite alright. Please don't bother yourselves. They are only an old pair."

"Don't worry. We won't strip them off you." Cue more hysterical laughter. Waving away their unwanted attentions and waiting for their glee to subside I tried to steer matters back towards my desired topic.

"Actually, the reason I came around today, unannounced, for which I do apologize, was to, er, to ask Molly if she would care to come to the theatre with me this evening; with your leave, Mrs. Carter, and unless of course you have other plans, Molly."

"Why yes, of course she can, no need to ask my permission I'm sure, Dr. Wilson." The mother seemed taken aback by having her permission sought in the matter of her daughter's activities.

"Yeah, I ain't got nuffing planned." Molly said brightly. "So, where you gonna take me then, Doc.?" she chirped, her eyes now gleaming.

"I thought I might escort you to the Haymarket. There is a new play there that you might find entertaining." A few weeks previously I had happened to obtain a pair of tickets for the Beerbohm Tree production of *Trilby* which had opened to ecstatic reviews and, knowing Holmes would not be remotely interested in such persiflage thought it opportune to use them for this occasion.

"Ooh, sounds smashing. Ain't been to the theatre for ages. You are full of surprizes, Doc."

"I am glad you are in favour."

"Right, well I'll get changed then. See you in a while, John. You did say I could call you John, didn't you?"

"Oh, yes, if you wish."

With that and a nod in the direction of her mother, she slipped out of the room and I heard her skipping up the staircase.

Mrs. Carter and I sat and stared woodenly at each other for a while, daring each other to make conversation.

"So where do you do your doctoring then? You did say you was a doctor, didn't you?"

"Yes, that's right. In Marylebone in point of fact. I have a fairly steady practice there." I said, not wholly accurately since patients had been conspicuous by their absence in recent months.

"Must be great being a doctor and curing all those people."

146

"Well, actually, I don't really cure people. No, not as such. I am what you might call a diagnostician."

Her jaw dropped.

"What's that when it's at home?"

"It's a doctor who analyses the pathology of disease."

"Oh, very good, I'm sure." She looked stumped.

"Do you and your daughter live here alone then?"

"Yes. Well, Jack, that's my boy," she pointed at a photograph on the side-table, "he's in the merchant navy so I only see him every few months and my husband's … away at the moment … on business, sort of."

This stilted colloquy continued for altogether far too long for my comfort. I was very relieved when Molly re-appeared through the doorway, now dressed in what was probably her smartest frock, a bright blue full length floral affair of silk or some such material, her hair elaborately coiffured, and what appeared to be distinct touches of make-up about her eyes and mouth. It was a wondrous transformation. I rose in unfeigned admiration.

"May I say how delightful you look, Molly."

"Why, thank you, kind sir." She dropped a mock curtsey in acknowledgement. "Shall we be off then?"

"Oh, er, yes certainly."

We moved out into the hallway. I bid Mrs. Carter farewell, promising that we would be back before twelve, and escorted Molly out into the street. Total darkness had now descended, relieved only by house lights and the street lamps. There was a slight fog. I was able to hail a hansom quite quickly and we sped off in the direction of Piccadilly Circus.

"I thought we might have a spot of dinner at the Café Royal first. The play doesn't begin until eight, so we have at least an hour or more to spare."

"Ooh, lovely." she chirruped. She was squeezing my arm tightly as she ogled out the cab window at the passing sights as we sped down Regent's Street.

At the Café Royal, I was relieved to be able to obtain a table fairly easily. I could see that Molly was slightly overawed by these surroundings.

"Ain't never been 'ere before. Seen it lots of times, though. Tom only ever takes me to the Bull's Head or some other pub."

As I feared she ordered some of the most expensive items on the menu, and was soon guzzling down the turtle soup, her spoon flying to and fro with wondrous rapidity.

"You evidently have an appetite."

"Well, yeah, been on the go since seven this morning cleaning the bedrooms, and then the lavatories and then the downstairs rooms and all."

I tried, as subtly as possible, to steer matters towards the *tagebuch*.

"Do you clean the office as well?"

"Well, sometimes, yeah, though usually it's Edna what does that. It's kept locked most of the time. Why?"

"Oh, just wondered. So, Molly, you say nothing was stolen in this burglary?"

"That's right. Really weird ain't it."

"But your employer, the Count, was sorely exercized?"

"Yeah, exercized alright. He was running up and down the stairs ranting and raving all bloody day." I recoiled slightly at the vulgarity of her language and was relieved that we were too far from other tables for it to be overheard.

"Was anything taken from his office?"

"Well, yeah, that's where they say the burglary happened, though people being a bit cagey about it. Tried to get Tom or Edna to tell me, but they don't know neither and Tom says Mr. F been told not to say nuffing about it to no-one."

"So perhaps the theft was from the safe in the office?"

"Well maybe. You seem to know a lot about it. You sure you wasn't the burglar?" she dissolved in fits once again.

"You really do seem to have the handcuffs on me." I had to wait for her mirth to subside. "Perhaps you should make a citizen's arrest."

"I'd take you into custody any time, darling." She said almost spilling a spoonful of soup into her lap. I could feel myself colouring slightly. I was struck as before by her forwardness and freedom from inhibition, which in its way was so refreshing and endearing. I changed tack.

"It's just that when I was visiting His Lordship, the Count, the other day I couldn't help noticing some of the exquisite items in his office. All that Frederick the Great memorabilia, for example. Some of it might be extremely valuable. Yet none of it taken by the thieves."

"Maybe they don't know its value."

"Perhaps not. But I mean those portraits, worth thousands I'd wager."

"Really? Maybe they couldn't get them out through the window."

"Well, yes, perhaps. And those volumes in his bookshelves; very rare some of them. That *tagebuch*, for instance, could be absolutely priceless."

"Target book?"

"*Tagebuch*." I spelt it out for her.

"No use telling me 'ow to spell it, darling, I can't read."

"Well, it's a large, black, leather bound volume on top of the central bookcase. It's weighted down by that bronze elephant. You must have seen it when you were cleaning?"

"Oh, I know. Yeah, that blasted elephant. Bloody heavy, it is."

"Yes, well I think that might be worth a great deal of money."

"The book or the elephant?"

"Ha, ha. The book."

"Oh, how much?"

"I'd say tens of thousands."

"Wow. You gotta be joking. For a book?"

"Oh, indeed. I offered to buy it from His Lordship but he wouldn't part with it. Sentimental value and all that."

"But why would anyone pay that for a book?"

"Rarity value."

"Sounds crazy to me. Must be millions going hungry every day and then people pay thousands for a book. Ain't no justice in this world."

"Well yes, you have a very good point there. So, I wonder if I could ask a small favour of you?"

"Oh, yeah? What's that then?"

149

"I would be prepared to offer a very large sum for it, but I need to know its contents, so that I can get it valued you see. I would pay thousands if it is what I think it is, but I can't be sure and until I can see the contents I can't know."

"Couldn't you ask him just to show you? I mean you say he's an old friend of yours." She may have been tipsy but she was still sharp as a needle.

"Well, I'd say an acquaintance rather than a friend and he's very reluctant to let anyone see it."

"So, what's this favour then?" I sensed that she was starting to view me in a more guarded light.

I proffered some more wine, pouring it liberally into her glass.

"I feel rather embarrassed even asking you, but, er, if I could just get a peek at it, that's all I need."

"You asking me to pinch it?"

"Not pinch it, no. Just remove it for a short while so that I could see it, and then you can return it. Next time you're in there dusting. He wouldn't notice. I mean you say he's going abroad any day. It could come and go without anyone realizing."

"Don't want much do you? Last time someone got caught nicking stuff he called the police in. She's doing time now."

"But no-one would know it was you, particularly if, as you say, Edna is the one chiefly responsible for cleaning the office."

I could see wicked thoughts crossing her mind.

"So, what do I get out of it?"

"What would you like?"

She placed her hand under her chin and fixed her glance upon the middle distance. "A diamond necklace," she averred decidedly.

"I am not sure I could supply that." I was reeling.

"Why not? If you can pay thousands for a book, you can afford a few sovs for a necklace, the way I see it."

"I will see what I can do in that regard," I said noncommittally.

"Only joking. You still can't tell when I'm teasing can yer?"

150

"Oh yes, you have taken me again. But I can assure you I would be most grateful. Would you care for some more wine? Let me say again, how very lovely you look this evening. I think you are quite the handsomest woman here."

"You're a bit of a devil, you are, John, you know that?"

"I don't know about that. I try to steer clear of sin, but it does tend to follow me around." Chiefly at the instigation of Holmes, I thought to myself.

She was wearing a powerful fragrance, but an altogether more tasteful brand than what I remembered from the Bull's Head. It was quite beguiling in its way.

"When do you want me to do all this, then?"

"Well, as soon as possible really. I mean if it wouldn't be too much trouble. You say your employer has deferred his going abroad but he might still go in the very near future and might take the book with him, so, er, would first thing tomorrow be acceptable?"

"Blimey, you in a hurry ain't yer."

I plied her with some more wine.

"Well, as I say, urgency is of the essence."

"Of the essence, eh?" she mimicked my voice, rolling her eyes upwards. "And how will I get in if it's locked? I ain't got a key, yer know."

"Perhaps you might be able to obtain a key. Your Mr. F might have one."

"Gawd. So, I gotta nick the key, then nick the book and give it to you, then put it back again. Don't want much do yer! I ain't the Artful Dodger, you know." She collapsed in laughter again. I chimed in as best I could. Her voice was getting louder and louder the more she drank and I tried to quieten her with a gentle shush, but luckily our table was too far away for anyone to be disturbed by her ravings.

"Look, I know I am asking a lot and I really don't want to place you in a compromising position, but as I explained I really am very eager to obtain this volume. As I say I would be very greatly in your debt. Now I come to think of it, there's an old friend of mine who deals in jewellery and I might be able to persuade him to part with something in the way of a diamond necklace."

"You for real, John? I was only joshing yer. Don't you worry; I'll do it for you. It'd be a giggle and I'd love to see the look on Mr. F's face if the Count finds it missing after everyfing else what's happened."

"Molly, you are marvellous. But I beg of you not to put yourself in any danger. If there is any chance of your being caught, pull out of the enterprize."

"Oh, I won't get caught. Nobody will know it's me what done it."

"But might not the Count notice it missing and try to find out the culprit?" The dangers of the enterprize were already rearing their ugly head.

"I dunno, but Tom says he's going away to his other house in Berkshire for a day or two, I fink, so he might not notice."

"If so that is a great weight off my mind."

"And a great weight off the book as well." She giggled uncontrollably at her little joke.

"Ha, ha. What a quirky sense of humour you have, Molly."

"So, 'ow do I get the book to you?"

"Ah. We can arrange to meet tomorrow morning or whenever you come off duty. I promise I can get it back to you very soon so that you can replace it before the Count will even realize it's missing. We could meet at the Bull's Head perhaps."

"Yeah, alright. You're a bit of a one, John." I could feel her knee nudging mine under the tablecloth. It made me feel distinctly uncomfortable and I glanced anxiously at the neighbouring tables to ensure that no-one had seen this but everyone was too enwrapped in their own conversations. I must say it gave me a strange sensation.

But I could scarcely credit my luck in managing to cajole her. Perhaps Holmes was right and I under-estimate my way with the fair sex. But this girl really was a treasure.

We walked the small distance from the restaurant to the Haymarket to attend the play which had Molly craning her neck forwards at the stage, enthralled throughout the performance, and, as we made our way back to Wessex Lane by hansom she couldn't stop talking about it; about how spellbinding Dorothea Baird was in the lead role, how fascinating the plot, and how elaborately staged the whole production was. I could not disagree with her, though I felt myself that Beerbohm Tree was rather over the top in the lead role; too many histrionics for my taste, but I was delighted that Molly had enjoyed herself so. We arrived back at her house by eleven-thirty, both of us in a state of joyful fatigue.

Approaching the house, I was startled to see none other than young Tom loitering in the vicinity, a black look writ large on his surly features. He accosted her as we reached the front door, casting a malicious glance in my direction before launching into a tirade of abuse and invective aimed at the girl, the gravamen of which was that she had stood him up and how dare she go off with me and what had she been up to. It was evident he had been drinking heavily. Such was the savagery of his language that I was moved to intervene on her behalf.

"I will thank you to keep a civil tongue in your head, young man. The young lady came out at my invitation, and I was not aware that she had any prior engagement. We have attended the theatre, if it is any business of yours, and I am escorting the lady home, and that is all there is to the matter."

He turned to me and replied in the profanest and most abusive of terms, casting doubt on my military history and threatening physical violence if I did not immediately depart. I protested vehemently at this un-called for treatment and stood my ground. He then grabbed the girl's arm, shaking her very roughly, and continued his abuse of her, prompting me to intercede once again, rather more forcefully this time. I shoved him hard, forcing him to release his grip upon her, whereupon he swung out at me with his fist, catching me a painful blow to the side of my face which sent me staggering backwards.

Flushed with anger I recovered swiftly to reply in kind, knocking him to the ground with ease, given his state of intoxication and general unsteadiness. He attempted to get back to his feet, but I stood over him with my fist primed ready to strike another blow if the need be. At this he launched into a further bout of invective at Molly from a crouching position at the kerbside, part rancorous, part self-pitying. She was herself now roused to fury and responded in almost equally intemperate terms.

All of this was attracting attention from passers-by and I feared that soon a constable would be called, notwithstanding the lateness of the hour, but after further exchanges of unpleasantries between them the young lout slunk away, shaking a fist in my direction and threatening retribution of a menacing but unspecified kind. I cannot deny I was shaken by all of this for, though I had been at the heart of the bloodiest of battle in my days in Afghanistan, it feels altogether different to be confronted with violence in a civilian setting when one is unprepared for it. I rallied to present a re-assuring front to Molly. She had calmed herself and now turned her attentions back to me. She came over to my side.

"You okay, John?"

"Yes, I am fine." I lied. "Are you alright?"

"I'll be alright, don't you worry, but you don't look too good. You got blood coming from your cheek." she said with evident concern.

And only now did I realize my face was cut from Tom's blow, the ring on his finger drawing blood.

"It's nothing really. Are you sure you are alright?"

"I'm okay, but you'd better come inside and let me do somefink about that cut of yours."

"No, really, I should be off. I have obviously caused you too much trouble already."

"Don't be daft. Get inside, you silly feller."

I complied with reluctance, shuffling in hoping nobody would see me, but the bystanders had drifted away, the excitement over. She grabbed my coat and steered me into the living room, and sat me down on the horse-hair sofa I remembered all too well from earlier in the evening, before scurrying off to the kitchen. She was quickly back dabbing my face with cotton wool doused in some stinging concoction. I mumbled my thanks and apologies.

"I really am most dreadfully sorry to have caused you all of this trouble; it is quite unforgivable of me."

"Don't fink nuffink about it, he's like that when he's had too much. He'll be normal in the morning."

"Are you sure you will be safe. I mean he won't come back will he? And you still have to work with him."

"Not tonight he won't. You scared him off good and proper; my knight in shining armour." Her emerald eyes were warm and inviting as she bent over me. I tried to shrug off her comments.

"It was nothing really. The least I could do under all the circumstances. But I must be going given how late in the evening it is, as soon as you have finished your ministrations. Perhaps we should forget all about what I said earlier. You need time to recover and I cannot possibly ask you to place yourself at any further risk for my sake." I tried to rise from the sofa, but she pushed me back down.

"Stay where you are. I ain't finished with you yet." She completed her nursing duties by applying a small bandage. She was very dextrous.

At length I again rose awkwardly from the cavernous depths of the sofa and protested that I must leave.

"You ain't going nowhere."

"What do you mean?"

"Come here you!" she was standing two feet in front of me in her stylish waist-hugging gown, incredibly fetching in the dim candlelight of the tiny room, with its flickering rays playing on her eyes of jade. She moved towards me and pressed her shapely little body tightly into me. Her trim little figure was sturdy and strong, her breasts firm and supple.

I gulped hard. I was trembling from a brew of shock and exhilaration. She slipped a strap off her frock, exposing the delicate curve of her pale shoulder and a hint of her bosom. It also revealed, to my further amazement, a tattoo. It was an anchor with a mermaid entwined around it. This little lady could provide no end of wonders. I was tantalized. Seeing my surprize she explained. "Mate of my brother's in the merchant done it for me. Good ain't it?"

"Bewitching." I said. "I didn't know women had tattoos."

"Probably lots of fings you don't know about women."

155

"Perhaps you should fill this lamentable gap in my education." I said discovering a boldness of attack I scarcely knew I possessed.

We found ourselves kissing, gently at first and then rapturously. Her lips were like honey. I ran my hand through her bush of reddish hair as it tumbled from its intricate mounting. It was softer and longer and lusher than I could ever have imagined. I ran my hands up and down her curvaceous little body, faster and faster, over her shoulders, down the small of her back and over her behind as she squeezed herself tighter and tighter into me.

"Coming upstairs, darling." she whispered.

"Surely you are not suggesting ..." I quavered.

"You don't want me?" she took a step back and gazed up at me coquettishly.

"But your mother ..."

"She's gone out for the night. Anyway, she won't mind. She's seen it all."

"But, but ..." I stammered.

"You don't need to worry about nuffing, darling, it's a good time of the month for me." She took me by the hand and guided me up the narrow little staircase after her.

I did not return to Baker Street that evening.

Chapter XII

The *Tagebuch*

I was awakened early by a series of muffled noises and peered about in bewilderment at my unfamiliar surroundings before the events of the night came flooding back to me. Molly was already up and beavering around the room dressing herself and cursing that she couldn't find what she needed. Women seem to have a curious knack for slipping from the passionate to the everyday with seamless ease. Perhaps it is a necessity for them; assuredly it must be for those of Molly's class.

"Good morning." I croaked.

"You roused yourself at last."

"What time is it?"

"Six."

"Six." I expostulated. I hunted for a clock to confirm this unlikely piece of information. "Come back to bed."

"Got to work, darling. I'm late already."

"What time do you start?"

"Six thirty, but I got to be there ten minutes before to get ready."

"Ready for what?" I said in bafflement.

"Ready for all the stuff I gotta do, like taking His Lordship his morning tea and lighting his fire and everyfing, what d'yer fink."

"Can't he do that for himself for once?"

"What planet you living on, John?"

I stumbled to my feet, searching for my trousers. I clutched a stretch of the bed sheets to cover myself.

"I've seen most of you already, darling, and you ain't got nuffing to be ashamed of. And even if you have that won't cover it. It's got holes in it." She giggled.

I laughed sheepishly and retreated back beneath the bedclothes. She was still bustling around, putting the finishing touches to her wardrobe of pinafore frock and mob cap and straightening her hair in front of a long mirror. She had not lit the gas lamp perhaps out of consideration for my slumbers and the room was dimly lit by a solitary candle.

"When do you come off duty?"

"One o'clock, if I'm lucky."

"Erm, about the book."

"Yeah, darling, I ain't forgotten. But I can't promise you nuffing."

"No, of course not. I fully understand. And as I said I implore you not expose yourself to any danger."

"Don't worry about me. The Bull's Head, okay?"

A thought had occurred to me.

"Might not a certain person be there?"

"Oh, Tom. Don't you worry about him. He's all talk. I'll handle him alright. Anyway, he ain't on duty today. Probably be sleeping it off until at least the middle of the afternoon if I know anyfing about him."

"Very well, then. One o'clock at the Bull's Head."

She was ready to depart but paused to look at me with a grin creeping over her face. She scuttled round to the bedside, bent over and kissed me on my cheek, causing a sudden re-awakening of the pain from the wound inflicted only a few hours before.

"Ooh, sorry darling, didn't realize it would still hurt." She rubbed the bedsheets covering my lower body and winked. "Is that better?"

I felt at a slight loss.

"Molly, may I express my gratitude to you for, er ... for last night."

This provoked another fit of the giggles. "Alright, no need to make a speech about it. We're not in Parliament. Takes two you know."

"If you will give me a few minutes I can be dressed and toileted and will accompany you."

"Don't be daft. Stay there long as you want, but I gotta go. Let yourself out, but don't slam the front door cos me mum's got in very late and she'll still be asleep."

She blew me a kiss and had swept out the bedroom door and down the staircase before I could get another word out. I heard the front door click shut. Peering out of the curtains I saw her scurrying away down the street towards Wessex Gardens, drawing her coat closer around her shoulders and disappearing amongst the general throng of morning workers trooping glumly to their labours.

I decided to rise, feeling uncomfortable lying there on my own and dressed hastily and untidily in the absence of proper light, for it was still dark outside. I poured some cold water from the large enamel jug on a side-table into a bowl to wash my face. I had no means of shaving not having brought my razor and kit, scarcely envisaging the startling course events had taken.

I made a cursory poke around her room, which I know a gentleman should never do, but curiosity about her circumstances got the better of me. It was modestly furnished and short of amenities and yet possessed a Lilliputian charm that spoke volumes of its occupant. There was an enchanting miasma of smells emanating from a jumble of perfumeries on her dressing table mingled with the more general odours of discarded clothing. Her evening dress from yesterday had been tossed over the back of a wooden chair. There were dainty displays of cheap knick-knacks and childhood playthings and a collection of rag dolls perched on top of a cupboard in the far corner of the bedchamber. Feminine paraphernalia was everywhere. There was a wardrobe and a couple of chests of drawers, undergarments spilling from them. I took the liberty of peeking into the wardrobe which disclosed an array of garments; severe and workaday on the one side and brighter

159

and gayer on the other; shoes of many descriptions were scattered on the floor.

I glanced at the photographs on her dressing table and picked up one, sepia and faded, surely of her as a little girl at the seaside with her parents and brother. I squinted and detected the impish features that had evolved so deliciously from the infant to the grown woman. Her mother, then still young, a somewhat plainer precursor of her now adult daughter. I smiled and carefully replaced it.

I crept downstairs. Thankfully there was no sign of the mother and I let myself out, the door locking shut automatically behind me.

I havered about returning to Baker Street for a proper wash, a shave and a change of clothes, but I was reluctant to confront Holmes, whom I could easily visualize saluting my return with a quiverful of caustic asides about my overnight absence, the more so after my tantrum of the previous day. If I could produce the *tagebuch* for him, however, that might cast matters in an altogether different and more favourable light. I hoped above all else that Molly would be able to fulfil her mission, though I was fearful for her well-being. Would she really be able to obtain this wretched diary without anyone noticing, and then replace it once Holmes had scoured if for clues? She was clearly a resourceful young woman but even so it was asking a lot. I chastized myself for exposing her to possible harm.

I made my way to the nearest workman's café where my unshaven and slightly dishevelled state, not to mention my cut and bandaged cheekbone, would not, I hoped, arouse adverse comment as it might have done in a more exalted establishment. I breakfasted well on sausages and bacon and, now fortified, felt altogether more optimistic.

It is a wearisome cliché to say I felt I was walking on clouds, but clichés become clichés because they are true. I cannot say exactly where I went and what I did but I managed to pass the time with a series of aimless and idle pursuits, before my watch showed it to be nearing one. I strode back to Mayfair and the Bull's Head with a sense of dread and expectation in equal measure, but my fears proved unfounded for, after a wait of ten minutes or so, Molly appeared, framed fleetingly in the doorway; a large bag slung over her shoulder which boded well. Once again, my heart skipped a beat at the sight of her. She exchanged banter with a small group of drinkers and spying me she made her way over. I was relieved also by the absence of Tom. I rose to greet her. She plonked herself down with a groan.

"What a bleeding morning. I've had no end of grief from Mr. F over this, that and the other. The coal didn't get delivered so I had to run all the way down to the merchants to find out why not and then when I get back I find the groceries didn't get delivered neither, and then Edna says to me ..."

"Yes, er, sorry to butt in but did you manage to obtain what I asked for." I said dropping my voice to a whisper at the end of the sentence.

"Oh yeah, well never mind about me then; your book is all that matters." Her voice was rising as mine was falling.

I pulled myself up sharp. "I am most dreadfully sorry." I castigated myself for the churlishness of my approach and fretted that we might have been overheard, but there was generally too much noise and conviviality for anyone to take any notice. "It's just that I am most anxious about the book, but, much more importantly, I am anxious about you."

"Well, I'm glad you said that cos I was beginning to fink you was interested in this bloody book and nuffink else. Convenient for you having me do all the donkey work, ain't it?"

"Molly, please, I care deeply for you. You must believe me." I reached out and clasped her hands within mine, before realizing myself and drawing back. "I know you must have a trying life, and I curse myself for imposing upon you in this peremptory way. It is all quite unforgiveable of me, and I should quite understand if you said you never wanted to see me again."

"Yeah, well alright, you don't need to make a performance out of it." The slight flutter of her eyelids told me I was forgiven. She was mollified. I amused myself inwardly by the curious appositeness of the word.

"Look, I got you this blasted book." She bent down to fish around in her bag and started to draw it out, a bulky black tome.

"Yes, yes." I hastily reached over to prevent her. "That's marvellous but we don't want anyone to see. We need to be circumspect."

"Circum what?"

"I know. Just leave the bag here when you go and I'll pick it up."

"Don't get into a lather; there's no-one here from number 4. Can't tell you how much bother it was. Had to sneak into Mr. F's cupboard to get the key, then found it was the wrong one and I had to go back, then realized the office weren't properly locked anyway cos the lock was busted from the break-in, and then I had to hide behind the door cos I 'eard someone coming. Phew! A right old two and eight I can tell yer."

"Has your employer realized it's missing?" I asked anxiously.

"No, like what I said to yer, he's gone away to his place out in the sticks; went off first fing this morning, long before I done the job."

"That is indeed fortunate. But when is he to return?"

"Mr. F says not till very late tomorrow evening."

"I must get it back to you before then."

"Yeah, I suppose. You seem more worried than me."

"So, where and when can I meet you?"

"Here? Seven o'clock tomorrow?"

"Why not earlier?"

"Won't get no chance till the evening. Gotta work all through the day tomorrow."

"Alright, seven. That will be splendid."

"Well, I hope it's worth it to you."

"Oh, my goodness me; I cannot begin to tell just how much."

"So, what yer going give me for it?"

I knew her well enough by now.

"Oh, all the riches in the world."

"Alright, then, but doesn't a girl get a drink first?"

"Oh, yes she certainly does. I do apologize. What would you like?"

"You can buy me the most expensive drink they got behind the bar."

"With pleasure."

I brought her a large brandy and water.

"Will I be able to see you again after tomorrow?" I said earnestly.

"Do you want to?"

"Why, yes, very much so. I mean you want to see me, don't you?"

I thought I had given a good account of myself as a man and was disappointed at her apparent indifference.

"So, it's not just the book your after?"

"Molly, no, no, I swear to you that I ..." at this juncture a man barged drunkenly into our table, causing me to spill my drink. He apologized with a rough courtesy but it had ruined the moment. Molly gulped down her own drink. We searched each other's faces for a moment or two.

"Look, I gotta go, John. Sorry."

We rose.

"And don't forget your book, after all the trouble I gone to."

"Oh, no definitely not." I looked around and seeing no-one I recognized from the house I grasped her hand once more. A flutter of her eyelids again.

"Come round the back with me." she whispered.

Obtusely, I almost asked her why. We scurried out to the rear of the public house which was largely deserted. Molly guided me towards a small alcove invisible from the main courtyard though I made furtive glances around to satisfy myself we were unobserved. I manoeuvred her against the wall and, confident we were alone, I slipped my arms round her waist; how shapely and robust she was, but pliable and yielding. She stood on tiptoe and flung her arms around my neck. We kissed; a long, slow lingering engagement. Her mouth was incredibly soft, her breath tangy from the liquor, her tongue curling its way to the back of my teeth. The thrilling sensations of the previous night came gushing back.

It seemed like mere seconds but it must have been several minutes when she at last pulled herself away.

"Sorry, John luvvie, but they'll be screaming for me back at the house. I'll see you tomorrow." she breathed.

"Seven?"

"Yeah."

I reluctantly let go her hand and she dashed away. I tried to shout some endearment to her but she was already scampering away, giving me a brief backward look.

I suddenly remembered the bag and feared it had been left in the pub, but as I glanced down there it was at my feet with the book protruding slightly from its open top. I looked back at Molly, but she had almost vanished, and then down at the bag again to reassure myself I was not hallucinating. I bent down and peered eagerly inside. I pulled out the book. It was a large, black leather-bound volume just as described by Holmes with a gilt title on the spine saying *tagebuch*. I had struck gold. In more ways than one.

It was a few moments before I could bring myself down to earth. I looked at my watch and saw that it was now one-thirty, and in my excitement I could hardly decide between running all the way to Baker Street or taking a cab, before settling on the latter so as to calm my nerves. I could scarcely wait to tell Holmes the good news, hoped he would be home, and that I would find him in a temperate mood. Now I came to think about it, I almost wished, perversely, that he would be in a foul humour such that my presentation of the book to him would come as a revelation. I mentally rehearsed the production all the way in the cab. I raced breathlessly up the staircase and then steadied myself for a few seconds before sauntering into the drawing room with all the nonchalance in the world. I was delighted to see Holmes at his laboratory in the far corner of the room. He didn't look up.

"Afternoon, Holmes" I said insouciantly.

"Ah, the wanderer returns. You were detained elsewhere last night I presume?" he muttered as he shook the contents of a test tube. He had adopted a tone of measured indifference. I suppressed my agitation and put my carefully crafted speech into operation.

"Yes, I was pursuing some enquiries of my own." I said offhandedly as I wandered over to my armchair and settled in, taking up my pipe from the mantelpiece. I briefly perused my newspaper, before coming out with my killer lines.

"Oh, by the way, Holmes, I chanced upon something that might be of interest to you." As casually as I could muster, I extricated the book from the bag and turned it over in my hands, peered inside it, closed it again and looked it over again until the spine faced towards him. I could see he was still resisting the urge even to look in my direction, but the production of the book was too much even for Holmes to maintain a facade of uninterest. He sprang to his feet and stood with eyes fastened on the volume in my hands. He sprang over and wrenched it out of my grasp.

"Watson! You are a phenomenon!"

He gaped in wonderment at me. Never did I think I would be able to impress Holmes in the manner in which he so regularly dazzled me, but I had done so and I savoured the moment for all it was worth. If I could salvage some morsel of consolation from the wreckage of this whole torrid affair it would be that look of unalloyed admiration. After a few seconds I could hold my pretence of languorous indifference no longer and we burst together into whoops of delight, Holmes almost dancing around the room in a transport of joy. I had never seen him so excited.

He dashed to his bureau and was turning the pages of his new prize in a fever of exultation, his eyes darting to and fro across the pages.

"But this is it, Watson! How? How?"

"A certain party was able to obtain it for me." I said cryptically.

"May I enquire as to the identity of this certain party?" He was unable to suppress a mischievous smile.

"It would be indiscreet of me to say more."

"This certain party seems rather uncertain. Is he, or should I say *she*, connected with your nocturnal absenteeism?"

"As I say. Indiscreet."

"So, Watson. You are the dashing lover after all."

"Oh, I wouldn't say that, but I am not without my wiles."

"And is this certain party in any danger?"

"I think not, at least for the time being. Luckily, it would appear that 'His Excellency' is away at his Berkshire retreat for a day or two."

"That is indicative as well as lucky. And you have been in the wars again." he said alluding to the bandaging on my face which I had almost forgotten about in the general excitement. "Is there perchance a connection?"

"It is a long story, Holmes."

"But doubtless one you will be retelling in graphic detail in your forthcoming account of the case."

"Perhaps, and perhaps not." I settled back in my armchair to bathe in glory.

A thought occurred to me.

"Holmes, if you say that the dates in the list cover a nearly fifty year period then how could this one volume be of much use? Surely you would need one for every year of his life?"

"Perceptive of you, Watson. You scintillate today. There is a remarkable effervescence about you if I may say so, though I cannot for the life of me imagine the cause. But to answer your question this diary appears to cover a much longer time frame than a mere year. It was originally a book of blank pages which has been drawn up and ruled in such a way that it covers many years. Let me show you."

I padded over to see what he was talking about.

"See here." Holmes pointed to the top of a page of the journal. "The year 1732 is indicated, with intermittent entries, and then it jumps to 1734, with entries for some days and not others and so on throughout the book. But it is at least chronological. Evidently he had started the journal early in his life and then let it go for long periods before resuming."

"But after all of this can you be sure it provides the key?"

"I cannot, but it is at least promising that the dates on the list all correspond, so far, to dates in the diary."

"Then, I shall leave you to it."

Holmes returned to scan the volume and was utterly absorbed. After I had calmed myself sufficiently, I remembered another salient aspect of the matter.

"But Holmes, I stress that the book must be returned by tomorrow evening at the latest."

"Tomorrow!?" he exploded. "Whatever are you talking about? You present me with the crown jewels and then announce that they are merely on loan and must be returned to the rightful owner by return of post. Are you trying to torment me?"

"It is imperative, Holmes." I thundered. "It is merely luck that von Runstedt is away for a day or two but he returns tomorrow evening and will surely notice the book's absence. And as you know all too well yourself, he may be leaving the country soon and may wish to take it with him. If he realizes it is gone it could be black indeed for Mol... for the person involved."

"I understand your concern, but even I cannot decrypt a document as fast as that."

"Could you not simply copy it then?"

"How fast do you think I can write? There are hundreds of pages of dense text here, and anyway mere copying might cause me to miss some vital element of the puzzle such as the spacing of the words, the script, their placing on the page, etc, etc. All sorts of superficially insignificant but potentially crucial detail would be lost to me. Don't you grasp that?"

"Yes, Holmes, I realize all of that. I will leave you to it then." I said submissively and left him to his devices.

And yet I could not in all conscience resign myself to this state of affairs. I prayed that Holmes might finish with the volume in a matter of hours or a day at most, whatever he had said, cracking whatever code it was, if indeed it be a code at all; but I knew in my heart that I was merely postponing the struggle until a later date. I dreaded being forced to contest him for possession of the book, and yet I could not leave Molly twisting in the wind, in danger of discovery, and retribution at any moment.

I occupied myself by taking a much-needed bath, had a shave, and donned a new suit of clothes. I went to the mirror to change the dressing on the cut to my cheekbone but, silly though it sounds, I decided to leave the dressing there, bloodstained though it was, as a keepsake of Molly. I found it impossible to think of anything other than her for the rest of the day; she infiltrated every nook and cranny of my thoughts; her entrancing little mannerisms flickered through my mind's eye like a cinematograph display, such as her habit of wobbling her eyeballs madly when excited. I could not settle to anything, and toured the house in fits of agitation, popping in to see how Holmes was progressing at frequent intervals, though it was impossible to be unaware of Holmes's annoyance at these trespasses upon his concentration.

By six o'clock, having had no word from Holmes, still closeted in the drawing room, I could contain my impatience no longer and barged in on him to enquire as to the extent of his progress. Predictably, he was needled by this interrogation.

"I have made some progress, Watson, though it would greatly facilitate my research if I were not subject to repeated interruptions."

But sensing my anxiety he softened his tone, perhaps glad to obtain a slight respite from his toil.

"Since you are taking such a keen interest in these matters let me explain some of the difficulties I have run up against. The dates in the list are sometimes hard to match up for the *tagebuch* is written in a deucedly obscure and eccentric hand, perhaps intentionally to confuse prying eyes and, given the passage of approximately a century and a half, it is only to be expected that the ink has faded somewhat in places adding to my difficulty. Moreover, the entries are not always strictly chronological for the great man has gone back and forth for reasons of his own, again possibly to confound the would-be spy. And even having located the relevant entry I cannot yet identify its significance. It may take many more hours, or even days, of intense study for it to yield up all of its secrets."

"I see." I said neutrally, but I could not contain myself. "Nonetheless, Holmes, I must insist that you return it to me by early evening tomorrow at the very latest."

"Impossible!"

"But it has to be! I will take it from you by force if necessary."

"My word, Watson, you are infatuated."

"Call it what you like, but I cannot permit you to hold on to it any longer than that."

"Oh, for God's sake, man, bring yourself back down to earth."

I turned on my heel and stormed out of the house to my club to calm my frayed nerves. I was assailed by further doubts. Would Holmes go to the abominable lengths of concealing the book from me rather than relinquish possession, especially if he had not yet deciphered it? No, he could surely not act so ruthlessly or dishonourably. But I was condemned to another restless night in which I tossed and turned seemingly without end. I relived in my mind as best I could the raptures of the previous night, yet this jostled with fears and uncertainties. I ardently desired to see Molly again as soon as possible, and not merely to return the book.

The following morning, I came downstairs resolved to be adamant, but if I was expecting another stormy contretemps such as yesterday's I was to be disappointed. Holmes had long since finished his breakfast, assuming he had even touched it in the first place, and had evidently been absorbed in the business at hand, perhaps all night long for all I knew, mindful perhaps of my anxieties in the matter of the book's return. The room was thick with his acrid tobacco smoke.

He had broken off from his studies and was leaning back in his easy chair and re-filling his pipe; a glazed aura of sublime satisfaction playing about his aquiline features. He pre-empted any declaration of intent on my part with his own gleeful announcement.

"Watson, it has taken me all night and an unconscionable quantity of the strongest shag tobacco known to mankind, but I believe I have broken the back of this accursed puzzle. And if I am right then I am now in possession of the identities and code-names of many of the Count's most important agents and, in some cases, even the means of communication between the Count and these same agents, not to say a great deal of other information besides."

"Holmes, I congratulate you!" The exuberance of the man's outburst had thrown me off my stride altogether and caused me to lose sight of my original objective. I found myself caught up in this orgy of self-congratulation.

"So then, Holmes. What are your conclusions?"

He sprang to his desk and beckoned me over. I padded over and took a chair next to his as he laid out the cryptogram side by side with the diary.

"I told you earlier that the numbers in the list corresponded to dates, and indeed they all match dates in the diary for which there are entries, covering quite a spread of years. It is, obviously, written in Frederick's (and the Count's) native tongue, with which, as you know, I am moderately conversant; but that is of little consequence in solving the puzzle."

"Why so?"

"I was entirely on the wrong track when I sought to pinpoint the significance of a particular date, for it is not the content of the entry but rather the words themselves, or more precisely their initial letters. Thus: to take one at random." He pointed to a set of dates on the list which he had underlined and then to the corresponding diary entry for that date. "Here the entry begins with: *'Was für ein herrlicher Tag im Leben Preußens'*, which with my limited knowledge of the language I would translate as: 'What a glorious day in the life of Prussia'."

"And?"

"But whatever spurs Prussia may have gained that day are of no relevance. It is the letter 'W' and nothing else that signifies! And now let us take another set of numbers, i.e. dates, from a few lines further on." And so saying he flipped over a wodge of pages in the diary to another entry which he had bookmarked with a piece of cord. Here we have: *'Schlechtes Wetter hat meine Pläne verzögert'* which I translate as: 'Foul weather has delayed my plans'. They insist on sticking the verb awkwardly at the end of a sentence, but again it is neither

170

grammatical peculiarity nor historical accuracy that signifies but rather the initial letter, 'S'. And so on, and so on." Holmes rushed through several more such dates and diary entries before reaching his peroration. "If we go through this whole set of dates and entries using that method, I end up with the name William S. Parminter." Holmes sat back with an air of profound satisfaction. I pondered hard, struggling slightly to share in his state of *nirvana*.

"So that is the key." I said at length. "But it seems a painstaking system. One has to go through thickets of dates just to get one name out of it!"

"Painstaking indeed! A name such as that, of seventeen characters including the Christian name and middle initial, requires one hundred and two digits, and since there are literally dozens of names and ancillary information here it is no wonder that we have such a very lengthy list of numbers. But it is damnably hard to crack, and that, after all, is the point."

"But is it really necessary to go to such extraordinary lengths when the information is safely tucked up inside a safe anyway?" I said.

"Well, it wasn't that secure was it?" he said pointedly, and we shared a laugh. "But it just illustrates how priceless this information is deemed for such draconian measures to be used to conceal it."

"It would appear so. It is certainly very ingenious. But Holmes, who pray is this fellow, William S. Parminter?"

"I thought the name rang a bell and, looking him up in *Whitaker's Almanack*, I confirmed that Sir William Parminter is the number two in the European section of the Foreign Office."

"Great Scot, Holmes. You mean to say you think that this man is an agent of the Count's?"

"It would seem so."

"But how can you be sure? Might it not be merely someone else with the same name? It is hard to believe such a senior public official could be a traitor."

"It is a relatively unusual name and though there may well be other 'William S. Parminters' in existence it is hard to believe

171

they enjoy the same eminence and would warrant their identities being so elaborately concealed."

I took time to digest all of this. The revelation that so distinguished a figure could be engaged in treason seemed far-fetched if not downright incredible, and I desperately sought an alternative explanation.

"But might not his appearance on the list be entirely innocent? He could be someone with whom the Count has merely been in correspondence on some innocuous topic, or with whom he has had social intercourse?"

"Then why go to such lengths to conceal his identity behind a barrage of cryptograms?"

I was forced to concede the strength of Holmes's argument.

"But then what damage might he have done to the country's interests?"

"Who knows? Perhaps very little, perhaps a great deal. One can only speculate."

"And you mean to tell me you have been through every set of dates and matching entries on that list?"

"Not all as yet; I have not had the time, but enough of them to reassure me about the correctness of my hypothesis. And what a labour of love it has been."

"And all these names on your list are agents?"

"All, I think, agents or accomplices of one stripe or another. And, in some cases, such as Parminter, they are names to conjure with. Several are known to me or suspected by me of being in league with the Bund, so I think I am safe in assuming the rest are likewise. One can only meditate on what role they play, or have played, or may yet play in the grand scheme of things."

"So, what is to be done now? Are you going to apprize the authorities of this document?"

"But then the conundrum presents itself. How do I convey it to anyone in authority without compromising myself in the process? It was, after all, obtained by unlawful means. And, moreover, what is the point of handing it to Scotland Yard, or the Foreign Office, or Uncle Tom Cobley only to have them dismiss my whole theory, however compelling, with their usual mutton-headed scepticism and probably then bury the document in a cubby hole somewhere for it never to see the light of day. If figures of the highest rank fell under suspicion there might well be an attempt to cover up the whole business to avoid embarrassment."

"Yes, I see the problem."

"No. I have other ideas."

"I had an intuition you might."

"I propose some spadework of my own. I intend to pay a visit to the vaunted Sir William to see what he has to say for himself. I have already got Billy to despatch a telegram to his house to request an audience."

"Surely he is unlikely to respond. Besides anything else he must be a very busy man. He may not even be at home at this time."

"I think he will respond because I quoted his code-name 'Jackal' which I had also deciphered. I feel that if that does not stop him dead in his tracks then nothing will. But we shall have to see."

"Well, I must say I am impressed, Holmes. Do I take it then," I added with hope rising in my breast, "that you have finished with this book and I can now safely return it to its rightful owner, albeit indirectly?"

"Good heavens, no, Watson! I have barely scratched the surface. I have extracted a few plums from the pudding but there must be plenty more where that came from."

I was cast down again, but Holmes, seeing my discomfort, added brightly. "But I may have extracted enough by the evening."

"I devoutly hope so. But I will leave you to it to speed your endeavours."

I occupied myself in various ways for the rest of the day and anyway I had another professional appointment at my surgery which at least kept me busy, and took my mind off Molly and the book.

Returning to Baker Street by the middle of the afternoon my worries were pressing in on me again, and I rushed into the drawing room to query Holmes on his further progress. The news was gratifying. Holmes was waving a small piece of paper in the air.

"Watson, I have received a reply from Parminter, in very short order I may say, agreeing to a meeting at his house this evening at five. Whatever affairs of state are consuming his working day he has put them aside to meet me. Suggestive is it not?"

"Well, well."

"Are you game to accompany me? Two would definitely be better than one for this exercize."

"When am I ever not game? But how are you going to play it? Simply accuse the man? Surely he will not confess?"

"He will, at the very least, be anxious to know what I have up my sleeve, and I will pretend to know far more than I do. It is amazing how often it works. It is three-thirty. Can you be ready in half an hour?"

"Assuredly."

Chapter XIII

Parminter

Within the half hour we were once more cantering briskly up Baker Street, this time in a northerly direction. Holmes had barked an address in Hampstead to the lethargic cabbie and at a quarter to five we alighted outside a large, detached greystone villa near the heath, pleasantly appointed with a well cultivated garden. The door was answered by a youngish fellow I took to be a manservant who showed us into the hallway before the master of the house appeared; a tall, stooping, distinguished, side-whiskered figure in his early sixties, wearing a dark, old-fashioned coat. He showed us into a tastefully furnished and subdued drawing room, bid us be seated in an exquisite eighteenth-century *chaise longue*, and offered us drinks which Holmes declined. He poured himself a whisky and soda. He was outwardly calm and unruffled by our presence but I sensed an inner tension. He seated himself opposite us and smiled benignly.

"I was honoured and not a little amazed to receive a request for an interview from such a celebrated figure as yourself, Mr. Holmes, but I cannot imagine how I might be of assistance in any investigation of yours." His voice was grave and well-modulated. "May I enquire the purpose of your visit?"

"To arrest you, sir." said Holmes evenly. The man was momentarily lost for words and gripped the sides of his armchair before recovering his composure.

"Is this some sort of joke? If so it is in extremely bad taste. Arrest me for what, may I ask?" he said giving off a forced chuckle of *faux* amusement.

"The theft and transmission of government documents to agents of a foreign power. Treason as some might call it."

"Treason!" He was gasping for air and seemed almost as if he was suffering an attack of some sort. He gulped down a great draught from his glass."

"This is outrageous, Mr. Holmes, if that is who you really are. I only have your word for it. I will have you thrown out immediately." He groped around for his bell and started to ring it frantically to summon assistance, half rising from his chair.

"I wouldn't do that if I were you, Sir William. For if we are ejected, we will instantly fetch the police and present them with the evidence."

"Evidence?" He ceased the frenetic ringing of the bell, which had in any case gone unanswered for the moment, and fell back into his chair. "What evidence?"

"Your name, address, code-name and various other particulars upon a list of secret agents, which I have been able to obtain. Agents of an organization in whose pay I presume you to be. I also have sworn affidavits from several persons."

"What list are you talking about? Where is it? I demand to see it." He was becoming agitated beyond measure, his suavity dissolving in the face of this onslaught upon his character.

"All in good time, sir."

"How do I know this list is not a fiction of yours?"

"You know from my telegram that I am aware of your code-name 'Jackal', and it clearly struck home to you or otherwise you would not have agreed to this meeting at such short notice. I know also of your contacts with Herr Kellmann and various other persons. How could I know that if I were not in possession of much else besides?"

"This is just some bluff of yours. The code-name, as you characterize it, is probably just something you have picked up somewhere that means nothing by itself."

"I don't think you can take the risk of calling my bluff. Your hand is not strong. Now, I should like you to answer a few questions of mine or I shall carry out my threat to call the police." Holmes had produced a foolscap sheet from his inside pocket and was scanning it.

"Questions? What questions? This is all quite outrageous. I will not submit to being interrogated and brow-beaten in my own house." His manner had superficially regained some of its former mastery, but it was plain he was a man whistling in the dark.

"Very well, if that is your attitude." Holmes rose from his chair and strode towards the door. "Come Watson. To Hampstead police station."

"You will be laughed out onto the street you fool." cried the man. "Nobody is going to believe a word of this."

Holmes turned back to him with his hand on the doorknob. "You must be aware that I have a considerable reputation in policing circles based on a wealth of successfully concluded cases. If the local constabulary are unwilling to believe the evidence, then Scotland Yard definitely will."

We marched purposefully out of the drawing room and into the hallway where we were in the process of donning our hats and overcoats when Parminter sprang out after us, displaying a swiftness of movement unsuspected in one of his years. He was gulping hard. The manservant had finally appeared on the scene in laggardly response to the summons but was curtly dismissed. "That's alright, Rogers. Back to your duties."

"If you would care to return to your seats, gentlemen. I think we should be able to talk this through in a civilized fashion." His severity of manner had wilted. Holmes cast a meaningful glance in my direction and paused. Slowly and theatrically he again doffed his coat and replaced his hat on the antlers of the reindeer hat-stand. I took my cue from him and we returned to the drawing room to resume our former positions. Parminter poured himself another large whisky and soda from the side-table with a shaky hand and slumped back into his armchair. Holmes stared inscrutably at his victim.

"So, let us start again, Sir William. Are you ready to satisfy my curiosity on these matters?"

177

"I will try to help you as far as I can, but I do not admit to any treachery as you so crudely designate it."

"Designate it how you will."

"And is it necessary for your companion to be present?"

"Assuredly yes. Dr. Watson is apprized of all of the facts and he will take notes."

"Notes indeed! I am not happy with that either."

"Your happiness is not my pre-eminent concern. Information and the accurate recording of it is."

The man harrumphed his acquiescence. I took out my notebook and pencil poised to record whatever transpired.

"If you already know so much, as you claim, then why do you need me to tell you anything?"

"Because I don't know *everything*. If I did I would not be wasting my time with you now."

"And why should I say anything that might be twisted in your hands to compromize me if you intend to go straight to the police with it?" he said searchingly.

"I may stay my hand depending on the extent of your co-operation. I am after bigger fish; bigger even than one of your high rank. If I conclude that you have made a clean breast of things then I am prepared to keep the information to myself."

"Then why do you want it?"

"To aid my enquiries."

The man seemed again to be engaged in a tumultuous internal battle with himself. Holmes was studying him keenly.

"You still haven't given me sight of this list of yours. I should be very curious actually to see it, if it even exists." Parminter said contemptuously.

Holmes paused to consider and then produced from his pocket a small sheaf of typewritten papers and laid a few of them down upon the low coffee table that separated Parminter from the two of us. They looked vaguely but not exactly like pages from the list. "These will not mean much to you because they are, as you might suppose, written in code; a code which I have been able to decipher." Parminter had put on his reading glasses from a leather case in his waistcoat pocket and feverishly scrutinized the sheets before him, his eyes darting to and fro across the pages. He made to pick some of them up but Holmes snatched them away at the last moment, scooping them back into a sheaf. "I will retain possession if you don't mind. We wouldn't want anything happening to them such as spillage from an inkpot."

"None of that is worth a brass farthing. Nothing more than an interminable set of digits that could be made to mean anything the reader wants. You will have to do better than that, Mr. Holmes." he said smugly.

Holmes then produced the foolscap sheet he had been playing with earlier and flattening it out, he laid that too down on the table facing towards his adversary.

"And this is a part of my translation of the foregoing." I could see the sheet was covered in writing in Holmes's own hand. "I have not yet had the opportunity to translate all of the sections dealing with your good self but that will come in time. By the way I must adjure you to disregard the bits pertaining to other persons which I really should have put on a different sheet but in my haste, I have lumped several together."

The man scanned this new sheet anxiously. His smugness was starting to evaporate, though he did not look wholly defeated. Holmes again snatched it away from him before he had had a chance to handle it and replaced it in his inside pocket.

"Your translation seems a little scanty to me. And how did you obtain those documents?"

"I am not at liberty to say but their provenance is extremely reliable and from a source at the heart of affairs who is willing and able to supply me with a great deal more. But I am losing patience with you, Parminter. Talk frankly or we depart," Holmes said pressing home the attack. He produced his fob watch. "I will give you five minutes to tell me all."

Parminter looked evasive.

"So, what is it you would like me to tell you?"

"I should like to know to whom you have passed information, what the nature of that information was, and when and where?"

"Even if there were any truth in these unsubstantiated claims of yours, and I am not admitting that there was, I cannot disclose the identity of any person."

"But you admit that you have passed information. That at least is a start."

Parminter heaved another great sigh.

"Look, I think I can explain all of this to you quite simply. It may well account for why my name appears on this supposed cryptogram of yours." Another lengthy pause followed and the man cleared his throat. "A while back, I met up with a chap I knew quite well at Balliol. He was a bit of a rum chappie, head full of nonsense even then ... got sent down after two terms for some misdemeanour or other, can't quite remember what, but we got talking and ... well ... he had ideas about the balance of power and so on; he thought England was too powerful *vis a vis* other nations, too big a navy etc. and there needed to be some redress of this precious balance to ensure harmony in Europe. I am sure you are familiar with all this radical claptrap."

Parminter paused his narrative to see the effect it was having upon his inquisitor, but Holmes gave no hint of his reaction to these admissions.

"Anyway," Parminter resumed his narrative, "we struck up quite a friendship and met several times over the next few weeks. Took pity on him to tell the truth as he seemed very down on his luck. But, anyway, during a rather heavy session at my club one evening I probably let slip a few things I shouldn't have. Nothing momentous you understand, just tittle-tattle, but maybe rather more than was wise." He glanced again at Holmes who was still a study in inscrutability. I was frantically scribbling this down as best I could in my laborious longhand, flipping the pages of my notebook at frenetic speed.

"Pray continue" Holmes said smoothly.

"Well, that was it really. I thought nothing more of it, but then, some while afterwards ..." his voice trailed off once again and his manner darkened. "We met up again at his instigation and he told me that he was working for a committee of some description dedicated to international peace. I can't remember the name of it, but he said they were very interested in what I had had to say and wanted more information. I said I wasn't in the habit of supplying information to unauthorized persons or organizations, but he persisted and said that I really should tell them more about the diplomatic situation or else … or else … they might reveal what I had said already in the public press, and the source of it. They had some organ of their own which they distributed quite widely, so it would be in my own interest …"

"You mean he was blackmailing you?" Holmes ventured.

"No, I wouldn't put it like that. It wasn't blackmail, but … as I say they felt anything I could tell them would help their cause, and I thought it reasonably harmless."

"Did you provide further information?"

"I passed on a few things; nothing of consequence. Actually, I made a lot of it up to put them on the wrong scent." He laughed weakly.

"Who was this person?"

"I would prefer not to say."

"And I would very much prefer that you did."

After another anguished pause the man relented.

"If you must know, his name is Carstairs. Jeremy Carstairs. There, does that satisfy you?"

"For the moment. But I will require his full particulars. What is his current address?"

"I don't know. I never asked him. I think he said he was living in lodgings somewhere in Middlesex."

"So where did you meet?"

"Various places. My club initially, and then some watering holes he favoured."

"So, if you didn't know his address how did you correspond?"

"We would arrange the next meeting at the time."

"What was the gravamen of what you told this man Carstairs?"

"It was, as I have said, trifling stuff, minor diplomatic spats, internal politicking, inconsequential all of it."

"It must have been of some consequence or else this man and those behind him would not have been interested."

"Yes, but ..." his voice trailed way. He was licking his lips and began mopping his brow.

At this juncture the door partially opened, and a rather frail looking grey-haired woman peered around it to address the man.

"Dinner will be ready in half an hour, William. Are your guests staying?"

"No, my dear, but if I am not there begin without me. I may be some time with these gentlemen." he said flatly.

"Very well, William dear." she whimpered and withdrew as noiselessly as she had entered. Certain that she had departed he continued.

"My wife. Anyway, as I was saying it was all very lightweight stuff; of no use to anyone."

"And for how long did these meetings continue? Weeks, months, years?"

"Over a period of a year or more."

"Are they still in progress?"

"Yes, but much less frequently now."

"They have bled you dry?"

"No, no, that is a ridiculous way of putting it. Actually, they probably realized that a lot of what I was telling them was rubbish."

"And you have given this man official documents as well, or at any rate, copies of them."

There was another lengthy hiatus. Holmes gave him a prompt.

"I know from my sources that you have, so there is no use denying it."

"Minor stuff again. Nothing of any great significance."

"How do you know?"

"You think I didn't know what I was passing on?"

"But they were still pressuring you?"

"Pressuring, no. But he was insistent."

"So why accede to his demands?"

"They were requests, not demands, and as I say I saw no harm, and it kept him off my back."

"So how were these documents passed on to your man Carstairs? By hand?"

"At first yes, but then he said he preferred them to be deposited at an agreed drop-off point. Didn't want us to be seen transacting business I suppose. I was willing to accede to that arrangement."

"And where is this depository?"

"A place on the heath, if you must know."

"I will require details."

"For God's sake, haven't I given you enough detail already?"

"Not yet. Who collected these papers?"

"I don't know. I merely left the stuff there and departed."

The man was taking longer draughts of his whisky and loosening up, now freed from the constraints of artifice.

"What sort of papers did you divulge?"

"I cannot possibly tell you. You are not in a position to assess the weight and relevance of government documents."

"But you can still tell me what their portent was."

"For the umpteenth time it was inconsequential."

"But who did you think was behind all of this. You must have known it was not some peace-loving body as Carstairs had tried to suggest."

"I didn't know."

"Good heavens man, you surely cannot be so naive as that."

"If you are so well up in foreign affairs then perhaps you can enlighten me."

"I cannot be sure, but it is highly likely that this was a front for an organization known as the Federation of the Black Eagles or *Die Bund der Schwarzen Adler* if you prefer the original, a body working on behalf of the *Auswärtige Amt*[1] of Imperial Germany."

The man started imperceptibly and emitted a barely audible intake of breath. He fell back in his chair and shook his head.

"Can you be sure of this?" he queried with the air of a man desperately hoping to be contradicted.

"It is as I said extremely likely."

---

[1] Foreign Office.

"What damage have I done?" he said despairingly, more to himself than to us.

"You tell me. If it was, as you say, trifling stuff then surely very little. My friend, Watson, here has been keeping notes. Perhaps now you could write down as much as you can recall of what documents, or copies of documents, you handed on and when." Holmes produced another sheet of paper, this time a blank one."

"You expect me to describe every little scrap I passed?"

"As much as you can." Holmes said remorselessly.

"I can't possibly remember everything. Most was, as I said, so piddling as to be instantly forgettable. And you would not be able to make anything of it? You could not assess the significance of anything without inside knowledge of affairs."

"I will give it my best shot."

"Oh, for heaven's sake, man." He groaned and shambled over to his desk in the far corner of the room clutching the sheet and started to write, at first hesitantly and then with greater fluency as, one assumes, matters were recalled to his memory. Holmes and I exchanged looks of suppressed jubilation, but we kept silent while the man scribed. I was glad of the respite for my hand was sore from activity.

"I hope you will not raise any objections if we smoke," announced Holmes as he produced his cigarette case and offered me a Virginia.

"It is of no concern to me."

"Would you care for one?"

"Thank you, no. I don't indulge. Mabel doesn't like it."

We sat in silence for ten minutes or more while the man produced his litany, periodically scratching his head. Eventually he had concluded and brought the sheet back over to us. "This is all I can recollect for the moment. As I said a layman would not be able to make much sense of it."

Holmes scrutinized the list.

"Are you still feeding information by this means?"

"No. I haven't done for quite a while. Some of the stuff I gave them in the recent past was fake anyway, as I think I told you. There have been no demands from them for some time. Maybe they have started to suspect it was phoney and have abandoned the attempt to squeeze me further."

"Hmm. Perhaps." ruminated Holmes. "And you still have not told me of the location of the drop-off point."

"Sounds ridiculous, I know, but it was inside an old hollow oak tree on the heath."

"Can you show me the exact location."

"I will draw you a diagram if you wish." he said half-jokingly.

"If you would please." Holmes handed him another blank sheet.

Parminter gave an ironic laugh, shrugged, and duly obliged.

"Splendid." said Holmes.

"Now would you sign and date these documents please." Holmes demanded. Our host looked horrified.

"I will do no such thing. You said you would not use any of this against me."

"And I shan't, on certain conditions, but all the same I require you to attest to the truth and accuracy of it. That is part of the bargain." Reluctantly, Parminter complied.

"And likewise, with Dr. Watson's notebook, if you please."

Holmes took it from my hands and passed it over to the man, suppressing a look of faint scorn at my illegible scribbling.

"May I see what your friend has written first?"

"Certainly." Parminter flicked over the pages, but was probably as bemused by my hieroglyphics as Holmes was, and eventually signed anyway.

"Doctor's handwriting, eh?" he laughed weakly as he handed it back to Holmes.

"What are you going to do with all of this?" the man demanded anxiously.

"Nothing for the present. Given your co-operation I will not use this information other than for my own purposes, but I must have your word that you have no further contact with this organization, save under my instructions, and that you give them nothing further. Do you understand?"

"Very well, I will swear to that." Parminter said resignedly.

"Excellent. You have been a damned fool, Parminter, but if what you say is true about the inconsequentiality of your treachery ... yes, I must use the word ... then little harm may have been done."

We saw ourselves out leaving Parminter wringing his hands in the drawing room. As we walked down the pathway to the roadside, I could see the twitch of a curtain from a front window as the wretched man watched us retreat.

"A good day's work I think, Watson. I may have extracted a lot of useful insights from this fellow."

"You would be a first-class poker player, Holmes. I don't think I should sit at a table with you."

"I have never indulged this fancy some people seem to have for gambling, though I am led to believe it can be lucrative or ruinous depending upon chance factors."

"What now?"

"I need to investigate this drop-off tree of his to ensure it really exists."

We made the trek across the windswept heath to the point designated on Parminter's hand-drawn sketch, easily located despite darkness having descended, because of its situation between a pillar box and a recently erected road-sign. Holmes examined the spot carefully, peering deep inside the trunk of the oak, but finding nothing deposited satisfied himself that it was not an invention of Parminter's. Holmes continued to survey the area in a ruminative manner. He seemed particularly interested in a clump of trees and bushes only thirty or so yards from the spot, diving into them for a few seconds disappearing from my sight altogether before emerging seconds later with a satisfied smile. I could not fathom the purpose of these activities and was wishing a speedy end to proceedings, the wind whipping up something awful and cutting through my bones.

"Concluded your examination?" I said swinging my arms about to keep warm.

"For the moment. Looks very promising, don't you think, Watson?"

"Promising for what may I ask?"

186

"For springing a trap."

"If you say so," I said.

"I may have further injunctions for our friend." With that we strode back the way we had come across the blustery fields and toward the house from whence we had travelled. I followed him as best I could. He rapped sharply upon the knocker again, and upon it being answered by the same valet as before he demanded to speak again to the master of the house. Upon being informed that the man was now at dinner and for the moment *incommunicado* Holmes became very insistent. Shortly Parminter re-appeared in the hallway, having presumably overheard the loud conversation.

"Whatever now?" he said querulously. "Can I not at least enjoy dinner in peace?"

"This won't take long. I just have a few requests, which I would be very grateful if you could accede to."

The man sighed heavily and led us dejectedly back into the drawing room. We remained standing. Holmes, satisfying himself that we were not overheard, continued in peremptory vein.

"How do you contact your man to let him know you have a document for him? Or does he just come to check the drop box every so often on the off chance?"

"It has been quite while, as I explained to you, but I put an advertizement in the personal column of the *Evening News*."

"How is it worded?"

"For God's sake man. You want blood. I simply say 'the jackal has landed'."

"The jackal has landed?" Holmes sounded sceptical. "And that is it?"

"That is it."

"So how quickly does any offering of yours get collected?"

"I don't know. I just deposit the item there."

"But don't you check that it has been taken?"

"Occasionally, and I have found it has been removed within twenty-four hours of my advertizement appearing, in my limited experience."

"Removed by Carstairs, or someone acting on his behalf?"

187

"I have no idea, but I can't imagine anyone other than he, or one of his agents, delving in there. It is a remote spot."

"Excellent. Here is what I require you to do. I want you to put your usual advertizement in tomorrow's edition of the newspaper. Then immediately deposit something or other. You can improvize, or even copy some trifle from your office."

"And then what?"

"You need do nothing further. I will take up the reins from thereon."

"And all the information I have given you?"

"Will remain privy to myself and Dr. Watson, so long as you do as I have indicated."

"But then how will matters be resolved?"

"They will be resolved, sir, you have my guarantee. Good day to you."

With that Holmes turned on his heel and we departed for the second time, leaving a dismayed Parminter in our wake. We had soon found ourselves a hansom and clattered back to Baker Street, Holmes wrapped in a reverie, but I could not fail to detect the sliver of a smile escaping his thin lips at one point. At length he opined; "Pretending to greater knowledge than one has can on occasion work a treat. In truth I was surprized how easily he was to bluff. The typewritten list I placed before him was not you may have guessed the real one."

"I thought it looked slightly different."

"I couldn't risk him doing something abominable with it in his desperation, and so typed up another in advance."

I marvelled at how Holmes seemed to cover for every eventuality.

"And as for the translation I included a lot of material about some of the other persons on the list, since I really had very little on Parminter himself, but I reasoned I could impress him with other names and details. He might even have known some of the persons, thereby strengthening the idea that I was in possession of more data than I actually was."

"But how can an English gentleman of that calibre commit treason?"

"A misplaced altruism perhaps. Who can really say? You heard his explanation. He was just drawn ever more tightly into their web of intrigue. Having taken one step, it was easier to take the next and the next. And I suspect he partly sympathized with their ostensible cause of peace and disarmament. It is a superficially attractive one. That may have helped drive him on. But who can really account for the immense complexity of human motivation."

"And you do not intend to report him to Scotland Yard, or to his superiors at the Foreign Office?"

"Yes, I gave my word on that and I will abide by it. I am prepared to believe the man when he says he only handed over unimportant stuff. He is a fool but not a traitor. And anyway, what would I say to the authorities? 'Here is a list of espionage agents that I have stolen from a distinguished and law-abiding foreign nobleman. Yes, I know it is only a list of typewritten numbers but by means of a diary which I have also obtained, also by dubious means, I can decrypt it to show that a senior public servant is a traitor.' I think not, Watson."

Back at Baker Street we dwelt upon the interview so recently concluded.

"What do you make of Parminter's catalogue of indiscretions?" I said alluding to the sheet Holmes was now mulling over in his spindly fingers.

"Mainly trifling, as he has pleaded. How many spoonfuls of sugar the Permanent Secretary puts in his tea seems to be gravamen of much of it."

"If he is playing straight with us, but surely he has every reason to downplay his malfeasance."

"That is true, but I am inclined to accept his version."

"So was the venture worth all the effort if you are not to make use of Parminter's confession?" I queried.

"If nothing else it proves the accuracy of my decryption of the list. And we have now sprung a trap for our Mr. Carstairs which could lead to who knows what revelations."

"So, you intend to keep a watch on this so-called drop-box. But it could be days before anyone comes, if indeed they come at all. If Parminter's offerings have been so meagre of late they may have given up on him altogether. And you surely cannot hope to follow this fellow Carstairs or whoever materializes for very long before he becomes aware of your presence."

"I will delegate the task."

"Not to me, I sincerely hope?"

"Don't fret. I have others in mind."

I did not disguise my relief.

"Delegate to whom, may I ask?"

"You will discover in short order." he said enigmatically.

I turned to wider questions.

"Do you intend to go through every name on the list and give them the same treatment as Parminter?" I asked, earnestly hoping for an answer in the negative fearing another onset of writer's cramp.

"Scarcely. Many of the names are unfamiliar to me and their role in the enterprize is unclear at best. I would not be able to track or trace them and they would not all be so compliant. Moreover, it may simply put the organization on alert and jeopardize a successful conclusion to the whole business."

"And what of Murphy. Can we nail the perpetrators of his foul murder? Would their names be on the list?"

"Very unlikely. The list comprizes those of Parminter's ilk … the agents, spies, informers and such like whose identities, and perfidy, must be kept hidden at all costs. Anyway, we already know their identities, Nayland and Barton, but alas we have no proof of their foul crime other than by virtue of our having being witness to it, which I do not wish to reveal. I do not want to move against the organization at this stage until I have much more thoroughly prepared the ground."

"Well, nonetheless, I am deeply impressed. But what of Murphy's note? The *Ich bin ein Hamburger* nonsense. Have you made any headway with that particular puzzle? Now that you have solved the riddle of the list you may be able to turn your attention to your other riddle."

"Yes, thank you for the instruction in the art of detection, Watson. That had not slipped my mind either, but even I can only grapple with one puzzle at a time."

I sat back in exasperation. Another salient point occurred to me.

"In all of this we do rather seem to have lost sight of the person who initiated all of this. Lady Diana. She must be in a state of barely controlled panic by now."

"I have not forgotten her at all. I have been keeping her apprized of developments by telegram."

"And what has been her response?"

"Her replies have been of necessity, brief but she expressed enthusiasm for the progress of my investigations and is content to wait upon events, confident in my ability to steer matters to a satisfactory conclusion."

"But she seemed to be mired in woe and confusion when here, and I can scarcely imagine that anything that has happened since has quelled her anxiety. She must be frantic for an early resolution to matters, however adverse to her own fortunes."

"It seems that she has mastered her desperation." he said meditatively.

"Well, this all so extraordinary. What is to done now?" I cried.

"The list has given me other leads to follow."

"Such as?" I said wearily.

"Another agent. One who, I would think, has been providing the Bund with information, and one with whose identity I am already familiar. Louis La Rothiere."

"Never heard of him."

"You wouldn't have. He is a free-lance who has been operating in this country for years with impunity. But I was able to decode the means of contact with this paragon."

"Which is?"

"An advertizement in the personal column of *The Times*.

"Another newspaper advertizement! Does nobody use these columns for innocent purposes?" I quipped.

Chapter XIV

The Baker Street Irregulars

The Parminter business had occupied much of the late afternoon and it was now fast approaching the hour of my rendezvous with Molly. My pulse was quickening at the prospect. Naturally I was anxious to return the volume to her, but I was even more ardent to see her again. I confronted Holmes once more.

"Now that you have deciphered much of the list to your satisfaction, I presume that you have no objection to my repossessing the *tagebuch*." I said evenly. He turned white.

"But I still have a wealth of decryption to undertake. I have uncovered quite a few names but there is a long way to go. I cannot possibly countenance its surrender as yet."

I was horrified to hear this and in no mood to acquiesce.

"I demand you give it to me, Holmes." I thundered with all the majesty at my command. I think my vehemence impressed him, or at any rate he took pity on my situation.

"Very well. Take the wretched volume." he said petulantly. "I will just have to work on the information I have extracted so far, but if it is insufficient for my purposes then I will hold you responsible."

"Fine. Hold me responsible. I will take the consequences." I barked as I snatched up the book from Holmes's desk. He threw himself back against the chair in a gesture of pique and frustration.

I placed the volume back in the bag in which Molly had given it to me the previous day; a day that now seemed aeons ago; and walked at a very brisk pace from Baker Street to Nightingale Square, looking repeatedly at my watch. I made it to the Bull's Head by a quarter to seven and rushed in breathlessly. To my consternation Molly was nowhere to be spotted, delayed at her labours no doubt. I ordered a drink and waited upon her arrival, clutching the bag close to my chest as if I half expected it to be torn from my grasp by some unknown agency. It reached seven and there was still no sign of Molly. I ordered another drink and waited and waited, growing ever more anxious. When it got to seven-thirty and she had still failed to appear my concern was great indeed. By eight o'clock I could contain myself no longer, and hot-footed it to her house in Wessex Lane, but there was no-one at home.

I began to fret and wondered if I dare go to the Count's residence and enquire after her there. It was a risky undertaking for I could not afford to be seen by the Count himself, though he was supposedly away, and feared that even if the door were answered by Fairbrother or another servant it might get reported back to him. Moreover, there was always the possibility of another encounter with the loutish Tom. But I felt I could really do no other for I feared far more for Molly's safety than for my own. Galloping to Wessex Gardens I knocked at the door which was answered by a doltish looking footman I did not recognize (was he the one with whom Holmes had dallied?) who informed me that Molly had not reported for duty that morning. This was disconcerting news indeed, for where could she have disappeared to if not home or the Bull's Head? Doubtless there were plenty of other places she visited on occasion but why should she not have kept her appointment with me? She could surely not have forgotten or regarded it as a matter of little importance. The more I thought about it the more discomforted I grew.

My unease was scarcely lessened by what I thought may have been the Count's personal carriage parked in the driveway at the front of the house. Had he returned earlier than expected, or maybe never even left? These were ominous portents indeed.

I returned to the Bull's Head, and then again to her house, but there was still no evidence of her. I was disquieted in the extreme, racked by nameless fears and apprehensions. Eventually I saw no alternative course than to return to Baker Street white-faced but at least still in possession of the book. If nothing else it meant that Holmes would get the accursed diary back and could continue his researches. I could not now be accused of prejudicing the safety of the realm in some nebulous way!

Holmes greeted my return with aloofness, scarcely concealing his displeasure at the Holy Grail being so peremptorily dashed from his lips.

"I take it your appointment was unfulfilled, since I perceive that you are still in possession of the book."

"You may scoff, Holmes, but I am very concerned for the girl's safety. Very concerned indeed!"

"Oh, but Watson, calm yourself. It is, I believe, not unknown for a lady to fail to appear for a tryst."

"This was not a tryst but a transaction, and a vital one for her own security in my estimation."

"Do not distress yourself, Watson. There is probably some prosaic explanation for her non-arrival."

"Such as?"

"She was detained at work. Asked to put in some overtime?"

"But the footman at the house said she has not reported for work today at all."

"Illness then?"

"But she was not at home."

"A better offer from another party then?"

"I really don't think so under all the circumstances."

"Do I detect egotism at play?"

"Holmes, must you!"

Seeing my all too evident discomposure he reined in his breezy optimism.

"My dear fellow, I do apologize most profusely for making light of your understandable concerns, but you must not allow your imagination to overwhelm you. There is probably a rational and innocent explanation. Have you reported her missing to the police?"

"No. I think it may be premature to do that."

"Indeed. I concur. So, let us then see what tomorrow brings, and in the meantime, if you have no objection, I will repossess that item in your hands and return to my analysis. And, I feel sure your sweetheart will re-appear safe and sound with some elaborate but implausible pretext for her vanishing act."

"I wish I could share your confidence." I said wanly. I suspected that Holmes feared the worst just as I did but was seeking to reassure me. I handed him the book with an air of resignation. The rest of the evening passed in silence between us for I was too mortified to speak. But what fate had befallen her? Ideas swirled around in my head without cease but nothing made sense.

Finally, I retired and left Holmes to continue his researches undisturbed. The following morning I was in pieces but events were to continue with relentless velocity. I was in a torment of despair. But it was worse than useless for me to mope around my chambers flaying myself. I decided I must take action. But where to begin?

The obvious place, it became increasingly certain in my own mind, was with the staff at the von Runstedt residence. One at least must surely know something concerning the circumstances of her disappearance. Even the accursed Tom perhaps? Especially the accursed Tom! A new and frightful spectre rose before me to the effect that Tom was the one responsible for her disappearance. And yet the more I toyed with this theory the more unlikely it became and I soon banished it to the ranks of the highly improbable. He might have confronted her again and some squalid encounter ensued but surely none so violent or terrible that could have caused her to vanish from the face of the earth. No, it must be the Count and his loathsome minions, but that was only to intensify the dread in my bones, for Tom was harmless by comparison with those ruthless operators.

I commenced my own operations first thing the following morning, forgoing breakfast in my haste, and evading any interrogation from Holmes as to my course of action. An enquiry at her house in Wessex Lane drew small solace or enlightenment from a fretful and hung-over Mrs. Carter who bewailed her daughter's absence without being able to offer any explanation.

I made my way to Wessex Gardens and concealed myself as best I could behind a zareba of foliage across the road from the front of the house and duly staked out the mansion for several hours, watching figures come and go throughout the day amidst the constant flow of traffic. Some figures I recognized, most I didn't, but they were, I reasonably assumed, chiefly servants engaged upon errands.

Was the Count himself in residence? It was hard to tell but I saw no sign of him. His carriage was no longer perched in the driveway but that could mean that he had now gone away, having delayed his departure for some reason, or that it was merely round the back. One or two more important looking characters came and went. Acquaintances of his perhaps? Which suggested him still to be *in situ*. After hours of this I concluded it was a fruitless exercize and devized alternative strategies. I tried the Bull's Head yet again but could see no-one familiar there. I went again to Molly's but knocking long and hard this time I met with no response. Forestalled in all directions I realized the sheer futility of the whole rotten exercize and returned gloomily to Baker Street where I was forced to confront Holmes.

"Ah, Watson. Pursuing your own enquiries, I imagine?"

"You know nothing of my movements surely?"

"No, I do not, though you seem to have draped yourself in such heavy raiment that I imagine it to be your attempt at a disguise, and that could only be if you were on the trail of the missing young lady."

"Well, what do you expect me to do? Sit and mope all day?" I sagged down into the armchair by the fire which I had stoked listlessly.

"No, I do not, but there are rather more promising avenues to explore than those upon which you are currently exhausting your energies. You may be interested to know I have been to see Mycroft once again to seek further information on several crucial points."

"And?"

"I told him of the Parminter business and he found it most intriguing. I did not apprize him of all of our recent gadabouts for obvious reasons. I am not sure exactly how tolerant of brazen illegality he might be, however nobly motivated our actions."

"Did you give him the list?"

"No, I assuredly did not."

"But why on earth not? I would have thought he would be the obvious means of conveying this information to the higher echelons without you incriminating yourself."

"Perhaps, but if I am to be completely honest, I do not entirely trust these higher echelons, as you dub them, to take the action they should. No, I am loth to relinquish possession and control of the list to parties whose identity and motivations I cannot possibly be sure. I still prefer at this stage of the game to pursue my own course."

"You mean you want the glory all to yourself."

"Watson, you are becoming very cynical in your old age."

"I find cynicism a useful defence mechanism when I am around you."

"If you really feel the need for defence. But now that I have had the benefit of your wisdom on these matters, I can tell you I made a few discoveries to our advantage."

"Which are?"

"For a start it seems that the Count's activities have been well monitored within governmental circles. Mycroft had made further enquiries on that point as a result of our first meeting."

"So, you are not alone in your suspicions."

"I did not really imagine I was."

"Anything else?"

"A few minor things with which I will not tire you. And you are aware that I have set in motion the trap for Sir William's old chum, Mr. Carstairs."

"Will Parminter have put the ad in the *Evening News*?"

"I have checked the first edition and he has."

"And then?"

"I shall put my hounds on the case."

"Your hounds?"

"As such I deem them." He plucked his hunter from his waistcoat pocket.

"And they are due any time now. Are you interested in taking part in this little briefing session?"

"Wouldn't miss it for the world."

"Excellent."

I was intrigued. My curiosity was soon sated for within minutes there came a series of belligerent knocks upon the front door and the thunderous tramp of what sounded like a herd of buffalo upon the staircase. There irrupted into our tranquil chambers such a rabble of unruly, scruffy and rowdy youngsters as I have ever had the misfortune to clap eyes upon. They were only eight in number though from the noise they made it could have been eight hundred. But their commotion subsided in an instant as Holmes stood them to attention with a few sharp words of command and, as if they were a platoon of well drilled infantry, Holmes had them lined up in order of size along the far wall of our drawing room.

"Silence now! Watson, may I present to you the Baker Street Regiment."

I stood in awe at this display of martial discipline conjured from apparent chaos.

"Master Wiggins!" At this the biggest and oldest of the boys took a step forward.

"Sir!"

"Very good, Master Wiggins. Anything to report?"

"No sir."

"Then let me give you your orders for today. You are each to receive two shillings in payment for your previous efforts in Mayfair, which were much appreciated, with the prospect of further remuneration in the event of success in the current venture." He handed a leather pouch to 'Master' Wiggins who then walked along the line dispensing two coins to each of the boys, ranging from the tall and gawky to the diminutive and fidgety. When he had finished Holmes continued.

"You are to proceed to a place which I will describe to you shortly and upon arrival to keep a very close watch upon a particular feature of it. The watch must be constant and unremitting; that is to say all through the day and the night, for however many days it may be, though I do not suppose you will have to wait too long."

He handed Wiggins a set of sheets for him to distribute and I could see they were maps of the Hampstead Heath area, and sketches of the drop-box and its precise location. Holmes had added to the sketch drawn by Parminter by including the clump he had investigated and other noteworthy features of the terrain.

"I want you to conceal yourselves in this clump of trees marked on the sketch and to maintain a constant watch upon the oak tree a few yards from it." He held up his copy of the sketch in front of him to point out the exact location of these features of the landscape. "Make sure you are well covered. You may have to wait a long time so I propose you do it in relays, with two of you at any one time, to be relieved every three hours. Bring sandwiches and bottles of something to keep yourselves fed and watered. Sooner or later, someone should arrive to take possession of a package from within the oak tree." He held up the sketch again to pinpoint the spot. "You must be situated so that you can see the tree clearly, but equally you must not on any account reveal your presence. That may require some periods of silence from you which I realize may be asking a lot, but it is essential. Now; when the person comes to take the item, I want you to take a very good look at him so that you may be able to give me a good description. Can any of you write?"

There was general muttering and a drooping of faces. Holmes looked despondent.

"Can any of you draw?" he said hopefully.

At this the mood of the assembly brightened and there were joyous shouts of affirmation as eight hands shot into the air simultaneously.

"As I thought." Holmes then handed to Wiggins for general distribution a batch of sketch pads and sets of coloured pencils.

There was great jubilation upon receipt of these artistic offerings and eager faces examined their new found instruments and started scribbling upon the pads. "Try to draw the man as best you can, with particular reference to height, weight, hair colour, unusual features and so on. Now, he may come during the hours of darkness which will make your task harder, but don't fret if you are unable to see him clearly, and do the best you can under the circumstances.

"Now, here comes the hard part. I want you then, as far as you find it feasible, to follow this man, at a discreet distance so as not to advertize your presence, but follow him as far as you are able and see where he goes and who he meets. I assume, though I cannot be sure that he will arrive by carriage, though he may be on horseback or on foot. If he is on foot, it may make your job easier, but do the best you can. Now to the question of transport. Unfortunately, there is no bus route along that stretch and it would be extremely unlikely anyway that a bus might chance along at that moment, or that it would be going the same way as our candidate. So, do any of you possess bicycles?"

"I do, sir." said Wiggins.

"Very good. Knowing your propensities some others of you might even be able to borrow a bicycle or two." He put an unusual stress on the word borrow. "If so, you can share the bicycles around between you, but ensure that whichever pairing of you is on observation duty both has a bicycle in readiness for use. If your man is in a carriage then cycle after him at a good distance. If he is on foot then you may need to be on foot also." instructed Holmes.

"Try to follow this person as inconspicuously as possible and observe and note where he travels to, who he meets and what he does with the package. And perhaps even attempt a sketch or two of such persons. Any questions?"

"What do we do after we've followed this bloke and everything, sir?" queried one.

"Then report back to me or to Master Wiggins, with whatever you have learned, complete with sketchbooks. Anything more?"

"How much do we get paid for all of this, Mr. 'Olmes?" queried another, middle-sized lad. "Only if I'm gonna be staking this place out for days on end I can't do no work."

"I have a good idea of what your work consists of Dubs, so that your absence from it may not be unwelcome to honest citizens in this fair city of ours. But have no fear. You will be well remunerated for your labours. There will be half a crown a day for all of you, plus five shillings for whoever can give me a good description and a satisfactory sketch of our target and another five shillings for any boy who can give me details of his itinerary, contacts and any other useful information." There was a general murmur of content and a few whistles of satisfaction indicating approval of this new contract of employment.

"Anything more?"

"No, Mr. 'Olmes." They chorused.

"Splendid. Then off with you and report back as soon as you learn anything, and don't make a racket on the stairs." he barked as an afterthought as they scurried out the room.

With that they tumbled down the staircase and were out of the front door before I had scarcely had time to walk to the window. "By Jove, Holmes, how do you manage to control them so well?"

"By dangling the prospect of reward, Watson. It works wonders on even the most unpromising of material."

"I assume that they are the same gallimaufry that created the disturbance outside the Count's residence?"

"Yes; I only have the one regiment to deploy."

As I watched them scuttling boisterously down the road, dodging the traffic and larking about, I could scarcely refrain from expressing my scepticism at their prospects of success in the mission they had been assigned.

"But can you really expect them to learn anything of value? I mean I can't imagine any of them being inconspicuous if they spent a lifetime practising it."

"Don't underestimate their resourcefulness, Watson. They have come up trumps many times before. What they may lack in the way of a formal education they more than compensate for with knowledge of the side-streets, the alleyways and the underside of metropolitan life. There are obvious advantages to using them as look-outs. It could be several days before anyone responds to Parminter's message in the *Evening News*, particularly if it has been a while since any communication and the trail might have gone cold. Who knows? I cannot be spending all day crouching in bushes waiting for someone who never appears. These boys by contrast will not attract attention as either of us might and could be able to trail someone without attracting suspicion, at least for a while. I have every confidence in them. Rarely have they failed me."

"Well, I hope you are right, Holmes. But I must say, what happens even if your boys are able to follow somebody successfully? Where does that lead you?"

"It may lead me to identify the agent concerned, and if they are able to follow him all the way to an address or a rendezvous with someone to whom he passes the package, then the identity of him also, perhaps a higher placed agent, and then … well I am not sure." he meditated, "but I am all the time building up my knowledge of the entire network."

"But what are you going to do with all this knowledge if you cannot admit to the source of it?"

"I am working on that point. I may have to end up by confessing all to Mycroft and handing him a fat dossier. But there may be other options."

"I cannot see what they might be?"

"I can only see dimly at this stage."

"And while you have delegated the business of the drop-box to these scouts of yours then what is your next move?"

"I think I had alluded to the existence of Louis La Rothiere and his habitual means of communication. While Wiggins and company are engaged on Hampstead Heath, I am going to set to work on Monsieur La Rothiere."

203

Chapter XV

La Rothiere

"So who exactly is this La Rothiere fellow? You said you had de-coded his name from the list."

"Yes, I have. But I knew already of his existence and his *modus operandi* from past cases. He is a free-lance agent. He slithers wraith-like through the portals of government ministries, picking up unconsidered trifles here and there by means fair and foul, overt and covert, and offering them for sale to the highest bidder."

"The highest bidder! You mean there are auction rooms where government secrets are bought and sold?" I cried incredulously.

"No, of course not Watson, don't be so absurdly literal. But there are means of communication between such agents that stretch across continents and prices can be matched against each other."

"So is La Rothiere a member of the Bund?"

"I fancy not, but rather someone who has had dealings with it as an independent purveyor of intelligence to all and sundry. I have been seeking to make contact with him for some time now, and I thought it expedient to redouble my efforts so I have placed an advertizement in the agony column of *The Times* as I mentioned to you. In addition to names and code-names the list contained, in respect of some agents, what was evidently a means of contact. In several instances this was transparently the personal columns of *The Times*, which I know from experience to be a popular means of communication among the espionage fraternity. I cross-checked the various code-names I had deciphered with notices in *The Times* for the last few weeks and I managed to find one match where the code-name 'Clown' appeared in the text. I then went back through previous issues to find other such messages that included that code-name and found a couple more. But the most recent was in an issue dated around the time when the so-called Transvaal Dossier went missing, which is highly suggestive, is it not?"

"So, your theory is that La Rothiere, or whoever the spy is, code-name 'Clown', had picked up the documents from the traitor in the Colonial Office and then contacted von Runstedt via that means to pass them on to him."

"Precisely so. Although I would envisage it would not have been von Runstedt himself but Kellmann, or another of his minions, who would have been the contact. There may be even more links in the chain so as to minimize the prospect of any connection being made between origin and endpoint."

"So that is the chain of communication. But then what is this trap of yours?"

"The message I have placed follows exactly the format and wording of the three messages I came across. These consisted solely of codename, time and date."

"No location?"

"No. That I presume would have been constant and pre-arranged, but never mentioned in the advertizement so as not to give anything away."

"I don't suppose that this list of yours contained any addresses?"

"Definitely not in regard to La Rothiere. That would really be asking for too much."

"But you knew Parminter's address?"

"Only because, as an eminent public servant, it was not difficult to ascertain. But with the likes of La Rothiere one can never be sure where he is domiciled at any given moment. His name is scarcely going to appear on any publicly available roll or register for he is careful to keep his whereabouts enshrouded in a fog."

"What does your advertizement say then?"

"Merely the date, namely tomorrow; the time, namely midday and the location, Nelson's Column. Plus his code-name and the single word 'Urgent' to spice it up!"

"How do you know the regular reconnaissance point is Nelson's Column?" I asked incredulously.

"I don't, but obviously I had to nominate a venue and that is as good as any."

"But will your fish bite? I mean, if you have stipulated Nelson's Column when normally no venue is mentioned won't that arouse suspicion in his mind? And normally, I imagine, it would be he who makes the initial contact not the other way around. Won't he realize it is a trap? All the more so if the person he normally liaizes with does not show up?"

"Yes, correct on all points. You have put your finger on all its flaws, but it is the only chance I've got. I feel he will rise to the bait out of sheer curiosity if nothing else, and on the off chance that the notice is genuine. But, one can imagine, he will be very wary for as you say he will suspect a trap. But this very wariness may cause him to give himself away."

"Wouldn't it have been preferable to have nominated a more out of the way location for Trafalgar Square, even at this time of the year, will be thronged? Somewhere more remote and esoteric would enable you to isolate and identify your man more easily?"

"Good point, Watson, but the problem is that our man, suspecting a trap, may scout the place in advance and spot us before we spot him. No such problem applies in the case of so busy a location as Trafalgar Square."

"But then how can you hope to pick him out amongst so many, given that you can't even know what he looks like?"

"Oh, I know what he looks like from several previous encounters. Our paths have crossed frequently, and sometimes our swords too."

"You indicated that this meeting is to take place at midday tomorrow?"

"Yes. Can you join me?"

"Wouldn't miss it for the world."

"Excellent."

"And what is your strategy if you succeed in making contact? The Parminter trick again?"

"With a twist. I shall offer to give him secrets rather than extract them."

"But what secrets?"

"I was able to get Mycroft to hand me a few official looking documents that he had with him as part of his consultancy work. It took a lot of persuading, but he finally agreed and I shall take these to Monsieur La Rothiere and offer to trade."

"And then?"

"We shall see what we shall see."

I spent the rest of the day in a deeply disconsolate mood. While Holmes was still preening himself upon his intellectual *tour de force* in deciphering the list and the seemingly successful outcome of his duel with Parminter I confess my heart was no longer completely in the enterprize, for I hungered to know Molly's whereabouts and to be assured of her safety and well-being, and yet the more that time dragged on the more pessimistic I perforce became. I was in a state of inner turmoil and could not desist from scourging myself for the rashness of my actions which may have wrought such a terrible nemesis upon a wholly innocent party. How could I have been so foolhardy or careless of the dangers to which I was exposing her? How could I have overborne my better judgment in nothing more than a fit of passion?

The following day, a Saturday, Holmes and I set off on foot at a brisk pace for our rendezvous with this mysterious fellow, La Rothiere. I think I went along with this latest project of his more as a means of taking my mind off Molly than because I felt deeply engaged in its prospects of success. We reached Trafalgar Square shortly before the appointed hour of noon. Holmes asked me to stand off to one side of the Square whilst he proceeded to take up a station beside the famous monument. He had given me a description of the Frenchman and had told me to keep my eyes peeled for any sign of his presence, but it was not an easy task given the masses of people of all descriptions, ethnicities and nationalities thronging the Square, tourists mainly.

I sat on the benches on the southern side of the square, facing toward the National Gallery and attempted to focus on Holmes but soon my mind drifted as I was soothed by the lulling burble of the fountains. Holmes appeared disconcerted by the failure of his man to materialize, and I wandered over to him. He was annoyed by my approach, which was in contravention of our plan, but I ventured the opinion that it was a hopeless exercize, and I could sense his tacit recognition of that truth. After a few more minutes even Holmes was sufficiently disenchanted with our prospects of success to give up the whole idea, when from nowhere there issued the sound of a greeting uttered with a strong Gallic accent.

"Monsieur 'Olmes. Why so disconsolate?"

Holmes and I spun round to look for the source of this disembodied voice. From amidst a largish group of sightseers emerged a small, dapper, moustachioed figure, draped in a cloak and a homburg and carrying a silver topped cane.

"Louis La Rothiere!" declared Holmes, scarcely able to conceal his surprize at being caught so unawares.

"How delightful to see you, *mon ami*. I suspected it was you who had placed the advertizement but could not resist the urge to satisfy my curiosity, however great the peril."

Holmes strode forward to greet this old sparring partner of his in surprizingly cordial terms.

"Good to renew our acquaintance. I must confess that you duped me with your newly acquired facial adornment."

"You are not the only one who can affect a disguise, my dear Monsieur 'Olmes."

"And you are perhaps the one man on the planet who can deceive me in such fashion."

"You do me too much honour, *mon ami*."

"May I introduce you to my dear companion and dedicated chronicler, Dr. John Watson."

I stepped forward to shake the man's hand, following Holmes's lead. It was silk-gloved and flaccid.

"I have heard much of you, too, *Docteur*. It is a pleasure to meet you. And so, what causes the great detective to seek to renew our relationship? Is it to go over old times?"

"Perhaps we could discuss this is in more congenial surroundings my fear fellow," responded Holmes. "There is an excellent restaurant not two hundred yards from here where we can discuss business over a fine brandy."

"How could I resist such an invitation?"

With that the three of us made our way to Henri's just off the Charing Cross Road, an old and venerated haunt of Holmes's where much business had been transacted in days past combined with the pleasures of the table. We were seated without too much delay, the waiter scuttling over as Holmes beckoned, familiar with his custom and the generosity of his gratuities. Settling ourselves down in a discreet corner of the establishment we ordered cognacs and matters took a relaxed and convivial turn. It was evident that Holmes and La Rothiere held each other in high regard as being men at the top of their respective games, and there was a great deal of mutual respect and admiration subsisting between them. The conversation was very different from that which had taken place with the wretched Parminter only two days before.

"I strongly suspected it was you who inserted the advertizement in *The Times* and I considered boycotting, but I could not resist the temptation. My curiosity overpowered me." declared the Frenchman.

"I gambled on precisely that."

"I took the bait but avoided ensnaring myself upon the hook." riposted La Rothiere. "It was obvious that the summons did not come from any of the usual quarters, for this has never been an agreed meeting place. Incidentally, how very droll of you to choose Nelson's Column to try to trap a Frenchman." he chuckled.

Holmes chuckled too. "I thought it might tickle your fancy."

La Rothiere's English was more than serviceable though he had the habit of sprinkling his conversation with slightly mangled idioms.

"Your summons was neatly worded but you are evidently not aware that the time stipulated in these announcements is always offset by an hour, so I had arrived fully sixty minutes earlier giving me ample opportunity to scout the surroundings from a safe distance. And then I see my old adversary arrive accompanied, I was relieved to see, only by his loyal amanuensis and not by any members of the Metropolitan force, thus making me not fear to disclose my presence."

"*Bravo*, Louis. You have excelled yourself in cunning and deception."

"The highest praise possible. But what is the purpose of this rendezvous, so elaborately contrived? Is it to enquire after my health?"

"Merely that I wished to discover what you have been up to lately, Louis, as if I did not already have some inkling."

"Oh, but I am just a humble foreign citizen, a guest in your country doing my best to observe your laws and customs."

"Louis, my dear fellow, if you confined yourself to that I would have little interest in you. I know of some of your underground activities and in particular your liaison with the Bund."

"The Bund?" the man affected a pose of mortification. "Why Monsieur 'Olmes, I am shocked; deeply shocked that you even suspect me of keeping such disreputable company."

"Come, come, I have heard much of your involvement with the gang. Indeed, I have hard evidence of it."

"And what pray can this hard evidence be? As I said I am merely a law-abiding visitor to your shores."

"I have obtained a document which identifies you as a purveyor of largesse to them."

"I should be most intrigued to see this supposedly damning document."

"And so you shall." said Holmes and he produced from his pocket his doctored version of the list, in similar fashion as forty-eight hours previously in a very different setting, but the effect here was very different.

"This is your hard evidence." he burst out laughing.

"It is in code but I have deciphered it and your name is unmistakeably there."

"Your English sense of humour never fails to amuse, Monsieur 'Olmes. If you plan to have me arrested and tried on that basis, I fear you have overplayed your hand. Your so-called deciphering would mean nothing to an English jury with its characteristic fair-mindedness and old-fashioned common sense."

"Well, well, Louis, maybe you are right. But I said nothing about any jury. I am sure there is no need for matters to come to such extremities as a criminal trial." Holmes said affably.

"And from where does this list come may I enquire?"

"Oh, did I omit to mention? I stole it from the safe of the Count von Runstedt one evening last week." Holmes said offhandedly, as if he were describing nothing more venturesome than a trip to the local tobacconist. He drew on his cigar and gazed into the middle distance to let the revelation sink in. La Rothiere could not conceal his astonishment.

"I congratulate you, *mon brave!* I would not have thought you capable?"

"You are not the only one prone to an occasional over-stepping of the boundaries once in a while."

"But what interest is any of this to me as I go about my lawful occasions?"

"I am keen to learn something of the Bund's activities in recent months. I am preparing a report."

"Indeed. Well, I don't know if I am to play a starring role in this report of yours but I hope, if so, that it unambiguously clears me of any wrong-doing, *mon cher* 'Olmes."

"It may not even mention you at all. I am happy to relegate you to the ranks of a spear carrier in the production, provided I have your co-operation. You may be eager to learn that I am empowered to offer you something in exchange."

"Exchange? So blackmail having failed, you now resort to bribery."

"Blackmail, bribery? Must you be so crude? You really do have a low opinion of me, Louis. And yet I hold you in the highest esteem."

212

"So then, just as matter of idle curiosity, what scraps do you expect me to scatter in your direction?"

"What you were able to supply the Bund with? From whom you received it? To whom you gave it? When and where?"

"*Sacre bleu*! You are not asking much, are you, Monsieur! Even supposing, *naturellement*, that I knew what you were talking about."

"I have a particular interest in the Colonial Office and anything forthcoming from that source." Holmes added smoothly, looking casually around the room as he uttered the words, but I caught him dart a glance in La Rothiere's direction just as he said 'Colonial Office' and I think neither of us failed to catch a near imperceptible tremor of recognition on the Frenchman's face.

There was a lengthy pause. "And if, for the sake of argument, I were able to go some way towards satisfying your enquiries upon these matters, what do I get in return?"

Holmes withdrew an envelope from his inside pocket, casting a furtive glance at nearby tables, but the occupants of these were all absorbed with their own noisy convivialities. The restaurant was now filling up with the early afternoon custom and there was quite a hubbub which tended to mask our conversation.

"I am authorized by Her Majesty's Government to offer you these documents." Holmes took some papers out of the packet and held them enticingly before the Frenchman's gaze.

"I did not know you were now an agent of the British government."

"There are some things of which even you are unaware, Louis. That may be one of them."

"May I peruse these?"

"That is why I brought them. This here is a copy of the latest Royal Naval deployments." He laid down a sheet on the table.

"You are revealing top secret papers to me. Oh, but I cannot believe it. It is absurd."

"Believe it or no, but here they are."

I had been sitting riveted by this contest of wits between these two sparring partners, but I could not believe that Holmes

213

was actually prepared to divulge such highly sensitive information to a known spy. Holmes had told me that Mycroft had furnished him with stuff to offer, but I could not credit it would be anything so high level. I struggled to contain my amazement and to hold my tongue in the face of these provocations.

"But you do not expect me to believe that you are really empowered to offer me anything so weighty. You must take me for a fool." La Rothiere expostulated. He contemptuously tossed the proffered documents back in the direction from whence they came.

Holmes laughed out loud. "But, yes, you are right, Louis. You must forgive my little joke at your expense. No, I cannot give you top secret government papers, but I can offer you something a little more modest which may yet redound greatly to your advantage."

"Which would be?"

"Information on the Bund itself and its network. Some other nations, perhaps even your own, would surely be interested to know of those in their midst who are in cahoots with the Bund and the government in whose service it operates. If, say, you were able to present your own government with such information; why it might even make you a hero in your own land. You might receive the *Croix de Guerre* for your pains."

La Rothiere dissolved in laughter to the slight perplexity, if not consternation, of Holmes.

"I give you credit for your ingenuity, Monsieur 'Olmes, but since you already suspect me of complicity with the Bund how can you offer me anything I do not already know? Answer me that?"

"But your knowledge is only fragmentary, based on what might be termed 'hole in the corner' dealings. You cannot know the wider picture such as whomsoever else might be in league with them. I, by contrast, have been able to obtain a great deal of such data and can allow you to share in the spoils. You might be more than a little taken aback to discover the identities of some of the Bund's informants. Figures of some note, highly placed within the French public service, for example."

"From this list of yours?"

"Exactly."

"Such as?"

"You first."

"Ha, ha, ha! You insult my intelligence, monsieur."

"I will give you one name free of charge, as a token of good faith, so to speak."

Holmes wrote down a name on a slip of paper and slid it face down across the table to La Rothiere. The Frenchman hesitated before picking it up and slowly turning it over to read the words written his eyes widened with incredulity. He paused and looked intently at Holmes.

"But how can you possibly be sure of this? After all it is only your gloss on this supposed list of yours."

"My decryption was good enough to enable me to identify you from it, your code-name and means of contact. Then why not others too?"

"But you could have guessed at mine from your crazed belief in my involvement in espionage."

"Your name perhaps but not the rest."

"But why should I, 'ow you say, play ball with you? What proof have I got that I can present to those in authority, at the Quai d'Orsay or anywhere else?"

"I can give you details of the code and the keybook, and a great deal else besides. Can you afford to turn down such an offer? It could make your fortune."

La Rothiere sat back pensively in his chair and drew long and slowly on his cheroot. Holmes allowed the man time to let the offer soak in and clicked his fingers in the direction of the nearest sommelier to order another round of cognacs. Before the waiter had had a chance to return La Rothiere had evidently made a resolution.

"When and where?"

"At my chambers in Baker Street in an hour."

"I cannot pledge myself to anything you understand."

"No, I understand perfectly." Holmes said urbanely.

"Shall we settle now?" the Frenchman's new-found eagerness was manifest.

215

"My treat, my dear Gallic confrere." declared Holmes as he waylaid a passing waiter.

"My God, Holmes." I cried as we rattled off back to Baker Street. "I cannot believe you are seriously contemplating giving this slithering worm of a man sight of the list."

"It will be a good trade, Watson. I can feel it in my bones. It can do little harm to let this fellow in on affairs, and I reckon what we may get in return will be worth far more. You caught his reaction to my mention of the Colonial Office, and unless I am very much mistaken he is none other than the conduit of the Transvaal Dossier. We may learn of the traitor therein, and perhaps even the whereabouts of the dossier itself."

"Well, I hope you are right." I craned my head around to see out of the side window to ensure that the carriage containing La Rothiere was duly following us. At Baker Street Holmes bounded up the staircase to prepare the ground and set out his stall. He laid out the relevant documents upon the table and positioned the chairs so as to ensure the sunlight, such as it was, played upon our guest. He could scarcely conceal his excitement. Within minutes we heard the clatter of La Rothiere's hansom arriving in the street below and the man himself was escorted into the drawing room by Billy.

"So, this is the beating heart of the master detective's operations." said La Rothiere as he peered around to take in his surroundings. "Ah, the much vaunted chemical laboratory." he said as his eyes fell upon Holmes's impressive array of scientific instruments in the far corner.

"Pray be seated." Holmes gestured towards the guest armchair. "A drink before we commence?"

"A brandy perhaps, if you have such a thing."

"I have a fine vintage. Watson, will you do the honours?"

I sprang over to the side board to pour out three balloons of brandy, one for each of us.

"Cigar?" Holmes held out his case of Havanas to the Frenchman.

"You are most kind." said La Rothiere as he carefully selected one and ran it along under his nose before Holmes cut the end for him and lit a match. The two men relaxed slightly though one could sense the underlying tension.

"Now, let us get to business, Louis. I have opened the bidding with my revelation earlier on. It is your turn."

I had positioned myself in a chair at the side of the room to oversee proceedings.

"I propose that we do it by turns. I have already vouchsafed you something in the form of ... well you know who. It is your move, monsieur." Holmes declared.

The two men were sitting opposite each other across the table, as if preparing to commence a game of chess.

"What do you wish to know?" La Rothiere queried.

"Did you take receipt of the Transvaal Dossier from someone in the Colonial Office?"

"I was offered some papers. I am not aware of their designation."

"But you must know what they contained. You cannot tell me you did not scrutinize the documents you were given."

"I noted their contents."

"And?"

"And, yes, I suppose they dealt with the Transvaal question."

"Progress indeed. And from whom did you take delivery?"

"Ah, but it is surely your turn, Monsieur 'Olmes."

"What I have already given you must be worth a great deal in return."

"But these pieces of information are not equal in their provenance, Monsieur 'Olmes. I have no way of knowing that your information is genuine, whereas what I can speak of I know from personal contact."

"But equally how do I know that any names you give me are genuine? And then what I am vouchsafing to you is surely of greater moment than anything you can give me."

"But it is all a matter of riddles and sphinxes from your side. You tell me you have this so-called ciphered list, and that you can make all sorts of fantasies spring from it, and yet I do not even know the cipher."

"You play a cagey game, Louis, but because it is you, I will reveal all." To my astonishment Holmes then proceeded to lay out to the man the secret of the code."

"Very ingenious indeed." said La Rothiere as he sat back to mull over these revelations. "But you still haven't given me any names."

"As I said it is your turn." Holmes declared obstinately.

"Very well. Because I trust you, *mon ami Anglais*, I will tell you the name of my contact within the Colonial Office." With that he produced a pencil from his waistcoat pocket and wrote down a name which he slid over to Holmes, with a wry smile playing about his lips. Holmes turned it over.

"Excellent. We are making progress. How and where did you make contact with this fellow?"

"But it is your turn again, monsieur."

"Oh, come on, Louis, none of this yet matches what I have already given you."

"You play a very hard game, my fiendish Englishman. Alright then. I was given this fellow's details by a man called Carstairs. I arranged to meet him at an agreed point and we did the deal. He passed me some documents which he said were highly compromising and I paid him."

"So, it was a mercenary transaction?"

"Oh, yes, the fellow had debts."

"Alright, Louis, you have earned yourself another name from my little list." Holmes wrote down some more particulars and slid them to La Rothiere. The Frenchman's eyebrows rose again.

"You do not fail to illuminate."

"And to whom did you transmit those documents and for how much?"

"You really are asking for the moon, as I believe your expression has it."

"Nothing so exotic."

"Very well. It was our mutual acquaintance, Kellmann. He paid me very well for it, much higher than what I had paid. It was a very profitable transaction from my point of view."

"I feel sure it was." said Holmes. "And now I need to know what Kellmann did with it?" Even the inscrutable Holmes could scarcely contain his eagerness as he felt himself to be nearing his ultimate goal.

"How on earth should I know?" the Frenchman shrugged his shoulders in an exaggerated gesture of ignorance. I am a mere conduit. A humble passer on of trifles." I could see Holmes's features sink slightly.

"But you must have some ideas?"

"Conveyed to his master, I presume. We both know his identity."

"But how and where are they now?"

"As I said I cannot possibly know, nor care. You said you had burgled the man's premises. I assume therefore you did not manage to locate these Transvaal papers upon which you place so much value." I felt the Frenchman could scarcely contain his *schadenfreude* at Holmes's failure in this regard. "But I have told you all I know."

"But you must have some idea of how these things are smuggled out of the country. As you are doubtless aware diplomatic baggages have been searched to no avail."

"Then these documents must still be in the country, or there is some other means of exporting them."

"I am tiring of this game. Tell me what other documents have you obtained and passed to Kellmann, or someone else in the organization?"

"Why nothing at all. I am as pure as the driven snow."

"Then our talks are at end."

"Oh, but we were just warming up. It was getting so interesting."

"Not interesting enough, I fear, Louis. If there is nothing more you can tell me there is nothing more I can tell you."

"Well, that is most regrettable. It has been a very agreeable discussion but all good things must come to an end, and I must be on my way. I thank you for your hospitality." He made to rise.

"Watson!" barked Holmes.

In accordance with our pre-arrangement, I barred his passage to the door and produced my revolver from my jacket pocket and trained it upon La Rothiere. I was unsure of what reaction to expect but certainly not the one produced. He chuckled mightily at my presumption, calmly brushed aside the muzzle of my weapon and pattered towards the door. He turned back to face us, his hand upon the door knob.

"I am disappointed in you, Monsieur 'Olmes. Surely you cannot think to strong-arm me into some sort of confession. You are not going to risk having a dead body on your hands. But, anyway, as I have said I know nothing." he added light-heartedly. Holmes's stern demeanour instantly dissolved into good humour and he joined in the Frenchman's mirth.

"Watson. Perhaps you would care to discharge your weapon in the general direction of our honoured guest."

I did as bidden, and pulled the trigger with the barrel pointed fractionally to his side, and the blank cartridge duly fired, creating a muzzle flash and a loud bang simulating that of a live round but otherwise causing no ill effects.

"I did not really think I could coerce you that way, Louis. You probably know nothing, as you say. You must forgive Watson and me our little prank."

"You English must have your joke, I understand." He said good-humouredly. There was general laughter and La Rothiere nodded politely at us before departing. I heard the opening and closing of the front door and watched him saunter across the road swinging his cane and heading towards Marylebone. I turned back towards Holmes, now seated by the fire, with some misgivings.

"Well, your trap seems to have back-fired, if you will forgive the expression. I was careful, by the way, to avoid aiming directly at him just in case there was a mishap. I cannot imagine what Mrs. Hudson has made of the noise, though I fore-warned her as you suggested. But even so, we are lucky she is not flying through the door demanding an explanation."

"I never imagined La Rothiere would be fooled by our show of arms. He is too cool a customer." Holmes said distractedly.

"Well, all very amusing, I am sure, but really, Holmes! Did you have to barter away these precious secrets so hard won?"

"Oh, but I think I have the better of the deal. I believe he is telling the truth when he says he knows nothing about the whereabouts of the dossier. There is no reason why he should once he has obtained the price for it. And I have got the most important nugget out of him which is the identity of the traitor in the Colonial Office. That is well worth the cost of giving away the names of a few foreign traitors who are of little concern to our own government."

"But can you be sure of the truth of what he says?"

"He is a wily old bird indeed, but I think I can trust him on some things."

"And who is this viper in the nest?"

"I do not know the name. Someone lowly in the ministry, I might hazard, particularly if the motive was monetary gain."

"And is this fellow on the list? Surely he would be if he is such a key player."

"I have not come across the name as yet, but then again I have not had the chance to decipher everything. I may yet discover it. And, it is always possible that this cove is such a recent accretion to the roster of agents that the Count has not yet added his name and details. At any rate I will look up the name in Whitakers, though if he is junior then his name might not warrant inclusion."

"And if and when you do identify this fellow do you propose to confront him as you did with Parminter?"

"No, that might be precipitate. I will hold off, awaiting further developments."

"Which are?"

"Let us see what tidings my platoon can bring. And in the meantime, perhaps I may yet be able to crack this other accursed riddle." he said, alluding once again to the Murphy fragment which he had retrieved from a drawer and over which he was again mulling, the recent dramatic events already thrust to the back of his ever-churning intellect.

Chapter XVI

Rowstock Gardens

Holmes returned to the study of his 'fragment'. I was left like a beached whale still convulsed with how I would solve my own riddle of Molly, but luckily for my peace of mind I did not have long to wait before the next round of activity. At about five o'clock that day a breathless Wiggins accompanied by two of his lieutenants scampered up our staircase, barely preceded by the page boy, and banged loudly on our door before Holmes granted them admittance. They tumbled in noisily trumpeting success in their mission.

Holmes was gleeful at so swift a response.

"Well, what have you learned?" he said addressing himself to the senior lad.

Wiggins eagerly produced for Holmes a batch of sheets of drawing paper. "We followed him, sir, or rather these two did, just like what you asked, sir, and got the drawings, though they ain't all that good under all the circs, you understand."

"Not to worry." Holmes avidly perused these artistic offerings. "Hmm. And what do you have to report? I require a complete account of events."

One of the boys started to issue forth in a babble. He was interrupted by Wiggins who was keen to demonstrate his mastery of the situation.

"Well, Mr. 'Olmes, it seems that little Dubs and Smiffy 'ere was watching the tree, just like you ordered, and at about midday some geezer come up in a carriage and leaps out and kind of fumbles around in this tree, looking around very suspicious like, but these two had managed to keep well hidden and quiet, and he gets hold of this envelope what was in there, looking really pleased with himself like, and then jumped back in the carriage and drives off. So, then these two followed on their bicycles about fifty yards behind and followed this carriage all the way for miles and miles and miles and ..."

Holmes interrupted this cascade of information tumbling out of young Wiggins at breathless speed and cast his gaze back over the sheets presented to him.

"And these are your sketches of the man?" he queried the two younger boys.

"Yes, sir, that's mine, sir, that one there." The boy Dubs said pointing at the grubby piece of sketch paper which Holmes was perusing critically. I could see from the other side of the room as I observed this performance that the drawing, whilst demonstrating artistic flair of a high order may have been lacking in the definition necessary for a good identification of the personage depicted. Nonetheless, Holmes affected admiration for the skills deployed.

"Splendid. As Master Wiggins has said it is a bold effort given the handicaps of time under which you must have laboured. Now, did you manage to note the route this carriage took?"

"Yeah!" effused Dubs. "It went all the way down Highgate Road, Leighton Road, Brecknock Road until it stopped at er ... er ... a house in er ... er ... Rowstock Gardens ... yeah that was it ... Rowstock Gardens." Dubs seemed mightily, and, it must be said, justifiably proud of himself at remembering all these road names.

"Excellent. But how did you manage to read the road signs?"

"Well, I didn't but I asked people what road we was in as I cycled past, or Smiffy did." Dubs announced proudly.

"And the number of the house?" Holmes queried hopefully.

"42."

"And then?"

"Well, this geezer went in and didn't come out for ages."

"Do you think this man noticed your presence?"

"I don't fink so, sir. He never looked out the back of the carriage or anything like that."

"That is very good. And did you keep a watch on the house?"

"Yeah. Like for ages and ages. Till finally this bloke comes out again and gets in the carriage and he drives off."

"Did you follow again?"

Dubs looked a bit awkward.

"Well sir, it was like he caught me at a bad moment, cos I had drunk a lot of beer and I was sort of otherwise occupied in the bushes at that moment if you know what I mean, so I didn't really see him go and then when we dashed off after him he had disappeared in the traffic."

Dubs seemed downcast at this forced admission and the other boy, Smiffy, got a fit of the giggles at his chum's recounting of this slight hitch. But Holmes was tolerant of this slight blemish upon an otherwise outstandingly successful mission.

And Dubs rallied. "But we got a drawing of the house, sir." He said offering up yet another dirt encrusted sheet for Holmes's inspection.

"Excellent. You have done extremely well. Did you see the householder or anyone he met inside?"

"Not really, sir. He was let in and stayed inside. Saw a few figures moving around in one of the rooms but couldn't draw them cos it was too dark in there and too many curtains."

"And are you sure you were not observed by this man on the journey or by anyone inside the house?"

"Yessir. We was hidden in the bushes the whole time."

"Magnificent work." Holmes then dished out monetary rewards to the three boys and sent them on their way with a reminder to stay in close touch in case their services were again required.

When they had left, I turned to Holmes to gauge his reaction. He could not conceal his delight.

"Watson, these are splendid tidings. We have probably discovered a safe house of this organization from where business is transacted. I presume the house to be Carstairs's residence and the man who collected to be either Carstairs or his aide. Let us just pray that our little friends were not rumbled, or else these two may take fright and decamp, lock, stock and barrel."

"Indeed. I must say, Holmes, you are placing great reliance on these youngsters of yours." I observed as I cast a critical look over the various dog-eared and dirt-encrusted sketches that had been handed over in the course of this debriefing, replete as they were with crude and garishly coloured depictions of personages; none, for all their artistic flair, sufficiently detailed or accurate enough to provide any real clue as to the true identities of these persons. "Are you sure they were really so inconspicuous the whole time?"

"I feel so or else our courier would not have led them straight to this ostensible safe house."

"If that is what it is?"

"I presume it for why otherwise would our man have spent so long inside, if not engaged on an elaborate inspection and analysis of the documents extracted."

"Are you going to investigate this house?"

"Without question. I must make enquiries of the house and its occupants and then decide how to proceed, but this could be our biggest breakthrough in the case. One thing has led to another with an inexorable logic, do you not feel?"

"Indeed. It is undeniable. And yet I cannot but feel that luck has been on your side throughout."

Holmes seemed distinctly put out at this suggestion, and I soon wished I had left the thought unexpressed.

"Luck, Watson? I do not see the role that luck has played. It has been a matter of clearing a pathway through thickets of uncharted terrain with the aid of a map and compass of my own devising." he said loftily. I forbore from contradicting him, and steered the conversation elsewhere.

"So, what role then does Carstairs play in the network or is he a free-lance like our Gallic friend?"

"I think he is intimately bound up with the organization and all its works and is probably a major source of intelligence to the Count, perhaps using his contacts of old such as with

Parminter to inveigle himself into spheres and extract confidences."

"When do you propose to visit Rowstock Gardens?"

"This evening. There is not a moment to lose for there is always the possibility to which you have adverted that my young accomplices have, in their zeal, inadvertently given the game away."

And, once again, during the course of this most extraordinary of all Holmes's cases we were soon speeding off, this time north-eastward to Islington and Rowstock Gardens. We arrived by which time dusk had long since descended and we stopped at the end of the road. We moved slowly and cautiously along the street until, nearing number 42, Holmes gestured to me that we should cross to the other side, though I doubt our identities could have been made out in the darkness. Concealing ourselves in some bushes that may well have been Dubs and Smiffy's hiding place directly opposite we looked across at the house that was now the focal point of our fascination. It was a large, three storied Georgian edifice. The downstairs front room on the right of the front door was lit, though there were heavy curtains rendering it impossible to discern the identities of any persons inside. There were lights on in the first floor rooms on either side, but again the presence of curtains made it impossible to see anything.

Traffic was light at this time of the evening, long after most citizens had made their way homeward from their daily labours, and we were left largely undisturbed in our little nest of foliage, but Holmes, even with the aid of his spy-glass could not divine much of value and at length he decided to call off the vigil, at least for the present.

"Our presence here is not yielding much in the way of useful data. I doubt if anyone ensconced within the premises is going to re-appear tonight."

We made our way back to Baker Street. The following day was a Sunday which I spent making further unavailing enquiries after Molly's whereabouts, but upon the Monday morning Holmes departed the breakfast table swiftly and re-appeared later that morning to say that he had made enquiries of a local land agent, and also of the council offices, and had discovered that the house was owned by a firm of property developers and leased to a Mr. Jones, who had sub-let some of the rooms. Further, more unofficial, enquiries of local tradesmen and neighbours had thrown up the fact that there were several persons living there and that there was quite a turnover of tenants, though none conformed to the description of the man who had been so skilfully sketched by young Master Dubs.

Thus far, so good, but, Holmes pondered, what was really needed was a permanent watch on the premises to see who came and went for this could surely be crucial in rounding up spies or intermediaries. He could not rely any longer on the Irregulars and would need a much more accurate means of identification of any suspects, and to that end Holmes announced that he had been in touch with a local practice of photographers, Messrs. Travis & Weston. They had agreed, upon the payment of a considerable fee in advance, to deploy a man or men, on permanent duty opposite the house, concealed within a stationary carriage, to take photographs of any persons entering or leaving, if at all practicable. I expressed astonishment at this proposal but Holmes was sanguine about its prospects of success.

He announced also that he had done some research into the man Carstairs and his organization, which he declared was apparently called the European Friendship League, and was ostensibly a body set up to promote good relations between the major western European powers and to seek to divert them from courses inimical to peace, fostering social, cultural and artistic ties between the various countries.

"Thoroughly commendable and innocuous on the face of it, I should have thought, Holmes."

"On the face of it, yes. But look beneath the surface and see what crawls under the flagstones and you may get a different impression altogether. I quizzed Mycroft and he seems to know something about the E.F.L. He, too, thinks it a front organization. Carstairs, it would appear, was sent down from Oxford, as indicated by Parminter, and then became active in politics, founding his own party which unsuccessfully contested a few by-elections before fading into well-merited obscurity. He then departed these shores for the Continent, spending a long time in Germany amongst other places, though little is known of his activities there, and he returned a few years ago. Since then he has been nurturing the E.F.L."

"Is there any evidence against him of treachery or disloyalty other than what you have obtained from Parminter?"

"None. He has been very careful. But I feel sure that he is a key piece of the jigsaw, feeding information to the Count gained from his various influential contacts."

"Such as who?"

"Leading figures in the spheres of business and international affairs. Probably, just like Parminter, innocently engaging in light-hearted banter, little knowing the use to which information may be put, though most of it just tittle-tattle. But you never know when seemingly insignificant details can prove devastating, especially if it is being sedulously collated. But if we can get images of some of these people actually visiting his abode then we will get a much clearer fix on things."

"Do you intend to make contact with Carstairs? Confront him even?"

"No, far too injudicious. It may just frighten him off along with those with whom he may have been associating. Far better to observe him surreptitiously. Who knows what eminent individuals may then be observed to come and go. Hence my decision to commission these photographers."

"You think there might be others of Parminter's ilk involved with this Carstairs fellow then? Equally senior figures?"

"Possibly."

"Not all guilty of treachery, surely?"

"In most instances, no. Mere social intercourse. But, if we can identify these figures, then who knows what other leads it may provide? Pick away at the threads of the garment and the whole conspiracy may unravel."

With that Holmes hastened off upon other errands and was absent for the rest of the day which left me to dwell once more upon the mystery of Molly and what had become of her. I again resumed an intermittent vigil upon Wessex Gardens and made enquiries of both her home and the local police who had by now been informed of her disappearance, but alas had had no leads to follow. It seems that members of the Count's household had been questioned upon the point without any light being shone on the matter. I returned no wiser and definitely no happier. But little did I suspect that events were to take another, even more, dramatic turn which at least for the moment eclipsed even my pre-occupation with Molly and her disappearance.

Chapter XVII

The Transvaal Dossier

I was awoken with a start by someone shaking me roughly. Gathering my senses it was Holmes, standing by my bedside, and barking exhortations at me to rise and shine.

"Watson, rouse yourself. The game is truly afoot!"

Unaccustomed to this treatment, even from Holmes, and blinking at my watch on the bedside cabinet which showed the hour to be well short of six I protested.

"What on earth." I croaked.

"Get dressed and be ready to leave in ten minutes. We've no time to lose."

"For God's sake, Holmes, what now?"

After the *sturm und drang* of the last few days I was yearning for a respite to lick my wounds, both figuratively and literally, and anxious too, to renew my search for the missing Molly, for whom I now felt the greatest apprehensions. But it was not to be and once again I found myself pitchforked from my domestic torpor into who knew what escapade.

I dressed and toileted as swiftly as I could under the circumstances, bumbling around in the gloom, and, poorly shaved and hastily attired I stumbled into the sitting room to present myself.

"Get your revolver?"

I rushed back to my room and snatched the weapon and some cartridges from the drawer and the next thing I knew we were off in the first hansom that presented itself, rattling away down the Euston Road in an easterly direction. So disorientated was I by all of this that it took me ten minutes to gather my wits sufficiently to query my friend about it all.

"Do you mind telling what this is all about? And where are we going?"

"To answer your second question first, because that is the simpler; we are going to Liverpool Street station and taking a train to the coast.

"And the first question?"

"Watson, I must be the biggest fool in Christendom. If there were a club for consulting detectives I should be drummed out for incompetence. This wretched dossier that everybody is so obsessed with is not going by the usual route out of the country. It would be too risky. As Mycroft has already told us, their diplomatic bags have been frequently searched, so they must be using some other method of spiriting it away, and what better than by means of an independent merchant or passenger vessel."

"And?"

"And that wretched note seized from Murphy. It didn't say *Ich bin ein Hamburger*, or anything of the sort. Murphy couldn't speak or write a word of German. Even writing English was a bit of a stretch for him. No! He had obviously written down some vital points and they were the ends of words on several different lines. Given what I just said about the means of export I realized that *Hamburger* might be the name of a ship. Amongst the periodicals to which I subscribe is *Lloyd's List*, and delving into it I came across the *SS Hamburger*; a German registered cargo vessel which plies between Bremen and … Harwich! *Ich* was not a German word but the end syllable of the name of that port. It took several pipes full of the strongest shag and a close study of the journal before this realization finally penetrated my skull sometime this morning. You can call me the damnedest booby not to have spotted it sooner. And further research indicates that this ship sails for the Continent on this morning's tide. God grant we are not too late."

"And what of *bin* and *ein*?" I mused.

"I haven't worked it out yet, but if we can find the ship it may reveal the rest of the mystery."

"Perhaps *bin* is the end of cabin?" I ventured.

"Very possibly. You scintillate again, Watson."

I shook my head at the sheer preposterousness of it all.

"It seems like a very long shot indeed to me, Holmes. Surely those words could have meant almost anything? Couldn't Murphy have been completely mistaken or, if he was suspected by the gang leader, given false intelligence to put us off the track? And even if you are right this dossier might have been smuggled out of the country on a previous sailing."

"All of that is so, but we have nothing else to go on, so we might as well persist. I don't think, though, that Murphy had been led up the garden path, or those murderous thugs would not have been so keen to get hold of the document and do away with him. They might have had him in their crosshairs, but wouldn't have wanted to prevent me knowing his story. And the list indicates that the SS *Hamburger* only sails for the Continent once a fortnight, so there may not have been an opportunity to smuggle anything out by that route before now."

"And I suspect you have had no sleep at all?"

"None, but I have stored up enough these last few months to give me deep reservoirs."

"Have you informed the police, for surely we cannot search this vessel without a warrant or some sort of authority?"

"There was no time to contact Lestrade or whoever might be on duty and, anyway, Scotland Yard would have no jurisdiction over shipping, nor indeed beyond the confines of the capital. And as for a warrant, I fear we may have to improvize." he said with a rascally air.

"But even if we are in time to stop and search this vessel, where do we even start looking?"

"That too, I am working on."

The enormity of the task ahead seemed insurmountable.

We reached Liverpool Street station at the eastern edge of the City at seven, and were just in time to catch the five minutes past train to the coast. Holmes had calculated to the minute the precise moment we should gain the station platform, given the speed of the cab and the density of traffic at that time of the early morning. We clambered aboard as the train was whistling its departure and flung ourselves into an empty carriage as the locomotive panted and groaned its way out of the grimy terminus and into the hard, intermittent winter sunlight. Holmes was eagerly studying his Bradshaw and snatched his watch from its pocket. "The journey takes two and a half hours, which should just give us time."

"Even so, we are cutting it deucedly fine."

"If I had but realized sooner. But there is no point worrying until we get there." Holmes sat back with a meditative sigh and closed his eyes. I could never be quite certain on these occasions whether this was for concentration upon the venture ahead or merely to take a cat-nap. At any rate I decided not to disturb him. We travelled like this for a quarter of an hour before his eyes suddenly snapped open and he proffered his cigar case.

I had compiled a series of questions.

"What of this ship, Holmes? Do the captain and crew know of their precious cargo, assuming that they actually have it? And if they do, we are scarcely going to get any co-operation. We could be attacked and end up suffering the same fate as poor Murphy. I have my revolver but even so!"

"I doubt that they have any idea of the villainy in which they are enmeshed. It is simply a roundabout means used by the Bund to smuggle documents out of the country of which the crew of the vessel concerned are totally oblivious. They are probably just common merchant seamen going about their normal business. The package will be picked up at the other end by the organization's contacts and conveyed to Berlin I would hazard. I doubt we will be in much physical danger. It is simply a matter of being sufficiently convincing."

"How can you be so sure of all of this? Might we just be embarking on a wild goose chase?"

"We might. But it is worth a try."

"And how can you be sure we have not been followed?"

"I can't be but that is simply a chance I have to take. If I were afraid of being followed every time I took on a new case then I would never leave Baker Street."

"And what if we find ourselves involved in another gunfight?" I am not sure my nerves can take another shoot-out."

"I think we are relatively unlikely to encounter physical opposition, for as I say it is probable the ship's crew are wholly unaware of anything of a criminal nature going on under their noses."

"I profoundly hope so. But if we are being followed by agents of this heinous organization of yours might it be they who attack us if they see we are onto their game?"

"That is a chance I am prepared to take, but my guess is we have been altogether too quick on our feet today and have thrown them off the scent."

"I don't share your confidence, Holmes. And are you sure you are really in a condition to hurl yourself into a further frenzy of activity after the attack upon you. How is your neck today by the way? Still very sore, I'll be bound."

"It will be strong enough to maintain my head on my shoulders, which is all I require of it." He rubbed his neck ruefully all the same.

I sat back, knowing it was useless for me to try to dissuade my friend from whatever perilous course he had charted. Soon we had left the city far behind and were speeding through open country across the flat and unvarying terrain of Essex, past farmlands and fields and small villages and towns. The station signs of Ilford, Romford, Brentwood, Chelmsford, Colchester and a litany of familiar and half familiar place-names flashed past. As I tried in vain to relax I noticed a discarded morning newspaper on the seat beside me, and picking it up I browsed the articles. I was brought up very sharp indeed upon espying on an inside page a story of a fatal shooting in the Whitechapel Road.

"Holmes, our shooting has made the papers." I gasped.

"It would have been remarkable had it not."

I was racing through the article to see if it disclosed the names or descriptions of any suspects but to my immense relief it merely reported that, though unidentified characters had been observed fleeing from the scene, they could not be described in anything other than the most general terms, and the police were working on a variety of leads.

"That means that they have no leads and are flailing around in the dark as usual. I shouldn't worry, Watson. We are in the clear."

"I wish I could share your confidence."

For the remainder of the journey Holmes discoursed upon topics as diverse as Pre-Raphaelite art, the different typefaces of regional newspapers and the prospects for the forthcoming winter festival at Cheltenham. As always, I was astonished at the range of his erudition and at his capacity to switch off the pressures of the moment. Eventually we chugged into the port town of Harwich on schedule, and flew from our carriages in the direction of the harbour. The weather on the coast was distinctly sharper and breezier than inland and we had to brace ourselves against a strong gale blowing in from the sea that cut through me like a hundred knives. We were greeted with a vista of ships and sailing vessels of all shapes and sizes and beyond them the vast dull grey expanse of the North Sea. Horns blared from all directions.

Holmes seemed already to know where the *SS Hamburger* was docked, and a few enquiries of locals bore out his surmize. The *SS Hamburger,* luckily for us, was a distance of no more than four hundred yards. It was a great rusting hulk of a steamship that looked as if it had served several decades and seen many better days; its hull, superstructure and funnel caked in soot and grime and the inscription on its portside barely readable for accumulated dirt and debris. We arrived at the boarding point, both of us struggling for breath, and grateful for a brief respite.

"Is this the object of all our exertions, Holmes? Not the most impressive of sea-going vessels." I opined.

"Probably the more mundane the better for it to escape scrutiny."

"So, what now?"

"We must find a way to get on board." Coming upon a clique of men lounging against a pile of sacks in the loading bay of the ship, enjoying a smoke, and assuming them to be crew members, Holmes approached.

"Where is the captain of this ship? I need to speak to him urgently." demanded Holmes of the group in English. These seemed to be a mixed bunch, German in the main but possibly with a smattering of Dutch and other nationalities represented, to judge by the snatches of conversation I could pick up. They were generally rather amused and slightly baffled by the sudden arrival of two discomposed English city gentlemen breathing heavily in their midst. One knew enough English to answer us.

"He is most likely on zee bridge by zis time."

Holmes needed no further invitation and took off up the gangplank, bidding me sharply to follow. I hesitated briefly to mumble thanks to the man in my probably laughable attempt at German and followed Holmes up. There were yells and bellows from one or two of the men, doubtless to the effect that we were not allowed on board, though the others just guffawed at proceedings.

Reaching the deck, we mounted by a series of awkwardly narrow and vertical wooden ladders to what I took to be the bridge and burst in upon a group of three men huddled over their charts and muttering in their native tongue.

"Am I addressing the captain of this ship?" Holmes demanded in English as we burst breathlessly in through the open door.

The assembly reacted with a mixture of startlement and perplexity at this sudden irruption into their counsels. One advanced threateningly towards us, but was held back by the oldest of the group.

"I am Captain Jacobus, and I am the master of this vessel." he voiced. He looked a mariner of the old school with the bushiest of grey beards and wore a chunky cable-knit jersey under a heavy blue naval jacket. "Who are you and what gives you the right to come barging your way in here? This is officers only!" he said angrily in a low growl. His English was quite serviceable though halting and heavily accented.

"My name is Sherrinford Hobbs of Her Majesty's Customs Board and this is Mr. Ormond Sacker of the Home Office. We are here on business of the utmost importance." Holmes said imperiously.

The man looked understandably befuddled. "What is this important business you talk of?" he asked sceptically.

"I need to inspect the cargo as a matter of the greatest urgency. Where is the consignment from London?"

"It will be in the hold with the rest of the cargo, but I cannot allow you to go down there no matter what your business might be. Who did you say you are and where is your authority?"

"As I said my name is Hobbs and I am here with a search warrant."

Holmes reached inside his coat pocket and with a great flourish produced an official looking document which he held up to the captain so that he might read it, though not permitting him to take hold of it. The man peered myopically at it, and started searching around for the spectacles which he had evidently mislaid somewhere on the bridge.

"It does not look like a search warrant to me." he declared assuming an air of command. "Now you must get off my ship straight away, or I shall have you and your friend deposited there by force."

The two men around him stirred menacingly.

Holmes assumed his most commanding of tones. "Captain, I cannot stress that this is a matter of the security of the nation. As I have previously stated I am a senior official of the Customs Board; this man with me is a senior official of the Home Office, and if you fail to comply with my directions the full majesty of the law will be down on your head. Would you care to face a charge of obstructing justice, and perhaps even of smuggling or worse?" Holmes thundered.

The sea captain looked momentarily thrown by this assertion of authority on Holmes's part, but, perhaps fearful of displaying any weakness in front of his officers he rallied. There was a conflab amongst the three mariners amongst themselves in their native tongue, the other two probably possessing no English and being informed by the captain of what had just transpired. He turned back to us.

"If you are here about the 'security of the nation' as you call it, how is it that you have no police officers with you?" he queried assertively.

"They will be here. They are following on the next train. We only got wind of this matter a few hours ago and had to round up people from all over London. Whatever else this ship must not leave port, or you will be held personally liable for whatever catastrophe befalls."

The captain looked slightly less certain of himself, but reluctant to back down in front of his officers.

"All right, but which consignment is it?" he asked uncertainly.

"May I look at your manifest?" Holmes demanded.

The man looked crestfallen once more at this further trespass upon his time and energy. He cast around at his crew to look for moral support in the face of this usurpation of his authority, but none was forthcoming from that source, his men probably lacking the English to comprehend the proceedings properly.

"Very well." he said reluctantly and retrieved a document from a cabinet at the rear of the cabin and handed it over to Holmes rather hesitantly.

Holmes cast his eye down it scanning the pages one after the other. Finally, he hit upon something.

"This is it! Drebbin. Take me straight to it." He gave the captain a look of the utmost severity. "This instant, if you please!" he said sternly.

The captain looked even less certain of himself and the situation, and there was a further intensive conflab with his fellow officers before he rather warily summoned one of them, the bigger and rougher looking of the pair, to follow him, whilst bidding the other to take charge on the bridge. He led us down to the main deck and then down a steep ladder into the depths of the hold, where we were led along past stack after stack of wooden crates and hessian sacks until we came to a section cordoned off by wooden staves. The hold was one of the dingiest in which I have been enclosed, and I have known quite a few in my time on the high seas in transit between Britain and her distant colonies.

"Here it is. Drebbin. What are you going to do now?" queried the captain suspiciously.

"Inspect it as I said."

The section contained just one medium sized wooden chest.

"With your permission, captain. Please assist me, Mr. Sacker."

We dragged the box into a more accessible position and snatching a crowbar Holmes started to lever it open. The captain and the accompanying mate looked on aghast at proceedings and started to renew their protestations.

"But look, here, Herr Hobbs, or whatever your name is, you cannot do that to registered property."

"I think you'll find we can. Pray do not obstruct us in the execution of our duties or it will go hard with you."

The captain shook his head at this reprobation and stood uneasily watching our endeavours with an air of mounting concern and frustration, exchanging fevered conversation with his mate.

Holmes was exhausted from his labours, as was I, the sweat cascading down our foreheads from the accumulated exertions of the morning; running, climbing and now lifting. As we broke the lid off the chest, which splintered open, we found bundles of straw, and not a lot else. Holmes delved further and deeper into the container, tossing the packaging material this way and that and finding little but beer tankards he visibly began to lose heart, but then with a cry grabbed hold of one of the mugs; a large, ornate specimen of the Germanic design with a hinged lid and thumb lever, and flipping the lid open he found to his intense delight buried inside some rolled up papers. He tried several other such specimens some of which yielded up similar contents.

"This is what we were searching for." he cried.

Rummaging furiously through the remainder of the crate's contents he satisfied himself that there was nothing more to be had and started to deposit the papers in his briefcase.

"This is what we came for. We are most obliged to you, captain."

"You cannot take that." growled the mariner, "It is private property. And where are all these other police then. I think you are just a thief and an imposter." He barked an order to his mate in German in which the phrase 'harbour master' was clearly discernible. The pair then advanced upon us with distinctly hostile intent and the mate yelled something more at the top of his voice, doubtless summoning reinforcements.

"Watson, your revolver!"

Needing no further injunction I produced the weapon from my inside pocket, glad that I had had the presence of mind to load it *en route* in the railway carriage when we were unobserved. I was even more relieved, and not a little astounded, to see Holmes produce his own gun, for I was unaware that he had even brought it and it was most rare for him to carry a gun. It underlined for me that he believed our enterprize to be a far riskier undertaking than he was prepared to admit to.

Now with two guns aimed at them the men froze in their tracks. I trained my revolver at the captain with as menacing a gesture as I could muster, trying to assume the mantle of one who was more than willing to use it. My performance was effective enough for the captain and his mate backed off slightly, exchanging anxious glances.

"Now if you don't mind, gentlemen, we will be on our way. The police will be here in a few minutes and can deal with the formalities." Holmes asserted with such an air of conviction, however unmerited by the circumstances, that the seamen were taken in.

We edged our way clumsily backwards towards the ladder of the hold keeping a beady eye on the pair with our weapons trained closely on them, and then strove to climb the ladder whilst keeping them so trained, a very tricky exercize. Reaching the deck we re-traced our steps very hastily back to the companionway, and then fled down it with the yells and curses of the captain and his mate, who had re-appeared on the deck together with the other officer from the bridge and who were screaming and gesticulating madly at their crewmen on the dockside to intercept us. Luckily for us the crew were too slow on the uptake to block our exit.

We were some way along the quayside before the crew had bestirred themselves sufficiently to try to engage us. As we hurtled away in the general direction of the railway station, we unavoidably bumped and barged into various dockside personnel. Fear and excitement overcame our exhaustion and yet my legs felt as if weighed down with a hundredweight of lead. As I slowed sufficiently to be able to cast an anxious glance back at the ship, now a hundred yards behind us, I saw that the captain and his officers had reached the shore and joined up with their men. They were gesticulating madly at them and pointing towards our fleeing figures, barking orders to give chase. We had both pocketed our guns upon reaching land but I now started to fumble for it again, meaning only to wield it to frighten, but Holmes seeing my intentions sharply bid me to keep it concealed.

"There is no need. We mustn't be seen brandishing a firearm in public or we really will run the risk of arrest." he gasped as we ran madcap along. He was surely right, and I cursed myself for my recklessness.

To my very great relief we easily outran the pursuing crew who, notwithstanding their relative youth and vigour, were on the whole poor runners on land, their gaits accustomed perhaps rather more to the very different rhythms of shipboard life. At Holmes's indication we used the cover of a large group of passengers from another ship crowding the shoreline at that point to dive into an old warehouse, fairly sure we were unseen by the chasing pack. Thankfully the building was deserted and gave plenty of room for concealment with its numerous chests, crates, and barrels. We made for the far corner and flung ourselves into a tiny niche formed by tea chests, fairly sure that our pursuers had not seen us take that escape route.

After a pause of perhaps ten minutes or more during which our hearts were in our mouths and we scarcely dared to breathe, we became reasonably confident we were not going to be discovered.

We were both sprawled upon the floor, Holmes clasping his leather briefcase to his chest for all it was worth, now crammed with papers and very securely fastened. When we had sufficiently calmed ourselves and completely regained our breath, we debated the state of play.

"What now? Back to London I very sincerely hope!" I said.

"Yes, but I think it may be best for us not to return by train, for who knows that our friend, the captain, will not have raised the hue and cry with the local constabulary, who may be scouring every train carriage out of the port from now until sundown. We must find an alternative route and means of transport. I think there may be nothing for it but a walk to the nearest village and then perhaps to hitch a lift on a cart or some such conveyance to get us back homeward."

"Dare we leave this building?"

"I think it will be safe by now, but I should prefer to take the back door here." I nodded assent and after deploying considerable effort to force it open, we peered out to see nothing but deserted alleyways and no sign of our pursuers. We made our way very, very warily out of the harbour area on foot and then out of the town completely, both of us wrapping our scarves around our faces with our hats pushed firmly down.

We trudged for weary mile upon weary mile along the steep, winding, dusty road out of the harbour town, darting behind roadside bushes or trees at the merest approach of any sort of vehicle from either direction, for who knew what forces might be on our trail. After what must have been two hours or more, we reached a village. I retrieved my fob-watch from its waistcoat pocket which showed it to be past midday. Finally, sure that we were clear of any danger we stopped at a wayside inn and, attempting as best we could to rectify our dishevelled appearance and affecting an air of nonchalance wholly at odds with our inner turmoil, we ordered refreshment from the amiable but quizzical landlord before collapsing into fireside armchairs. We must have looked a very disreputable pair, or, at the very least, slightly suspicious and there were looks of curiosity and dark mutterings from the regulars seated at the barstools by the counter.

Taking a long and deeply satisfying draught of the foaming mug presented to me I sought to gather my thoughts.

"Holmes, I don't know how but you've pulled off another masterstroke." And, indeed, for cunning, guile and sheer bravado he had surpassed himself. "I presume you are going to hand this stuff over to the authorities, though how you are going to account for your acquisition of it puzzles me."

"I have my own plans for these documents."

"Oh, good grief, Holmes, whatever next? And, by the way, what exactly was that 'warrant' you produced?"

"Oh, just a little something I knocked up using some police stationery I happened to have in my possession, and some rather convincing looking seals. It was good enough to convince our seafaring friends, at any rate, at least for a time."

"Holmes, you would have made a master criminal, I do declare, with forgery and imposture to add to your burgeoning list of talents."

"I think perhaps I already qualify for that designation. Anyway, detective and criminal. Opposite sides of the same coin."

"So, what do you make of it all? The clues in the note must have made sense?"

"Perfect sense. As I suspected the *ich* and *Hamburger* bits fell into place, whilst a perusal of the manifest made it obvious that *bin* was the end of Drebbin, the probably fictional personage in whose name the consignment was sent, and the final piece of the jigsaw was *ein* which was, I hazarded, the end of the word stein, the German model of beer tankard. A most ingenious means of smuggling any material out of the country, which the organization have probably used on many occasions, though when they discover their ruse has been rumbled, I doubt they will do so again."

"And Captain Jacobus and his crew?"

"In all probability totally unaware of their unwitting complicity in these nefarious matters."

"But why should German tankards be sent back to Germany?" Surely they would be imported not exported."

"Surplus to requirements perhaps. Just a convenient vessel of conveyance and, besides, nobody is going to be sifting through the contents of the crates to note the anomaly."

"Except for you, Holmes," I said wryly.

"Except for me," he replied.

"And your poor ally, Murphy, somehow managed to discover all of this."

"Yes. He must have been able to glean some inklings of their methods, perhaps from another gang member, after my promptings, and wrote it all down in his clumsy hand to give to me, when we were so rudely interrupted."

"Poor fellow."

"Poor fellow, indeed. And it makes me even more determined to bring this dastardly gang to book for their crimes." Holmes rarely showed any emotion but it seared through his sallow visage.

"And what of these invaluable documents you have liberated? Do these constitute the much vaunted Transvaal Dossier?"

"Well, obviously I have not as yet had an opportune moment to go through them but I shouldn't wonder if is the very same. It would be ironic if they are not, for it would mean we have exposed ourselves to the greatest jeopardy for no good reason."

"Ironic is not the word that springs most readily to my lips. Well, aren't you going to examine them now? You must be straining at the leash."

"I must confess I find it hard to restrain those impulses, but it may be wiser to do so in more secure surroundings than a public hostelry. We don't know what prying eyes or ears are around."

"I take your point, Holmes. Should we be away?"

"Yes, I think we must depart soon, for much as my bones demand rest, so my mind demands enquiry. Let us polish off our meal and be away."

"Since we cannot risk the railway what is our best alternative?" I mused. "Surely you are not proposing that we walk all the way back to London. My weary bones could not take it." I protested.

"I will make enquiries of the publican." He called the man over when he had finished serving at the counter, and asked him about the possibilities of the hire, or even purchase, of a horse and cart from somewhere in the neighbourhood, to be told that there was a farm not two hundred yards away where we might be able to negotiate some such agreement. Holmes thanked him and we trudged off once more to find the farmer somewhat curious to receive such a request from a couple of city gentlemen, who might have been expected in the ordinary course of affairs to be making use of the railway service. But he obliged us all the same to the tune of several pounds for the purchase of a broken-down old dog cart, and an equally decrepit mare to pull it, which was apparently all he could spare us. But we were happy enough in the circumstances to accept his terms, and Holmes handed over the money to a beaming seller. We took our seats on the rickety vehicle and set off.

"Do you know how to drive a cart?" I wondered aloud to my friend.

"It cannot be that difficult."

I could not conceal a smile.

"We will see."

Holmes bristled a little at my sarcasm, but after a few blunderings about, to the amusement of the farmer as well as myself, we were away down the road, clip- clopping along at a steady rate. We made our way back to the metropolis via the most circuitous route imaginable, having to stop for directions more times than I can recount. We perforce stayed overnight at a hostelry somewhere in the depths of the county, the homeward journey taking far longer than could have been imagined given the obsolescence of our transport. The following day we offloaded our new acquisition onto a needy traveller somewhere in north London, selling horse and cart at a large loss. We then got a hansom all the way back to Baker

Street and fell in a heap into our armchairs. Mrs. Hudson, caught a glimpse of us as we laboured up the staircase and issued forth with her habitual tuttings of disapproval at whatever we had got up to.

After a long soaking in the bathtub Holmes spent the rest of the day poring over the fruits of our larceny. I hoped he thought it was worth it. I queried him about the documents. He had spread them out on his table and was surveying them intently.

"So, is this bundle of stuff the much vaunted Transvaal Dossier?"

"I very much think it is." There was a gleam in his eye. "This is potent stuff alright. Some of these papers emanate from the very highest levels. Mycroft was not exaggerating when he spoke of the momentous nature of these documents, and the potential damage to the international standing of the country if their contents were to become public knowledge, not to mention the catastrophic diplomatic consequences that might ensue. No, it is well that they have stayed under cover."

"May I have sight of these?"

"Feel free." Holmes tossed some of the papers casually in my direction and I scanned them with a slightly uneasy conscience.

"I suppose we should not really be reading this material at all if indeed it is top secret, or even mildly confidential?"

"I should not worry too much on that score, my dear Doctor, for that would be a minor misdemeanour compared to some of our other mischief. And anyway, how can we assess the significance of the stuff if we don't first read it? It might after all turn out to be a lot of innocuous scribbling which barely merits any attempt to interdict it or seek to return it to its source. Why should we risk compromising ourselves over something of little or no moment?"

"You always have the clever answer don't you, Holmes."

"Better than a stupid one."

I saw the logic of Holmes's case and anyway needed little encouragement to tuck in. The papers were mixed in their content, much of it obscure and esoteric, though the broad thrust was unmistakeable. There were typed memoranda with pencilled marginalia, initialled by different hands some very exalted indeed, correspondence between various parties, telegrams, accounts and much else besides, and all of it focussed on matters pertaining to southern Africa. It was, as Holmes had indicated, potent. I skimmed through several of the documents and I could only gasp in wonderment at the enormity of the proposals contained in some of the memoranda. At length I laid them aside, feeling gorged.

"Flammable material, Holmes. But how did these documents transport themselves to the coast?"

"Probably via several different hands, including those of La Rothiere."

"And the Count behind it all?"

"Presumably. And this back channel a sure means of evading scrutiny. They may, or may not, have passed through his or Kellmann's hands. It is of little significance. There is no doubt his network is behind the whole escapade."

"And what happens now? How are you going to get this dossier of material back to its place of origin? Will you go to the authorities yourself with them?"

"Definitely not. As you have pointed out, I would be exposing myself, and you, to all sorts of jeopardy. There is no guarantee I would not be accused of taking them myself, or of being the initial contact, and then perhaps backtracking when I discovered no market for them or simply getting cold feet. And even if I explained the true state of affairs and it were to be accepted there is a possibility of our being prosecuted for all of the misfeasance committed along the way. Purity of purpose is not a total defence. No, I have an altogether different plan in mind."

Chapter XVIII

Shepherd's Bush Revisited

I slept more soundly that evening than I could have hoped, tiredness and relief overcoming whatever other emotions crowded my head, and I awoke to a sense of anticipation that we might at last be nearing the conclusion of all of this.

Upon arriving at the breakfast table, I found Holmes already finishing.

"Suitably refreshed after your recent exertions, I hope, Doctor." he said puckishly.

"Indeed. I can still not quite believe what you, or rather we, have done. But what is your next move, Holmes? What are you proposing to do with this so-called Transvaal Dossier? As you have already explained, in regard to the list, you can scarcely go to the authorities with it and all the dark secrets it holds, for you would assuredly be exposing yourself to a battery of criminal charges. Acting in the interests of national security may be strong mitigation, but scarcely qualifies as a defence in law."

"Precisely. Therefore, my next move must be an even bolder one than the last. I, or rather we, if you have not yet despaired of the game, must venture out once more. I regret that we must revisit the site of our original gruesome discoveries."

"Holmes, you don't mean we have to go back to that wretched house in Shepherd's Bush!"

"I am afraid so, for I cannot see any other way forward."

My heart sank once again.

"Holmes, I cannot for the life of me see what good is to be achieved by returning to that vile abode and the bloody presence within. If we are to do anything in respect of that we should, at the very least, inform the police of the presence of Kellmann's body."

"I concur. The police must indeed be made aware and very forcibly so, but there are a few slight adjustments I need to make first."

I was more perplexed than ever.

"Dare I ask what might be the nature of these slight adjustments?"

"You can ask but, since I have not completely formulated my plan, I fear I may have to withhold an answer for the present."

"As usual you insist on wrapping enigma within enigma. So, when do we venture out to Shepherd's Bush?"

"I prefer this evening, or very late afternoon, at the earliest. Cover of darkness is desirable."

"And what then is your itinerary for the hours before?"

"I will need to study these documents more closely to decide upon the most appropriate means of disposal."

I tried to work out Holmes's intentions but gave up. Since I was once again at a loose end for the bulk of the day, and had no appointments of a professional nature to fulfil, I resolved to use these hours to resume my quest for Molly. Fears as to her fate were gnawing away at me madly and incessantly, notwithstanding the excitements and distractions of the last few days, the more so now that she had been officially reported missing.

Were there any sightings of her and did the police have any new leads? I took off for Wessex Lane and was able to speak to Mrs. Carter, who woefully informed me that there was still no news of her daughter's whereabouts. Further enquiries of frequenters of the Bull's Head yielded no glimmerings of enlightenment, and I knew it was pointless to call at the Count's residence. I had no other lines of enquiry to pursue. It was becoming all too easy to imagine the turn of events, if indeed the Count had returned earlier than expected from his sojourn, realized the *tagebuch* missing, so vital to his enterprize, and launched an investigation which had fingered Molly as the culprit. She may have been seen by one of the other servants as she purloined the book, or had simply broken down under interrogation from the Count or his minions. What may then have transpired? It was too horrible even to contemplate. And yet what other explanation was there for her disappearance? I tried desperately to conjure up an alternative scenario, but it was a pathetically futile exercize.

I returned to Baker Street in a very downcast frame of mind which I did not attempt to conceal from Holmes, not that I could have done so, no matter how brave a face I were to put on it. He saw my distress and commiserated solicitously with me, but I could tell that he was focussed on the latest stage of his plan with an all-consuming intensity of purpose that brooked no interference.

*****

At six o'clock, for Holmes insisted it must be done under cover of darkness, we were once more trailing across west London, a repeat of our earlier journey to Shepherd's Bush some two weeks previously. Holmes had, I knew, brought the dossier with him carefully packaged, and he had complemented this with some of the documents he had relieved from von Runstedt's safe, though not the prized list. But why had he brought them? They would surely have been safer kept under lock and key back in our rooms. As always, I knew it was useless for me to penetrate his thought processes. He stopped off at a post office half way through our journey, leaping out of the cab without warning, giving me no explanation for this diversion.

We reached Shepherd's Bush well before seven and as before we alighted at the end of the street, and paying off the cabbie we strode back along this road of awful recollection.

"Let us pray our corpse is as yet undiscovered, or all my schemes may go awry."

I would have been more impressed by this comment if I had had any idea at all as to what these schemes were, though they

251

evidently involved the documents he had brought. By the time of our arrival the street was sparsely populated. The building was exactly as I had recollected it, as grim and forbidding as in my memory. We wedged our way in through the gates as before, I, at least, feeling a sense of dread at the prospect once more of seeing that ghastly corpse. I almost hoped it might have vanished courtesy of some benevolent but unspecified agency.

We advanced cautiously, as before, up that fearfully creaking staircase bracing ourselves for the sight that must surely meet us. In that same upstairs room Kellmann's corpse lay as before, but even whiter than previously, and there was now the putrid stench of rotting flesh, inevitable given the passage of time as I knew all too well. I put my handkerchief to my face. It took some pluck once again to have to face this ghastly apparition, now even more pallid and spectral than in my recollection, for there was also, as I had feared, some evidence of the rats in residence there having eaten away at fleshier parts of the body, though happily they were absent for the present. I had considered warning Holmes of this, but he was blithely unconcerned and carried on about his pre-conceived business. There was no sign, at least to my untutored eye, of any disturbance to the arrangements of a fortnight before, so that we could be reasonably sure that no-one beside ourselves had yet discovered the corpse.

I now observed with a mixture of horror and stupefaction as Holmes set about his business. Surveying the corpse, he crouched down beside it. Donning gloves he drew the documents he had brought from his briefcase and carefully tucked a few of the flimsier specimens into the inside pocket of Kellmann's coat, and others into an outer pocket, whilst a few more he scattered about the floor. These I recognized as part of the von Runstedt haul, and I supposed them to be among the less important of the documents from the Count's safe.

I could now see, all too clearly, what Holmes's game was about and marvelled at the ingenuity of it, and yet I felt an onrush of moral revulsion. Though I cannot attest to any strongly held Christian faith I felt there to be something almost sacrilegious about Holmes's actions, desecrating, as it seemed to me at the time, the body of the dead for secular and base purposes. Kellmann was doubtless, by all accounts, a thoroughly corrupt and detestable individual and yet still, I reckoned, worthy of more respect than this in death. Nonetheless, I forbore to intervene, and found myself instead unable to do anything but shake my head in disbelief and mortification, as I stood galvanized by this scurrilous routine of Holmes's devising.

He continued in this vein, doubtless one he had planned in the minutest detail, swiftly placing a folder of documents on the table near the body. He even went to the extraordinary lengths of taking hold of Kellmann's lifeless hands and rubbing them over the cover of the folder and some of the documents within, presumably with the possibility in mind that fingerprinting techniques might be brought to bear; a technique pioneered by Holmes and which he had urged upon Scotland Yard, though they had yet to adopt it, and which therefore seemed to me to be a wasted exercize on his part.

He completed the picture by overturning a few items of furniture and disturbing some ornaments, designed obviously to create the impression of a struggle having taken place. When this pantomime was complete, Holmes straightened up and surveyed his handiwork with an air of satisfaction. I could restrain myself no longer.

"Holmes, are you doing what I think you are doing?"

"I am attempting to fell two birds with one stone, or at any rate to fell one, and maybe in the process keep the other on her perch." he said with bitter humour.

"So, we are to dishonour the dead to save the honour of the living?"

"There may not be much honour to lose in the case of the charming fellow here." He seemed almost to treat my reservations with contempt. "And how else am I to accomplish matters? I cannot, as I have explained, go to the police with my treasure without risking the full might of the law upon my own head, and yet how else am I to bring these matters to the attention of the appropriate authorities? And if we may, by a side-wind, provide our client with an alibi then it may be forgivable."

"I see all too well your reasoning, but I must register a protest all the same, Holmes."

"You may think my methods unorthodox or even damnable, Watson, but I fear one cannot always play by the Queensberry rules, especially when our opponents have thrown away the rulebook altogether. I may have a lot to answer for here, but let us hope I am justified."

Seeing my look of utter detestation, he moderated his asperities. "And, dear chap, I fear that in my haste and single-mindedness I have once more implicated you in criminality, for which I do most sincerely apologize. I should fully understand if you wish to leave now."

"No apologies necessary, Holmes. You wish me to corroborate your story. Well, I might as well add perverting the course of justice to my charge-sheet."

"Once again I am deeply in your debt, old fellow."

"What happens now?"

"We have set the stage very nicely for our expected visitors. Let us pray they take up the invitation."

"And they would be?"

"Scotland Yard's finest!

"Which I assume was your purpose in stopping off at the post office to send a telegram?"

"Quite so. There is little we can do now but possess our souls in patience."

We made our way back downstairs and into the dingy drawing room, where we settled in as well as we could in all the circumstances, nestling uneasily into the old and grubby furnishings on offer.

"Would you care for a cigarette?"

I badly needed to calm my frayed nerves and took a proffered Virginia from his silver case. I sat back and reconciled myself to the impending course of events.

"Can you be sure that Scotland Yard will answer your summons?"

"I cannot be sure, but I phrased matters so enticingly that I cannot believe that any self regarding and reasonably ambitious Metropolitan officer would not be here hotfoot, whatever his other commitments."

"Let us hope so."

We then waited in as much comfort as we could muster in the grim surroundings. I was glad that I had at least had the foresight to bring my hip flask, and offered Holmes some refreshment from it for which he was grateful. We passed the time in conversation upon several diverse topics, none related to the matters so tantalizingly at hand for Holmes would still refuse to be drawn on it. After half an hour we heard the thud of several pairs of boots in the courtyard, accompanied by much kicking of obstacles and curses, followed by a heavy pounding on the front door, and there appeared framed in the doorway the lean and hound-like figure of Inspector Lestrade, with Sergeant Parker and a couple of burly constables in tow.

"Ah, Lestrade. So glad you could join our little soiree."

"What's all this then, Mr. Holmes? he growled. I got your telegram saying it was urgent and that you had some desperado cornered. Bolted down my dinner I did to get here, and all I find is you and Dr. Watson in this hellhole. You'd better have a good explanation."

"My dear fellow, I could not explain much in the little missive I sent, but in a room upstairs you will find a gentleman whose tracks I have followed keenly for some considerable time. I had received intelligence that he was transacting some business from these premises, so I dashed round hoping to catch him red-handed, but I fear I found him in the unfortunate condition in which you will find him yourself if you would care to look upstairs."

Lestrade looked momentarily bewildered, casting his eyes towards the rickety staircase, and duly despatched Parker and the constables, deciding to follow them up himself. We caught a muted cry of horror from one of the party, as they surveyed the scene. Holmes and I then mounted the stairs ourselves, exchanging expectant glances.

"What has happened here? Who is that man?" demanded Lestrade, striving visibly to control his horror as he stood over the prostrate figure of Kellmann.

"His name is Dieter Kellmann and he is the aide to a certain Count von Runstedt, a German who has been resident in this country for some years. I found him just as you see him now. He had obviously been dead a long time, and there was nothing we could do for him, as Dr. Watson will confirm." Holmes explained to his audience.

Lestrade looked aghast at the spectacle but was striving to conceal it. Holmes continued.

"I endeavoured not to disturb anything as I know you to be particularly mindful of the need for careful preservation of evidence. I confess I did, however, take a brief look at the body and I noticed some papers in his pockets, which seem to be of the same provenance as those laying about the floor near his body and possibly also of that folder upon the table. I cannot be sure of their significance but they look to be of a very weighty nature if you ask my opinion and may well have some bearing upon matters of State. I have not touched them, awaiting your arrival."

Lestrade barked orders at one of the young constables to go off to the nearest police station so as to contact Scotland Yard immediately for more men and the police surgeon. His domineering manner may, I suspect, in part have been an attempt to conceal any discomfiture at the sight of the mangled body, a rarity in all probability even for a seasoned officer such as Lestrade. He bent down over the body, and after a cursory examination, rather gingerly removed some of the papers alluded to from the man's inside pockets and gathered up the loose papers from the floor. He glanced over them and seemed more perplexed than anything.

"Looks like it might be important stuff."

"If, as I suspect, he is an agent of some description then I would strongly advize you to contact the Commissioner immediately for these could be matters of concern to those in the highest circles."

"You may be right, Mr. Holmes, but I wish you could have informed us of all this beforehand." Lestrade straightened up, still perversely unable to remove his gaze from the horrid spectacle before him, much as we had been ourselves.

"Yes, I am sorry that I did not contact you before now, but I feared the trail might go cold if I wavered. May I suggest you keep these papers very secure indeed. The safety of the realm may depend upon it."

"Well, yes, if you really believe them to be that important, but I am not sure how you can be so certain. So, what has transpired here?"

"I strongly suspect that a deal was in progress between this man and another and that he had stolen these papers from his master, the Count, with a view to selling them and then there had been a double cross of some sort, in which this fellow came off the worse."

"Well, yes, all of that is transparent to me. This man, Kellmann, or whatever you say his name is, has stolen some documents and was in the process of doing a trade with a person or persons unknown when a fight ensued, over the money I would guess, and he was bludgeoned to death in all probability."

"I am sure you have put your finger on it."

"But what I don't understand is why they fled without taking the documents since that is evidently what this is all about?"

"A good point Lestrade and one that I knew you would instantly seize upon with your characteristic acuity. I suspect that they must have feared disturbance during the tussle, or had already taken the bulk of the documents on offer and then fled in haste failing to check he didn't possess further material about his person."

"Yes, that must be it, Mr. Holmes. Well, that clears that up, I am sure. Although I must say we have had no report of any theft of sensitive documents from this Count of yours, or indeed anybody else, in the last few days."

"But that is unlikely, because as yet they may not have been missed, and it is probable that their theft would not be reported if the documents were of a highly sensitive nature. The owner might not want to admit to even possessing them."

"Yes, yes, I see that very clearly. Any idea of who the other man, or men, were?"

"I fear that the birds had flown long before our arrival for obviously the killing occurred some considerable days, or even weeks, ago to judge by the extent of the body's decay, though here your police surgeon will doubtless be able to make a more precise estimation. There seems to be little here to enable one to identify the killers, despite my having examined the crime scene with some thoroughness. Perhaps you should seek witnesses in the area, though you must appreciate the perpetrators may have adopted disguises."

"Yes, you are probably right again, Mr. Holmes, I will put enquiries in hand. Perhaps you would you care to probe further. We are always grateful for your contribution to our investigations."

"I am afraid not on this occasion, for I am deeply involved in another case at the moment, as I said to you at our previous meeting a few days ago, and I simply cannot spare any time at all. But you know where to find me if you want a statement or any further details."

"Yes, of course, Mr. Holmes. But is this not your present case then? And is this to do with the questions you were asking me about other murders and burglaries and the like?" Lestrade seemed to be on a roll with this line of questioning and was gazing earnestly at Holmes.

"Possibly."

"Well, this is all highly unsatisfactory. If you had information, you should have told me at our last meeting. You could be accused of concealing evidence, or even perverting the course of justice."

"But, my dear fellow. I knew nothing of this the other day when we spoke, and as I have explained I only discovered the body just today by pure chance. It was merely coincidental that I queried you about other murders."

Lestrade did not seem convinced, but his evident zeal at coming across a murder and the retrieval of apparently vital documents, all of which would, he calculated, redound to his credit, overbore any resentment at Holmes's disregard for the niceties of the law.

"I suppose in the light of everything you cannot be accused of any offence, and you did alert us to this body and the documents at the earliest opportunity."

"I am glad you think so."

"But what about the Whitechapel Road murder I talked to you about? Is that linked to this in some way as you speculated?" Lestrade peered even more intently at Holmes.

"Once again, it may be, but I have no hard evidence, either way."

"I see." Lestrade pondered hard, his hand stroking his chin, and was evidently trying to process all of this new information and theorizing at some deep level of his limited intellect. He ended up coming down on the side of Holmes.

"Yes, well it is probably as you say, so I suppose I should be grateful to you." he begrudged.

"That is most good of you. Characteristically generous, I should say. So, if you have no objection, we will be off. But may I say that all of his could be quite a feather in your cap Lestrade, catching a spy and all."

Lestrade permitted a beam of self-satisfaction to escape him and bounced up and down on the balls of his feet a few times to emphasize his deep contentment.

"Yes, I suppose so. But I will require a statement from you in due course, Mr. Holmes."

"Nothing would give me greater pleasure."

"Oh, by the way, Mr. Holmes, *apropos* your query about any other murders committed recently. After a welcome drought, if I may be forgiven for characterizing it as such, we seem to have turned up three dead bodies in as many days."

"Ah, really, Lestrade. Can you tell me more?" Holmes said as casually as he could manage.

"There is the Whitechapel Road murder and now this."

"And the third?"

"Well, it seems that the body of a young woman was fished out of the Thames near London Bridge early this morning. I was not personally involved in the discovery of the body but I have heard reports from others at the Yard. Yes, it seems that this unfortunate woman had had her throat slit and her body disposed of by dumping it into the river."

"Do you know the identity of the woman?" Holmes queried evenly, though I think he, almost as much as I, feared a terrible revelation was to dawn. Lestrade glanced down at his notebook and flicked over a few pages with an agonizing methodicalness, and as he did so the blood froze in my veins for deep down I knew already the answer he was to give.

"Well, it seems that she had been stripped of all her clothing and personal effects before her body was disposed of, probably so as to prevent her identification. But there was one thing that might help us identify her. Yes, apparently she had a very unusual tattoo on her shoulder of an anchor and a mermaid."

A cry of horror escaped me. I staggered backwards and nearly collapsed under the blow of the news. Holmes, seeing my distress, instantly surmized the cause.

"You know this person, Dr. Watson?" Lestrade queried seeing my reaction.

I was unable to speak. Holmes interjected to cover for me, though he too was shaken.

"You must forgive Watson. He has not been feeling well all day and it's been a long and trying one. I fear the shock of seeing the body upstairs may have been a little too much for him."

"Oh, I see. It's just that you look as if you have been pole-axed, Doctor. I would have thought as a medical man you would be conditioned to this sort of thing." He was regarding me with concern tinged with suspicion. I had slumped into the nearest chair. My head was swimming, but Holmes retained just enough mastery to handle the situation.

"I think it's just the combination of factors. I am sure he will be alright in a moment."

"Very well then, if you are sure your companion is not too badly stricken. Lestrade seemed unconvinced. "So, you don't know this woman then, doctor?"

"No, no." I muttered distractedly. "It's as Holmes says … just the shock of finding the body upstairs, but as you say I should be used to it. I'll soon be fine."

"So, if there is nothing further, Lestrade, we will take our leave of you. I think Watson has recovered enough to make the journey home. Just to emphasize what I said before, those documents you found about Kellmann's person I am convinced are of the greatest import. Come Watson, pull yourself together," he added quietly, taking my arm and hauling me up and out of the house.

As we left, I vaguely recall seeing Lestrade strutting around imperiously within the house and barking orders, no doubt preening himself at his accomplishment in recovering items of such potentially great significance. Holmes hailed a hansom and shoved me aboard. I could see further police vehicles arriving on the scene as we sped away, but my mind was everywhere and nowhere.

"Watson, my dear chap, I assume from your distress that this poor girl with the tattoo is your Molly?" His tone had softened from that of Olympian disdain, which he so often assumed in the presence of Lestrade or police officials in general.

"Yes. It must be." I said sorrowfully, my head in my hands. "What have I done?"

"You have done nothing except what I urged upon you. If anyone is to blame, it is I for strong-arming you into all of this. And, first and foremost, Count von Runstedt, for it must surely be his handiwork. He must have discovered the loss of the diary and identified her as the thief. And, though I fear to think too precisely upon it, he must have thought her an agent trying to expose him and had her murdered. What an unspeakable blackguard! If ever I have had motive to bring a man to justice it is now."

Holmes's pathetic attempt to spare my feelings and exculpate me from blame were of no avail. I sat with my head in my hands all the way back to Baker Street, where Holmes almost had to help me up the staircase and into an armchair before pouring me a very strong drink. It was all I could do not to weep.

"You must not lacerate yourself, Watson."

"But what else can I do? I have taken an innocent young woman and thrown her to the lions, and all for what? To aid and abet you in this fantastical attempt of yours to prove a conspiracy, which may all be a figment of your over-active imagination, and in which no-one will ever believe."

"Oh, but there is a conspiracy of that I have no doubt. The bestial murder of this poor girl proves it if anything ever could. But you have a profound point, Watson. I sometimes wonder whether the game is worth the candle. In our efforts to triumph over crime we may be committing so much incidental damage along the way that when the two are weighed in the balance it is not clear which side will be the heavier."

"Incidental damage!" I almost shrieked. "You call the horrific murder of an innocent girl incidental damage." I could scarcely contain my rage, unable to find its true target, now directed wildly at Holmes.

"No, no! A desperately poor choice of words on my part for which I apologize from the depths of my soul. This act is monstrous, unforgiveable, but have no fear the fiend will pay for his crime. I will make sure of it if I do nothing else for the rest of my days," he said.

"I will not wait a moment longer, Holmes." I had recovered enough of my sanity and self possession to form a resolution. "Are you with me or against me for, dare I need to say, it is one or the other!"

"Watson, I am with you as ever. You must know that. The Count will assuredly receive his just deserts. But don't you see, we must not act precipitately, or all our work will be as nought? Remember the French adage that revenge is a dish best served cold."

"Served cold, be damned." I cried. "If we dawdle any longer it may be off the menu altogether. If this black-hearted scoundrel decamps to his native soil he may prove untouchable. I will have my vengeance now!" I yelled, and dashed upstairs to my room, wrenched my revolver from its drawer and began to load the weapon, my hands still shaking with fury. I had the avowed intention to march on the Count's house and confront him with the heinous crime of which he was assuredly the architect. Returning to the drawing room thus armed I made a bee-line for the door. Holmes threw himself across my path.

"Watson, I beg of you, no!" he roared. "We must do nothing yet. The fellow may not even be in residence and may have already left for the Continent. And we have no evidence that a court of law would for a second be prepared to entertain." I was so incensed I barely registered his words though their import must have penetrated. "If you descend upon his lair and create havoc the overall result would be you charged with murder or assault at the very least, and the wreckage of all my schemes to bring the man to book. No, we must prepare our ground. I beg of you to see sense."

He was gripping me by the shoulders with all the animalistic strength of which he was capable, for he knew that nothing less would have stopped me from charging out of the house and into the street. We tussled frenziedly for a few seconds as I tried desperately to thrust him aside and he, with equal resolve, clung on to me. His eyes were piercing like gimlets into mine as if to drive reason into my brain. At last, my fury cooled and my energy subsided just enough for me to cease the fight. I collapsed, weeping, onto the nearest couch, my Webley flung to the carpet. Holmes flew to the drinks side-table and poured another whisky. He raced back to the settee and sat beside me, steadying my still shaking hand to ease the balm down my throat. His manner had changed utterly from the cold, calculating machine I knew all too well, and the deeply buried but very genuine man of empathy and compassion now rose, unbidden, to the surface.

"Watson", he declared as the drink worked its sedative effects, "If you have any trust in me and my modest powers, and I should not blame you for one moment if you have lost faith in them utterly and totally after the fiascos of late, then I entreat you to listen to me now. I know I am in large part to blame for all that has happened for which my heart is heavy with shame. Sometimes I recoil with horror at my own insensitivity, but you must try to accept that even I, on occasion, do not fully gauge the true depths of wickedness that can be summoned."

I gave a snort of derision.

"It is of little comfort to you I know, but I think I have already successfully accomplished the first part of my plan, for Lestrade will, I sincerely believe, pass these Transvaal documents on to higher authorities and we may, if nothing else, have brought a diplomatic debacle screeching to a halt."

I was profoundly unimpressed by Holmes's apparent sense of satisfaction.

"You are all too right. It is no consolation to me at all in my present pass, Holmes." I sobbed.

"I realize that my dear fellow." His tone was more affectionate than I had ever known in the long years of our sometimes stormy alliance. "It is of little moment when weighed against the murder of an innocent person."

Minutes passed in silence as I wrestled to master my emotions and Holmes looked on benignly, gently rubbing my shoulders as he plied me with another draught of Scotch. We had been through hell and high water together and our relations had had its ups and downs and had, on rare occasion, soured, yet I never doubted his integrity nor the depth of his friendship.

"So, tell me then, Holmes." I asked at length when I had recovered a measure of composure, "What is the second part of this grand scheme of yours? We seem to have been up hill and down dale over the last few weeks without any real advance. You keep insisting you are gathering evidence, but then say you cannot make use of it. Isn't it all utterly futile?"

"Futile. No, never! I can tell you that in another day or two I hope to bring these matters to a conclusion of sorts, though how happy a one I cannot foretell."

"Really?"

"I can inform you that our client is due to arrive for another interview the day after tomorrow, and I shall be able to give her a complete picture of events to this date."

This seemed an utter irrelevance. "I am pleased to hear it, but, frankly Holmes, so what?"

"We shall have to see. In the meantime, I must impress upon you with all the force that I can muster that you must do nothing rash or intemperate to prejudice affairs. I must have your word that you do not approach the Count or his residence in the next two days."

I fell back against the cushions of the sofa as my sighs indicated acquiescence. I gulped down the last of my whisky. I began to contemplate wider questions.

"I cannot even bring myself to view her body at the Scotland Yard mortuary, or wherever it is now. But there can be no doubt that it is she."

"You should not do so for it might only arouse Lestrade's suspicions if he gets to hear of a visitation from yourself."

"And what am I to say to Mrs. Carter? She will be even more devastated than I at the news, if she has not already heard. The shock might destroy her."

"She may not have heard yet, for surely you are the only person who can be aware of the identity of the body at present? The police will eventually match up bodies with reports of missing persons, so that Mrs. Carter will doubtless be called in to make an identification, but that may not be for some time." He averred.

"Yes, as you say. It is too ghastly to try to imagine her reaction, but there is nothing I can do to soften the blow. Any explanation would only exacerbate her grief."

"And if it be established that the victim is who she is then there will be a murder investigation encompassing the Count and his staff and associates, the prospect of which may surely cause the whole organization to go to ground. This is why it is imperative for matters to be concluded as soon as possible, and ideally before identification has even taken place."

Holmes was as calculating as ever, notwithstanding his genuine remorse at the turn of events. We fell to silence. Finally, there being nothing left to be said between us, or what needed to be said being best left unspoken, I retrieved my gun from the floor and trudged upstairs to my room, though sleep was an impossibility. I raged at the Count, at the foul perpetrators of Molly's murder, at Holmes for instigating all of this, but most of all I raged at myself. I knew that whatever the assurances I had given Holmes I could not rest idle with anger boiling within me. I had promised him I would not approach the Count, but I had given no such undertaking in respect of others within his entourage. The last thing I wanted was to sabotage Holmes's schemes, yet I felt I must know the truth of Molly's demise if nothing else or the rest of my days would be consumed in a pitiless quest for answers and a bottomless quagmire of anguish and self-recrimination.

Chapter XIX

Nayland

That night as I tossed and turned I resolved upon my course, however unwise and foolhardy, for I knew I could do no other. I was equally resolved that I would say nothing to Holmes of my intentions, for there could be not the slightest doubt as to his reaction, nor that he would find the means to thwart any schemes of vengeance that might be festering within me.

He had gone to the lengths of issuing me with a written schedule of activities with which I was to occupy myself the following day, chiefly involving extensive archival research at the library of the British Museum to augment his knowledge of certain arcane points relating to Prussian history, gently counselling that work was the best antidote to grief. But I knew that this was merely a ruse; that he feared some reckless action on my part and was seeking to keep me otherwise occupied. I rose not much after dawn, being in any case unable to sleep and made sure I slipped away before Holmes had risen so as to avoid any inquisition, leaving a note mendaciously assuring him of my compliance with his wishes. Nonetheless, he must have entertained deep suspicions of my true purposes and in my mind's eye I could visualize him tracking me to Great Russell Street only to find me absent. I could not help relishing the morbid humour of this image.

I wrestled with myself to the point of mental dislocation upon the question of whether I should view the body at the mortuary, if only to assure myself that it was Molly, but there could really be no doubt and, quite apart from Holmes's strictures, I knew I could never face the sight that would inevitably meet my eyes were I to do so. I was equally certain that I could not face Mrs. Carter nor reveal anything to her of what had passed between Molly and myself. Could I be sure of who had committed whatever foul, devilish, and unspeakable acts that had led directly to her death? Unquestionably von Runstedt had been the instigator. But it could reasonably be assumed from everything that I knew and had witnessed of this ghastly imbroglio, though I lacked hard evidence, that it was Nayland and or members of his gang who had carried out the deed, though I could scarce even bring myself to speculate further upon the means.

And so it was, at an early hour and in damp and chilly conditions squatting uncomfortably amongst some bushes opposite the house, that I resumed my vigil outside number 4, Wessex Gardens. Who or what did I expect to see, and what did I intend to do? I could not really have said. I was laboriously though unobtrusively garbed as before, not merely as a form of disguise, however inadequate by Holmes's standards, but to keep out the bitter cold. These measures were aided by frequent recourse to my hip flask filled with a fortifying spirit and my wrapped-up sandwiches, which I had polished off by mid-morning. I had brought my newspaper, but however much I strove I found I was incapable of concentration. I had come prepared, armed also with my old army issue binoculars around my neck, a memento of my days in Afghanistan.

Before departing I had delved into Holmes's files on the Nayland gang, but it yielded up little for my comfort or enlightenment. I had no clear notion of what I intended nor, even if I succeeded in exacting some form of retribution, how I would explain myself to Holmes to whom I had given such binding assurances of good conduct; assurances which under normal circumstances I should never have conceived of reneging upon. Perhaps in some twisted way I meant to pay Holmes back for his having initiated the whole process which had led so ineluctably to Molly's terrible demise. All of these thoughts and innumerable others ran through my fevered brain as I once more took up my post near the outcrops of the von Runstedt residence. But one thing I knew. Inaction on my part was not an option if I was to retain any shred of my sanity or self respect.

After tedious hour upon tedious hour of fruitless observation, and after I had seen innumerable nondescript figures, familiar and unfamiliar, come and go by the front door and the tradesman's entrance, I was at the point of giving it all up as a futile exercize. But then I was electrified by the sight of a burly figure lumbering along the pavement in the direction of the house. It was the man with the scarred face; one of the murderous pair of felons who had so viciously descended upon poor Murphy, the man I now knew to be Frank Nayland, brute and murderer of the first order, and, crucially, I told myself, Molly's killer. Though I lacked any hard evidence of the latter, I was so blinded by rage and hatred that it scarcely gave me pause. I could not believe my good fortune, if as such it could be described. I put my field glasses to my eyes to verify the fact, but it was unquestionably he. His garb and general demeanour were very different from my recollections of our one previous encounter, and yet I could not mistake that fearsome and malignant countenance in a hundred years if I tried.

He came up to the main entrance and to the front door, and after a few glances around, perhaps to ensure he was not observed, the door was answered by an unseen hand and he slipped inside. I was transfixed. I strained every muscle and sinew to stay alert for his re-appearance, whilst disciplining myself not to give away my presence by any untoward action which might attract attention. This was an opportunity I dare not let pass. And what was the purpose of his visit? I speculated feverishly. Was it to brief his master on the killing of Molly or some other foul enterprize, or to be briefed on some new assignment? Who could know? Perhaps, somehow, I would manage to extract answers from him in the fullness of time.

After what seemed aeons but was probably no more than twenty minutes he re-emerged through a side entrance, perhaps having been advized to take that route so as not to advertize his attendance upon the Count and I resolved that, whatever else, he would not slip through my fingers. But what was my intention? Extracting a confession? Demanding answers? Exacting a terrible vengeance? I could not have said! Only that I was driven onwards.

As he started to walk off down the road I broke from my hiding place, creaky from prolonged inactivity and my outer clothing slightly soggy from ground moisture, and tried to settle in to a pace that matched his at a gap of maybe thirty yards. Turning the collars of my coat up around my ears and ramming my hat firmly down upon my crown to make myself inconspicuous, no unnatural act given the wintry conditions, I set off on the trail of the man. He strode bulkily down the road, discarding a cigarette end along the way and stopping briefly to exchange jovial banter with a couple of passers-by with whom he was evidently acquainted. I ground to an abrupt halt to avoid catching him up and overtaking him and was forced to improvize a bit of business, rolling myself a cigarette and striking a match, whilst casually surveying the life of the street. I preened myself on my thespian prowess, which I felt could not have been bettered even by Holmes himself.

He resumed his swaggering stride, chuntering idly down Wessex Gardens and off into a side road from where he hailed a hansom, lurching clumsily into the interior and grunting orders at the driver which I did not hear. I was fortunate to be able to catch a cab myself almost immediately afterwards and gave instructions, for the second time in recent days, for the driver to follow the cab ahead but not to get too close. The cabbie seemed to derive a wry amusement from these enjoinders. I was reasonably sure that Nayland was unaware of my presence on his tail, for I felt I had been commendably unobtrusive.

We clattered off as the cab in front made its tortuous progress through the crowded London traffic in an approximately south-easterly direction. At every twist and turn of the cabs' progress I feared that we would lose contact or that my driver would get it confused with another, so that the whole exercize would turn into an excruciating fool's errand. But no!

I paid the closest possible attention to every detail of the vehicle ahead; scribbling down the cab number and striving to capture every little peculiarity of its design such as where the paintwork was scratched and the contours of clotted mud that clung to its huge wheels and of the piebald horse that pulled it, not to mention the appearance of the cabbie with his short, rather tattered cloak. I prided myself that Holmes could not have done better in the realms of observation. There would be no mistake!

Almost fearing to take my eyes from the road for a second, I plucked my watch from its waistcoat pocket to discover it to be already afternoon. After a crawling passage through the centre of the capital we eventually made it south of the river crossing Waterloo Bridge into Southwark and then through Bermondsey, Deptford and various obscure south London districts until we finally came to rest in Blackheath. The whole journey had been one of perhaps no more than eight or nine miles yet had occupied two hours or more given the traffic congestion. I was sorely vexed that the driver of the cab ahead might at some stage become conscious that the same cab had been behind him every inch of the way to Blackheath, but to my relief not once did he look behind so intent was he on the task of steering his slightly wayward horse.

Realizing that we had reached the endpoint of our journey I bid the cabbie to stop at a distance of fifty yards or so back, and stepped out warily still endeavouring to retain my anonymity. Fortunately, darkness was already descending and a fogginess seemed to have encloaked the whole of south London. I paid off the cabman, who thanked me and helpfully enquired if I didn't still need a cab for my further progress. He seemed to watch my departure on foot for a considerable time before retreating back to his duties.

I continued to trail Nayland along a busy street bristling with homeward bound pedestrians and attempting to maintain the optimal gap between us. It was not easy. I bumped into one person after another, offering profuse apologies to each while staring fixedly upon the object of my pursuit. I began to understand that surveillance was a craft not easily mastered.

At length, and as I began to fear I must either lose contact or stumble almost on top of him Nayland suddenly, and almost to my relief for I was footsore, dived into a raucous tavern in the centre of the high street; a rather unsavoury looking establishment. I felt I was sufficiently incognito, covered as I was in layers of heavy garments, to enable me to follow him in without betraying my presence. Nor would my presence have advertized itself given the poor lighting inside the tavern, with its crammed and disorderly custom and the fact that my man found himself swiftly engulfed in noisy banter with some cronies. This was evidently a regular haunt of his. Were these characters members of his gang or merely boon companions? Not possible to say, but probably the latter, and I definitely could not, with confidence, have identified any of them as the second man present at Murphy's slaying, though some of these fellows looked as if they could handle a knife or a cosh with as much ease and readiness as they could the pints of ale they were presently downing with gusto.

I snuggled down in a corner of the pub with a glass of ale, having ordered from the counter well away from the Nayland group. I was glad of my pipe for not only did it provide solace, but its billowing fumes added a further layer of concealment and blended with the scene. As I drank and watched I could observe my man swilling pint after pint and engaging in rowdy but good-natured altercations, though such was the general noise level in the place that it was hard to discern anything of his conversation. At several points he disappeared into the dingy recesses of the establishment only to re-appear shortly afterwards; evidently natural breaks necessitated by the copious quantities of his liquid intake.

After two or three hours of this, during which I had downed a plentiful quantity myself, it was evident that the man's socializing was drawing to a natural close and he started bidding his chums farewell before staggering out into the street. One or two others came out with him, but I was massively relieved to see them depart in different directions. As inconspicuously as I could manage, I swigged the dregs from my glass and shuffled out the door after him, still keeping a good distance. Even at this late stage of affairs I could not, in all honesty, be sure what my intentions were, though I was determined that the man would not escape my clutches. The drink had given me extra courage though my mood was so black I scarcely had need of it.

He took a swaying, wobbling course along the badly mended pathways; I assumed making for his home wherever that was, probably not too far from the pub, clearly much affected by drink if not totally intoxicated. I was far from completely sober myself but nonetheless, and crucially, in a better state than he. The wind was very chill and the evening very dark for the street lighting in these parts was sparse and intermittent. A few vehicles swept by, but pedestrians were few and far between. He turned off the main road after a few hundred yards and down a side-street. There was almost no-one about and I had to drop further back to avoid any danger of his seeing me, though I suspect in his condition he would barely have noticed if I had been literally breathing down his neck. I adopted a noiseless, shuffling gait, in imitation of a drunkard, should he chance to look back, but he never did.

After five minutes or so he turned off again into a dingy, dank alleyway, muttering to himself; probably an attempt on his part at song, the lyrics of which were incoherent. I now saw my chance for this was as deserted and isolated a spot as one could hope for. Emboldened by drink, my blood was up. I rushed up behind him and seized him by the shoulders. He was startled indeed and turning unsteadily round he bellowed some oath at me or the world in general.

"What the ..."

"Frank Nayland?"

"Who wants to know?" he slurred.

"You don't know me but I know you." I said, finding my voice more commanding than I had imagined it could or would be.

He peered at me with a mixture of alarm and confusion and staggered backward trying to gain a fix on this assailant. I shoved him hard against a brick wall. He was large and stockily built, having several inches and a couple of stones or more advantage over me, and yet in such a deteriorated state that he at first offered little resistance. He almost crumpled to the ground. I was gripped by his features, swarthy and menacing with the livid diagonal scar and piercing blue-grey eyes, now watery with inebriation. Gathering himself he made to come at me, swinging wildly, but I was ready for him and struck him a hefty blow with my malacca cane, which sent him reeling backwards clutching his arm. Fear now started to swamp his features.

"I asked if you were Frank Nayland?" I could scarcely credit my own boldness and daring.

"Yeah, what of it?" he grumbled incoherently. "Who might you be?"

"I witnessed you kill Declan Murphy, though you probably won't remember me."

"Murphy?" he muttered vaguely, still slurring his words badly but trying desperately to sober himself for what was shaping up to be a tough encounter in prospect. He was peering at me as he swayed, screwing his eyes up to try to identify me.

"Yes, Declan Murphy. You remember him. The man you murdered in cold blood." I spat.

"Dunno no-one called Murphy" he mumbled.

He cast his intense eyes over me with a mixture of fear and hatred.

"Why do you care?" he was beginning to regain some semblance of understanding.

With what I fondly imagined was a dramatic flourish I produced my revolver from my coat pocket, at which the fear and hatred manifested itself in heightened form. He was still in a crouching posture against the wall and tried to back away further but there was nowhere to retreat. I trained the gun on him.

"What's this all about?" he was sobering up fast.

"It's about you and your activities, you murderous scoundrel. I am minded to gun you down now like a dog, but I will spare you if you confess all."

"Dunno what you're talking about." he said recovering some of his bravado. I raised the weapon very slowly and deliberately and fired a shot into the wall beside him, a few inches from his slouching body. I was taking a huge and unnecessary risk for there could have been people in the vicinity who might rush to the cause of the commotion, but I was desperate to show that I was in earnest and not thinking completely straight. I was again lucky in that no-one came on the scene, despite the crack of the gunshot echoing thunderously within the confined space. Clumps of brickwork were flung into the air, which sprayed the both of us. I was scarcely conscious of the pain shooting up my arm and into my shoulder. The shot had caused him to cower once more, his hands up in front of his face as if trying to fend off any more bullets.

"You're a bleeding maniac," he shrieked.

"The next one won't be wide of the mark." I raised the revolver once more and aimed it straight between his eyes. Terror now supplanted alarm over his features, but I realized that further shots would surely rouse householders. I had been dimly aware of a wooded area not far off. I directed him towards it with a flick of my revolver.

"That way or I shoot you down right here." I hissed whilst keeping my voice low as possible. "Get up and move." I hissed again. He began to shuffle off in the direction indicated with me thwacking him hard on the back with my cane to speed his sluggish progress whilst keeping my gun trained between his shoulder blades.

I was again fortunate that no-one seemed to have responded to the sound of the gunfire and we made it to the wood within a few minutes, he glancing behind every so often as if to gauge his chances of overpowering me. I shoved him roughly into a brambly area into which he crumpled and confronted him as before. I repeated the question I had put.

"It was you who murdered Murphy, wasn't it?" I gritted.

"No, no, you got the wrong bloke." he blurted, his hands outstretched towards me, palms outwards as if both to protest his innocence and ward off bullets at the same time.

"I haven't got the wrong bloke, you swine. I couldn't mistake that face of yours in a million years. No-one could! You've got precisely three seconds to admit it, or the next bullet will be in your leg, and the one after that straight between your eyes." It was as if some alien agency had taken over my brain and was dictating my words. I cocked the Webley and aimed it with as unwavering a hand as I could summon.

"Alright, what do you wanna know about Murphy? It was just orders. He was an effing squealer." He gibbered.

"Orders from whom?" I continued though I knew the answer but wanted to test the man.

"The boss."

"You mean the Count?"

"Yeah, whoever he is. Foreign bloke."

"Anyway, I know all about Murphy. I was there, though perhaps you don't remember me. I want to know about Molly."

"Molly?" mystification crossed his face.

"Yes, Molly Carter! The chambermaid at your boss's house. What did you do to her?"

He looked evasively to the side, as if seeking inspiration from some invisible source.

"Dunno nothing about any Molly Carter."

"Yes, you do. I already know you were responsible, and I have evidence, but I want to know the details from you."

"Nothing to do with me, guv'nor," he said with a vain air of innocence.

"Like Murphy was nothing to do with you! Look; I have five bullets left and if you don't talk, I will fire one into each of your limbs in turn, and the fifth and final one will be between your eyes." I could scarcely believe the words that were coming so readily to my lips, and yet I am sure I meant every one of them.

"Who's this Molly then?" he said playing for time. His eyes were darting to and fro as if hoping desperately for the appearance of an accomplice from somewhere.

"I told you. The chambermaid. The girl you killed only a day or two ago. The girl from Wessex Gardens!" I rasped and raised the gun, fully intending to discharge it into his leg if I didn't receive a satisfactory answer.

"Oh, that girl." he replied with a pretence of dawning realization.

"Yes, that girl! If you want to stay alive one second longer tell me exactly what you did to her."

"We just took her to this place we use … yeah, the boss told us to take her to the usual place. But we never killed her, I swear."

"Where is this place?"

"An old warehouse, up in north London somewhere."

"So you admit you abducted her?"

"Well, yeah, sort of, if that's what you want to call it."

"So what happened next?" I screamed.

"We asked her about this book what the boss said she nicked and where had she hidden it."

I felt slightly encouraged that I was making progress with my interrogation and that I was correct in assuming this blackguard to be the perpetrator, or at any rate one of them.

"But how did you know she had taken this book?"

"The boss told us she had."

"So was von Runstedt … the boss as you call him … was he there?

"No, he just told us to get on with it and get some answers from her."

"And what form did this questioning take?"

"Just questions, you know."

"No, I don't know. Tell me."

"Well, she wouldn't say nothing at first, just started cheeking us and ended up spitting in my face, and I admit things got a bit rough."

"A bit rough! How? What then?" I yelled.

"Well, then finally she admits it. So then we ask who told her to take it, but again she wouldn't say nothing, and some of the lads getting a bit riled up by her, you know. I mean I couldn't stop them. I tried but things just got out of hand. But it was her own fault for not saying nothing and just giving us backchat all the time. Fiery little minx she was." He seemed to catch himself, realizing his words were not assisting his cause and reverted to pleading.

"So how was she killed?" I raged.

"Killed? What you talking about, guv'nor. She's alive I can tell you for sure."

"You damned liar. I know her to have been murdered, and you either tell me exactly how it happened, or I will carry out my threat." I raised my gun again.

His hands were shaking and the sweat was now pouring down his face, forming rivulets in his scar. His pathetic attempt to exculpate himself and lay the blame on nameless, faceless others enraged me further, and revealed him for the snivelling coward he was beneath all the swagger. I still strove to control my emotions.

"I dunno what you're talking about guv'nor, she's very much alive, just a bit knocked about. But she's fine really," he added hastily.

He wavered again, breathing very heavily, the sweat pouring down his temples, his eyes swivelling, his whole body in the throes of some sort of convulsion as he threshed around from side to side.

"But she was killed. Her throat was cut and she was fished out the river only two days ago," I insisted.

"You're wrong matey, I swear on my mother's grave."

His words came faster and faster, louder and louder, perhaps hoping that they would be heard by someone, anyone, who would come to his rescue. But, at this last outpouring, my fury so overmastered me that any vestiges of self-control were lost. I discharged the Webley for a second time, shooting blindly. It was almost an involuntary act. The bullet missed his foot by a fraction of an inch causing him to recoil instinctively and yell out, screaming for help. The crack of the bullet caused a great flurry of activity as birds whooshed away from tree-tops and unidentifiable mammals, hitherto hidden, scurried off madly through the undergrowth.

I cursed myself for my loss of control, the more so now that the fiend was starting to talk. I made a huge effort to calm myself, slowing my breathing, but it was a mighty struggle to rein my emotions back in. And alas, this second gunshot, unlike the first, was evidently heard and evoked a response from someone somewhere who must have been passing. The voices; there were more than one; seemed to come from a hundred yards or more from our secluded woodland nook, probably from pedestrians passing alongside the main road even at this late hour. Gradually the voices grew louder and gained in clarity as they approached nearer.

Hearing them Nayland grew emboldened and screamed out for help. I growled at the man to be silent or I would shoot him dead on the spot, and he then fell silent again, though extreme agitation was writ large upon every line of his gargoyle of a face. I resumed my questioning, but now *sotto voce*, for fear of being heard by the approaching group, and more hurriedly, knowing my time might be cut short.

"How was she killed? Who did it? Tell me, or I vow I will shoot you now."

"You're talking nonsense mate," he pleaded in anguished tones.

He havered again playing for time in the hope that these interlopers, invisible to both of us in the darkness, but trampling weightily towards us through the drenched, rain-sodden field that separated the road from the woods would reach him soon; his eyes darting in the direction from where the voices were coming, still some distance off. By now the voices were close enough to be intelligible.

"Halloa there. Is everything alright?" an uncertain, querying, male voice could be heard, piercing through the void, though its distance was hard to judge. It was supplemented by another higher pitched, female voice, conversing with the first and possibly urging caution.

"Who killed her? How and why!" I demanded with the maximum vehemence I could summon without raising my voice above a gritted whisper.

I kept darting glances of my own in the direction of the voices but could still see nothing. But this distraction gave him his one and only chance. I had turned momentarily away, but in that instant he hurled himself upon me with a speed and venom I could scarcely believe. He was a powerfully built fellow indeed and scarcely unaccustomed to the use of physical violence and yet so far gone in drink that I should barely have credited him with the muscular strength and purpose he brought to bear upon me at that moment. Doubtless the prospect of imminent death at my hands had sobered him to such a great degree. He surged forward from his crouching position into my midriff, knocking me completely off my feet and sending the pair of us tumbling to the floor of the wood, locked in a furious struggle for possession of the gun, still in my grip, but only just. My cane had been sent flying several yards from the scene and could be of no aid to me now in this extremity.

We wrestled furiously on the floor of the wood for what seemed like ages but must have been no more than a few seconds. His demonic strength was such that he soon gained the upper hand, manoeuvring himself on top of me, his hands now locked round my throat with a grip of steel, a diabolical glint in those eyes. I could hear the voices and shouts of the people approaching, now relatively near at hand, doubtless further alerted by the grunts and oaths emitted by Nayland, the pair of us locked in a deathly embrace. I was now the one to hope despairingly for their appearance, but I was unable to emit a sound with the man's fingers pressing into my windpipe and throttling the life out of me. I prayed for salvation.

And then it happened. I had managed somehow to retain hold of the gun, its hammer still cocked from before, my forefinger all this time curled around the trigger. It was wedged between us and under the impact of the tussle with our bodies grinding and bumping against each other the trigger was forced back and the fire-arm discharged with an anti-climactic crump, its sound muffled by several layers of clothing. I sensed my adversary's grip tighten convulsively for a couple of seconds and wondered absurdly if it were I who had been shot but then his clench released itself totally, his eyes went blank and his massive, sprawling torso collapsed on top of me. I forced him off in a spasm of revulsion and he rolled over lifelessly. It was unclear where the bullet had struck home but its effect was instant and fatal. There was not even a groan.

Chapter XX

A Reckoning

The voices were still discernible in the middle distance, but upon the sound of another shot there were gasps and shrieks and then an eerie silence. Fright must have frozen them in their tracks and discouraged any further approach. There was a low, fevered conversation, and I sensed a scuttling away, with the audible swishing of the long, wet grass diminishing in volume as the party retreated. I lay for several minutes in that posture flat on my back, choking and wheezing uncontrollably and trying to raise myself upright. I was scarcely able to credit that I was still alive and breathing, albeit only just. I must have lain there a long time before managing to prop myself up, still gasping for air, my head spinning.

It may have been fifteen minutes, or half an hour, or an hour for all I knew or cared, but eventually I recovered just enough of my strength and composure to make a survey of the scene. Nayland lay motionless, blood pouring from a wound somewhere from his chest area. My coughs and spluttering had eased to the point that I was now hardly aware of it. Stumbling to my feet I groped around for my cane, partially obscured nearby in the under-matting of the woodland. I realized I was still gripping the Webley in my sweaty, trembling hand, my fingers locked around it with such a grim and deadly resolve that I found it almost impossible at first to break my grip on it, as if psychologically wedded to the weapon, my forefinger still on the trigger. It was lucky that the mechanism was stiff enough for it not to have discharged again in the course of the struggle. The barrel was still burning hot, and I laid it carefully on the ground, pointing away from me.

After the storm the calm. I found a weird serenity and detachment descend upon me, as if in a dream-like state. I imagined the fight to have happened to someone else and to not me. My hand was not even shaking, and I was breathing more steadily. I felt released from some awful burden. I am a man of medicine or I am nothing, and so I checked for Nayland's pulse as a matter of everyday routine, tearing the man's sleeve to get at his wrist, and sure enough there was none. Blood was everywhere on his upper body still escaping from his wound, and, ripping his heavy outer garments asunder, closer investigation revealed that the bullet had penetrated the chest, by the left-side intercostal muscles covering the heart. Blood had spread to my own clothing and must have dripped to the ground, but it was impossible to tell in the darkness and it would soon be soaked up and made invisible to the naked eye, or at least the untrained naked eye; one not already searching for it.

I was reasonably certain that none of the fatal struggle had been visible; what with the cover of darkness, a still all-pervading fogginess and the density of forestation, and that these potential witnesses would not investigate further, at least for the time being. I decided my best course was to drag the inert body by its feet, deeper and deeper into the woodland so as to conceal its presence for as long as possible. I found a niche for it within an elaborately wrought clump of trees where the branches had intertwined. Using all my strength I pushed and manoeuvred the body into the middle of this growth. Where I found the energy for these further exertions, I cannot say so great was the weight of the corpse. I covered it up with as much brush and foliage as I could lay my hands on from roundabouts and then lit a match, fumbling in my pockets for the necessary, took a step or two backwards and held up the match to the clump to admire my handiwork. I felt it to be such a masterpiece of concealment for it not to be readily discoverable for a long time, even by those minded to search for a body. I had considered the alternative of digging a shallow grave but I possessed neither the implements, nor the further reserves of energy for such an ambitious undertaking, and so decided to leave the job at that. I permitted myself a grim, macabre laugh of satisfaction at the effectiveness of my burial operation. The corpse would not be found, at least not until well into the following day by which time I hoped I would be far away from the scene. How I found the wit to accomplish all of this I could not say, but the actions came to me as of instinct, military experience perhaps coming to the fore in this extremity.

What did I intend to do then? I really did not know.

I slumped to the ground against a tree and took stock. Dried sweat was coating my face. I had sustained numerous cuts and bruises to the face and body, and heavy bruising to my throat. I ached all over and my shoulder would have been a torment to me under normal circumstances. My clothing was filthy from head to toe and torn in places. But none of this concerned me at that moment. I could scarce believe what had taken place, but I could not say in all honesty that I felt any shame or remorse, nor that I did not think that Nayland had received his just deserts. I could at least console myself with the thought that the death was unintentional and in self-defence. But whether or not there was to be a reckoning in a court of justice there would unquestionably be a reckoning with Holmes.

What was I to do now? I could not think of sleep for, however great my tiredness and exhaustion, my state of mind permitted neither rest nor peace. Only now did I start to become aware of the coldness of the evening. I gathered my possessions together in my satchel as best I could, hoping to leave as little trace of myself as feasible. I thrust the Webley, now cooled, deep into my coat pocket. I then wandered aimlessly for a while in a state of utter confusion through the woods, deep into its impenetrable heart until reaching an outlet somewhere a long way from where I had entered several hours before and, I fervently hoped, a very long way from the scene of the struggle. I plucked my watch from its waistcoat pocket. Its glass had been cracked in the fight, and the hands stopped, but I didn't need my timepiece to tell me it must now be very late in the evening.

There was little or no prospect of a train back to central London, even if I could have located a station. Moreover, I could scarcely consider using public transport in my present wretched condition; bruised, bloodied and dishevelled. I could not be sure if and when Nayland's body would be discovered but I had to assume that those strangers might go straight to the police who would then conduct an immediate search and initiate a manhunt. Although there would have been no good description, if at all, of myself, but I would nonetheless have stood out in a crowd.

I contemplated bedding down in the woods for the night, with my coat as my blanket and my scarf as my pillow, but I knew I would only manage to sleep fitfully if at all, and was desperate to remove myself as far as possible from the scene of the crime. I had the nous to realize, also, that whatever else were now to happen I must inform Holmes as soon as humanly possible, for my reckless actions might prove devastating to his carefully wrought plans. It must now have been close to midnight, or even well past, though I could not be certain, and I made the decision, crazy though it may seem, to make my way back to Baker Street on foot. Tiredness was utterly driven out by excitation.

I hauled myself homeward for what seemed an interminable distance, probably not taking the best route for I was unfamiliar with the geography south of the Thames, until finally I crossed the river at Tower Bridge.

I kept my collar well up and my scarf around the lower portions of my face, though given the hour I did not encounter a single soul upon the journey until reaching the City, and even then the only sightings of humanity I had were with the odd drunkard and itinerant.

It must have been nearly three o'clock by the time I got back to Baker Street, and I have never felt so glad to be home. I ached all over and part of me wanted to topple into bed, for it had been a very long day indeed, but the other part told me I would find no solace in sleep and that I must tell all to Holmes without further delay. I dreaded the prospect, and had rehearsed how I would play it every step of the way home, my thoughts switching wildly between snatched recollections of the fatal struggle just ended, and imagined exchanges between myself and Holmes shortly to come.

After letting myself in with my latch-key as quietly as I could, for Mrs. Hudson was a notoriously light sleeper and her rooms were on the ground floor, I crept up the staircase, paced to and fro about the drawing room for a minute or two to stiffen my resolve and marched to Holmes's bedroom. I tapped softly on his door and, unsurprizingly, receiving no response I knocked more boldly and croaked out 'Holmes' loud enough to wake him, but, I hoped, not loud enough to wake Mrs. Hudson. Still receiving no response and knowing Holmes to be a deep sleeper, I called his name again rather more loudly and this time my summons was answered for the door was flung wide and Holmes stood before me in his night clothes, a look of thunder writ large across his aquiline features, occasioned I knew not by the interruption to his slumbers but the supposition of what I had been about.

"Watson, what the devil is your game! Dare I even ask for I fear the very worst if your appearance is to be a guide?"

And, indeed, it scarcely required one with his unrivalled powers of observation to surmize that I had been through the torments of hell.

"Holmes, I must admit everything to you!" I cried in a hoarse whisper.

"Wait there!" he commanded. The door was closed and I could picture Holmes on the other side of it throwing on his night-dress and striving to focus his acute brain upon the business now at hand. Within seconds he had re-emerged attired in his velvet dressing gown, wrapping the belt around his waist, and making an effort to smooth down his ruffled hair.

"The drawing room!" he barked and we swept speedily and noiselessly, me first with he close on my heels, to take up our familiar chairs by the fireside, its embers now long dead. Holmes reached for his briar from the pipe rack and the strongest of his tobacco from the pouch nailed to the mantelpiece.

"A drink I have no doubt?"

"Brandy. Gallons of it!"

Holmes leapt to the drinks cabinet and poured large measures for both of us. He snapped up his cigarette box and proffered it to me. I needed no invitation and took a clutch. After Holmes had lit his match for me, he resumed his seat, lighting his own pipe. He sat staring at me with such probing intensity that I felt as if he could see right through my brain and penetrate to the very back of my head. Several seconds passed in complete silence, broken only by the ticking clock, before he uttered.

"Well?"

"It is a long story, Holmes."

"Then pray tell it. All of it if you please, with as much accuracy as possible. Omit nothing." His tone was cool and forensic, and yet I knew him to be suppressing a deep inner rage. And I could not blame him.

I proceeded to recount the events of the day just gone with as much detail as I could recall, though things came tumbling out with a jagged edge to them. I faltered several times in my telling of the story, and I must have repeated myself time and again, and yet forgot vital aspects. I took frequent draughts of the liquid tonic at hand and got through several of Holmes's finest Virginias.

I took him through my morning vigil outside Wessex Gardens, clapping eyes on Nayland, following him to Blackheath by hansom, then the tavern, the confrontation, the fearful struggle, and the killing. Finally, I described how I had managed to conceal the body and of my trek homeward. The whole telling must have lasted half an hour, given that my rendition was circuitous and repetitive, and sometimes involved reverting to an earlier stage as I would suddenly recall some detail that I had initially forgotten. Holmes sat mostly silent throughout, puffing quietly on his briar, his face typically offering no clue as to his reactions even at the most terrible points of the narrative, only occasionally interjecting to demand clarification on some aspect he considered important. I kept expecting Holmes to blurt out some expletive or a cry of shock at the extraordinary turn of events, but I should have known better for he remained outwardly imperturbable throughout, his emotional self-control a marvel to behold. He would allow nothing to sidetrack him from a cool appraisal of the facts, as best as I could supply them. When I had finished there was another prolonged silence.

Holmes finally turned his austere glare from me and rose from his chair pacing about, smacking the bowl of the briar into the palm of his hand as was his wont when in deep contemplation of a matter that required urgent attention. He turned back toward me.

"Watson, you have been an imbecile of the first order! I prostrated myself before you with pleas for restraint, yet you barged ahead with this crazed scheme of vengeance, and your temerity has now imperilled everything. Don't you see? Did you not consider the consequences for even one second, man!?"

I was fazed and yet Holmes's reaction had reignited my own anger.

"Yes, I considered the consequences, damn you! But did you consider the consequences when you first got me to entangle that poor girl into your grandiose schemes? Oh no! Human happiness is a trifling consideration when set against the great Sherlock Holmes and his plans to save the nation!" I blazed.

"Keep your voice down." he said, as a sort of holding mechanism to quell my fury. I realized that I had been roused to such a pitch that I was shouting, as were we both, but he was visibly taken aback at the vehemence of my outburst. He circled about the room again pummelling his briar into his hand. But I was not finished.

"I didn't really expect any sympathy or understanding from you Holmes, but surely even you must have appreciated my distraught state these last few days. I sometimes wonder whether you have blood in your veins or machine oil. How did you expect me to react?"

"Yes, you were in flames! But did you really have to go to these lengths. I could have rolled up this entire organization, hide and hair, in a matter of a few days but this new madcap escapade of yours has put everything in jeopardy, don't you realize. This man's death will put the whole network on alert and they may go to ground as fast as you can say Jack Robinson."

"Well, I had to have my revenge, whatever you say, Holmes. I do not repent of it. I would do it all over again if I had the chance, even knowing the outcome as I do, and I would do it with relish. Yes, with relish!" I said, meaning every syllable. The ardour of these assertions on my part clearly affected him. I could sense him wrestling with himself as he continued to pace about the room. I strove to read his face and detected a gradual softening of his demeanour. Finally, he stopped in his tracks.

"Watson. I feel I must offer apologies." he said with a note of contrition in his voice that I seldom heard, but which was all the more affecting for its very rarity. "You are right. I do not always take into account the effect that my actions may have on others, especially upon those less able than I to appreciate the necessity for absolute rationality at all times."

This *mea culpa* was, I felt, considerably devalued by its allusion to my own implied shortcomings.

"It is not so much my own lack of rationality as the girl's innocence which I had in mind." I snapped.

"Yes, you are right again, my dear fellow." His asperities had softened to the point of tenderness. "I have allowed my own dedication to the cause to blind me to so much else in the course of this whole affair. I shall curse myself to my dying day for the havoc I may have brought down upon blameless parties. And yet even now I cannot shrink from what I conceive as my duty."

"Duty, be hanged." I cried.

"Watson, I beg of you to disregard my admonitions to you entirely but I must be apprized of certain hard facts. How effectively did you conceal this body? Is it likely to be discovered at the first search, for the local constabulary must surely be on the case if and when your would-be interceders report the matter?"

"I cannot say. It may stay hidden for a while. Perhaps even a day or two but it depends upon how painstaking a search is put into operation." I reflected.

"I think we must assume that it will be discovered sometime today, perhaps in only a few hours, and then the rats might scuttle from the sinking ship leaving only their droppings behind. A murder enquiry will be afoot, word will surely reach the Count that one of his chief henchmen has been killed, and the whole organization disappear off the face of the earth as if it had never existed. It means I will have to advance matters faster than I had intended ... there is not a moment to lose."

"Holmes, I naturally have no choice but to report everything to the authorities."

"For God's sake man! Do no such thing. What are you thinking of?"

"But Holmes ..."

"I need you at my side at this critical juncture and, anyway, what would you be confessing to other than deeds that would meet with nothing but hurrahs from any red-blooded Englishman?"

"That's as may be, but in law I am guilty of manslaughter."

"There is not a court in the land that would convict you."

"Should we not leave that to a jury?"

"I am second to none in my support for the English system of justice as you well know, Watson, but there are exceptions to everything in this world."

"But what is to say that I won't be arrested anyway? I may have been identified by somebody at the scene."

"But you said yourself that these passers-by never got close enough to see you or Nayland, and it was very dark and densely wooded. And is it at all likely that you could have been identified by someone at some point along the journey or in the tavern?"

"Very unlikely. I have only rarely travelled to south London, and I think it highly improbable that anyone would have known me there."

"Exactly. So, you are most likely in the clear."

"But what of the cabman to whom I gave such memorable instructions?

"Ah, yes, indeed. We must hope he is not questioned and does not come forward of his own volition if matters receive wide publicity, but if you were as hugger mugger in your dress and demeanour as you suggest, then he may not even be able to point you out as his fare. And as time passes memory fades. Are you sure you left none of your effects at the scene? That is a point of vital importance."

"I am fairly certain I managed to gather everything up. I have examined the contents of my bag and there is nothing missing."

"Excellent. You have done well to cover your tracks. And what of your trusty Webley? You must clean it as soon as possible to remove any traces of recent usage. In the very unlikely event that you have been identified the police will come knocking and may wish to examine the weapon. And your clothing. It may be expedient to dispose of both for there must surely be traces of the man Nayland's blood upon them."

"If you insist, but I think you are assuming the police to be as fastidious in their investigations as you are yourself."

"I think that they are rapidly adjusting their procedures so as to adopt some of my own methods, which I can scarcely object to, and indeed wholeheartedly commend, but in this case I might for your sake wish them to be a little tardy. But as I say, identification is improbable. So be of good cheer! And in the meantime, you must get some rest. A long, hot bath will do you good. Do you need medical attention?"

"No, I think not. I am bruised and battered but there are no breakages, and it may be best not to involve anyone else."

"That is what I wanted to hear, my dear fellow, for you are as invaluable to me as ever. I cannot have you hospitalized or incarcerated as we come to the climax of these grave matters."

I rose stiffly from my chair and we faced each other, each of us doubtless considering how our friendship stood in the light of these further dramatic exchanges. Now, as never before in the long annals of our adventures together, I think we recognized the deep bond that existed between us which had withstood so many twists and torsions over the years and yet held firm in spite of, or perhaps because of, our very contrasting dispositions. We shook hands heartily, and then Holmes did something I had never known him do before. He clasped me

290

firmly by the shoulders and hugged me with a warmth I could never have envisaged. I reciprocated and I cannot deny I was moved by these tokens of our deep mutual attachment.

After all of this I staggered into the bathroom, drew as much water as was left in the tank, lukewarm though it was, cast off my clothing and plunged in. I needed so desperately to bathe not merely for the sake of hygiene, but to cleanse myself of the foul stench, both literal and figurative, of the beast with whom I had been locked in deadly battle and whose malign essence seemed still to cling to me. I allowed myself to soak in that bathtub for a very long time, drifting off to sleep, before rousing myself and hauling myself to my bedroom. I fell into a deep and well merited slumber. Whether Holmes had returned to bed or whether, as would have been so characteristic of him, he had forsworn further sleep and was already embarking on some fresh set of initiatives in the light of this dramatically altered picture of affairs I could not be sure.

Chapter XXI

Carstairs

When I awoke several hours later after a deep, though troubled, sleep I felt momentarily refreshed, but instantly the horrifying events of the previous evening came flooding back to me in a ghastly montage of images. And yet I could not say exactly what I was thinking. There was a deep ambivalence. I did not regret the death of Nayland one iota and cared little for my own fate, and yet I was sorely troubled by how all of this might impinge upon Holmes's doubtless carefully laid plans. I scarcely knew what to expect next, and almost imagined that the police would be downstairs ready to arrest me.

Gingerly, for I was aching all over, I changed into a fresh suit of clothes and made my way to the drawing room, now very conscious of the pangs racking me from every inch of my body. My neck, in particular, was very stiff and my throat as sore as blazes. I found Holmes already abuzz, darting from drawer to drawer and riffling through documents, his half-eaten breakfast still upon the table. I was braced for another round of chastizement for the folly of my exploits, though I need not have worried on that score.

"Watson, I must offer you thanks as well as apologies for it has been your initiatives, however unwise, that have spurred me to act sooner than I intended, but no sooner than is necessary. I have temporized for too long, seeking to extract more and more juice from my plucked fruit, but letting precious days pass in which the villains may be securing their escape tunnel.

"And now there is this!" he snatched up the newspaper and flung it down on the table in front of me with a melancholy expression. It was folded in such a way as to frame a particular article. I half feared it would be a report of the discovery of Nayland's body, though it could not possibly have been as yet, but to my almost equal consternation it was the story of the death of someone altogether different. My brain cranked into action as I devoured the contents of the article headlined by the bald statement that a senior Foreign Office personage had been found hanged.

"My God! Parminter," I cried.

"Indeed," Holmes looked grim.

"Holmes, what are you doing? What are **we** doing? It is as if we are destroying lives left, right and centre with our every move." I could not contain my distress at these awful tidings. "First Murphy, then Molly, and now Parminter. Would any of these people be dead if not for your interventions?"

"I have a lot to answer for here, Watson," he confessed ruefully, falling back into his chair.

"More of your incidental damage," I said caustically.

"Your sarcasm is wasted Watson for I am already racked by misgivings. How variegated are the fruits of treachery! Our man Parminter commits suicide over mere indiscretions and yet a real traitor in the Colonial Office acting out of greed still walks free. But I can only say that having come this far we must go all the way. We are near the end of the road."

"Well, I am at least gratified to hear that, for the truth is I am not sure I can bear the burden of all of this one moment longer than I have to, Holmes, just as I suspect you cannot yourself. I still feel I should admit all to the police immediately."

"I beseech you to do no such thing. It would only lead to the ruination of all my plans, and then these terrible deaths would have been in vain."

"So, what then?" I implored.

"I have been rounding out my investigations. I received sometime yesterday, while you were otherwise engaged, a batch of photographs taken at Rowstock Gardens by Messrs. Travis & Weston who have followed my instructions with great dedication and thoroughness. They make for very interesting viewing indeed with Mr Jeremy Carstairs and other figures prominent."

"You mean you recognize some of the other persons captured in these photographs?"

"No, but there are those who may be able to identify them. At any rate it may be an invaluable source."

"For whom?"

"For whomever I pass all this material to. Would you care to see the photographs?"

"Very well, if you insist." I had lost any real enthusiasm for the game but felt I must humour Holmes. He handed me the file containing these plates, and I scanned them in a desultory fashion.

"You may also be interested to learn that I had arranged an interview with our client for next week by which time I had hoped to have built up a much fuller picture of everything but in the light of all that has now transpired, thanks in no small measure to you Watson, I have felt impelled to bring matters forward, and so have despatched a messenger to her house to request her presence here tomorrow, or at any rate her very earliest convenience."

At that there was a knock on the front door and Holmes whisked himself to the window. "Here is the post-boy now." In seconds a missive had been sent up. Holmes ripped the envelope open to scan its contents.

"Excellent. The fair Diana has answered my summons in the affirmative and will be here at ten o'clock promptly tomorrow morning, and then we may see some resolution of affairs."

I was perplexed. In truth I had almost forgotten about the lady such had been the fearful whirligig of events over the previous week or so, but it was she who had sparked all of this into motion, and it was she to whom Holmes had, of professional necessity, to give an account.

"But Holmes, I realize you want to keep her apprized of events, and she must be anxious indeed to know how matters stand, but is it not a distraction? If you are now so seized of the need for urgency and have all of this devastating evidence in your possession, I should have thought it imperative to contact Mycroft or someone in authority."

"It may be anything but a distraction," he asserted meditatively. "Mycroft is a fine analyst, I acknowledge, second to none in my estimation, but he is too inclined to sit on matters, and may merely pass things on to others who will in turn merely sit on them, with the net result being torpor and inaction."

"Well, I suppose you know best," I said with weary resignation.

I fell to re-reading the account of Parminter's death, the report stating that the death was unexplained but not suspicious, a phrasing frequently employed by the press to signify probable suicide in cases where they were reluctant to state it before the outcome of the inquest.

"And I made another little jaunt yesterday," Holmes announced proudly. "Would you like to hear about it?"

"Very well."

"I attended a meeting of the European Fellowship League, no less, at the University of London."

"And?" I said distractedly, still engrossed in the newspaper. I had turned to Parminter's obituary.

"Our man Carstairs was there, giving a speech. He is, after all, the secretary of the body and its leading light."

My interest in what Holmes had to say was re-kindled.

"I posed as a journalist and asked a few questions at the end of his talk. I then managed to get to chat to the man himself afterwards over a few drinks. I think some of my questions unsettled him, and, perhaps, even annoyed him."

"So, you have actually met this sinister figure. In some form of disguise as usual, I take it?"

"Of course. I could not risk having him identify me."

"So then, what were your impressions of him?"

"A superficially charming and highly intelligent cove, but one from whom one instinctively recoils."

"Why so?"

"Something a little too shifty and oleaginous. A little too plausible and overly sincere."

"A typical politician then?" I mused.

"You may think so, Watson. I should say that our conversation ranged far and wide. It seems he is a highly erudite fellow acquainted with a variety of influential persons to whom he is not shy of offering advice, nor chary of receiving confidences."

"Just as might be expected. But did you learn anything of significance from him?"

"Depends upon what you mean by significance. He is all too crafty a character to let anything slip of an incriminating nature, no matter how much I tried to draw him out. But I was able to learn a few things from other members of his coterie present there. I gathered a lot of information about his friends and associates, and of the so-called Fellowship Union itself, which for all of its outward pretences of being a purely social and cultural body is really, I am convinced, a front organization for German diplomatic ambitions."

"Well, this is all quite fascinating, Holmes", I said trying to sound more enthusiastic than in truth I was. "But does it take you any further forward in your investigation?"

"Very possibly. As I said I was able to observe some of those with whom he socialized at the meeting and picked up snatches of conversation. I also followed him on foot from the meeting."

"And he didn't spot you?"

"No. I know how to trail a person without advertizing my presence. You are not the only one skilled in those arts, Watson," he added mischievously.

"*Touché*, Holmes. So where did he go?"

"He walked northwards toward Fitzrovia, which is where his London residence is located, and I kept a close watch on his house for the rest of the day to see who, if any, were his visitors."

"And?"

"I think I may have recognized one or two of his callers."

"So, was it profitable?"

"It helped me to flesh things out and gain a better picture of the whole operation. I think one can visualize much. He is able to use his contacts to gain information and, in the case of a few, such as Parminter, more or less blackmail them. Meanwhile the Count and his henchmen run a more secretive and hard-nosed operation, stealing documents and so on, or obtaining them via the likes of La Rothiere. It all builds up."

"Indeed. Did you mention Parminter to him?"

"No, that would have been too risky and would have set alarm bells ringing in his head, particularly if he were already aware of the man's death, which he may well have been."

"Yes, I see."

"So, that is the state of play, Watson. And now, unless you have any more queries, I will endeavour to complete my deciphering of this list. I am nearing a conclusion and may be able to complete the task within twenty-four hours."

"So, this whole wretched farrago may finally be drawing to a close?" I asked hopefully. "Have you uncovered any more names of distinction?"

"None as distinguished as that of Parminter, if that is what you mean."

"But what about this perfidious fellow at the Colonial Office? The man who passed the dossier to La Rothiere."

"He does not seem to rate a mention, but, as I said before, it may be because he is a very recent addition. And, incidentally, I made a few little enquiries at the Colonial Office yesterday about this personage, but such is the level of secrecy that has descended there now that I could not obtain any information about him."

"So, no more lives to destroy," I said acidly.

"I have already expressed my deepest regret for Parminter's death, though I cannot really say remorse. And, no, I am not going to seek any more direct encounters with any of these individuals whose names I have teased out, even if that were possible or desirable," he explained. "Except perhaps one more." He added reflectively.

"Then I shall leave you to it, but I can only say that I most sincerely hope matters will be resolved somehow in the very near future."

"I think you can depend upon it, Watson," he said firmly.

Chapter XXII

Surprizing News

I was left to my own devices for the remainder of the day, having no professional engagements, for which I was thankful because I would have been utterly unfit to discharge them conscientiously given my frenzied state of mind. I was still trying to recover from my battering at the hands of the fearful Nayland, not to say my psychological battering at the hands of fate. But this merely left me more time in which to brood, lament my misfortunes, and stare into the abyss of my future prospects. In the last couple of weeks, I had ridden a roller-coaster but one that had terminated by dumping me on the reefs of despair. I could not see where all of Holmes's machinations would lead, and in the meantime I could almost sense the fell hand of the law upon my shoulder at any moment. And, of course, I grieved endlessly for my dear Molly.

Late that afternoon there came loud knocks upon the door which I recognized from Holmes's previous description to be those of Lestrade. We were both still in the drawing room, Holmes bent over his studies and I still listlessly perusing my copy of *The Telegraph* from that morning. I thought to impress Holmes.

"Sounds like Lestrade," I ventured.

"Excellent, Watson, you are learning very fast."

Sure enough the lean policeman and his sergeant were soon brought up and admitted to our chambers. Holmes was still labouring upon his precious list with, he insisted, many pages still to be deciphered but with Lestrade's entry imminent he hastily covered up the documents, spreading his newspaper over them, and strolled over to the fireplace to greet the officer with a casual affability.

"Lestrade. Always a pleasure. How may I assist you?"

"Actually, Mr. Holmes, it was Dr. Watson I came to see," he announced portentously, and turned his gaze fully towards me. His posture stiffened markedly with Parker by his side emulating his superior.

It was the moment I had come to dread, but which I feared must surely arrive. Evidently proof had now emerged of my presence in Blackheath, but of how much more? Did they know the full story, or were they merely acting upon suspicion? I resigned myself to my fate, but wondered how I should handle the situation so as to minimize the damage to Holmes's plans. My best course I resolved to was to exercize my right to remain silent. I rose slowly from my chair to meet the policeman's glare. I could see Holmes out of the corner of my eye, tensing almost as much as I was myself.

"Yes, Dr. Watson," Lestrade pronounced. "I believe you were present ..." I tried to control a sharp intake of breath, "... at Shepherd's Bush when the body of this man Kellmann was discovered the other day."

"Yes, you surely know that, Inspector," I said weakly.

"Yes, well in the light of that we shall require a statement from you as well as from Mr. Holmes. So, if you would be good enough to make an appointment at Scotland Yard in the next few days, we would be much obliged."

"Er, is that all?" I said, trying to control my relief.

"Yes, well did you expect something else?" he queried.

"No, no, not at all. No, I should be only too happy to co-operate with your enquires, Inspector," I said as I sank back into my armchair.

"Splendid." He turned his attentions back toward Holmes and the room in general.

"Yes, gentlemen, it seems that this Kellmann business has really disturbed a hornet's nest. You were right, Mr. Holmes, about those documents found on and about his person being of interest to the top ranks. Got called up to the Commissioner's office first thing yesterday to give a fuller account of the case. He was with somebody from the Home Office and they were both very keen to know how I had uncovered everything. Got a lot of praise for my sharp work," he said rocking back and forth on the balls of his feet, and glancing in Parker's direction to seek corroboration of his little triumph, though, to Lestrade's evident irritation, the latter was blankly unresponsive. "Yes, got quite a pat on the back. Of course, I was careful to acknowledge your role in the affair, Mr. Holmes. I couldn't take all of the credit."

"No, of course not. It was very good of you to mention my own small part in the matter." Holmes said amiably.

"Unfortunately, the case has now been taken out of my hands and passed on to some specialist people, but the Commissioner was kind enough to say that I should probably get a commendation for my efforts, all the same."

"I am sure it is thoroughly deserved." Holmes said, beaming.

Lestrade's fulsome self regard faltered slightly.

"But I am still slightly puzzled as to how you got on to all of this in the first place, Mr. Holmes?"

"It is a very long story, my dear Inspector."

"Did you know what these documents were?"

"I had an inkling. But I will be able to explain it all when I come to make my statement."

"Yes, yes, of course. I quite understand. Well, I must be off now if you will excuse me. Been given another big case to deal with. Yes, I am quite the sought-after man down at the Yard now."

"As indeed you should be." Holmes said.

Holmes and I both sought to suppress sniggers as Lestrade moved toward the door, but just as he was leaving, with his hand on the doorknob, he turned back.

"Oh, yes, there was one other thing."

"Yes, Lestrade?" Holmes queried.

"You remember I mentioned to you about that poor woman fished out of the Thames?"

Having been spared one torment I found I was to be starkly reminded of another.

"And?" said Holmes.

"Well, you might be interested that we've been able to make an identification of the body." I groaned inwardly.

"Yes, apparently it was an Annie Rafferty."

I leapt from my chair.

"Annie Rafferty." I cried, almost shrieking the name as I stared at the Inspector in disbelief.

"Yes, do you know her then?" Lestrade queried, looking at me intently.

"No, I've never heard of her in my life." I said, desperately trying to conceal the overmastering joy in my voice.

"You seem to be getting very excited over the death of a woman of which you've never heard, if you don't mind me saying, Doctor."

"I, I ... no, it's just that I thought for a moment you said ... I thought you said **Abbie** Rafferty. I knew someone of that name, daughter of an old army friend." I stammered, improvising desperately. I could sense Holmes willing me to be silent.

"No, no, definitely **Annie** Rafferty." Lestrade re-affirmed. "She was a common prostitute operating in the Mile End district who had been reported missing a few days before. It's a ghastly business but it sometimes happens to these women of the night. They have little protection, and there are some crazed and murderous types out there." Lestrade said woefully.

"Oh, well thank God." I breathed. "I mean, of course, one is deeply sorry for the death of this other woman, but you understand."

"Yes, of course, I regret if I have caused you any alarm, Doctor."

"But are you completely sure it is this Rafferty woman?"

"Oh yes, no doubt about it. She was identified by one of her associates. A very distressing scene, I believe."

"But the tattoo you mentioned before?" I cried.

"Hmm? Oh, yes, the tattoo. Well apparently a lot of them have tattoos. Quite the fashion it seems amongst that class of woman, and that particular tattoo is very popular, or so I am told. Your friend's daughter didn't have one did she?" Lestrade asked in bafflement.

"Oh, er, well yes I believe she did."

"Good heavens. A lady of repute? What is the world coming to? Smoking, drinking, having tattoos done. They'll be getting the vote next." He shook his head in mock disapproval. Suddenly a light dawned above the man's head. "Is that why you got so upset the other day at Shepherd's Bush, because I mentioned the tattoo, and you thought it might be this other Miss Rafferty of yours?"

"Oh, no, no Inspector. It was, as Holmes said, merely a minor ailment of mine, brought on by overwork. No, I could not have believed it was Abbie at the time for she rarely if ever travels to London, but then when you mentioned the name just now, and I misheard ..."

"Yes, I see. Well, as I say, I am sorry if I worried you, Doctor. And if you would remember to make that statement down at the Yard."

"Yes, yes, of course."

Holmes swiftly interceded, seeing that I could scarcely contain my state of excitement. "Let me show you down, Lestrade." He cast a fleeting glance in my direction, tacitly bidding me to say no more and the three of them disappeared from the room and down the staircase. I paced about the room dementedly, crying and laughing at the same time, as I saw Lestrade and Parker depart on foot down the street. Holmes swiftly reappeared in the room, the wind now clearly in his sails.

"This is excellent news, Watson," he said.

"It is wonderful news!" I erupted.

"Oh, yes, of course. You mean about the deceased woman not being your Molly. Yes, yes, I am delighted for you. But I meant that the powers that be have sat up and taken notice of these documents, and with any luck they will find their way back to the Colonial Office from whence they came. I have at least accomplished the first part of my strategy," he said pacing about the room and pummelling his fist into the palm of his hand, a characteristic gesture of his as he contemplated further action.

I emitted a snort at his cavalier approach to death and to my own travails, which he picked up and took as a reproach. He made amends by rushing over to clasp me by the shoulders.

"I do apologize for being so insensitive, my dear fellow. I really am so very happy for you."

"Thank you, Holmes, but I can hardly believe it," I sobbed with joy and collapsed into my chair.

"But did it never occur to you that there might be another female with that tattoo, or one very similar?" he said.

"Why should it? It never occurred to you."

"To be frank it did, but I was reluctant to say anything so as not to raise your hopes."

"But you urged me not to view the body."

"Yes, I did. I feared that if you, or I for that matter, had made an appointment at the mortuary it would have led to raised eyebrows at the Yard, and questions from Lestrade or a colleague of his that I would not have cared to answer. So, you must blame me for prolonging your agony. Once again I must offer you the sincerest of apologies."

"I do not blame you, Holmes. At least not for that."

"No, but you do blame me for getting both you and she snarled up in the cogs and wheels of my schemes, and you are right to do so."

"No, Holmes, I blame only myself."

"It is good of you to try to spare my feelings. I don't deserve such careful treatment. But I beg of you not to raise your hopes too high. It was not she they found in the river, but we still do not know of her true fate."

"She may still be dead?" I said voicing the real meaning of his words.

"It is pointless to speculate." He poured a drink for the two of us. "Let us at least celebrate a small mercy."

I gulped down the brandy.

"So, what now? I must try to find her. Nayland said something of a place she had been taken, but I cannot remember for the life of me if he said where it was." I paused as the full implications sank in. "So, he was telling the truth when he said she was still alive! I have killed an innocent man."

"Innocent! You have rid the world of a foul and pestilential murderer, who may just have been guilty of one murder fewer than we thought. And he would surely have killed her anyway, or had her killed, once he had got the information he wanted from her. There is no way they would allow her to live and tell the world what has happened. No, there is nought for you to grieve over in that respect."

"I suppose not, but then that means that if she is being held captive and they manage to extract something from her then she in the greatest peril. It is all the more imperative I find her."

"But there is no way you would be able to locate her. You could search from now until kingdom come and not discover her whereabouts."

"I must at least try."

"Where would you start? No, no. Think rationally, man."

"But the longer this goes on the more likely she is to be murdered. She may talk at any time and then her usefulness is at an end, as you just said yourself. We must tell Lestrade all and set a search in motion. With the resources of the Metropolitan force they must surely stand a good chance." I implored.

"No, no! If the Nayland mob were to get any idea the police were about to swoop that would merely sign her death warrant for they could never allow her to give evidence against them. It is all the more vital I try to draw matters to a close my own way."

"How?"

"I have already said that I now have an interview with our client first thing tomorrow."

"But that is an irrelevance!"

"I think far from it," he declared cryptically as he fixed his gaze into the middle distance.

Chapter XXIII

Endgame

The following morning, I arose with a sense of hope such as I had not experienced since the outset of this affair, a huge weight of guilt and remorse lifted from my shoulders after the revelations of the previous day. A renewed sense of purpose was coursing through my veins, though I still was still deeply troubled and would not permit myself too much rejoicing which could easily prove all too horribly premature. I eagerly anticipated, also, the expected arrival of Lady Diana for her interview, and hoped that once that aspect of the matter had been disposed of Holmes could concentrate on the really vital elements.

At breakfast Holmes seemed very much on edge. He was occupying himself with yet further research into his list, probably nearing the completion of his deciphering of names and data, and then he engaged in a sedulous arrangement of papers into envelopes. Mrs. Hudson's housemaid scurried about removing the remnants of breakfast from the table and lighting the fire, a dire necessity given the unrelenting chilliness.

Holmes, I imagined, was finalizing his conclusions, presumably for presentation to the lady, though how much he was prepared to divulge to her I could not be sure. He was certainly taking a great deal of care over everything and was, I sensed, more nervous about the forthcoming encounter than I would have expected. I imagined, though, that she would be delighted, or at the very least immensely relieved, to know that Holmes had, effectively, found a means to exonerate her of blame for Kellmann's demise, and had provided an alternative, and wholly plausible, explanation for the death which would be satisfactory to the police.

And would Holmes explain more to her? Again, probably not, if she were content with the knowledge that she would not be exposed in any way. I did not envisage that Holmes would apprize her of any of the other dramatic occurrences and revelations which had unfolded themselves, none of which were of any real relevance to her situation. It would, I felt, be Holmes's intention to leave her in the dark about the espionage business and simply to explain that he had satisfied the police that Kellmann's death was the result of a gangland feud or some such.

"It is nearly ten o'clock, and I think I hear her carriage wheels now. I trust you will be happy to sit in on our little *tete-a-tete*."

"Verily." I was utterly drained mentally, physically, and spiritually, and yet I knew I must stick to Holmes's side.

My friend was correct and within a few minutes her card had been sent up and the lady herself glided through our portals once more, though on this occasion she was on her own. I had forgotten how beautiful a creature she was, and today she shone as brilliantly as on our first meeting, radiating a demure elegance and sophistication. And yet her attractions were very largely lost on me in my over-wrought state.

She greeted Holmes and me with an air of pleasant, almost bright, expectation, very different I sensed from the nervous agitation she had manifested only a couple of weeks before. Holmes motioned her to a seat near the fireplace where she would be facing the hard winter sun now streaming in through the far window. She slipped off her coat, and draped it carefully over the back of the armchair and then sat squarely forward with an air of eager anticipation, her hands folded in front of her around her handbag, her face alert and receptive. She wore a high-necked white satin blouse, held at the throat by a copper brooch, the flounce of her balloon sleeves accentuating the breadth of her shoulders and a long flowing cotton skirt that subtly delineated the contours of her figure.

I stoked the fire a little to stir its embers into more vivid life. Holmes broke the silence. "You are unattended by your maid today, milady?"

"Unfortunately, Elsie is indisposed and there was no-one else, but my man Meadows is in the coach downstairs."

"Oh, I see. Well, that is most unfortunate. Please convey my best wishes to her for a speedy recovery from whatever ailment she is suffering." Holmes carefully planted himself in the seat opposite her and slowly and deliberately lit one of his Turkish cigarettes which he tended to favour on the occasion of the more gravitous of his interviews. I settled into a hard-backed chair at the side of the room, presuming that Holmes would wish me to be witness to any proceedings without projecting myself into them. "I hope you do not object if I smoke?" he enquired of her.

"No, of course not, Mr. Holmes, these are your rooms and you are surely free to do as you please."

"I am obliged. Oh, I do apologize for my inattentiveness. Would you care for some refreshment?" It was unusual for Holmes to be the one to consider these niceties.

"Thank you, no. I have already breakfasted and would prefer to get down to affairs as quickly as possible. I should say that I am obliged to you, Mr. Holmes, for having kept me so well informed of how the case has been progressing up to this point for I have read all of your telegrams and letters most avidly. And when I received your invitation this morning, accelerated from tomorrow, I was only too ready to comply, assuming that you must have news of a compelling nature. I trust you have something very noteworthy to report and can only hope that it is not too unfavourable to my situation?" she queried with a suppressed agitation.

"Indeed, I do. First of all, let me relieve you of any doubt as to the fate of our mutual friend, Herr Kellman. He, alas, is deceased, as you so vividly described to us, and his body now taken possession of by the authorities."

The lady looked both shocked and relieved at the same time, clasping her cheeks in her hands as she listened to this.

"Well, that is distressing news, but it does at least settle the matter and put my mind at rest in one respect."

"You may also be relieved to hear that I made no mention of your participation in the manner of his death."

"Oh, thank you, Mr. Holmes. Words cannot express the extent of my gratitude." she said, relaxing markedly.

"But there are quite a number of other points arising that you may be interested to hear about."

"Why yes, I should be most intrigued to know as much as you are able to tell me." she said, with what I felt was a slight uncertainty creeping into her voice.

Holmes settled back in his chair.

"You may be interested to know that I paid a visit, after hours so to speak, to Count von Runstedt's townhouse, and though I shall not go into detail upon the means, I was able to obtain some documents in his safe-keeping. The bulk of these have been handed to the authorities also." The lady now looked distinctly fazed.

"That is extraordinary, Mr. Holmes, but why on earth would you have done so? I never suggested anything of that nature." She looked crestfallen and even a little annoyed.

"You must pardon me, 'Milady', for I was not aware that I required your authorization, but I can assure you I had my reasons which will become apparent in the further course of my account. Perhaps you will permit me to continue without interruption, if you would be so kind." he said smoothly.

"Why yes, as you desire." The lady looked abashed and settled back uneasily in her chair. I was dismayed that Holmes was being so candid with her, and that he was apparently willing to reveal so much to her of the background to the case.

"There was much in these documents, some of peripheral interest, but one document in particular struck me most forcefully."

"Please continue."

"It was evidently a coded sheet which I could not at first decipher, being exclusively numerical in character, but strenuous mental labours finally brought their reward, and I was able to make a complete translation."

The lady looked even more startled.

"I have it here." He produced two batches of sheets from the foolscap envelope on the table beside him. "This is the original document, and this is my translation of it."

"May I see them?" she leant forwards excitedly.

"In a moment, but perhaps I should first add my gloss to them. The sheet appears to contain a list of names, and I suppose them to be agents run by our mutual acquaintance, the Count von Runstedt, together with other information pertaining thereto, including means of communication and what I presume to be codenames." He paused to take a long pull at his cigarette, sending its smoke spiralling into the air.

"Agents?" quizzed the lady. She looked distinctly discomforted. "Agents of what, pray?"

"Agents of an organization run by the Count, which goes by the soubriquet of *Die Bund der Schwarzen Adler*. Perhaps you are familiar with it?"

"But why on earth should you suppose me to be familiar with such a bizarrely named organization? Is it an ornithological society or something of that nature? Really, this is quite mystifying, Mr. Holmes. I wish you would come to the point."

"Rest assured that I shall. Several of the names that I was able to decrypt were already familiar to me, confirming many of the suspicions acquired in the course of previous investigations of mine into a variety of criminal activities. Several of these names occupy quite exalted positions in spheres of government and business. There is, for example, Herr Klaus Stoltenberg, the well-known armaments tycoon, and Signor Luigi Massini, the Italian financier, and several others. And there was that of Sir William Parminter, so very recently deceased, one must presume by his own hand. But I will not bore you with a complete list of all the names."

I was amazed that Holmes was so keen to reveal such highly delicate information to her; information that he was apparently reluctant to disclose to official sources. He continued urbanely.

"There was, however, one name on that list that did come as a surprize to me."

"And whose was that?" she said uneasily.

"It was yours, Lady Diana."

There was a lengthy silence.

I nearly rose from my seat in astonishment. This was not the *denouement* to the affair I had expected.

The lady's composure scarcely faltered, but she seemed temporarily unable to speak. The two principals seemed locked in position with no flicker of emotion registered by either.

"You appear to have the drop on me, Mr. Holmes. What do you make of this revelation?"

"I have not quite come to a conclusion in that regard. But there are a number of other conclusions that I have drawn. Would you care to hear them?"

"You have my rapt attention, sir." she said after a slight pause. Her manner seemed to me to have changed subtly, but perceptibly, from eager-eyed contentment to something cooler, more detached, and almost steely.

"There were many aspects of this case that troubled me from the outset, and the deeper I delved into them the more troubling they became.

"First of all, there was the matter of Herr Kellmann's body. It was evident from the very detailed examination that I undertook of the corpse that the violence upon his person was far greater than would have been inflicted by mere concussion from banging his head upon a table and from the relatively light tussle between he and you. Bruises were extensive over much of his body, consistent with a prolonged and very violent struggle, and the infliction of the fatal blow to the head may have come merely as a *coup de grace*. Moreover, the angle, nature, and extent of the head wound was not consistent with being struck a glancing blow by the corner of the table, but rather the product of being struck a sharp blow from a blunt instrument. On the other hand, despite the extensive bruising generally, there was a notable absence of bruises about the shinbones that might have been expected on the basis of your description of you kicking at them. And though there were deep scratches upon his face that were consistent with you having clawed at him, as you recounted, the marks were not those that would have been inflicted by fingernails. There was no sign of the calcium deposits I might have expected to have been left by finger-nails. Rather there were indications that the marks were caused by a serrated blade of some description, made perhaps to simulate scratch-marks.

"And the posture of his body was so strange and awkward as to suggest it had been placed there, a theory supported also by the fact that his coat had been buttoned up incorrectly as if he had been dressed very hastily by other hands, and there were no keys upon his person, as might have been expected. I found his keys in a drawer at his lodging. Odd that he should leave the house without them."

I sat tantalized by this unfolding melodrama, so different from the more prosaic business I had been expecting from this interview. I quite forgot about my own travails for the moment. Holmes was far from finished.

"But these are not the least of the curiosities. I carried out a very detailed forensic examination of various specimens of blood, including those from his head wound and from the surrounding area. Extraordinarily, the blood taken from the skull was of a different type from that on the floorboards beside him. To be particular the latter was non-human blood! On the other hand, there were traces of blood on the staircase and the downstairs rooms which did match those from the skull. It seems, I think you will agree, that we had ourselves a very lively corpse indeed; one that walked downstairs and then back up again before expiring and gave itself a blood transfusion of a different, non-human type of blood. Remarkable wouldn't you say?

"Then there was the matter of the dispersal of the dried blood deposits in the vicinity of his head. These were not consistent in pattern and range with what might be expected on the basis of scientific study of such phenomena, but seem rather to have been configured somewhat randomly."

I had half risen from my chair in astonishment at Holmes's words. But the lady sat impassively; not a flicker disturbed her *sang froid*. Holmes, however, was still not finished.

"I made a very thorough examination of Herr Kellmann's lodgings and made further discoveries. There was evidence of much cleaning and scrubbing having gone on there, and bits of carpet were missing, perhaps because they contained traces of blood, and yet despite all of this there were definite residues of blood on pieces of furniture and even on the curtains. And as I mentioned I found his keys in a drawer there. This led me to the belief that our friend met his end, not at Oil Drum Lane, but at Acol Road, and that, for some inexplicable reason, he had been moved from one location to the other. But whoever did the moving encountered a snag. There was no blood on the floor next to the body as would have been expected had the death occurred there and then. Perhaps a rat or two was slaughtered for the purposes of supplying the missing blood."

"Holmes, surely you are not suggesting ..." I had risen half to my feet, but Holmes waved aside my expostulation with a flick of the hand that commanded my silence. I resumed my seat. He proceeded impassively with his analysis.

"And, turning to wider perspectives, there was always something rather implausible about the whole account you gave. I have made enquiries of those with an insider's knowledge of high society, and it is evident that you are an independent lady with, shall we say, considerable breadth of experience. You move in Bohemian circles in which sexual adventurism is taken for granted. I do not really imagine that the revelation of an affair with our noble friend would have caused any embarrassment to you, or serious damage to your reputation, or certainly none that you could not have brushed aside with contempt. And, as for the Count wishing to keep it a secret because of his engagement. Baloney! Enquiries of my correspondents abroad confirm that he is not, and never has, been engaged. And this tale of sorrow and woe was so theatrically presented to us by you and your maid, if indeed she is your maid, which I doubt! The damsel in distress sobbing into her handkerchief? No, no! It simply did not fit. Here was a lady of a very different mettle."

Our client continued to sit with an air of imperturbability before this onslaught upon her character. Not so much as a flicker of discomposure escaped her.

"And then we come to this business of blackmail. Kellmann may well have been coercing you in some way, but over something rather different. Now I find your name amongst this list of agents, and it is not difficult to ascertain the reason for all the coercion. There was the recent resignation, in clouded circumstances, of Sir Henry Tremayne, late of the Admiralty, a man known to have been associated with you, and it becomes easy to see cause and effect. You are, I infer, a purveyor of secrets, wafted from pillow to pillow, if you will pardon the expression. Perhaps Kellmann was threatening to expose you as a traitor. To judge by his circumstances, he may have been in need of money, which you possess in no small quantity.

"Whatever the cause, you decided he must be disposed of. You, or you and your confederates, perhaps this bulky Meadows fellow, went to his house and did away with him, bludgeoning him to death. But things went wrong. You were seen by the landlady, the eagle-eyed Mrs. Agnes Grimthorpe, despite your attempt to remain in the shadows. What were you to do? His death would be bound to come to light and you would be implicated, and probably identified as having been present at the scene. What more would then come out, of treachery, murder, and who knows what else?

"So, you devized this charade. You moved his body elsewhere and then fabricated this cock and bull story to exonerate yourself. And who better to confirm your story than myself, the great detective, the soubriquet which, in all modesty, I believe some have bestowed upon me."

There was another and much longer hiatus, an unbearable silence pervading the room. I could not imagine what was going to happen now. I looked from one to the other to see who would crack first. The lady rose very slowly and stood glacier-like before him. He rose to meet her and the two stood opposite each other like gunslingers locked in a duel. I looked again from one to the other in a state of enthralled anticipation. She seemed unable to contain herself any longer. Her eyes were now ablaze, a fierce, flint-like cast upon her lovely face. The three of us stood there motionless for what seemed like an age. The only sounds were the ticking of the clock, the faint rattle of carriages in the road, and the spattering of rain upon the window pane.

But when it finally came her response was even and well modulated.

"You are a very clever man, Mr. Holmes. Some of us doubted your brilliance, but I never underestimated you for a second." She said smoothly. Surely, she was not about to confess to the truth of these allegations? "You have spun an ingenious theory, but even you do not know the all of the facts. You have told me a good story. Now, if you have the time and the patience, I will tell you another, an even better one. You hold a strong hand but I may yet trump your ace."

Holmes gazed at her intently, and after a brief pause waved her to be seated again, and we all three resumed our positions in readiness for the second round of this contest. It was turning into a game of cat and mouse such as I had not experienced before in these quarters.

"May I trouble you for one of your excellent, rather aromatic cigarettes, Mr. Holmes? Turkish are they not?"

It was highly irregular, in my not inconsiderable experience, for a lady to smoke, certainly not for one of her high station, but I sprang over to oblige, proffering Holmes's silver box and lighting a match for her. "You are very kind, Dr. Watson." She leant back in her chair, and drew languidly upon the Murad before commencing her narrative.

"It was foolish of us … of me … to try to deceive you. I must take much of the blame. But matters are not quite as you suppose."

She drew again on the Murad, and exhaled very slowly before resuming.

"I suppose I should start at the beginning, which I find is usually the best place, though it is not always easy to say where the beginning is." She paused again, rolling the cigarette in her long fingers and contemplating the middle distance. "There is a branch of the Home Office dedicated to the surveillance of suspected foreign agents and saboteurs. You may be aware of its existence, though it has never been officially acknowledged, its funding being concealed in government accounts. Its offices are located just south of the river and it is known colloquially, in a sort of jest I suppose, as the Oval. It is headed by a distinguished figure known simply as 'Z' whose identity I cannot reveal."

Holmes and I had settled back in our chairs in enthralled silence.

"I was recruited to their service ... no, that is too formal an expression ... it would perhaps be more accurate to say I was invited to assist them. This was some time ago. I will not go into all the details, but suffice it to say the powers that be knew of the Count's covert activities, and of my one-time friendship with him.

"The fellows at the Oval had gained knowledge of a network of agents operating from Berlin and when Wolfi, the Count, moved to England two years ago he was already strongly suspected of being at the head of this network, and knowing, as they did, of my former relations with him, I was prevailed upon by a mutual acquaintance of Colonel ... of 'Z' to renew my friendship and to seek to garner what evidence I could of the man and his activities. I succeeded very well, as I described, and soon gained his confidence, and I may say became the object of his ardour. We resumed our former romance, but now with a greater intensity ... I, now being freed from the constraints formerly imposed upon me."

I marvelled at how free of embarrassment the lady appeared to be in connection with such intimate matters.

"I learnt a great deal about his associations, though, naturally, he never suspected me of having any ulterior motive, and was therefore slightly careless in concealing matters from my attention. I may say that the flow of information was not all one way. Pillow talk can travel in both directions you know, Mr. Holmes. The Oval carefully fostered the erroneous impression of my liaison with a senior figure in the Admiralty, Sir Henry, to whom you alluded, which gave credence to much of the fictitious material I divulged to him. Things are, as I said, not how they seem in the world of espionage and diplomacy. It is a chamber of distorting mirrors. We were perhaps all too successful in passing on misinformation, and we now fear that *Wilhelmstrasse* has discovered some of it to be false or, at any rate, find it all a bit too good to be true. Perhaps that is the reason for his being summoned back to Berlin, to explain inconsistencies. But we cannot be sure."

Holmes and I were electrified by this revised narrative. Holmes's demeanour had lost some its self assurance. He had finished his cigarette, and now reached for the Meerschaum and the tobacco pouch. He slowly filled his pipe as he listened, never averting his eyes from the lady.

"I fear that, like you, I exceeded my brief. I was informed a few weeks ago that very important documents had gone missing from the Colonial Office, and it was deemed highly likely that the Count and his organization were behind the theft. I was requested to try to retrieve them, or at the very least attempt to discover their whereabouts. Previous, rather desultory, efforts on my part to locate his safe had been unsuccessful, but I was now urged to make a renewed effort given the urgency of the situation. So, one day I contrived to invite myself into his house when I knew him to be absent, and only the servants were in residence. I began to search his office seeking for the safe, the location of which you seem to have discovered by some guileful means, Mr. Holmes. But I was caught *in flagrante* by the wretched Kellman, who had descended upon the house unexpectedly and unbeknownst to me. He came upon me in the act of riffling through the drawers of the Count's office desk. He threatened me with exposure to his master and said that he knew all along I was working for London, or at least suspected it, and now this confirmed his suspicions. I protested my innocence but he would have none of it.

"But then his manner softened, and he said that he was prepared to overlook it in return for money. I agreed, or pretended to. He also made a clumsy attempt to seduce me, which I hurled back in his face. I played for time and said that I would consider his proposition. I reported back to the Oval. We pondered what to do. We did not want to jeopardize the great asset we had in my intimacy with the Count. We thought that if Kellmann was trying to milk me then perhaps he could be persuaded to work for us if a sufficiently generous offer were to be made.

"Consequently, it was arranged for a pair of senior officials to go to see him. We already knew his address from our investigations. It was felt desirable for me to be present, or he might not be very welcoming to such an intrusion upon his privacy. Our little delegation duly proceeded to his Kilburn rooms that Saturday evening and, after a rather awkward introduction he agreed to entertain us. We settled down and opened negotiations, I, perforce, admitting to be in governmental employ. Eventually, I left the house, my presence no longer necessary, with Kellmann and our men still there engaged in intense discussion and barter. However, I was careless enough to allow my face to be seen by that busybody of a landlady as I descended the stairs, having omitted to put up my hood in time, but I did not think it would matter."

Here she faltered slightly from her hitherto calm and unflinching account.

"I subsequently learned that Kellmann had been killed, though I truly do not know the precise circumstances. Whether because they could not agree terms and matters suddenly flared into open confrontation, or it was decided he was too great a liability and had to be put out of the picture. You must pardon my crudity of expression, but that is how things stand in our line of business. I am not absolutely certain of how it happened, but I had no hand in it, of that I swear, Mr. Holmes. But we at the Oval were in a quandary. We did not want to squander the advantage we had, and yet if his body turned up it would be obvious to the Count and his political masters what had happened, and our whole operation would be blown asunder."

Holmes and I were listening ever more intently to this narration. I found it hard to credit the veracity of it all but followed Holmes's lead in keeping my counsel so as not to disturb the flow of the lady's account. Holmes was clearly processing this blizzard of information at some deep level of his analytical brain. She continued calmly and unhurriedly, drawing casually upon her cigarette all the while.

"We devized a scheme to move his body, which would in any event have been taken to our safe house at Shepherd's Bush for the time being, pending a plan of action. The last thing we wanted was for Berlin to suspect what had happened … the repercussions for our own agents in Germany would have been too awful to contemplate if it were believed that we had had one of their own murdered. And with diplomatic relations at such a pivotal juncture. We, or rather I, came up with the idea of dressing it up, if you will, as a blackmailing business concerning the Count and myself. Matters were so arranged to look as if Kellmann had met his death at the safe house, though clearly our chaps made a blundering mess of setting things up. I hope you will forgive me, Mr. Holmes, if I say that I congratulated myself upon the ingenuity of the scheme, but we should have realized that you would instantly see through our little pantomime."

Holmes permitted himself an almost imperceptible nod of the head in recognition of her compliment, and continued to draw imperturbably upon his Meerschaum, smoke now billowing up so as almost to obscure his features from his interlocutor.

"But we knew that if the police were to investigate and come to the desired conclusions it was unlikely to be credited by our adversaries who would surely interpret the whole thing as a fabrication by the authorities to conceal the sordid truth. It was surely preferable for it to be investigated and confirmed by somebody from outside conventional circles. Somebody who could not be accused of complicity in government intrigue. Somebody such as yourself, Mr. Holmes.

"I say, these Murads are frightfully good. May I have another?" She cast a look in my direction since Holmes was immobility personified. I leapt to my feet to do service once more.

"Thank you, Dr. Watson.

"In truth, we were not sure how you would react. But we already knew of your keen interest in the activities of the Count and his organization and decided we might succeed in harnessing it to our own purposes. Perhaps you would be able to confirm our manufactured account, and I would decide to confess to the police at the last, with you to confirm my account, and no charges be brought. Or, preferably, you might take the initiative and conduct enquiries in, er, your own inimitable way, as indeed you appear to have done."

At this the hint of a wry smile played upon Holmes's lips.

"The point is that as an independent actor we knew that you were free to conduct enquiries in ways that would have been debarred to us at the Oval, for the possibility of one of our number being caught in an illegal act would have been disastrous to our cause. I must admit, though, that we did not expect you to go to quite the lengths to which, evidently, you have. I had not yet heard of the theft of documents from the Count but if it is true then it is indeed a brilliant coup and likely that you have rendered a great service, though we cannot be sure of the outcome at this stage. It seems also, from what I have heard from colleagues, that the object of our quest, the purloined government papers have turned up in an unexpected quarter. If so then the nation owes you a great debt of gratitude."

Holmes maintained his silence. But every new revelation struck me like a thunderbolt. The lady sailed on.

"I must make another confession to you, namely that we had kept you under surveillance, or tried to, though I hear that you gave our man Sandham, though you know him as Beecham, rather a rough ride and we largely abandoned it after that. You certainly led us a merry dance. Fortunately, we always equip our men with false papers to prevent identification in case they are rumbled.

"And we did, as a matter of routine, keep the safe house under constant observation. You may have noted the presence of a coal merchant's dray. We also have one or two hansom cabs and their drivers at our service to follow those of interest to us. It was not always possible in your case as you were sometimes too quick on your feet, and you gave us the slip too many times."

She turned her attention towards me. "Amusingly, Dr. Watson, you found yourself the fare of one of our operatives for we had naturally also maintained a watch on Wessex Gardens, and it seems that another of our cabbies found himself giving a ride to you all the way to Blackheath. It is not clear to us what you were going to do there, Doctor, for it seems our man was unable to follow on foot after he had set you down, but judging by your appearance I am assuming that matters came to a desperate pass with Frank Nayland. The fellows at the Oval do not tell me much, officially, other than what they think I need to know, but I can usually wheedle a lot more out of them if I want to. But you should not be too concerned about whatever may have occurred, Doctor. Our man's lips are, I assure you, sealed," she said, favouring me with a re-assuring smile.

I was staggered by these further disclosures of hers, and had to engage in a frantic mental exercize of re-evaluating events so recently past.

"And so we presented ourselves to you, Elsie and I, or should I say my old friend, Sarah, from my days in the theatre. Quite a stellar performance in a supporting role wouldn't you say, though I think she overdid it just a mite? If the day comes when they give awards for acting she will surely merit a nomination.

"As to this list of yours, there may be many reasons for my appearance on it, if indeed one is to accept the accuracy of your translation, but of one thing I can assure you. I am not a traitor, nor a murderer, and have never acted against the interests of our country.

"So, there you have it, Mr. Holmes."

She leant back in her chair with an air of finality and a raised eyebrow, scrutinizing Holmes intently to gauge his reaction to this sensational account. And yet Holmes's face, shrouded in the fumes from his pipe, still gave no clue as to his feelings, though there was a tautness about his features. He drew very hard upon his Meerschaum, but no response was immediately forthcoming. At length he sprang sharply from his chair and strode over to the window. The lady and I watched his movements, transfixed. After a while of peering outside he turned back to face her, and held forth in a rather subdued mode.

"A very intriguing and colourful account and, more or less, the one I expected you to offer up in your defence." He said neutrally. He resumed his contemplative silence and drew again upon his Meerschaum whilst continuing to gaze at the street outside. Neither Lady Diana nor I presumed to interrupt this reverie. At length he spoke again. "I may say also that I am prepared to accept it. I had speculated upon the possibility of you being, as I believe they say in the lingo of the espionage world in which you purport to move, a double agent, and decided to test you out."

"And have I passed your test?"

"It depends upon the means of examination," he said smoothly. His manner darkened. "But I may say that I do not take kindly to being treated as some sort of a cat's-paw in these games of yours. I am not to be played upon as an instrument, yet you would seem to know my stops and sound me from my lowest note to the top of my compass. Had you been frank at the outset we would not have needed to play out this ridiculous melodrama, though I suppose it has at least provided some entertainment value."

"I must offer my sincerest apologies to you, Mr. Holmes. In retrospect we were wholly wrong not to let you into our complete confidence in these matters right from the outset. But I am sure you understand the delicacy of our position." She said persuasively.

Another hiatus, the third, and even longer than the previous. I tried desperately to read Holmes's face but not the merest twitch offered a clue. But at length the lady broke the silence.

"So, you have two stories, Mr. Holmes. Which do you prefer?"

"It is not a question of preference, madam, but of truth and falsity."

"And how do you decide upon truth, may I enquire?"

"By reference to the facts, madam."

"But you have so many facts to choose from. Which are you going to select?"

"Those that fit the case."

"But fitness is surely subjective. So, is it not, after all, a matter of preference?"

"Do not presume to fence with me, madam. I accepted your brief and I have fulfilled my commission. Let that be an end to the affair."

"So, may I ask what you intend to do now, Mr. Holmes? What of this ciphered list of yours and its translation?"

A further pause.

"You engaged me to act for you in this matter and I accepted your commission. It has produced what it has, and I offer you the fruits of my research." He moved back to his chair and took up the papers from the side-table. "In addition to the list and my gloss upon it, I have been able to procure a set of photographic plates showing persons entering and leaving premises in Islington of which I have unimpeachable evidence to be a safe house of this organization. You and your colleagues may find it a mine of useful information. I have documented all of my research in a further paper which you will find enclosed together with the photographs. You and your colleagues at this Oval place of yours may wish to scrutinize them, but I would advize you to make haste for members of this organization may prove to be very swift on their feet.

"A few other things. I have included also a signed statement from the late Sir William Parminter, detailing his involvement with one of the leading conspirators, Jeremy Carstairs, the occupant of this safe-house. I had promised not to reveal it to anyone, but his death has altered the complexion of matters in that regard, and I feel released from that pledge, though I would earnestly desire that you protect his reputation by not publicizing it. The man Carstairs seems to be the linch-pin of all of this and merits very close scrutiny. I also have details divulged to me by Louis La Rothiere, with whom I dare say you, or your colleagues, are familiar."

Holmes picked up the envelope containing all these documents and proffered it to her. She rose to meet him, paused for a second; her eyes still fixed upon his, and then reluctantly took hold of it. He kept a grip of it for a merest second, both their pairs of hands upon it.

"I am in your debt, Mr. Holmes." she said softly.

"Then our business is concluded. I bid you farewell." he said reverting seamlessly to his normal briskness of manner.

He hesitated a moment.

"I will, you understand, require payment for my services. I have prepared an invoice which I have enclosed here." He handed her a second envelope. "My normal terms are payment within two weeks."

She seemed a little taken aback by this sudden terseness.

"Yes, certainly, sir."

"Excellent. Good day, My Lady."

He nodded perfunctorily to her, turned swiftly on his heel and retreated to his bedroom from whence he did not emerge. I was left alone with our client, embarrassment vying with confusion. I coughed awkwardly. She acknowledged me with the slightest of curtseys, plucked her coat from the chair, and swept from our chambers clutching the envelopes. I heard the swish of her skirts upon the staircase, the click of the outer door, and watched her carriage cruise off up Baker Street.

Holmes had disappeared for the day into his sanctuary and did not emerge. I knocked once or twice but got no reply, and so fell back upon my own resources for the rest of the day, though my head was awhirl with confusion and speculation. There were a thousand questions I wanted to ask.

On the morrow there arrived a small package that bore a Kensington postmark. After a brief perusal of the cover Holmes put it aside with a look of studied indifference. He continued silently with his breakfast, brooding over his boiled egg and toast, before carrying the little parcel away with him to his bedroom. It was not difficult to surmize the identity of the sender, and I was avid beyond measure to know its contents.

Later that day Holmes took off from our rooms with no more than a cursory mumble to the effect that he was going to pay a further visit to Mycroft at his club. It is, I freely confess, vastly to my discredit, and yet it was more than flesh and blood could stand for me to desist. I sneaked into his room, and a furtive search of the drawers of his bedside cabinet disclosed a cheque drawn upon a government account in payment of Holmes's fee and an accompanying letter from the lady herself detailing profuse thanks for services rendered and a lengthy apologia for the deceptions. But there was something else, a beribboned medal with insignia. The inscription was in Latin, and I had just enough of my schoolboy learning sticking in my head to translate it into what I knew to be the motto of the Olympia Society – 'Liberty, Equality & Sorority', together with a sub-inscription welcoming a new and honorary member.

I was desperate to go through everything that had happened over the preceding two and a half weeks for I have never known anything quite like it, notwithstanding the many adventures we had shared together, but it was days before I finally managed to corner Holmes, for he seemed strangely reluctant to engage in discussion. When he finally did condescend to answer my questions, he admitted that he had suspected from the outset that he was being manipulated by shadowy forces, but could not be absolutely sure of what their game was and so played along. He was effusively apologetic that he had, as so often, excluded me from his innermost thoughts, but said he felt it desirable to use me as a kind of sounding board. I waved aside his apologies as unnecessary and, anyway, I was used to this treatment from him.

He said he had decided upon a resolution to affairs by confronting our exalted client with his knowledge. Much of the evidence he confronted her with, he conceded, was speculative, including that of the blood analysis, but he felt she was scarcely going to question it. It was a bit of a bluff, he conceded, *a la* Parminter. He was intrigued to see how she would react, for if his suspicions were correct she would surely now have had to come clean, as indeed she did. It had been a fascinating tussle, he averred, concluding a truly extraordinary case and, when all was said and done, he felt he regretted little of it and savoured much of it.

"But what would these intelligence service fellows have done if you had not forced the pace in the way you did? They could surely not have allowed matters to drag interminably?" I said, still frothing with queries.

"No, but I suspect they would have come out into the open at some point. Maybe they were planning to move against the *Bund* in the very near future anyway, and were hoping I could provide a bit of extra ammunition."

"Well, I think you provided some very explosive devices indeed."

"I think I probably did."

"And how much of our own activities were being monitored by these people?"

"Some, no doubt, but not all. As I said previously, I think we were a bit too light on our toes for much of the time. But I doubt that you or I have anything to fear from the forces of the law." He said re-assuringly.

"Let us hope not."

Holmes's mood through the days and weeks succeeding these transformative events was hard to read, as so often in the wake of some exceptional case of his, but I fancy that more than once I saw a look of indescribable contentment descend upon him, as if a warm and glorious sun had escaped from behind the clouds. It was such as I had not witnessed for many a year, at least not since his dealings with a certain other lady of dubious memory. And, upon the evening of the day in question, as I lay on my bed, I heard his footfall in the drawing room and the sound of the violin case being opened. The listless and dissonant scrapings of recent times gave way to the sweetest of melodies.

Chapter XXIV

Fall-out

I must recount the events of the next few days and weeks as briefly as I can for though events proceeded at a quicksilver pace, I had little role in them and nor indeed did Holmes, for all that he had given rise to them.

It seems that, acting at least in part upon the information passed by Holmes to Diana, which she duly delivered to her overseers at the Oval, long prepared operations were put into effect. Many arrests were made, including those of Barton and other members of his gang, and prosecutions followed in respect of a host of foul crimes, Barton ending up on the gallows. The Count's residences in Mayfair and Berkshire were descended upon by police and intelligence officers, and thorough searches made therein for any material of a compromising nature, though the man himself had vanished, almost certainly for his native soil and by unknown means. His household was, in due course, broken up by virtue of his absence and passed eventually into other hands. Servants sought and found employ elsewhere.

Carstairs, it seems, was charged with offences of an obscure nature pertaining to the transmission of unauthorized government documents and received a lengthy term of imprisonment. Several senior figures in government resigned, or were dismissed, from their posts, including at least one from the Colonial Office who was also subject to prosecution. Other eminent personages fell under investigation and some were, in the fullness of time, charged with and in some, though not all, cases convicted of offences against the safety of the realm. Much of this was kept from public view. Louis La Rothiere continued on his serene path of clandestine activity undisturbed by the forces of the state.

It was revealed, via Mycroft, that this Oval intelligence service, having long harboured the profoundest suspicions of the Count's extra-curricular activities, had managed to place an operative of theirs in the household of No. 4 Wessex Gardens in the form an ostler, the large turnover of staff there affording the opportunity eventually to insert someone on the inside via the local domestic service agency. This fellow reported back regularly on proceedings so far as he could gauge them, albeit that he was mainly employed on duties external to the house. He was in frequent but irregular contact with one or more 'cabmen', also in the service of the Oval, who hovered in the vicinity, rotating themselves so as not to arouse suspicion. Many of the comings and goings had been observed by these 'cabmen', though I think Holmes and my little 'adventure' there had thankfully gone unnoticed since even they, with their limited resources, called off their vigil at night-time when a loitering cab might have been too noticeable.

I learned much of these doings second, third, and even fourth hand via Holmes, Mycroft, and others. After much urging and exhortation on my part I was able to glean some of the circumstances surrounding Molly's abduction and rescue. It seems that on the evening of the day when she had purloined the volume the Count had returned prematurely, and unexpectedly, from Berkshire to discover it missing and had carried out an enquiry of whirlwind ferocity amongst the servants. Molly had been fingered, perhaps dobbed in by her arch-nemesis Edna. Refusing to admit her hand in the theft she had been handed over to the tender mercies of the Nayland crew to extract a confession by fair means or foul, and was carried off to a den of theirs, as extorted by me from Nayland. The ostler had got wind of her abduction, signalled to the cabman on duty who duly followed her to this safe house where her ordeal at the hands of Nayland and others was to take place. They could not bring about a rescue without giving the game away, but maintained a constant watch upon the premises.

When word came through, a few days later, that the long-awaited round-up operation was to be put into effect a raid was carried out on this venue by armed police acting in concert with these intelligence agencies; Barton and others were arrested after a fearful struggle in which he suffered serious gunshot wounds and Molly was found within, badly bruised and battered after ill-treatment at the hands of these vile thugs, but still very much alive. It may well be that she had withstood torture knowing that to say anything would have been fatal, in which case one can only marvel at her fortitude and strength of character. She had spent several days of treatment and recuperation at the local hospital, before being discharged to her home where she was interviewed by the police as a prime witness against Barton and other gang members implicated in her kidnapping. Nayland's body had by then been discovered and the Count himself had, as previously recounted, contrived to effect his long prepared disappearance.

When I learned of all of this, I was relieved beyond all measure and deeply anxious to visit Molly at the first opportunity, though apprehensive as to the reception I might get, given that I was, after all, and as she must have known all too well, directly responsible for all that she had had to endure. Racing over to Wessex Lane I was met at the door of No. 69 with a volley of invective and abuse from her mother who told me in no uncertain terms that I was not welcome and that Molly did not wish to see me ever again, blaming me, quite rightly, for her ordeal and hating me for having lied to her. I mumbled my apologies, though my words were weak and fruitless. I did not know the full extent of what Molly may have vouchsafed to her mother of the run-up to these fateful events, but could only imagine, and I scarcely blamed her or her mother for viewing me with loathing and distrust. Though I was deeply thankful for her deliverance I felt wretched beyond the power of words to describe.

But I could not leave matters resting there in that awful state of suspension and uncertainty and resolved upon getting to speak to her, even if she was to respond with vilification, for even that was preferable to the aching void in my soul. I went round to her house the following evening and kept a lookout for her. Eventually I saw her, no longer, of course, engaged at Wessex Gardens, which household was now effectively liquidated and its staff scattered to the four winds, but having seemingly found employment of a similar nature elsewhere. She looked glum and ashen-faced as I watched her withdraw into her house and I yearned to reach out and talk to her, yet I could not summon the courage to approach, nor would I have found the words if I had. I went home and brooded and resolved the next day to confront her, whatever the consequences. Again I saw her returning home and I am sure that this time she spotted me. She glanced uncertainly in my direction and paused as if wanting to speak, but then, as if thinking better of it, switched demeanour to confer a look of utter disdain before striding onwards, ostentatiously avoiding my gaze.

On the third day I decided there would be no hesitating nor backing down and, in the early evening, I stood in a little porchway some small distance from her house awaiting her arrival and as she hoved into view I took a step forward. But as I did so I saw that she was with someone, an upstanding, good looking young man I vaguely recalled seeing at the Bull's Head, a footman at one of the other residences in the area, I would assume. They were laughing and joking, and she was staring lovingly into his eyes, and he into hers. I took a step back into the shadows, and as I watched them skip gaily along I welled with warmth and gladness for her, though I had to fight back a tear for myself. I realized that this was the way things had to be. I never saw her again but think often of her.

I returned to Baker Street where Holmes greeted me.

"You have been to Wessex Lane once more?"

"Yes. The natural order has been restored," I said abstractedly, and Holmes knew exactly what I meant. He favoured me with a benevolent and understanding smile.

"Probably for the best," he said quietly.
"Yes, Holmes," I said.

Postscript

I must endeavour to conclude my account of this most melodramatic and, I do not hesitate to say, ill-starred of all Holmes's cases by wrapping up the loose ends as best I can, though some things remain forever ambiguous. I am writing this postscript at a distance of several decades and yet the reader may appreciate, all too readily, that it has at times caused me anguish in the highest degree to recount these events in such stark and unremitting detail; though I have at least the consolations of my successful second marriage to sustain me through my advancing years. But I have felt compelled to do so out of a sense of mission so as to lay on record all of Holmes's extraordinary cases in order that future generations may be enthralled by the exploits contained therein and, dare I suggest, educated by the forensic methods deployed.

No arrests were ever made, nor charges preferred, in regard to the unexplained death of Dieter Kellmann and, though arrests were made in respect of the murder of Declan Murphy these did not lead to any charges or prosecutions, hard evidence being lacking. It is unclear as to what strings were pulled at the highest levels to prevent any exposure of these and other matters to public scrutiny.

I might add with a sense of relief, tempered with a modicum of shame, that the shooting of Frank Nayland produced no arrest, charge or prosecution either. I have occasionally felt the urge to admit all to the authorities of my own, by no means inconsiderable, role in these matters, but I have managed to resist these promptings of my conscience; reinforced in this 'omerta' by Holmes's forceful adjurations as to the folly of such a course. Shortly after these climactic events I was visited by a mysterious figure who handed me my binoculars which I had discovered to my mortification were missing. He fixed me with a meaningful stare and told me that I should be more careful where I left them in future, before departing as swiftly as he had come.

Nothing was ever made public of a burglary in Mayfair nor of a seizure of goods from a cargo ship on the Essex coast. The coroner's verdict on the death of William Parminter was suicide while the balance of his mind was disturbed by factors unknown.

The days and weeks immediately following saw events progress swiftly but clandestinely, with the arrest and trial of several influential and highly placed figures, including Jeremy Carstairs, the suspensions or removal from high office of assorted others, and the expulsion from the our shores of a clutch of alien persons, though all of this was conducted behind closed doors, and was largely invisible to the general public.

Count von Runstedt vanished from our shores for perpetuity shortly before these episodes, and disappeared into obscurity in his native land, dying under mysterious circumstances many years later.

Holmes, himself, became the object of official attention, not for the first time in his illustrious career, and was visited some days after the tumultuous events described in the foregoing pages by government officials and, I believe, recruited to government service in some undefined capacity. One heard rumours of the doings of Diana Conquest, and though her activities were the subject of speculation they were always shrouded in mystery.

International affairs proceeded at an ever swifter rhythm leading to the controversial events of the following month in South Africa and, it may be argued, fixing Europe and the world upon a dread, unalterable course leading, like a fast flowing river to a cataract, to the catastrophes of the next century.

I have forborne from publishing an account of this very singular case for a host of obvious reasons, and have made no mention of it in my telling of his numerous other adventures, and do not intend to do so until all parties have passed away.

These events are now a distant memory, yet there are nights when my dreams are filled with a terrifying kaleidoscope of images; of Nayland and his scarred face swooping upon Murphy, and of my own horrific struggle with him; of the contorted features of Kellmann upon the floor of that old house and the icily charming evil of von Runstedt. I awake with a jolt, sit up ramrod straight, and see Molly standing at the foot of my bed with her mischievous smile and dancing eyes.

Dr. John H. Watson, M.D.

Acknowledgements

I would like to thank Baker Street Studios Limited for agreeing to publish this novel, based on the account by Dr. Watson of one of Sherlock Holmes's most extraordinary cases.

I would like also to acknowledge the role played by the Sawbridge Words Writers Club under the inspiring leadership of Emma Vandore and J. S. (Jacquie) Watts and for their advice and their encouragement of my writing endeavours.

I am very grateful to Diana Jones for her penetrative comments on the draft, having given her sight of it on a chapter by chapter basis (*The Strand Magazine* fashion), and for rescuing me, at times, from verbal infelicity.

I am glad, finally, to have completed the novel, courtesy, at least in part, of the Covid lockdown, though, on occasion, having to contend for control of the keyboard with my cats, which may account for some of the neologisms and eccentricities that appear.

Simon R. Trelawney

Essex